Into The Fae

Book 1, Gypsy Healers Series

Quinn Loftis

Published by
Quinn Loftis

Photography KKeeton Designs
Cover Design Mirella Santana

Dedication

For my son, thank you so much for all your smiles.
You truly are my sunshine.

Acknowledgments

There are so many people who need to be thanked, have their hand shook, a pat on the back, a hug, some form of appreciation shown to them for how much support they have given me, not only on this project but on all of my books.

I praise my God for loving me and sacrificing his Son so that I might live a full, abundant life full of love, grace, forgiveness, and hope.

I thank my incredible husband for all the hard work that he puts into my books. I thank him for the long hours he works on my books, for every thoughtful Nerd slush (new at Sonic, you have to try them), for being the most wonderful father ever, for doing laundry, and for bringing me a coke zero every morning before my feet hit the floor, but most of all I thank him for choosing to love me. It is because of his choice that I am able to write characters that fight for something that is so very hard to do but so very worth it.

Thank you to Nancy for reading Into the Fae as I wrote it and cheering me on. Thank you for the sticker wars on Facebook, for the thoughtful texts, and kind words. Thank you for lifting me and my family up in prayer.

Thank you to Candace Selph for being the most amazing PA in the history of Pas--I know I checked. Thank you for reading my books over and over again, for loving the characters, for helping me remember when I can't keep things straight and for reminding me to not freak out. You are truly a blessing.

Thank you to my Beta readers, I truly appreciate all of your comments and insight; it helps more than you realize.

A special thank you to Heather, a wonderful young woman who is a fan of the Grey Wolves Series books and also the inspiration for the character "Heather" in this book. Thank you so much for your help and for reaching out to me to share your story.

There are so very many people who have made this book possible and I hope that I have made sure you know, either by e-mail, text, Facebook message, or some other communication, just how much I appreciate you.

Thank you to the readers! If I could shout that from the mountains and know that every single one of you would hear it then believe me I'd be climbing right now. I have never met such wonderful, caring, kind people as those of you who have taken a chance on my books and, through that chance, come to love these characters as much as I do. There truly is no way for me to express just how much it means to me that you all take your time to read my books. Thank you with every fiber of my being. Thank you and God bless you all.

Sincerely,
Quinn

Books by Quinn Loftis

Prologue
"It has been said that with great power comes great responsibility and that is true. However, what should have been added to that saying was that with great responsibility must come even greater self-control. For those with great power often seem to lack the power of self-control. Not that I have any such difficulty."
~Perizada of the Fae

I am over three thousand years old. I have seen civilizations rise and then crumble like sand beneath the evening tide. I have watched kings be exalted on their thrones, only to be ripped down and trampled upon as the next great name is being written over the fallen. I myself have fought in battles and felt the warm spray of my enemy's blood upon my face as I cut them down. I have laughed in the face of danger, danced on the edge of death with the warlocks, played chicken with the wolves, riddled with the pixies, and yet, the thing I fear most does not come at the end of a sword. The thing I fear most comes at the will of another. It is not something I can force, it is not something I can change, and it is not something I can control. So, in short, I don't like it.

At this point you might be asking yourself who I am and why anything I say matters. Well listen up and listen good because I'll only say this once. Don't bother to point out to me that you can come back to these pages and read it over again, it will only piss me off, and the last thing anyone needs is a member of the high fae pissed off at them.

I am Perizada, a member of the council of the high fae. I was chosen long ago by the Great Luna, the creator of the werewolves in case you were wondering, to be an ambassador if you will—between the fae and the wolves. You see, the fae are the most powerful of all the supernatural beings. Therefore, the Great Luna saw fit to make us the overseers and law enforcers of the supernatural world. I did as the Great Luna asked and became the go between for the Wolves and the council of high fae.

As time passed, the werewolves' vulnerabilities as a species, their tendencies toward divisiveness and territorialism, began to weaken the packs. In an effort to aid the wolves, the Great Luna, in her infinite wisdom, presented the packs with a gift—gypsy healers. These are humans with an affinity for healing magic. So it was that a gypsy healer was chosen from the tribes of gypsies and given to each pack. It was then that the Great Luna decided that it would be best if the high fae were assigned a certain number of packs and healers to oversee. I was given the packs in the region of Romania. At one time they were divided into two packs but after the werewolf wars, the two became one and now are under the rule of one great Alpha, Vasile Lupei. That is how I came to be the liaison to the Romanian pack. But that is not really where this story begins, for that we must go back a little further. Now I will condense this as much as possible to bring you up to speed so that you don't feel the need to stab yourself in the eye out of boredom.

Before the great werewolf wars, there was a powerful fae, the most powerful in fact. His name was Volcan. You might say he is our dirty little secret, yes, even we mighty fae have them. His power—and lust for more of it—became an obsession. Unbeknownst to the high council, he began to create witches with his dark magic and began releasing them into the human population. By 1605 it was evident that the witches were out of control and we, meaning the Fae council, knew we needed to step in. This is where the story gets hazy. Not many know that once the Great Purge, that's when all the witches were wiped out, happened, Volcan was not destroyed. His power was so weak that we, the council, decided that a more fitting punishment was to let him wither away in his castle in the dark forest. So for an entire century we left the evil wizard to his own devices, checking on him occasionally to make sure he was still harmless. Towards the beginning of 1700, we began to feel so magic growing around the dark forest once again. We continued to monitor it and even attempted to put some binding spells around it. By 1705 it was evident that Volcan was once again attempting to create witches. We had underestimated his determination and ability to fly under the radar. We realized our mistake in having not destroyed him during the Great Purge and we knew we couldn't be lenient again, he had to be stopped. A desperate battle was fought between Volcan and an alliance of wolves and fae. Volcan's castle was raided, and at the cost of many lives, he was defeated.

If this story were a movie then that would be the end, the happily ever after for the wolves and fae alike, but alas real life often sucks sour lemons. The happily ever afters never come or if they do it is at too high a price. Unfortunately somehow evil continues to rule in the hearts of those who think they are superior to everyone else. Volcan's evil had permeated the dark forest so completely that it had to be sealed off, and the knowledge of it blocked from the minds of those who had been involved in the battle. There is more to that part of the story which will surely unfold as we continue forward.

For my part, which this is about me so really the most important information you need right now is my juicy details. When we sealed the dark forest, we unknowingly imprisoned a pack member of the Romanian wolves and not just any pack member. We unknowingly confined none other than Lucian, Vasile's brother. For centuries he lived in darkness, surrounded by malevolent magic that has no place in the fae realm. Now, ages later, circumstances, horrible circumstances mind you, that involved my own sister trying to kill me, for which she will pay, led to his release. Now I am not begrudging Lucian of that, far from it. I am however disturbed, rattled beyond anything I have faced before, and let me tell you I have faced things your puny minds cannot even begin to fathom, because upon his release and thanks to the Great Luna and her bloody love-fest, the wolves are able to find true mates with the fae and you guessed it—yours truly is the true mate to one Lucian Lupei. In the words of the great John McClain, Yippee Ki Yay, Mother--, and I'll stop there lest someone get their panties in wad.

So now that you're up to speed, for the most part, I suppose we can get this party started. Things are going to be moving fast so if you need to get some beauty rest before you start this journey with me, I suggest you do that right about now. But if you're ready and you think you got what it takes to keep up with me, then keep reading, (insert creepy voice), my pretties. We have a psycho bitch fae to catch, a mate to deter, and lives to save. There is no time for dilly dallying or wishy washy pansy ass whining. If you're in this with me, then you are in it 'til the end. And the first one of you that cracks a joke about the whole being mated to a werewolf thing will be farting out of their mouth every time they hear the word gas and burping from their butts every time someone laughs for the rest of their stinky, noisy existence.

As my good friend Jen would say, let's do this. Okay she would say *him*, but we're going to go with *this* in an effort to keep things rated PG.

Chapter 1

"There's so much noise, so much life and light and chaos. For so long I have been trapped in silence, surrounded by death and darkness. Even though I'm now surrounded by all this light, I find that all I want is her. In the midst of all the reunions, there is only one my soul cries out for, but she is the only one who won't let me near." ~Lucian

"I'm tired, Costin," she whispered to him.

"Lay down, Sally mine. I'm here with you."

Peri watched helplessly as the little healer lay on the ground, her breaths growing shallower by the second. She couldn't move. She couldn't get to her no matter how she tried. She was pleading with the Great Luna not to let this light be taken from the world, but her only answer was the final breath that rattled from Sally's lungs.

"She shouldn't have done that," she heard herself say as she stared at Sally's still form. "Not for me." These young ones had no idea how old she was, how long she had lived and how many lives she had spent. They couldn't comprehend fifty years, let alone thousands. She had screamed at Sally to stop, to not put the pill in her mouth and just like the bloody wolves were apt to do, the healer had ignored her wishes. And now she was dead, taken from this world much too early in her young life and it was Peri's fault. As she watched Costin wrap his arms around his mate, tears stained his face and pain that Peri knew she'd never experience, wracked his body. She didn't have a mate. She had no clue what it would be like to lose someone that you loved so completely. And as she watched the wolf before

her crumble over the loss of his female, she knew she would never want to love like that, not if it meant experiencing that kind of pain.

"Wake up, beloved. It is only a dream. The healer lives, and you have a mate," a deep voice rumbled into her consciousness pushing away the heavy sleep.

Peri sat up abruptly in her bed. The material of her sleep clothes clung to her sweaty skin as her heart pounded in her chest and her breathing came in shaky gasps. It had been the same dream she'd been having for weeks. And just as always, the same deep voice had interrupted it, pushing her to wake from the nightmare.

"I have asked you politely to stay out of my head," she spoke into the dark room.

A chuckle whispered through her mind causing goose bumps to break out across her skin.

"So telling me to get a damn life and leave you the hell alone is your version of polite?" Lucian asked.

She rolled her eyes and began gathering her long shimmering white hair into a pony tail and then twisting it up until it was all tightly gathered. She used her magic to hold it in place.

"I didn't throw anything at you and I didn't stab you. So yes, that is my version of polite," she snapped at him. She felt silly talking to her empty room but then she didn't want to use the mental link between them, something that only happened between true mates; it felt much too intimate. She had tried to block him and been successful for a while, but their bond had only grown stronger despite her neglect. Eventually, he had been able to force his way in. When she had pointed out how rude that was, he had pointed out that it was rude of her to yell and curse

13

him. He was right, of course, but she wasn't about to tell him so.

"I do not know why you are fighting this, Perizada. You are my true mate; you have the other half of my soul and I have yours."

"You can keep it. I've gotten along fine without it for all this time."

"I could help you with the nightmares," he murmured into her mind.

"I don't think my nightmares are afraid of the big bad wolf—sorry to disappoint."

"You underestimate the healing power of love. Love mends many things; it could mend the brokenness inside of you."

"Bloody hell, did you get that off a Hallmark card?" Peri laughed, unable to stop herself as she imagined the big, intimidating Lucian, with his six foot four frame, blonde unruly hair, and stoic glacial stare, standing in the greeting card section of a store scanning cards for the perfect words.

"What's a Hallmark card?" The confusion in his voice only made her laugh harder.

This time she heard a low growl before he spoke. *"I'm glad that my ignorance amuses you. At least you're laughing instead of cursing at me."*

Peri's laugh was halted immediately, not because of what he'd said, but because of the way he sounded when he said it. He was hurt by her efforts to push him away. She closed her eyes and let herself open up to the bond just a little, just so she could feel him, feel what he felt. But though she had opened it just a fraction, the power of his emotions was like a tidal wave. They crashed into her, busting the door wide open. Then, he was everywhere.

He surrounded her, his love, his fear, his confusion and pain—it was all there—pushing into her, causing her to fall from the bed to the floor under the sheer weight of it. *How does he live like this,* she thought to herself as she closed her eyes and tried to breathe. *How could anyone feel so intensely and not be buried under it all?* She clenched her hands into fists and bit her lip to keep from crying as his grief washed over her.

"Bloody hell," she rasped as she leaned forward, pressing her forehead into the cold, stone floor of the room she used while staying at the Romanian pack mansion. The door to the room flew open just as the darkness that lived inside of him smothered her, driving away all of the emotions and leaving something even worse, utter despair and loneliness.

"Peri," Lucian's voice pierced the silence as his arms came around her. He picked her up effortlessly and held her in his lap as he sat on the edge of the bed. "I'm sorry, beloved. I didn't know that would happen. I didn't know our bond would open all the way."

Peri knew she should push him away. She shouldn't encourage such touchiness, but she found herself buying her face in his chest and relishing his big, warm hand rubbing her back with a gentleness that she knew he had not been shown in a very long time. She felt her eyes begin to fill with tears, tears she had still not allowed herself to cry. Wrapped safely in Lucian's arms, however, she found herself finally letting go. She gripped his shirt tightly as the sobs broke through the usually tightly controlled appearance. His arms tightened around her and she felt his breath on her neck as he whispered to her in

15

Romanian. She was familiar with his language and caught a few words but she was too far gone to get it all. Instead, she latched onto the sound of his voice and used it as her center, to refocus herself as she tried to pull it together.

"You have to let it out," Lucian told her even as she tried to lock it all back up. "You can't keep carrying all of that inside of you. You can let go, Peri. I've got you, and I won't let go. I won't let you fall apart."

Peri choked back a sound that she was sure would have had all the wolves headed their way as she fully grasped what it was Lucian was saying to her. She wasn't alone.

"Never again," he whispered and then pressed a gentle kiss to her forehead. "Whether you want me or not, I am yours and you are mine."

The tears continued to fall as she finally let go of the grief she had been carrying ever since she had been in the dark forest. She cried for the things she had seen, for the pain she wasn't able to prevent and for the loss that she could never restore. She cried for the sister who had turned her back on her and their people. She cried for fear of all the emotions that were swirling around her, comforting her and protecting her. All the while, as the tears continued to fall, Lucian held her.

Lorelle slowly pushed the door to the old castle open, cringing at the loud, creaking hinges in the silent, deserted forest. With Reyaz, the warlock she had aligned herself with in order to destroy Perizada, out of the picture, and her betrayal known to, well, everyone, she'd had to make a hasty retreat and the dark forest, empty of all her enemies was the perfect place for her to lie low. She knew the council would be coming for her. They wouldn't let her crimes go unpunished. After all, how would it look to the rest of the supernatural world if the ones who are supposed to be in charge can't even police their own?

She took a step through the doorway, half expecting some sort of residual magic to strike her. But when nothing did, she took another step, and then another, until she was all the way into the foyer. She turned in a slow circle and whistled appreciatively at the grandness of the entryway. At one time, before Volcan had been attacked by the wolves and the fae, his castle had been magnificent. As she took in the now drab, grey stone walls, the torn window dressings and dusty floor, she had to admit it was a far cry from the majestic palace it once was. Still, it had potential.

"Potential for what?" She asked herself out loud as she walked over to the staircase and sat on the third step up. "I mean, what do I honestly plan to do here?"

Her sister was dead, that's what she had wanted, right?

"Yes, but I hadn't planned on getting found out by the council," she answered herself. "I had planned on getting my sister out of the way so that I could become the powerful high fae that I should have been. Instead, I'm still living in her shadow."

Lorelle felt a rush of cold air blow across her face and ruffled her hair. She stilled, barely breathing as the air continued to swirl around her. She wanted to think that it was nothing, just a breeze because she had left the door open, but she was no fool and she knew the touch of magic when she felt it.

"Show yourself," she demanded.

"I would…if I could," a deep voice rasped at her, only slightly louder than a whisper.

She felt the air brush the back of her neck and she abruptly stood, hoping to put some space between her and whatever it was that had joined her.

"What does that mean?" She asked the voice.

"I would show myself to you if I could," it responded.

She rolled her eyes and folded her arms across her chest. "Fine, if you can't show yourself, tell me who you are or who it is that commands you." Lorelle fought the urge to shiver as she felt the temperature drop. She refused to show weakness, especially when she didn't know if this voice belonged to friend or foe.

"There is no one who can command me," the voice growled. "There are none great enough to wield power over me."

She snorted. "If that's so, then why am I only hearing your voice and not seeing your form? If you are so powerful, so great," she bit off the word, "then why aren't you standing here before me?" She held her breath waiting for a response. When several minutes passed without an answer she began to wonder if she had finally cracked and the voice was only in her head. Then, for a brief panic attack inducing minute, she considered that it could be Perizada's spirit. She would not put it past her sister to haunt her for all eternity if she could find a way. As she pondered the terrible implications of this thought, the castle walls began to shake.

Lorelle backed away from the stairs as loose rocks tumbled down from the rattling walls. The ground rolled beneath her and she was sure something was going to sprout up out of the floor at any moment. She held her arms out to catch her balance and then looked up ominously at the huge chandelier that hung from the high ceiling. It swayed threateningly and Lorelle took a big step back, attempting to get out of its line of fire should it decide to fall.

"I am ancient. I have created power and sent it out into the world to spread my essence. I have battled numerous foes and still I survive. Do not think to insult me in my own home, Lorelle, *formerly* of the high fae, sister of Perizada."

Lorelle felt her heart literally drop into her feet as his words bore into her mind, drawing up images of the facts he spewed. She felt her head begin to shake. *No*, she thought to herself, hoping with everything inside her that this wasn't real. It was surely just a dream. She had fallen asleep on the steps and she was so tired and so unsure of what to do next. Her eyes squeezed closed tight as the voice finally spoke his name, and she felt any future that she might have had slip away.

"I am Volcan."

∞

Peri stood, blessedly alone, in her room staring out of the window. Lucian had finally left after she had threatened to turn him into several unsavory rodents. But she knew he had only left because she promised to have breakfast with him. She let out a lengthy exhale as she thought about the events of the night. She had to admit that she felt better after her mini—okay so it might not have been so mini— meltdown. It was as if a festering boil had been popped and now that all the infection was out, though it still hurt, it would heal. Knowing she would heal, that she *could* heal, gave her much hope, even in the face of the difficult task before her.

She finally turned away from the window. As she headed for the door, she caught her reflection in the mirror. She chuckled as she took in the dark jeans and trendy top. Jen, one of the American female mates of the Serbian pack alpha, had gotten a hold of her and told her in no uncertain terms that while she was in the human realm she was bloody damn well going to look human. Peri had let her have her say because though she would not admit it to Jen herself, she liked the crazy female. She supposed she looked alright for someone several thousand years old. Her smile turned a tad wicked when she considered what Lucian would say when he saw her jeans. He wasn't just from a different era. He was from *several* different eras ago and in his time, women never wore trousers. They were considered indecent because of the way they hugged the curves of the female form.

Knowing that her clothes were bound to aggravate Lucian put a bounce in her step that hadn't been there before. She pulled the door open and headed towards the dining hall where she would have to make her announcement that tonight would be her last night in the Romanian pack mansion. She had yet to discuss it with the Great Luna, and she knew she would have to soon since it was the goddess who had put her over the Romanian wolves all those centuries ago.

Her thoughts wandered as she walked without thinking, her feet had grown so very familiar with the home. She felt a pang in her heart as she realized that is exactly what she considered it, her home. She shook her head as she stepped up to the doors of the dining room, trying to get her emotions under control. It wouldn't do for her to walk in crying like a blubbering fool. "Wouldn't that evoke confidence in them," she snorted as she pulled the door open and walked in to join the others.

Without any preamble she announced, "I feel it is necessary that I take a leave of absence, Vasile." Peri's voice pierced the silence that had settled over the dining room upon her arrival. Vasile sat at the head of the table with Alina to his right and Sorin on his left. Her quick glance around revealed Decebel, the Serbian pack Alpha, was visiting again. Next to him sat Lucian and across from Lucian sat Fane, Vasile's only son. There were others, all male she realized. *Huh,* she thought as she looked back at Lucian who was now standing, *that must be why he's looking at me like I've just walked into this room in my most revealing lingerie.* She cocked an eyebrow at him, daring him to say something about her jeans. She didn't have to wait long.

"What are you wearing?" He asked through their bond.

"Though you are not from this century, or the one before it, I still trust that you are an intelligent male and can figure out what I have clad myself in," Peri answered dryly.

21

Lucian's scowl deepened at her. She simply shrugged her shoulders at him and said, *"Just because we had a moment last night does not mean I'm going to make this easy on you."*

"I'll remember your words when you are begging for my touch, mate," his voice grew deep as his eyes narrowed at her.

Peri wanted to stomp her foot like a child and whine about how it wasn't fair that she didn't know all the facts behind the mate bond. Sure, she may have observed them over the centuries, but observing and taking part were two very different things. She felt at a distinct disadvantage with Lucian. If there was one thing that Peri didn't do well, it was lose. No, she was not a graceful loser and so she knew she was going to have to start researching the true mate bond and what all it entailed.

"Will you join us, Peri?" Vasile spoke up, pulling her from her thoughts and drawing her attention from Lucian.

"If that is what I must do to seem agreeable, then fine I'll sit, I'll eat, and I might even listen, but then I'm going." She walked down the side of the table Lucian sat on and took the seat he held out for her. As she started to reach for a roll she heard Lucian growl at her. She pulled her hand back and turned her head slowly to glare at him.

"What is your problem?" She whispered as she leaned towards him. She heard low chuckles and laughs disguised as coughs around her but she didn't take her eyes off of Lucian.

"I will fix your plate," he told her simply.

She considered arguing with him but he was already doing exactly what he said and really what was the point? *Pick your battles, Peri,* she told herself. As the huge male set her plate, overflowing with a ridiculous amount of food, down in front of her, she added *there will be many.*

"I'm assuming that you want to be relieved of your duties with my pack in order to hunt down your sister?" Vasile asked.

"That is correct, Alpha. She is my responsibility and her treachery must be dealt with," Peri said coolly.

"Is the council not sending anyone after her?" Decebel spoke up.

"I'm sure they will," Peri shrugged, "but it is by my hand that she should be punished. It is my right."

"Are you sure you want to be the one to do it, Peri?" Vasile's voice was filled with sympathy. "The taking of life is not easily undone. You will have to bear that cross for the rest of your very long existence."

She snorted. "Are you questioning my ability to kill my sister, after she was involved in the murder of not only my life, but your wolves?" She shook her head in irritation. "You clearly have forgotten how cruel I can be when it is deemed necessary."

"Any of us who have been on the receiving end of your wrath would never doubt your ability to deal out punishment, Peri," Vasile pointed out. "However, dealing out punishment to our own flesh and blood is an entirely different matter."

Peri dropped her fork and it hit the plate with a loud clank. The wolves in the room stilled as she slowly pushed her chair back and rose from her seat. "Do you presume me weak, Vasile, Alpha to the Romanian pack? Do you challenge my ability to do my job?" Her voice was cold, calculating and maybe a tad overdramatic. *Peri, you have got to get your crap together,* she growled to herself as she watched Vasile go very still.

"Leave us please," he said not taking his eyes off of Peri.

Lucian stood but didn't move to leave. His eyes were narrowed on his brother as he took Peri's hand.

Peri nearly jumped at the contact. She had been expecting Lucian to leave with the others, but instead he took up a position in front of her, shielding her from the Alpha's glare. She rolled her eyes at his overprotectiveness, but in her heart of hearts she was honored that he would think to try and protect her.

"Lucian, I know she is your mate, but you are not bonded yet. No blood rites have been performed and, therefore, you have no right to stay when I have ordered you to leave." Vasile's voice was calm, not demanding and not cruel. He was just stating the facts.

"Do you want me to stay?" Lucian asked her.

Here heart warmed by his thoughtfulness and seemed to swell in her chest. It had been so very long since someone had worried about her, had tried to protect her. Though it was not necessary, it was still a nice gesture. *"If he asked you all to go, he must have a reason. He will not hurt me, Lucian."* She squeezed his hand affectionately and then released it.

He turned to look at her. Though she was tall, he was taller still and she had to look up at him to meet his eyes. He leaned down and pressed a kiss to her forehead and whispered, "I will wait for you just outside."

She knew he had said it out loud for his brother's benefit and that made her chuckle under her breath. Her mate the maverick, back in the living only a couple months and already bucking the system.

When the door had closed behind Lucian, Peri let out a deep breath and sat back down. "Okay so I'll admit that was a tad childish."

"A tad?" Vasile asked with a raised brow.

She huffed. "Oh blow it out your ass, Alpha. I was killed, brought back to life, and discovered that I had a werewolf for a mate, and not just any werewolf but one that was supposed to be dead. Forgive me if I'm slightly testy."

"I concede," he said holding up his hands. "You have every right to be childish, testy, or any other emotion that strikes your fancy. You have been through a lot. There are some things that I wanted to talk with you about, and I hope that it might help decrease the number of childish episodes you might need to have."

Peri gave him a dry look at his words but made a motion for him to continue.

"I know that you have been around the wolves and mated pairs for a very long time, but even still there might be things that you don't know about being a true mate or being mated for that matter."

Peri actually sat up straighter as she folded her hands in her lap. "And pray tell, what does this have to do it the fact that I just bit your head off because I thought you were questioning my power?" She asked him pointedly.

"It has to do with you acting, as you said, a tad childish. You feel out of your depth, Perizada. I've known you a very long time, my old friend, and if there is anything I know about you, it's that you don't like to be uninformed or misinformed. So I'm going to help you get your bearings. The rest is up to you." He paused and folded his napkin as he seemed to gather his thoughts. He laid it down next to his near empty plate and then began to speak again. "You know that the males are possessive, and jealous to a fault. You know that they carry a darkness inside of them and without their true mate that darkness slowly takes over. What you may not know is that once a male finds his true mate, the need to be with her, to bind her to him and to take care of her, is overwhelming. It's nearly all he thinks about. For my brother I believe this desire is going to be even…let's see, what's the word…," he rubbed his chin as he thought, "intense."

"Great," Peri drew out under her breath.

Vasile smiled sympathetically. "He, as you know, comes from a *very* different time than the one we live in now. Even though women in the Canis lupis world were held in high esteem, they were never outspoken, nor did they dress in clothing so revealing. Our current culture is desensitized to these things, but that wasn't always the case. Also, you have to remember that women were considered lower than men in the 1600s. That was *never* the case in our world. Our females have always been treasured—considered precious. Lucian is going to be much more modest in many ways, and he will seem so much more overbearing than the males who have changed with the times. I ask that you be patient with him."

"You say that as if I've already agreed that I will be his mate," Peri challenged.

Vasile gave her a coy look. "What would you do if he were to look at another woman?"

"Gouge his eyes out with an ice pick," she answered without thought or hesitation.

"And if another female were to touch him?"

"I'd beat her with the bloody stump of an arm that I had just ripped from her pathetic body. Holy crap, I'm phsycho!" She leaned forward and gripped the edge of the table. Her eyes were wide as she realized the intense anger she felt was simply because Vasile had planted the idea of another women being near Lucian. "Is this what true mates feel like all of the time? This need to kill anyone who might show interest in their mate? Because, if so, then seriously, Vasile, we need to get you all some counseling." She asked sounding every bit as shocked as she looked.

Vasile chuckled as he watched the usually calm fae attempt to catch her breath. "It gets better once the Blood Rites has been completed," he told her. Then he cleared his throat and with a slight blush added, "and once other things have been consummated."

Peri shook her head as she looked at Vasile from the corner of her eye. "Are you seriously blushing? Bloody hell, man, we're not teenagers. Hell, we're not even twenty-somethings. Call it what it is, sex. S-E-X," she spelled out, "Doing the deed, bumping uglies, hittin it, tappin that…,"

"I thought you said we weren't teenagers?" Vasile interrupted her rant.

"Sorry, I watch way too many movies. And I've been around Jen. Okay, so being around Jen is probably the reason for the immature references to sex that seem to always imply some form of physical punishment." Peri leaned back in her chair and steepled her fingers under her chin. Her eyes met Vasile's and they stared at one another silently for several minutes. He was waiting for her to admit it. If she were honest with herself, then she would just fess up and admit that there was no way in any hell that she would let another woman near Lucian, which meant she was going to have to do this whole mate thing. *Honesty is so overrated,* she thought as she let out a deep, resigned sigh.

"Let's just say, *for arguments sake,* that I am willing to be his mate and do all the Blood Rites and yada yada. What then?" She asked.

"Then you would have to learn to live with each other," Vasile smiled innocently.

Peri's eyes narrowed at the Alpha. "Do you have any idea how many times I've wanted to turn you into a turd and flush you down the toilet?"

"I imagine that my brother will somehow surpass whatever number that is many times over," he told her smugly, then added more seriously. "It will ease the possessiveness somewhat, if you complete the bond. He won't feel the need to claim you in front of every new person you encounter and it will free him of the darkness he wrestles with. For you, it will help you not want to rip off the arms of other females and beat them with their bloody stumps."

She shrugged at that. "Well at least that's something."

There was a knock on the door and then Alina's head poked in. She smiled at Peri and then looked at her mate. "You called?"

Vasile motioned for her to enter the dining room. "I've told her from the male point of view what I can, but I think perhaps she needs to hear things from your side of the bond." He stood and met his mate halfway down the table. He pressed a kiss to her lips tenderly and then headed for the door. Before he closed it behind him he added, "And be careful, mate, there's been talk of turning wolves into turds and flushing them."

Peri rolled her eyes. "Not wolves, just you. Geeze," she glowered, "dramatic much?"

Alina laughed as she sat across from Peri. She leaned back in the chair looking relaxed and composed, as usual. Peri had always admired that about the she-wolf. Here this woman lived in a mansion full of possessive, bossy werewolves and she rarely even raised her voice.

"Alright, Luna," Peri finally said, "what's your take?"

Alina's head tilted ever so slightly to the right as she took in the high fae before her. Her lips twitched as she seemed to fight the grin that threatened to bloom at any moment. "Before we begin I just want to know one thing. What's driving you crazier, the fact that you are mated to a wolf, or the fact that you want to, I think Jacque put it best, jump his bones?" she spoke at last.

Peri let out an exaggerated huff as she met the Alpha female's eyes. "Why are you and your mate suddenly so interested in my sex life?"

Alina laughed. "So Vasile went there, did he?"

"Oh yes, but he was much less crude than your daughter in-law, or even myself."

"Consummation?" Alina asked knowingly.

"The one and only," Peri answered dryly.

Alina sobered and her voice grew serious as she leaned forward in her chair. Peri could see that the Alpha wanted her to listen, and to hear well what she was about to say.

"There is no walking away from your mate. I'm not saying that to challenge you Peri and I'm not saying it to scare you. I'm telling you because you need to fully grasp how permanent a true mate is. You, who have been alone for so long, will never be alone again. I only know Lucian from the stories that Vasile has shared with me. But if he is anything like Vasile, then he will do anything to take care of you, to provide for you, protect you and love you. That doesn't mean it will be easy, but you don't have to fear losing him."

"What about all the bossiness and broodiness?" Peri asked. "You yourself said it. I have been alone a very long time, doing my own thing. I don't take orders. I won't be caged and the word 'submit' is pretty much a death sentence to the one saying it."

Alina smiled at Peri as if she was a cute little dog that had performed a trick. "For one so wise, Perizada, you can be awfully dense."

Peri pointed a long finger at the she-wolf. "See, that is why you should all be turds."

"Any relationship is give and take," Alina continued as if Peri hadn't spoken. "Sacrifices must be made by both parties. You both will have to make changes and allow the other to make mistakes. As for submitting, well, you know what pack life is like. There has to be a balance of power. There has to be an Alpha, and those beneath him must submit. But your mate will never ask you to submit to him, not unless he truly felt it was necessary and a compromise could not be met."

"And I would just have to do it?" Peri snapped.

"I would hope that your relationship at that point would be one of deep trust and love. I would hope that if he was asking that of you, then you would trust his judgment, and trust him to take care of you. Submission was never meant to be a negative action. Submission is an act of love and service because someone must lead, and the others must follow. Your greatest act of love to your mate is when you submit and that comes in many forms. Think of it like this," she scooted forward and laid her hands on the table between them. "For a wolf to give another his stomach is an act of ultimate submission, right? The stomach is the most tender and vulnerable place on the body and puts the wolf at the greatest risk. So what do you think it means to Vasile when I, his werewolf mate, lie in bed with him? How much trust does he see from me when I sleep on my back, vulnerable to him? Are those not forms of submission? Do they demean me in anyway?"

Peri sat speechless across from Alina. The air from her breathing seemed too loud in her ears as the words the she-wolf had just spoken ran through her mind. She had never looked at the relationship between true mates in quite that way. They were wolves, she got that. But then, she realized that she totally didn't get it at the same time, because, once again, she was not a wolf.

"I'm going to blow your mind one more time," Alina interrupted her epiphany moment. "Now that you realize what it means to submit and what it means to your mate, ask yourself this; how much trust and

31

love must he feel when he gives his stomach to you? You have the greatest treasure of all, Peri. Lucian will only ever fully submit to you. He will only ever lie in your bed on his back, exposing his stomach and neck to you. He will only ever trust *you* with that. How great his love and trust must be for one so proud, so strong, and so dominant to yield to you."

Peri didn't hear Alina leave. She sat in stunned silence as she considered her words. Lucian submit to her? It was nearly laughable. But then, how did any relationship survive if not for the bending of two wills? Alina had said there was no getting around it. She was Lucian's true mate. It was a bond that would not be denied, one that no one walked away from. After several minutes of thought she stood, straightened her shirt, and let out a deep breath.

"The way I see it, I have two choices," she told the empty table. "I can accept that I'm going to be mated to a werewolf, or I can accept that I'm going to be mated to a werewolf." She shook her head as she turned to leave the room. In a final huff of resignation she mumbled to herself, "Damn if I don't like either one of those."

Chapter 2

"When I gave my creation free will, I worried that they would never fulfill the destinies that I had planned for them. I was sure that they would turn their own way and disregard the path I had laid out for them. My one defense against this was love. Love is what helps them make the tough decisions, what guides them when they've lost their way. True, unconditional, selfless love can soften the hardest heart, cleanse the filthiest soul, and quench the driest spirit." ~The Great Luna

"I don't understand why you need so many square boxes that do all the same thing," Lucian said as he held the contraption that Costin had handed him. A *cell phone* was what he had called it and Costin said he could use it to speak to people all over the world. Lucian had laughed.

"Well you don't want to attempt to carry a television around with you, and a tablet is too big to use as a phone. You see, even though they do similar things, it's having various sizes for various circumstances that matter."

"Okay, when I walk into a room and hear one dude talking to another dude using words like various, and sizes that matter, I have to admit I'm a tad intrigued," Jen said as she strolled into the library with a burp rag slung over her shoulder.

"Quit being modest Jen," Costin laughed. "You're more than intrigued, you're practically salivating at the sexual innuendos coming together in that wicked head of yours."

She shrugged. "What can I say, it's a gift." She motioned to Lucian who was still staring at the phone in his hands. "Since we know you guys weren't really talking about the size of your junk, what exactly were you talking about?"

Lucian's eyebrows rose as he looked up from the phone to pin his stare on Jen. "I truly do not understand most of what you say."

She laughed. "Neither does my mate, but he's learning and so will you. Now as interesting as I'm sure that cell phone is to your poor, neglected mind, I want to know how things are going with you and your fairy." She plunked herself down on the couch and pointed across from her indicating for him to sit.

"Jen," Costin started.

She held up a finger to stop him and turned her head slowly to look at him. "I'm going to meddle so don't bother telling me not to meddle because, frankly, it's a waste of oxygen. You know as well as I do that they are going to have to complete the bond because at some point his darkness is going to take over. What happens if another male makes advances on Peri and he doesn't have the darkness under control?"

They heard a crunch and looked over at Lucian who now had a crushed cell phone in his partially human hands. He looked down at it and frowned.

"What male are you talking about?" Lucian asked with calmness that Jen knew all too well.

"I'm not saying that there *is* one, Lucian. I'm just saying that if there was one, things could get messy." She groaned dramatically, "Ugh if there was just one person here that could appreciate the things I could do with that sentence." She looked back at Lucian and motioned once again for him to sit. He walked over and took the seat she indicated but he held her gaze the entire time. Jen finally relented and dropped her eyes. "Stupid Alphas and their power games," she muttered.

"I am not an Alpha," Lucian pointed out.

"Maybe not, but you have the dominance to be one. Now, about Peri…," she prompted and then waited.

"She is coming to terms with it," Lucian finally spoke. "She just needs time, and that is something I can give her."

"You know that she wants to leave, to go after her sister?" Jen asked.

Lucian nodded.

"And you're okay with her going?"

Lucian's lips twitch in amusement. "She can go anywhere she wants," he paused, "but I've made it very clear to her that where she goes, I go."

"And how did Peri fairy respond to that?" Jen grinned.

"I would not repeat such language in front of a female," Lucian told her with a gleam in his eyes that had Jen laughing.

"Oh man this is awesome," she ground out with a clap of her hands. "Our little Peri is all wrapped up with the big bad wolf, totally priceless." She stood and smiled down at the wolf. "Hang in there, brother wolf. She'll come around."

Lucian smiled and it was all teeth. "Do not worry, mate to Decebel. We wolves are very, *very* patient hunters."

Jen cackled as she turned to leave and called out over her shoulder, "Don't I know it."

"Sorry about the cell phone," Lucian told Costin as he stood and held out the plastic mess.

Costin chuckled. "You can imagine that we go through quite a few phones; we have really good insurance." Costin tossed the phone in the trash and then glanced back to Lucian who was now staring out of one of the many windows. "I'm headed to the training area to get in a workout. You can join me if you want. Sally's with Rachel doing healer stuff so I'm having to figure out how to entertain myself." He shook his head. "It's hard to believe that for sixty years I was capable of getting through the day without her, but now," he exhaled, "now every minute away from her is torture."

Lucian nodded. "Like you are seeing the world in black and white until she walks into the room and suddenly everything is in color; rich, vibrant colors that reflect her light."

"Exactly," Costin agreed.

"I appreciate the offer, but I think I had better bow out of training today," Lucian said politely. "I fear I would be too aggressive to be safe."

"As Jen said, hang in there. Peri is a proud fae, but she is not stupid. She will come around." Costin left without another word.

Lucian glanced back out the window and his eyes landed once again on his mate.

He agreed that she was indeed proud, but he was beginning to question whether Costin was right about the not stupid part. She was on the very training ground that Costin had just spoken of and she was now wearing clothing that revealed every enticing curve, every defined muscle. She was sparing with another fae female that he recognized as Elle. Peri landed a powerful forward strike, leaving Elle sprawled on her back. Lucian saw a male figure step forward from the group that was now forming around them. It was Sorin, one of the wolves, and also Elle's mate. He looked about as happy as Lucian felt.

Elle waved him off and readied herself once again for Peri's attack. They continued sparring, moving with a speed and grace that fae alone could accomplish and soon they had an entire group, female and male, circling around them watching the bout. Lucian's jaw clenched as Elle conceded, bowing to Peri and then stepping back. He watched as Peri motioned for someone else to step up to spar with her. After several seconds one of the younger males stepped forward. He didn't remember his name, but he recognized the face as being one of the Serbian wolves.

"Mate, I am asking that you not spar with that male," Lucian reached to her through their bond as he tried to hold back his wolf. His hands trembled under the strain that it took to hold the phase back. He watched as Peri stiffened as she heard his voice and her head slowly rose until she was looking at him through the window. He knew his eyes would be glowing, but there was nothing he could do about that. All he knew was that if that male put his hands on Peri in any way, be it to harm or give pleasure, his wolf would kill him. There was no doubt in his mind. If he let his wolf out, he would not be able to control him.

"Perhaps you could take his place?" Peri's cool voice was like a refreshing breeze across the hot marshes of his mind.

"I do not think it would be wise of me to engage in any form of violence right now." Lucian tried to let her see just how difficult it was for him without flooding her with all of his emotions. He saw the moment she picked up on it because she took a step back from the male. She gave a low bow indicating that she was withdrawing from the fight and then disappeared.

"It's only going to get worse isn't it," her voice came from behind him. She had flashed from the training ground to the library. Judging from the looks on the faces of the group still on the training ground, they were still just as bothered by it as the first time Peri had done it.

He turned to face her and bit back the growl that wanted to pour out of him. She was beautiful—her face flushed from the work out, her hair shimmering in the light, her form perfect on display in her training clothes.

"Do they make clothes that do not fit so snug?" He asked her, unable to hold it in any longer.

She laughed. "You want me to accept this bond between us? Well then you are just going to have to accept the clothes of this day and age."

"I do not think that is a fair exchange. Why should I be alright with your feminine form being on display for other males to see?"

"The key word in that statement Lucian is *your*. You have just stated that it is indeed my feminine form that is in question, and since it belongs to me I am the one in charge of it," Peri said coyly. "Now if you will excuse me, I need to go shower said feminine

38

form lest it becomes smelly. I don't do smelly." She turned on her heal and left without another word.

Lucian wondered why she bothered walking anywhere when she could flash. He decided to tuck that question away along with others he had been forming to ask her. He would save that to ask while they were on their journey to find her sister. He hoped that during their search he would be able to get to know her better and for her to get to know him and, hopefully, to fall in love with him. He would have much rather completed their bond and blood rites before their departure, but she just wasn't ready and he would not force it on her.

Laughter out in the hallway caught his attention and he walked over and stuck his head out. Jen sat precariously perched on the balcony railing that looked out over the entryway to the mansion. Her mate, Decebel, stood several feet away holding their new infant daughter in his arms. Lucian's lips twitched at the large male holding the tiny child with such care. But his shoulders tensed at the angry expression he saw on Decebel's face. It was so inconsistent with the gentleness in which his arms held the babe that it caught Lucian off guard.

"Jennifer, get down from the railing." He heard the Alpha say through clenched teeth. It was obvious that he was trying to stay calm because of his tiny burden, but his mate was truly putting his control to the test.

Jen dangled one leg over the edge, her balance perfect, her body relaxed. "But this is what I wanted to show you," she whined. "Jacque and I have been seeing how many of our wolf traits we can use while in human form, and get this," she held her hand out in excitement, "cats aren't the only ones that always land on their feet." And with that she pushed up with her legs and threw her body back high in the air above the entryway.

Lucian was out the door and running without realizing it as he watched in part horror and part awe as the female did a back flip off of the railing. As he and Decebel both reached the rail and looked over, he saw that she had indeed landed on her feet. She threw her hands in the air in celebration and then proceeded to dance to some tune that she was now singing.

Lucian quickly looked away from the Alpha's mate's gyrating body. He looked at Decebel when he heard an exasperated huff leave his chest.

"You might want to check into a return policy before you complete the bond with your mate," Decebel told him wearily.

Lucian shook his head feeling every bit as tired as Decebel looked. "I don't understand her. I don't like the way she dresses, her temper is legendary, and she is constantly threatening me with bodily harm, and yet I would rip out my own heart before I would give her up."

Decebel chuckled and nodded knowingly. "And just to be clear brother, you *do* like the way she dresses, you just wish you were the only one who got to enjoy it."

"I will never admit such a thing," Lucian said stoically as he fought to keep the smile from his face.

Decebel turned at the sound of his mate coming up the stairs. Lucian watched as Decebel growled at her, his good humor seemingly gone.

"Dec babe, you know I don't like you to threaten me unless there is going to be some follow through. So don't be throwing around things like *spank you* and *over my knee* unless you got the gumption to back it up." Jen leaned around Dec and gave Lucian a wicked wink as she grabbed her mate's free hand and pulled him down the hall. All the while Lucian could hear the Alpha grumbling to his mate about trying to give him a heart attack and at least she kept her clothes on. *Bloody hell*, Lucian thought, *I do not even want to know what that is all about.* He supposed he should be thankful that Perizada didn't dance in public or attempt to take her clothes off. He heard Jen's laughing again and sent a silent prayer to the Great Luna on Decebel's behalf. From what Lucian had seen and heard of Jen, the Alpha would need all the help he could get.

Showered, refreshed and ready to get on the road, Peri reached out to Elle and Adam. As a high fae, Peri had the ability to connect mentally with others of her kind and, until now, she had never thought twice about invading their privacy when she needed them. Of course, until now she had never had to share them with anyone. They were her soldiers, sent by the Great Luna to help keep the supernatural world in balance. Peri could never have guessed that the Great Luna would cause the fae and werewolves to become compatible as true mates, forever changing the fates of both species. Adam, who had at one time been quite the flirt, became true mate to Crina, one of the female werewolves in Vasile's pack. Adam had been shocked, but he gave in willingly. Now, months later, he hardly leaves Crina's side. He had even developed the markings that were common on the wolf males that indicated he was a dominant and then Crina's mate markings had appeared and matched Adams.

Elle had also been chosen to be the mate to a wolf. She was given, Sorin, once the Guardian of the Alpha's son, and a dominant. Elle hadn't been quite as sure as Adam and had initially run from Sorin. Peri smirked at the memory of Sorin, calm, collect Sorin, having a regular werewolf tantrum when Elle had disappeared right before his very eyes. Peri had been the one to go talk to Elle, much to her own surprise and the surprise of pretty much everyone.

Now she was contemplating supernaturally communicating with Adam and Elle through their minds, something fae are accustomed to doing. But the fact of the matter is that a mental bond in the werewolf world is a much more intimate affair than in the fae world and she felt like she was going somewhere that only their mates should be allowed.

"Dammit, Perizada," she snapped at herself as she headed for the door, "it's not like you are walking into their bedroom while they're going at it. All you're doing is slipping into their mind to give them a message and then just slipping right back out again." She walked to the hall where their rooms were located as she reasoned with herself. But she knew she wasn't going to win this battle, not after sharing the mental bond with Lucian—her conscience wasn't hearing her.

She let out a resigned sigh as she stood in the hallway. "ELLE, ADAM!" She yelled, knowing that

42

her strong voice would make it through the walls and doors. She waited, not patiently by any means, as her foot tapped and she chewed on her lip. *I'm chewing on my lip, good grief what's next, nail biting?* She admonished herself inwardly. Finally, two doors opened almost simultaneously.

"Good grief it took you two long enough," Peri grumbled.

Adam stepped into the hall with a knowing smirk on his too handsome face. "You still haven't given in and taken that male of yours to task have you?"

A single brow rose on Peri's face as she looked at the male fae. "Did you just refer to the intimacy of mates as taking them to task?"

Adam laughed. "Okay, you're right, it's so much funnier when you say it."

Crina slapped his arm. "Be nice."

Adam pretended to be hurt as he put on the pouty face that seemed to make Crina laugh; it only made Peri want to smack it off.

"But *she's* never nice." Adam blinked big puppy dog eyes at his mate. She giggled.

Peri rolled her eyes and smacked herself on the forehead. "Please tell me this is not what I have to look forward to?"

"Oh no, Peri, it gets worse," Elle said as she walked up to stand next to Adam with Sorin, her mate, at her side. "Nauseatingly worse," she said wickedly and laughed at Peri's look of distress.

Peri took a deep breath and let it out slowly, all the while telling herself that she would never allow herself to be that wrapped around Lucian's little finger, the way her fellow fae were with their mates.

"I actually sought you both out for a reason and much to your disappointment it was not for your input on the ins and outs of being mated to a werewolf."

"Can I touch that one?" Adam interrupted.

Peri knew exactly how Adam's mind worked. He was basically the male version of Jen, in short, a pervert. "Not with a ten foot pole," she glowered. He held his hands up in surrender but the grin remained.

"What do you need, Peri?" Elle asked.

Her tone indicated to Peri that she still recognized Peri's authority and would perform whatever task was required of her. Peri wondered how Sorin would feel about that. *Guess we're about to find out,* she thought.

"I'm going after Lorelle. Her crimes are a death sentence and since she killed me, and even though the Great Luna spared my life, I feel obligated as her sister to return the favor. I would appreciate your help and Adam's as well. You both have very useful skills that would be of great importance to such a mission." Peri tried not to look at their mates to gauge their reactions, but instead focused on the two fae who had served her and been her friends for centuries.

"Are we going to be traipsing through a forest, sleeping on the ground, battling other supernatural beings or killing a witch or warlock?" Adam asked.

"Considering we have recently killed the last evil witch left on this earth that I know of, I think it's a safe bet that I can say no," Peri said dryly.

Adam acted disappointed as he slumped back against the wall. "Well in that case, no, sorry I can't in good conscience go on any missions where my life isn't in some sort of danger. That would be boring. I'd rather stay here and see how un-ladylike I can get my pretty, furry mate to be."

"Okay, first off, I think I just vomited in my mouth," Peri's face twisted into one of obvious disgust. "And secondly you should know by now that anytime I have to spend more than a day in your company your life is in danger. So problem solved and you," she pointed at Crina who was staring at Adam like he had just invented social media, "shame on you. Come on, girl. You're giving the rest of us a bad name panting after him like he's the last popsicle in hell."

Crina blushed and laughed. She was usually nearly as snarky as Jen and Jacque but her mating to Adam had softened her. Peri was giving her a hard time, but she wasn't about to tell Crina that her mating agreed with her, that she looked happier and healthier than she ever had.

"What about you?" Peri asked Elle.

"Honestly we've been waiting for your call," Elle answered. "We're ready to go when you are."

"Sorin, you are okay with your mate continuing to work with me?"

Sorin smiled slyly. "You ask me that as if I had some sort of say in the matter."

Elle elbowed him in the stomach and though he pretended to be hurt he was laughing.

"I do need to ask," Sorin spoke up again having corralled his mate's stabbing elbows, "will Lucian be joining us?"

"Yes," Peri answered curtly. "Is that a problem?"

"Just like to know the pecking order if you know what I mean," he told her with a wink.

45

Peri rolled her eyes. "You wolves and your dominance games, you all should seriously consider making it an Olympic sport."

Sorin shook his head. "I have no desire to play games, Perizada. I do, however, have a strong sense of self-preservation and part of keeping my mate safe and staying alive is knowing who the more dominant wolves in the room are and how to avoid angering them."

"Or you could just learn to fight dirty," she replied. As she turned to go she added, "We'll meet at the edge of the forest at midnight."

"Um, why midnight?" Elle asked her retreating back.

"Because that is when the things that go bump come out to play. Lorelle is most definitely a thing that goes bump in the night. Don't be late, I do not want to have to come drag your writhing bodies from your beds, because it would make me puke and I dearly hate to puke," she called out over her shoulder not bothering to see the looks on their faces.

Chapter 3

"If you are a villain, eventually there will come a day when you finally admit that you like the taste of all things evil. You like doing evil deeds you take joy in others pain, and you seriously struggle not to turn every idiot you meet into a beetle that you can then step on with a satisfying crunch. But when the day comes that you finally encounter an evil darker, and fouler than your own, the taste you so dearly cherished becomes bitter ash in the back of your throat."

~Lorelle

"Why have you come to my home, Lorelle?" Volcan's voice echoed off the cold stone walls. Lorelle looked around her, feeling vulnerable because she couldn't see him and yet he could somehow see her. "I found myself in need of new lodgings," she told him casually.

She heard his chuckle and knew the nonchalant tone in her voice hadn't fooled him.

"Come now, it's rude to be dishonest when you're a guest."

"Isn't it *always* rude to be dishonest?" She asked.

"In the face of murder," he let his words set in before he continued, "what's a little dishonesty?"

Lorelle immediately pushed up mental walls to cloak her thoughts from the ancient fae. She hadn't even considered that he might be able to read her mind. "If you already know the answers, then why even bother to ask me questions?"

"Perhaps I wanted to see if you would be honest with me." There was another pause and then he

47

finished with, "And perhaps I wanted to see if you could feel my presence."

"How is it that you…,"

"Ah-ah," he interrupted. "No more questions from you until you begin to answer my own. It seems the Fates have brought you to me. I cannot leave this place thanks to the Fae Council and their bloody binding spell."

Lorelle chuckled but tried to quickly cover it with a cough.

"Is something amusing?" Volcan asked her.

"Well it's just that you called it a *bloody* binding spell and I couldn't help but find that ironic since it took blood for the spell to work," she explained though her humor had dried up by the time she was done.

"Yes well I imagine your sister had something to do with that part of the spell. She was always quite powerful."

Lorelle bristled under the praise of her sister and couldn't believe that even after she'd killed the egotistical wench she was still getting more accolades than her.

"Now, tell me the truth or I will rip it from your mind and it won't be pleasant," the voice of Volcan growled at her.

"Hence the whole ripping part," Lorelle muttered.

He made an exasperated sound and Lorelle could almost picture in her mind the face he would be making.

"I guess I should start with *hi my name is Lorelle and I killed my sister.*"

∞

Lucian stood outside of her door, his hand poised to knock. He hadn't seen her since their encounter in the library and he was hungry for the sight of her, but something stopped him from knocking. Instead he stood there listening for her movements, and not for the first time feeling very unsure of himself. It was not a feeling he was used to and he found more and more that he did not like it.

"You are acclimating well to this environment," a soothing voice came from behind him. He turned and knelt all in the same motion, bowing his head to his Creator.

"Great Luna," he rumbled.

"But for all your acclimation, you hesitate at the door of your true mate. Why?"

Lucian didn't miss the reprimand in the Great Luna's voice and fought the urge to cringe at the picture she painted. He, a dominate male, and an Alpha in his own right, stood like a scared pup outside the door of his mate instead of claiming what was his.

"She doesn't fully understand the bond and I won't push her before she is ready," he explained and though it made sense to him, it sounded like an excuse as he said it out loud.

"Perhaps you aren't giving her enough credit. Peri is a strong female, which is why I picked her for you. She has shouldered many burdens and dealt with much evil in her time. I have a feeling she is plenty up to the challenge of an Alpha male werewolf. Stand, Lucian," she commanded gently.

Lucian rose from his position on the ground and looked at the Great Luna. His eyes met hers briefly but then dropped in humility. He decided to voice what he knew his Creator already knew. "What if she doesn't want me? What if she doesn't want the mate bond?"

He felt her hand on his shoulder and her warmth, love and comfort from that simple touch.

"You aren't asking the right questions. What you should be asking is what if she does?" She tilted his chin up so that he had to look at her. "I know that you were in the dark for a very long time and that has affected the wolf you are, but do not let it affect the man I created you to be. The struggles that you endure in your life can either chip away at the goodness inside of you, or they can cause you to grow stronger, fortifying your character. Don't let that time in the Dark Forest ruin the good things I have in store for you. Don't allow yourself to be robbed of joy because of fears that might never come to fruition. I made you wolf I have a purpose for you but I cannot fulfill it. That is something only you can do. I gave you a true mate; now you must claim her. Love her as she needs, be the servant male that she has never known and watch the walls that she has built up around herself come crashing down only for you."

Lucian stood there looking at the empty hallway for several minutes after the Great Luna's departure. Her words struck something deep inside him and he felt his wolf stirring, answering his Creator. He turned to look at the closed door he had been standing in front of full of indecision and saw it for what it was, a barrier between him and his mate. He was done with barriers.

∞

Peri paced the room checking the clock for the umpteenth time and growled in frustration when she realized that only three minutes had passed since she checked it last. It was only eleven o'clock; she still had a bloody hour until she would meet up with the others. She hadn't seen or heard from Lucian, not that she had attempted to reach out to him through their bond, but it would have been nice if he had checked in on her.

"Oh hell," she groaned as she sat with a gracelessness that was uncharacteristic of her race, on the edge of the bed. "I like him," she admitted out loud, granted only she could hear her admission. That could be the only explanation for wanting to see him or hear from him. *Well not the only*, she conceded, but she refused to even give thought to the other four letter L word. Liking him wasn't the end of the world she decided. He was, after all, a nice male and nice to look at, that certainly didn't hurt.

She had assumed after their little interaction in the library that he would seek her out, but to her surprise and irritation he hadn't. He had said that he would go with her when she left. Now she was beginning to wonder if maybe he had changed his mind just as she stood up to resume the pacing that seemed to be her tendency of late, the door knob on her door twisted until the lock in it popped and broke. Peri gathered her power but before she could strike out at the intruder Lucian walked in.

Peri's breath caught in her throat as his eyes met hers. He was cloaked in his usual confidence but there was something more. Something stronger seemed to shimmer on the edges of his being. He stalked towards her and didn't stop until he had a strong arm around her waist and a large but tender hand held her chin still so she was forced to look at him. She could feel him in her mind, searching as his silver eyes stared into hers.

"You missed me," he finally spoke. There was no smugness in his voice. He was merely stating what he had found when he used their bond and she didn't deny it.

"Yes," she told him.

"Why did you not seek me out?"

Peri's lips parted but no words came out. What was she supposed to say? *I'm too proud to admit that I need you, that I want you near me?* And even as she thought the words, she realized they were true, and she felt so very ugly in that moment. Standing there in the arms of a man ready and willing to be whatever she needed of him and she hadn't even had the courage to ask him how he was when all she had done was think of him nonstop.

"I don't know how to do this," she finally blurted out. She tried to look away but his hand held her captive.

"Do what?" He asked gently.

"This," she indicated with her hand between them. "I don't know how to be a mate. I've been number one in my life for thousands of years, and now suddenly there is someone else who has feelings I should consider."

"So you are saying that you are selfish?" A slight smile danced on his full lips. "We all are, but the beauty of having a mate is that they will love you regardless. I want you, even with all of your selfishness. With all of your ages of baggage, I want you. Do you want me? I know that you are unsure about doing the blood rites, and completing the bond, but in this moment looking at me, can you say that you want to be with me?"

"Yes," Peri didn't hesitate, what would be the point? She couldn't lie to herself any longer and she was sick of denying the ache inside of her chest. She wanted Lucian. She didn't know where it would go from here or how quickly she would let it progress, but she was done pushing him away.

He closed his eyes and let out a low, possessive growl as his arm around her pulled her more tightly against him, her body flush against his igniting a flame of desire in her that no other ever had, and she knew without a doubt ever would. "Finally." His eyes snapped open and then his mouth was pressed to hers. Peri swore she could hear all of nature shouting, a chorus of angels singing and quite possibly even that Elvis guy from the grave singing that falling in love song, as Lucian, her mate claimed her lips, her heart and her soul. He deepened the kiss as he tilted her head to the side and her lips parted without a conscious thought. The sensuous stroke of his tongue on her own woke urges that she didn't even realize she had. Peri felt her arms raise and her hands wrap around his neck, her fingers tunneling through the hair on the back of his head drawing a deep moan from him. She lost herself in him. All rational thoughts flew out the proverbial window as his hands gripped her hips, *holy hell when had his hands made it there*, she asked herself. He lifted her and she automatically wrapped her legs around his waist as he walked until her back was pressed to the wall.

Lucian pressed closer to his female, holding her effortlessly against the wall as he drank from her lips. Her scent was swirling around him calling to his wolf. He felt his canines lengthen and he had to be careful not to cut her as he kissed her. He needed to get control of himself, but as he felt her thighs tighten around him he felt his resolve for that control slipping. He could have her here, now, she would give herself to him, he could feel it in her mind and his wolf urged him to claim her. *Bite her*, his wolf growled in his mind, *she is ours, she should bear our mark*. Lucian's lips slid from hers down her jaw and neck to the tender place below her ear. He licked her and kissed her several times until Peri's head fell back and she submitted to him. He stared at the spot on her neck calling out to him through a haze of lust, need, want and instinct. He felt a snarl rising in him as he fought his wolf for control as the thoughts of the man broke through. *Not like this*, he told the wolf.

"Lucian," Peri's needy voice helped clear his mind and he looked up from her neck into her pale green eyes.

"Is something wrong?" She asked him through swollen, glistening lips, flushed cheeks and hair all askew from his hands ravishing it. He could feel her chest rising and falling against his own as she fought to catch her breath.

He let out a deep sigh and set her feet on the ground. He didn't let go of her, but he put a little space between their bodies so he could continue to regain his reasoning. There was only so much a man could handle before he was tempted beyond reason and gave into his primal urges, especially a man who also carried the soul of an animal inside of him.

"Yes and no," he told her honestly. "That was…it was," his breathing was still ragged as he tried to gather the words. "I've been told intimacy with your mate is indescribable and I'm inclined to say I agree even though all I've had the privilege of doing is kissing you. That was not wrong okay; I need you to hear that Peri. What we just shared was beyond anything even I could and have imagined with you."

"Okay, so then what *was* wrong?" She asked him carefully.

"My wolf doesn't think like I do. He doesn't reason the way a man does. He smells your desire and goes crazy to be near you, to touch you, taste you and possess you. He doesn't stop to wonder if you want him touching you, he just assumes it's his right and you will like it."

Peri let out a snort of laughter. "Sounds like a man to me."

Lucian tapped her nose playfully. "Behave, mate," he teased. "He wants to mark you, needs to mark you. I barely stopped myself from biting that luscious neck of yours. When you tilted your head back that was a clear sign to the wolf that you were submitting to us, basically he read it as *I want this so do it now*. I have never had to fight him so hard before."

"So *you* don't want to mark me?" Her voice was tentative and unsure even as her stare held his in her usual straightforward confidence.

Lucian's eyes narrowed as a frown crept over his face. "No that is not what I am saying at all. Peri, if you said to me *bite me* now this second and I knew you meant it, truly wanted it, I would gladly lay you on that bed and take what is mine and give you what is yours. I would bind you to me irrevocably right now, body and soul, but you are not ready. You want me, lust for me, ache for my touch and enjoy my company, but you have not fully come to terms with the mate bond yet. That's why I did not bite you. That is why I have not claimed your virtue." His hands that had been resting on her waist moved up to gently cup her face. "What are you thinking?"

"I'm getting there," she told him as she looked up at him. "I know that I don't want to be without you. So I'm moving in the right direction." She rose up and pressed a soft kiss to his lips and as she pulled back Lucian struggled not to pull her into his arms and pick up where they left off. The woman was too desirable for her own good.

"I'm glad to see that you are making progress." A voice said from behind them.

Peri bowed her head to the Great Luna as she stepped to the side of Lucian. He turned and wrapped an arm around her waist, determined not to let her put space, be it physical or emotional, between them, not with the forward motion they seemed to be in.

"Great Luna," Lucian's voice rumbled not revealing his surprise at seeing her again so soon.

"Perizada," she stepped towards them and held her hand out to the fae. Peri went to her without hesitation and took the goddess' hand. "You have never fully understood your worth and I hope you will let this male show you just how worthy you are. I do not make mistakes, Peri. I gave him to you for a reason, him and no other."

Peri understood what the goddess was saying, and she knew that she would be wise to heed her advice. Did that mean she would comply right away? Probably not, she seemed to like to suffer unnecessarily. *Idiot,* she thought to herself.

"But I have come for another reason. Long ago I made you the mediator for the wolves. You have done your job well. I also put you over the healers and though have not been present for some time, their time is coming. There are healers even now that have not been exposed to the wolves and so their true nature has not surfaced. I know that you wish to go and take vengeance on your sister. You seek justice and as honorable as that is I need you elsewhere." She paused as she looked out into the night. She stepped away from Peri and pointed out into the forest beyond the Romanian mansion. "There are five gypsy healers out there, living their lives completely ignorant of their heritage. Much like Sally, the gypsy blood of their ancestors flows through them, but knowledge of their heritage has been lost over time. Healers are precious and they have power that can be used for good or evil. I'm asking you to find these healers. I will designate a place for you to take them to train them, to teach them their heritage. Then they will need to be introduced to the packs because they have mates that need them. You know that the mate of a healer is always a dominant, they have to be strong enough to protect them, but that also means the

57

darkness in them is stronger. These females range from ages sixteen to twenty, so they are of courting age."

Peri waited for more and when the Great Luna didn't continue she asked, "Do you have a location for any of them?"

The Great Luna turned and looked at her with a small smile. "Perhaps you would like me to go gather them up for you as well?"

Peri laughed. "Have you been hanging out with Jen?"

"The purpose is not in the outcome but in the journey. One road often leads to many places, Perizada, and this journey, this road will take you where you need to go and teach you what you need to learn. No one, not even me, can do it for you. You need to have your mate with you, you need to trust him and let him lead when necessary. You have always been willing to make sacrifices for others; I ask that you would do so again and save these healers. They need you both, they need my wolves and we need them."

Peri stood looking out the window after the Great Luna left as quietly as she had come. For the first time in her immortal life she was struggling to do the right thing. The right thing would be to do what the Great Luna had instructed her to do and go find those healers. But what she wanted to do was hunt down her sister first and *then* go find the healers. Surely it would be safer for her to find the healers after the threat was dealt with.

"Hey," Lucian's deep voice came from behind her just as his arms wrapped around her and pulled her back against his chest. She bit her tongue to keep from groaning out just how good it felt to be held and she went more than willingly.

"I can hear you, you know?" Though she heard his voice in her mind, she felt his chuckle in her back as his chest moved with it.

"Yes, I'm aware of the fact that you use frequent flyer miles in my mind gathering up information and such," she said attempting to sound irritated. But the purr in her voice only made her sound like a slightly ticked off kitten. *Lovely,* she thought.

"I am not sure what frequent flyer miles are but if you mean I am often in your mind then yes you are correct. As much as I like to use our bond, I like it even more when you willingly talk to me. What are you thinking?" He asked her.

"I'm thinking that the Great Luna didn't disclose everything to us," she answered honestly. "I'm not saying that I think she is being deceitful because that isn't in her nature, I just mean that I think she didn't reveal the whole puzzle."

"We live in a world full of evil, a fallen world. She knows that we know we are going to face that evil whether it is spelled out for us or not. She also knows that we will defeat it."

"Do you think I should let my sister go?" She asked him quietly.

"No, but I think you should do it in the right order. If Lorelle finds out about these healers she might try to take them. You and I both know that there have been other powerful enemies who have wanted healers for their own use. If Lorelle truly has turned away from the light and embraced the darkness, then abducting a healer to use her power would just be the next step in her evolution."

Peri let out a slow deep breath and reluctantly stepped out of Lucian's hold. She turned and looked at him. "And here I thought this would all be cut and dry. Hunt down my sister, bitch slap her for being stupid, sentence her to death and then live happily ever after."

Lucian's head tilted to the side as he looked at his mate. "Sometimes you say the most unorthodox things."

"Now you're just showing your age old man," she teased him. She let out a weary sigh as she headed towards the door. "Well we're supposed to meet my partners in crime at midnight to leave on our hunt; I guess I will have to tell them there has been a change in plans."

"Peri," Lucian's' voice brought her up short of pulling the door open. "Can I ask why you do not just flash where you want to go? Why do you walk so much if you do not have to?"

Peri smiled as she turned and looked at her mate. "Do you honestly think this incredible figure would be possible if all I did was pop in and out of places? Immortal or not, all this," she motioned to her frame, "takes work."

Lucian let out a low huff of laughter. "Whatever you say, love." He took her hand and led her from the room.

They found the two couples at the edge of the forest where Peri had instructed them to meet her. The way they were draped over one another made them look more like two teenage couples after prom, rather than elite fae hunters and werewolves waiting on a mission briefing.

"Don't you all ever give it a rest? I mean I seriously think you are worse than Jen and her fur ball and really that's saying something," Peri grumbled as she approached the pairs.

Adam pulled his lips away from the spot on Crina's neck that he had so dutifully been giving all his attention and looked at Peri. "All work and no play makes for a cranky fae, Peri. You're frown and the frustrated look on your mate's face is a testament to that statement. Perhaps you could learn something from us and the Serbian Alpha pair."

"Are you seriously giving me advice now on my…,"

"Peri," Lucian's voice cut her off before she could continue. "Perhaps you should tell them what the Great Luna has revealed."

Peri folded her arms across her chest as she eyed Adam and then Elle. "If you two think you can pull yourselves from your mate's body parts for five minutes then I will gladly fill you in on what Lucian is talking about."

"I think she's getting crankier," Elle told Adam.

Adam nodded. "Agreed."

"The Great Luna has given Peri a new mission, one that doesn't involve going after her sister at this time," Lucian spoke up interrupting any more play by play between his mate and her long time comrades.

"She's just going to let Lorelle go?" Elle asked incredulously.

"No," Peri spoke up. "I'm not just going to let her go, but I am going to do as the Great Luna has instructed and then I will go after my sister."

"What could be more important than taking out a murdering high fae?" Sorin asked.

"Gypsy healers," Peri responded.

The group gasped at her answer as their eyes widened.

"There are more?" Crina asked.

"According to the Great Luna there are five females, ages sixteen to twenty that need to know of their heritage and be trained," Peri explained. "She wants me to find them and bring them to a safe place for Rachel and I to teach them, and then she wants them introduced to the packs."

"True mates," Crina said in awe.

"Exactly," Peri agreed.

"How are you going to find them and once you do, how are you going to bring them here?" Sorin asked. "Some of them are minors; you can't just take them from their families."

Peri rolled her eyes. "You've forgotten a tiny detail, Sorin," she paused for effect and then said with a sly grin as she pointed to herself, "High fae, ûbber powerful. I think I can handle causing five gypsy healers to disappear with no problems."

"So when do we start?" Elle asked.

"This isn't going to be some exciting, adrenaline inducing, life threatening hunt," she looked from Elle to Adam, "you still want to help?"

Adam shrugged as he wrapped an arm around Crina's waist. "I suppose one tame mission a year isn't too much to ask."

Peri chuckled, "How magnanimous of you Adam."

He grinned showing perfect, white teeth. "I have my moments."

"I will talk with Rachel and Sally tomorrow and see if any of their magic can help locate others of their kind. We'll meet at lunchtime and go over what I've learned and decide the next course of action."

"Do you want to involve any of the other high fae?" Elle asked.

Peri thought about the question, considering the possibility that having others with considerable power might help. But then something inside her told her that she needed to keep the knowledge of the young healers as quiet as possible for as long as possible. "No, I think this information needs to stay among us. Rachel and Sally will be the only others that know. Healers are valuable, and until they are safely under our protection it would be better if others weren't made aware of them."

"Sounds like a plan," Adam said as he took his mate's hand. "Since we won't be leaving tonight, Crina and I are going to turn in. We'll see you all tomorrow at lunch." Without another word he flashed and he and Crina were gone.

"We will take our leave as well," Sorin said as he wrapped an arm around Elle and she flashed them from the field.

Peri look from the empty space where the couples had stood to Lucian. "I can't believe Adam left without any bedroom commentary," she shook her head, "I almost feel as if he's going to suddenly pop up and say something completely disgusting."

Lucian frowned slightly. "I am not used to everyone being so open about their intimate relationships with their mates." His frown deepened as he continued. "When we arrived Adam was practically…,"

"Licking his mate like a man on death row licks the fork of his last bite of his last meal?" Peri interjected.

Lucian eyed her dubiously. "Exactly. Wolves touch their mates freely and often, but I do not ever remember seeing mated pairs talk so open about their intimacy."

Peri tried not to laugh at the confused look on Lucian's face. "Well, you might want to get use to the whole touchy feely thing because more than likely we'll be going to America in our hunt for the healers."

"What does that mean?" he asked as he took her hand and they once again headed back towards the Romanian mansion on foot instead of flashing.

"It means you ain't seen nothing yet. And I totally mean that literally."

Chapter 4

"There shall only be certain females chosen in a bloodline to become healers. The healer's spirit will be pure and her heart will be selfless. Life shall flow out of her like healing water into the Pack that she serves. She will bring hope where there has been none, light where darkness has taken over and peace where turmoil has reigned. She is to be treasured and protected from all malevolence because there is no greater depravity than to take something meant for good and use it to glorify evil." ~The Great Luna

"There are no more witches left alive?" Volcan asked Lorelle for the third time.

Lorelle was beginning to think that being alone for the past several centuries hadn't done anything to improve Volcan's sanity.

"Desdemona was the last of her kind and Vasile, the Romanian Alpha, killed her just a few months ago," she told him yet again.

She could feel disbelief and anger flowing around her and she was surprised by the amount of power his spirit seemed to wield. Not that she frequently came in contact with non-corporeal beings that were supposed to be dead, so how would she know how much power they should or should not have?

"Focus, Lorelle," Volcan's voice snapped her from her musing. "The situation is grimmer than I had originally thought. But no matter, that won't change our plans."

"Our plans?" Lorelle asked hesitantly not really wanting him to elaborate on it but understanding she needed to know just how deep she was in.

"You didn't come here by chance, Lorelle," Volcan's voice took on a story teller like quality. "You were brought here by your subconscious, answering a call that I sent out. You see, I need a body to possess until I have the power to get my own back. There is only so much of my magic that I can use without a physical form. So I sent out a call and you, my dear, are what answered it."

"I don't remember hearing a call," Lorelle said trying to keep the fact that he had just completely creeped her out, from her voice.

"Like calls to like, Lorelle, you know this. Your own black heart is drawn to the darkness in others and it heard the call even if you did not."

"That really brings a whole new meaning to the term *follow your heart*," Lorelle muttered under her breath.

"I see that you are blessed with the same foolhardy wit that your sister had. That's too bad for you," Volcan said dryly, obviously not impressed by her sarcasm.

"In case you have forgotten so soon after having been told, I am the one who killed my sister. I'm not exactly harmless," she snapped.

"Then there is hope for you yet. I will need to possess your body to cast a seeking spell."

"What are we seeking?"

"Gypsy healers," he answered.

"We don't have to seek for any, I already know of one. There were two, but one of them took her own life to save the lives of her pack mates," Lorelle explained with no emotion in her voice."

"You must not understand the value of a healer if you allowed one to die," Volcan challenged.

"How valuable can they be if they aren't willing to cooperate? It's not in the nature of a healer to harm; how can you possibly use their magic if they won't bend to your will?" She asked.

"Everyone has a weakness, Lorelle, and if you can exploit that weakness you can get them to do just about anything."

Lorelle crossed her arms in front of her chest and rested her hip against the wall. She looked around the foyer, trying to see if she could get a read on his magic. If she could pinpoint his spirit, she could locate him, but her mind was such a terrible mess that she couldn't focus. She knew there was no way out of the castle now that Volcan wanted her here. She wouldn't be allowed to leave until his will released her. Like it or not, she was stuck.

"I have been informed that there are several young gypsy healers out in the wide world as we speak. They are unaware of their heritage, and not under any protection. You are going to retrieve them for me." Volcan's voice had taken on a purring quality as he spoke of the healers.

"Informed by whom?" Lorelle asked.

"I have eyes and ears all over, Lorelle. You might want to remember that once I send you out to do my bidding. I may not have a physical form, but that does not mean I cannot wipe your pathetic life from existence."

She fought the urge to do something totally childish and human like flip him the bird, and settled for a frown and sullen silence instead. Not as satisfying, but quite a bit safer she was sure.

"Now," Volcan's voice was close again, right next to her ear. "If you will just relax this will be painless, but if you fight me, then it will be quite the opposite."

Lorelle braced herself for the invasion and tried not to think about the consequences of letting another magical, powerful being have access to her own magic and power. She tried to seal off any parts of her mind that she didn't want Volcan to have access to but as soon as she felt his power begin to push its way into her body, she knew it would be useless to resist him. He was incredibly strong. Her blood felt as though it were a wire pulsing with electricity through her veins. Her skin warmed and the hair on the back of her neck stood on end.

She expected to lose herself once he entered her mind, but she was still there, still able to move her arms on command and turn her head. At the same time, she was fully aware of him in her consciousness. He was right there, as if he were standing next to her, and when he commanded her brain to blink, she blinked.

"Why can I still control myself if you possess me?" Lorelle asked.

"It can be a battle of wills, or you can freely allow me to give your mind commands. If you do not readily submit then the stronger one of us will prevail," he explained.

"Fine," she huffed, "let's just get this over with." Lorelle didn't want him to get to cozy inside of her body lest he decide to commandeer it for good. She heard Volcan's voice again, only he was not addressing her, he was chanting.

"Ancient blood flows through their veins,
Healing magic in them reigns.
Gypsy born yet they live a lie,
For their location I now scry."

Lorelle felt a sharp cut across her hand and gasped as she looked at the slice in her palm. Then she was holding stones in her bloody palm. She felt her hand shake and then she tossed the blood coated stones to the floor. Her body knelt down, seemingly of its own accord, but she knew that it was Volcan who was calling the shots. She looked at the stones now scattered on the floor and watched as Volcan discerned their meaning. She had never scried before, it was blood magic and fae did not practice blood magic unless it was absolutely necessary.

"The stones say to go West. The healers reside in a land barely in its infancy—a young land where technology and industry rule instead of magic."

"America," Lorelle muttered.

Volcan stood back up and closed her eyes and she felt his power beginning to swell inside of her.

"The fae have always been the Great Luna's tool in protecting the healers. I call on the blood of this High Fae Lorelle and command your obedience."

Lorelle's heart began to pound like a two ton boulder against her chest as Volcan's words took power and wrapped themselves around her blood. He was using her own magic against her and there was nothing she could do to stop him. She felt violated as he took control of something as sacred as her magic. He had sliced her hand and had her blood to do with it as he pleased. *Stupid Lorelle*, she thought to herself.

"Find the healers in this young land,
Make their blood a beacon in the night,
Draw them out, place them in her hand,
Wrap them up so she holds them tight."

Lorelle felt him leave her body and didn't try to stop the sigh of relief that fled her lungs. She squeezed her eyes closed and concentrated on expelling the last bit of his magic that lingered. Then suddenly she felt a pull inside of her and she knew immediately that Volcan's spell was working. The healer's blood was crying out to her, calling her to them.

"You will follow the pull and, one by one, you will bring me those healers," Volcan commanded.

Lorelle gave a curt nod instead of answering because she knew if she opened her mouth whatever came out was just going to get her killed, sooner rather than later.

"Go," Volcan's voice growled at her.

She flashed from his castle to the edge of the dark forest and felt instantly lighter once she wasn't in the presence of the evil that was Volcan. Lorelle took several deep breaths and closed her eyes. She focused on the magic that was flowing in her veins, foreign to her body because it wasn't her own. In order to do what Volcan had commanded, she was going to have to listen to it and follow its lead. The sooner she got those healers to Volcan, the sooner she could begin devising an escape plan to get away from the fae who had taken evil to a whole new level.

∞

Peri watched as Rachel, the Romanian Pack gypsy healer, pulled an old and rather worn book from the shelf behind her desk. Rachel set the book down and a layer of dust puffed out from between the pages.

"I take it this isn't one that you refer to very often?" Peri asked.

Rachel smiled her sweet smile and replied in her soft spoken manner, "It isn't very often that I have to use my magic in a non-healing manner."

"Pssht," Peri scoffed, "Now you're just telling lies. Ever since you and your mate came out of hiding you've been using your magic for all sorts of things besides healing."

"Guided by you," Rachel countered. "You are asking me to do something without your assistance that isn't healing. That's going to take a little research."

"Well, by all means, please consult the big, old, dusty book." Peri hopped up onto one of the long counters, pushing beakers and plants out of the way. She crossed her legs and prepared to wait while Rachel attempted to figure out a way to seek out their quarry with the use of her magic. Peri's mind drifted after several minutes to the conversation she'd had with Sally, the Serbian Pack healer, earlier that morning.

"I wish I could help you Peri but I just can't leave right now," Sally had told her in her sweet southern voice.

"You aren't even staying with your pack, what does it matter if you leave the continent for a few days?" She'd asked, even though she had known what the healer would say.

"Jacque is pregnant; you know that if there is a healer with her the chances of a successful birth are much greater. If you are taking Rachel, then I need to stay."

Peri knew she was right. Jacque needed a healer with her, especially when she went into labor. Jen hadn't had one with her when her child was born and it was a miracle that she lived. Of course, Peri was convinced if the little girl was anything like her mother then she was just too ornery to die. Truth be told, Peri was being selfish because she figured if she had two healers then they would find the five girls more quickly and then she could get back to taking care of her sister. That's what it all came back to— Lorelle. But then, what did she expect when her own sibling tried to end her life? Those with immortality tend to be quite stingy with their life, and usually get pretty freaking ticked off when someone tries to take them out. Peri was beyond ticked, she was hurt and confused and that just made her all the angrier.

"I think I might have found something that will work," Rachel's soft voice broke through Peri's thoughts.

Peri pushed herself off of the counter and walked back over to Rachel's desk. "Let's hear it."

"It's an ancient finding spell used by the gypsies when the clans suspected that there was a healer among them that hadn't been revealed," Rachel explained as her eyes continued to scan over the yellowed pages. Her eyes narrowed and then her lips tightened. "Sally isn't going to like this."

Peri cocked a hip out to the side as she crossed her arms in front of her. "Why? Do you have to sacrifice a puppy?"

72

Rachel's furrowed brow deepened. "Well no," she said quickly.

"Castrate an elephant?"

"No."

"Hold Jen's baby on a cliff overlooking the animal kingdom and sing Circle of Life?"

Rachel let out an exasperated breath. "Are you done?"

Peri shrugged. "After the things I just said, I'm betting it doesn't seem so bad now."

"We both have to give up one of our ovaries," Rachel blurted out.

"I stand corrected. Sally is going to hate that and all my ideas were way better," Peri conceded.

Suddenly, Rachel started laughing. "I was joking, Perizada; we don't have to give up one of our ovaries."

"I totally knew that," Peri said dryly. Rachel continued to laugh and when Peri cocked a single brow at the healer she finally pulled it together. "Now really, what is it that Sally isn't going to like and why is she going to be involved anyway?"

"Her magic is getting stronger every day and will only continue to do so the more she uses it. It will help if there are two of us casting the spell," Rachel told her, then let out a deep breath. "The spell will open up a mental bond with the healers. That is how we will be able to find them."

"You're wrong then. It isn't Sally that won't like it. It's her bartending, possessive mate that isn't going to like sharing her mind with others."

Rachel nodded. "I agree, but the reason I said that Sally wouldn't like it is because she is going to be the one who has to deal with her possessive mate

73

complaining about her mind being shared with others."

"Too true," Peri chuckled. "They do tend to get annoying when they start complaining about something that isn't in their power to control."

"Speaking from experience now, Peri?" Rachel asked with a sly smile.

"Oh no, healer, we aren't having a counseling session on mating 101. Vasile and Alina have already given me their little tidbits. Damn Alphas always meddling," she muttered.

Rachel stood up as she nodded her head. "Yes, they tend to do that. But it's only because they care so much."

"I could totally stand a little *less* caring, wouldn't hurt my feelings *at* all."

Rachel laughed and shook her head. "Perizada, you may not see it now, but you are exactly where you need to be, and with whom you need to be as well."

"Was that an attempt at being profound, gypsy? Because I'm going to have to go with a big fat fail on that," Peri teased.

"Make yourself useful and get Sally while I get the things we need to do this spell," Rachel told her as she made a shooing motion with her hand.

"Mated to a werewolf and suddenly all my respect goes out the flipping window," Peri grumbled as she flashed from the room.

"Sally, you're being summoned by Rachel," Peri said as she flashed into the library where the healer sat with her mate and Jacque.

"I thought we already talked about this, Peri," Sally said without standing up.

"Don't get your herbs in a boiling beaker, gypsy lady. She just needs your help casting the spell, that's all." Peri said as she pointedly looked at her finger nails, inspecting them closely.

"Why do I feel like there is more to it than that?" Costin asked.

"Look," Peri said shortly. "What I can guarantee is that you don't have to sacrifice a puppy, you don't have castrate and elephant and you don't have to reenact the Lion King with Jen's baby held up in the air over a ledge with a bunch of hungry beasts hoping you will drop it, while singing a song about the circle of life. Oh, and you don't have to give up either of your ovaries. So how much more to it can there really be? Now, Costin, you aren't needed so you can stay here." She grabbed Sally's arm and flashed them back to the healer's room before Costin could react to her statement.

"You really shouldn't have done that," Sally said as she stepped away from Peri and further into the room that had become a second home to her. "He's going to be…,"

"Perizada!" Costin's deep growl rolled through the door way just before he came into view.

Peri glanced at the door and flicked her wrist towards Costin. His body rammed into an invisible wall, preventing him from entering the room.

"This is a peaceful healing room, Costin,"Peri taunted him. "We don't need your negative energy in here."

"Let me in, Peri," he snarled.

"Oh give it a rest," Peri snapped. "Your mate is right there," she pointed at a very worried looking Sally. "She's not in any danger, and she sure as hell doesn't need your paws distracting her while they cast this spell. So pipe down and I might not turn you into a fantastic coat the next time you phase."

"Peri, is that really necessary?" Sally asked.

"What? The coat? Well I really could use a new fur coat."

"No," Sally huffed interrupting her, "keeping him locked out."

"Oh, it will be."

"Why?" Sally said with warning in her tone.

"Well, because most males don't like to share the mental bond they have with their females."

"I'm going to be sharing my mental bond with someone?" Sally's voice grew a little high with each word while Costin let out an ear ripping growl.

"No, no," Peri attempted to sound reassuring but it was ruined with she finished with, "You're going to be sharing your mental bond with five someones."

Chapter 5

"I've had the responsibility of so many lives in my hands for so long. Now I will be adding five more innocents. I will be taking them from their safe homes and bringing them into a world where, more often than not, bloodshed is the norm and darkness lives inside the very mate they will each one day take. How am I to justify that? How am I to tell them that I can offer them nothing other than the promise of the love of a Creator and the wolf she made for them? Is that enough? Or is it too much to ask?" ~Perizada

"Can you please tell me why the young wolf is cursing you so profusely and give me a very good reason not to cause him harm for disrespecting my mate?" Lucian's voice rumbled through Peri's mind as she stood staring indifferently at a snarling Costin. She caught a glimpse of Lucian's form in the shadows beyond Costin and her heart leapt at the thought of seeing him.

"I stole his mate," Peri admitted.

She heard Lucian clear his throat and saw a slight twitch of his lips. *"Why exactly did you steal his mate, love?"*

"Because we need her for the finding spell and when Costin realizes what the consequences of said spell are, he is going to be quite unhappy, well unhappier."

"What are the consequences, Perizada?" This time Lucian's voice was out loud.

Peri grumbled under her breath and let out an exasperated huff before she answered. "In order for us to get a lock on the gypsy healers, Rachel and Sally both will have to open their bonds up to the magic of the other healers. They will create a mental link with them."

"Why?" he asked, clearly unhappy about her explanation.

"If we weren't mated it wouldn't work," Rachel answered. "There has to be a mental bond connection. Because we already have that opening through our mate bonds, we can use it to latch onto the magic that lives inside the minds of the healers."

"There is no other way?" Lucian asked.

Rachel shook her head. "Not that I could find."

"How does your mate feel about this?" Costin growled.

"He isn't happy but he's accepted that it is part of the role I play as a healer."

"Costin," Sally's sweet voice seemed to bring the growing tension down several notches. "They will all be female. And it's not like they are going to know that there is a mental link open. They aren't going to hurt me."

"It's sacred, Sally mine," Costin's voice lost most of its growl as he talked to his mate. "It's only supposed to be between a male and his female."

"Well, I'm sorry but you aren't just mated to a female, you're mated to a healer."

Their eyes stayed locked and Peri could tell they were using their bond to speak privately. She turned to look at Rachel and saw that she was almost finished setting up an assortment of plants and liquids. It looked like some elaborate experiment. Which, Peri supposed in some ways it was.

"Peri, please let him in," Sally turned to look at her. "He's not going to keep me from doing what I need to, but he needs to be in here. Please."

Peri looked at Costin who was still staring at his mate. The longing in his eyes was desperate enough to even pierce Peri's usually impassive heart. She knew it had been cruel to keep Costin from entering, especially when weeks ago he had watched his mate die before his eyes. Costin had become a tad clingy since Sally's death. Thanks to the Great Luna, she didn't stay dead long, but it had been enough to do quite a number on the young wolf.

She waved her hand and the invisible barrier was gone. Costin was through the doorway wrapping his arms around Sally before she could even blink. Lucian also entered, though in a calmer fashion than the other male. He walked straight over to Peri, ran a gentle finer across her cheek before turning and facing Costin, keeping his body between his mate's and the emotional male wolf.

"Sally, are you ready?" Rachel asked.

Sally gave Costin a reassuring smile before walking over to stand next to the other healer.

"You two will not interfere," Peri narrowed her eyes at Costin and Lucian, who had turned slightly so he could see her while still keeping Costin in his sights.

"Don't make it necessary for me to interfere," Costin challenged.

"I will only stand for so much disrespect towards my mate, young one." Lucian's voice was low as he watched Costin. His words and the effort in which he spoke them were calculated and even had a chill running down Peri's spine.

79

"Enough!" Rachel growled. "We are not in danger. Costin, I understand that you are especially overprotective of Sally, but please trust me." She turned to the other problem in the room and huffed, "Peri, quit baiting the wolves."

Peri shrugged, looking bored as she leaned against the counter and proceeded to watch as the two healers began to mix the herbs and liquids.

Twenty minutes later both healers held small glasses of smoking liquid.

Sally looked at the glass in her hand with a pinched expression. "Well," she held the glass up, "bottoms up." She downed the fluid in one big gulp and then slammed the glass down onto the table. She shook her head as her mouth took on the tight look of someone who had just sucked on a lemon.

Rachel followed suit and downed her own drink, and held her own sour face when the liquid was gone.

Peri waited, standing as still as a statue along with Costin and Lucian. They stared at the two females, waiting—for what they weren't sure.

"How do you feel, Sally?" Costin spoke up finally, his eyes imploring his mate to be unharmed.

"Aside from a nasty taste in my mouth, I feel," Sally was on her knees with her hands pressed to her head before she could finish what she was about to say. Rachel was right behind her. Both women let out cries of pain and Costin was by Sally's side in an instant.

Peri started towards Rachel but was pushed out of the way by a large form. Gavril had come crashing into the room like a gale force wind. Peri backed up quickly and found herself pressed against a familiar chest.

80

"Are they going to be alright?" Lucian whispered in her ear.

"I," Peri started but then her mouth snapped shut. She didn't know what to say. She and Rachel had no way of knowing what would happen when they performed the spell. Magic was sometimes volatile and unpredictable, but usually gypsy healer magic wasn't dangerous.

Sally squeezed her eyes closed as she struggled to gain control of the thoughts ripping through her mind. After the initial onslaught she had figured out what the pain was. It was emotions, too many all at once bombarding her brain like a deadly assault. She needed to just slow everything down and then hit the mute button. She tried to focus only on the thoughts and images in her mind and gradually the pain began to subside and she was able to use her own magic to compartmentalize the new information.

"What is that?" Costin's voice broke through her concentration.

"You can hear them?" She asked him.

"Female voices, too many of them," he confirmed.

"Five to be exact," Sally clarified.

"Yes, well, that's five too many. There should only be yours." She felt Costin's hand on her back rubbing her gently and she leaned into his touch. She found she was able to handle the chaos of the voices much better when he was touching her.

"You could have just told me you wanted me to touch you more, beautiful," he teased, *"You didn't have to go and open up our mental bond to a bunch of strangers to get it."*

"That just sounds so bad," Sally groaned out loud and felt her cheeks warm.

"Whatever do you mean, Sally mine?"

"Costin, shut up," Sally said dryly.

He grinned at her, his dimple making an appearance as he pulled her into his arms. Sally looked over at Rachel who was also in the arms of her mate. Their eyes met and Sally could see that Rachel was experiencing the same sort of invasion that she was.

"You alright?" She asked the other healer.

Rachel nodded. "I forget how busy the minds of adolescents are."

"It worked," Peri piped in seeing that the two healers where no longer writhing in pain. "You connected with them?"

Both healers nodded.

"Great, where are they?" Peri asked as she stepped away from Lucian and rubbed her hands together eagerly.

Sally rolled her eyes. "That's not how it works, Peri."

Peri huffed. "Fine, tell me how it works then, Sally, because I need five healers as of yesterday. So could you please enlighten me as to how we figure out where they are?"

"We're going to have to do a little digging in their minds because short of them thinking my name is Jane Doe Healer and I live at 500 Easy To Find Avenue, the information isn't just laying out there on the surface."

Peri's head tilted to the side as she eyed the young healer, she let out a snort of laughter. "I think death agreed with you because you are a lot funnier since you came back."

Costin let out a low growl.

"Oh put a bone in it, flea bag," Peri waved him off, "It was compliment, and she isn't going to just drop dead because I brought it up."

"Peri please try and play nice," Sally begged.

"Nice is so over rated," Peri grumbled. She turned away from Sally who was consoling her mate and noticed that Lucian was staring at her. "What?" She asked him.

"You're breathtaking," he told her simply.

Peri didn't know how he did it, but just two words from him and she found the ache inside of her for him growing painfully larger. His lips tilted up ever so slightly and she knew that he completely understood the effect he was having on her.

Movement on the other side of the room caught her attention and she turned away from the mesmerizing gaze that was her mate.

Rachel had grabbed a piece of paper and handed it along with a pen to Sally, and then gathered the same for herself. They both stood, leaning over the table with pen and paper, their eyes closed clearly concentrating. Sweat broke out on both of their brows as they began to feverishly write. Several minutes of silence went by when Gavril finally said, "Enough, Rachel."

It was then that Peri noticed that Rachel had blood dripping from her nose. She stood up straight and Gavril pressed a handkerchief to her face to help stop the bleeding. Sally too had blood coming from her nose and Costin was attempting to help her staunch the flow.

Peri waited as patiently as she could as the two women collected themselves.

"Okay, for now this is what we have, Peri," Rachel spoke up. "Basically I told Sally to find a name and once she had a name she wrote it down. I then thought of that name until I connected to the mind it went with. We both focused solely on that one female and sought out as much information from her as we could without alarming her to our presence in her mind and without separating ourselves from our own bodies."

"Is that a possibility?" Peri asked.

"I didn't think so, until I actually tried to search inside of someone other than my mate's mind. Now I believe that it is a distinct possibility, especially with our bond so stretched," she explained. "If these females were aware of the magic that lives inside of them they could use it against us with the mental bond open between us."

"Well, let's try and keep them from ever being aware of your presence then," Peri agreed. "So, now that we are aware of what not to do, tell me what you got."

Rachel looked down at the piece of paper and began to read what she had written. "Anna, New Orleans, Little Shop of Horrors, lonely."

"I feel like I should respond to that with something like; *What is an American gypsy teenager?*" Peri said with a snort.

"Well it's not like she thinks in complete sentences or full paragraphs. Basically we were pulling stuff out of her memories," Rachel told her.

Sally nodded. "We're lucky we got that much. Her magic is strong."

Peri looked from Rachel to Sally as she took in the information she'd just been given and realized she was going to have to make a change of plans.

"Okay Sally, I understand that you want to be here to take care of Jacque,"

"Peri we aren't going to go over this again," Sally interrupted.

Peri held up her hand to stop the healer from saying anything more. "As I was saying, I understand that you want to be here for Jacque because of the pregnancy and I agree a healer should stay but I don't think it should be you."

"I agree," Rachel spoke up. "You are an American, and you are young enough to be able to relate to these girls," Rachel continued. "It only makes sense that you would be the one to help Peri convince these girls to trust her. I mean let's face it, Peri by herself will most likely have the girls running in the opposite direction."

Sally laughed at that. "Too true. Okay," she let out a deep breath. "I understand what you're saying and I can't say that I disagree with your logic. So Rachel, you are going to stay here and take care of my best friend?"

"She is pack, Sally. I will always take care of pack. You need not worry about her," Rachel reassured her.

Sally turned to look at Costin who still had his arms securely wrapped around her. "How do you feel about taking a little vacation to America?"

"I'm always up for an adventure, brown eyes, as long as you're by my side then I'm game. I can get someone to cover for me at the bar."

"Alright then, we meet in the dining room at lunchtime and we'll leave from there. Adam and Elle will be joining us along with their mates. There is really no need to pack anything because unlike the times before when we've traveled, this time we will be flashing to where we are going."

Sally raised her hand and Peri clucked her tongue at her. "Sally, how many times am I going to have to tell you that you don't have to raise your hand when you want to ask a question?"

Sally shrugged. "I'm a product of the public school system, old habits die hard. Now, what I was going to ask was, is flashing across large distances that include bodies of water safe?"

Peri grinned. "I can promise you it's safer than a huge, heavy, steel, cylinder held up in the air by the engineering of fallible humans."

Sally frowned. "I know that should reassure me, but it also insulted my species so I'm having a hard time feeling reassured."

"You'll get over it," Peri said flippantly as she took the hand Lucian was holding out to her and let him pull her from the room.

Sally shook her head as she stared after the retreating fae. "Does he even realize what he's in for by being mated to her? I mean I seriously think she is going to be worse than Jen."

Costin chuckled. "I would agree, but I would also bet that Lucian, who has been alone for so very long, does not care how much of a handful his mate is bound to be. He, like all of us males who have true mates, is just overjoyed to have found her."

Sally continued to stare at the now empty doorway, still sitting in her mate's arms. "I just hope Peri will realize her own worth. For all of her flashy confidence that she portrays, she truly doesn't believe she is worthy of having a mate."

Costin kissed her hair tenderly. "Don't worry, Sally mine, Lucian will be more than happy to show her just how worthy he finds her. I think you know from firsthand experience just how much we males like to prove your worthiness to us." Sally pinched him and blushed causing him to laugh as he picked her up in his arms.

They waved to Rachel and Gavril who had been quietly talking and headed to say their goodbyes to their pack mates, before embarking once again on another mission. This one they both hoped wouldn't turn out to be as dangerous or deadly as their past experiences had been. But then they both also knew that you had to expect the worst in the supernatural world, and then jump for joy when something less than the worst happened.

Chapter 6

**"I've constantly spent my life waiting for the
other shoe to drop. With every corner I turn I'm
always expecting to be smacked in the face and
with every new person I meet I'm always waiting
for them to yell *You've been punked*. Call it
superstitious because I'm a Gypsy, or call it
paranoia because I watch way too many
Supernatural Saturdays on BBC, or you can just
call it the ugly truth; I'm not normal." ~Anna**

"I'm sorry but we're closed," Anna called from
the back of the store. It had been a slow day and she
had dozed off and slept right past closing time, also
known as *lock the door so the crazies don't come in* time.
When no one answered her she grabbed the can of
Mace spray she kept at the counter and made her way
around the book shelves and display racks.

Her feet came to a sudden halt causing her black
Converse to screech on the dingy linoleum floor. Her
mouth dropped open only to then close again as she
stared at the odd group of people standing crowded
together at the entryway door. She knew something
was off because unlike most shoppers who walk in
and immediately start browsing, this group simply
stood there. They weren't looking at anything in the
store, but instead were staring right at her.

"Okay, before you spray us with that can of burn
your eyes out, perhaps you can just listen to what we
have to say?" The tall woman, with long white hair
that shimmered as though it were lit by thousands of
tiny lights spoke up. Though she was tall, Anna

noticed that she wasn't big by any means. She wore a simple blue dress that cinched at her waist and then flowed down in layers to her ankles. The sleeves were long and see through in the same color blue as the dress and hung gracefully off her shoulders. Her frame was thin and delicate looking but the ancient look in her eyes betrayed that delicacy. This woman was a predator. Her hands were held loosely in front of her, clasped together. Her shoulders were relaxed and her lips were turned up in a slight smile, but all it took was one look in those pale green eyes to know that she was deadly.

"I take it you aren't here to buy a voodoo doll?" Anna asked nervously.

The white haired woman laughed and the sound was so light and beautiful that Anna wondered if it was real. "Only if you have them in the shape of wolves," the woman answered.

A low growl emanated from one of the others but Anna couldn't tell which. A young girl about her age cleared her throat and quickly stepped forward. She was average height with long brown hair, golden tan skin, and huge brown eyes. She was wearing shorts, a sleeveless shirt that tied in the front and sandals. She had a very gentle look about her, and Anna would never have put the brown eyed beauty anywhere near the deadly white haired lady. Just then a large, obviously strong arm wrapped around the brown haired girl's torso pulling her back against a large chest. Anna looked up to see who owned the arm and her breath caught when her eyes locked with shockingly hazel ones set against tan skin and a face too handsome for words. Anna was sure he couldn't be more handsome, but then he grinned and a deep dimple appeared and she was wrong.

"Shuck a duck," she muttered slowly under her breath.

"You're going to give him an even bigger ego if you keep that up." Anna's eyes snapped away from the handsome man back down to the brown haired girl standing in front of him. "Please don't misunderstand, I'm not upset, I mean let's just be honest, he gorgeous. But if you keep that up he's going to be impossible to live with." A small smile formed on the girl's lips. "I'm Sally Miklos, this is my husband, Costin," she motioned to the GQ model standing behind her. "And I'll introduce the rest of our ragtag bunch as soon as you understand that first of all we aren't here to hurt you. Do you believe me?"

"Isn't that what the bad guy always says to the stupid blonde chick in horror flicks?" Anna asked skeptically.

"Good point," Sally conceded.

"Oh good freaking grief," the white haired deadly woman groaned irritably. "Look, we're here to take you to a safe place and teach you all about your Gypsy heritage and magic. We don't want to sell you on the black market, we don't want any of your organs, and if you're lucky you will even get one of those," she pointed to the guy named Costin, "of your very own. Okay?"

"Oh, okay," Anna replied.

"Really?" Sally asked.

"No," Anna said dryly. "Not really."

"Oh I like her," a laugh came towards the back of the group from a guy every bit as handsome as

Costin, but with sandy brown hair and sharp eyes that seem to see everything.

"Would you be willing to meet with me and Crina?" Sally pointed to a beautiful dark haired girl standing next to the sandy brown haired god. "In a public place of course."

"To talk?" Anna asked.

Sally nodded. "Yes, just to talk. Don't mind Peri; she has no bedside manner."

"Sally dear, I would remember if we'd been to bed together and since I don't swing for our own team, I know we haven't. So how would you know anything about my bedside manner?" Peri retorted.

Sally blushed. "And she has no couth either."

"So she's generally honest then?" Anna asked, not able to help the small smile that appeared despite her reservation towards the group.

"Brutally so," Sally confirmed.

Anna glanced hesitantly towards the group and then back to Sally. "I can meet you in twenty minutes. There's a Starbucks just a block up the road."

Sally smiled and nodded. "Great, we'll see you in a few then."

Anna watched as they all filed out of the store. The door finally swung shut and the chime that usually didn't even register to her ears was like the warning bell in a boxing match. Round 1 had just ended and round 2 was coming. As she hurried forward to lock the dead bolt on the door before any other oddities could come through, she tried to figure out her next move. Did she go and meet with Sally and the girl she called Crina? Though they looked normal enough, the others that had been standing in that bunch were definitely not normal. The one called

Peri had mentioned Anna being a Gypsy. How would she know that she was indeed of Gypsy dissent?

Her mind was a chaotic mess as she counted her till and closed down the cash register. As she went about her usual closing routine her thoughts continued to bombard her with *what ifs* and *what should I dos*. She wished, not for the first time, that she could call her mom and ask for some guidance, but true to her Gypsy heritage, her mother was a nomad. As soon as Anna had graduated high school two weeks ago she had taken off. She said it made her antsy to stay still for too long, that it would draw evil spirits to her if she didn't keep on the move. *Whatever that meant,* Anna thought as she rolled her eyes. She might be a Gypsy and she might work in a voodoo shop called Little Shop of Horrors, but she didn't buy into all that magic mumbo jumbo. Anna was a realist. She believed in what she could see and touch. Since her mom was so frequently out of touch with reality, one of them had to be firmly fixed in the here and now.

With all of her closing chores completed, she glanced at her phone to check the time. She had five minutes until it was time for her to meet with Sally, if she was even going. She paced back and forth in front of the door with her purse slung diagonally over her shoulder. Her loose, dark brown curls were thrown up into a messy bun as the humid heat of the New Orleans's June evening clung to the back of her neck.

"Okay," she finally stopped, facing the door her hands held out dramatically beside her. "I'm going. We'll be in a public place," she continued to talk out loud as she took a step towards the door and reached to unlock it. "What's the worst that could happen?" As she exited the shop and relocked the door she muttered to herself. "The last time you asked yourself that you wound up in a belly dancers costume on a float with a sign on it that said *Gypsies do it for the five finger discount*. So ask yourself again, do you really want to do this?" Anna was lost in her thoughts and didn't notice that someone had joined her until the female voice hit her ears.

"Do you always talk to yourself?"

Anna jumped and her hand flew out to catch herself against the side of the building. "HOLY CRAP!" She hollered. Her breathing was heavy as she leaned down with her hands braced on her knees. She looked up and was instantly hit with a sense of familiarity. This woman hadn't been with the group that had come into the store, but she was definitely a member of their weird club. She reminded her of the white haired one called Peri. She had the same delicate features, her hair was the same white color but it didn't shine with the same intensity and her eyes were pale blue instead of green. She was wearing some sort of cloak which Anna might have found odd if she hadn't been from New Orleans.

"You really should pay more attention to your surroundings," the woman said in a cool, detached voice.

Anna didn't respond. She righted herself and straightened her purse and started walking again. "I told your people I would meet you in twenty minutes, I don't need an escort," Anna told her tersely. She was irritated that she had allowed herself to be so distracted that someone had snuck up on her. This part of town is not a place to find yourself caught unaware after dark. She had lived here all her life and knew better than to let her guard down.

"What do you mean, *your people*?" The woman asked as she suddenly appeared right in front of Anna causing her to stumble and take several steps back or run straight into her.

Anna once again righted herself and folded her arms across her chest. She pulled her shoulders back and straightened to her full, albeit unimpressive, height of five foot, three inches and met the woman's hard gaze. "I mean the group of people that showed up at my shop just a little while ago spouting off about Gypsies and magic. You can't tell me that they weren't with you because one of them looked just like you."

"What do you mean just like me?"

Anna rolled her eyes as frustration began to dance across her nerves. "Do you speak the same language as me? Because you keep asking what do I mean, when I'm making myself pretty stinking clear."

"I will ask you one more time, healer," the woman practically growled, "what do you mean just like me?"

"Hellfire and brimstone," Anna muttered, then added in an equally irritated voice, "I mean as in related like maybe your sister. She looked like you."

∞

Lorelle stood frozen, staring at nothing as the healer walked around her. She should follow her, or at least turn and see where the girl was going but she couldn't seem to move. Her heart was pounding in her ears and for some reason her lungs didn't seem to want to work as she struggled to take a breath. *Like*

94

you, the healer had said, someone that looked like her had been to see her today and not only did she look like Lorelle, but she looked as if she could have been her sister.

Lorelle turned suddenly just in time to see the young healer slip into a coffee shop. Her mind was jumping rapidly from past to present. She remembered the forest and Peri dying, yet this gypsy was giving her reason to think that her sister was alive. Oh, no she didn't say Peri's name, but there was nobody else who the girl would have compared to Lorelle's appearance, as if they were sisters. She had to know. She had to know if Peri indeed was still sucking up precious oxygen instead of feeding the maggots like she should be. Lorelle cloaked herself in her magic, making herself invisible to those around her and practically sprinted across the street to the coffee shop. She would like to say she wasn't shaking like some pathetic human junky craving their next fix, but then she would be lying and frankly her sins were beginning to rack up.

As she pressed her face closer to the glass window her eyes landed on the Gypsy and then quickly moved past her to the brunette sitting on the other side of the table.

"No," Lorelle gasped quietly, her warm breath fogging the glass in front of her. She took a quick step to the left and blinked several times to make sure that her eyes were working properly and hadn't just suddenly taken a detour to the twilight zone. But still, there she sat, Sally Miklos, gypsy healer, mate to Costin and weeks ago dead to the world. If Sally was alive, then the odds of Peri being alive had just increased exponentially.

"This is going to put a damper on things," Lorelle muttered to herself as she quickly flashed away from the coffee shop. She reappeared at the edge of the Dark Forest and began pacing as her thoughts raced. All the while the pull of Volcan's magic to find the healers tugged at her insides like a hook caught in the gut of its aquatic victim. With each tug she felt the rip and tear of the foreign magic, but even that discomfort was nothing to the knowledge that her sister had somehow escaped fate. Now not only did she have Volcan to contend with, but she had to kill her sister—again.

"This time, sister mine, you better damn well stay dead."

∞

"She's frazzled," Sally sent the thought to Costin through their bond as she watched Anna walk into the Starbucks where she and Crina currently sat. He was sitting in the outside dining area, no doubt with a frown on his handsome face because he had lost the Rock, Paper, Scissors game to get to come inside the restaurant. Sally didn't want Anna to be scared, and though Costin wasn't as big as Lucian or Decebel, he could still be very intimidating when he wanted to be.

"Well I would be better able to help you decipher what is wrong with her if I were inside with you instead of sitting out here like a dork," Costin huffed.

Sally bit back the smile that threatened to inch across her face. His Romanian accent coupled with American terms had become a big source of amusement to her, though for some reason he never seemed to find it as funny as she did.

"Quit pouting, it's not attractive."

She heard his chuckle in her mind. *"Now you're just telling lies love, you think everything I do is attractive."*

Sally sent him a mental eye roll but didn't respond because Anna had taken a seat across from her.

"You didn't have to send someone to get me," Anna said with obvious irritation. "I said I would meet you and I keep my word."

Sally looked at Crina and then back at Anna. "Um, sorry but I don't know what you're talking about."

Anna's head tilted ever so slightly and Sally could tell that she was trying to decide if Sally was blowing smoke up her butt or not.

"You didn't send someone to walk me here?" Anna asked.

"No," Sally answered shaking her head. "What did this person look like?"

"Like the woman you called Peri, only she seemed dim, like a washed out version of Peri."

"Lorelle," Crina spoke the name Sally had been thinking.

"This is not good," Sally murmured. *"Houston we have a problem,"* Sally sent to Costin.

"I'm not Houston, but I imagine I can help," Costin retorted playfully.

"Lorelle is here," Sally relayed. *"Anna said she showed up at her store."*

"I'm on it," Costin growled.

"So she isn't with your group?" Anna asked.

97

"No," Crina answered. "She is quite the opposite of being with our group."

"But you know her?"

"Not exactly," Sally rejoined the conversation, feeling slightly better that Costin was making sure that Lorelle wasn't hanging around outside waiting to ambush them. "It's quite a long story but the short version is that she's evil."

"Wicked," Crina confirmed.

"Psycho," Sally added.

"Diabolical."

"Maniacal."

Anna's head bounced back and forth between the two as they tossed out adjectives.

"What their trying to say is she's bat shit crazy and she will stab you in the back with a spoon, dig your heart out and feed it to the vultures," Peri's voice came from behind Anna.

Anna turned to look at the woman who did bear a striking resemblance to her sister, but now that Anna was before her again she realized that the one key difference between Peri and her sister was their eyes. Not the color, though that was indeed different. Peri's eyes were alive. They danced with light and mirth. They were perceptive and alert but there was no malice in them. Her sister's eyes had been the eyes of someone with a soul that had withered and dried up inside of them and all that was left was an empty husk.

Sally looked up at Peri and smiled tightly. "So glad you decided to let us have this private meeting with Anna so that we wouldn't overwhelm her, Peri."

Peri rolled her eyes and took the empty seat next to Anna. "My sister killed you, and *me* for that matter, just a few weeks ago. Now she's in the same city, on the same street, talking to the same person that we are, that sort of changes things, healer."

Anna's eyes had widened at Peri's words. She looked at Peri and then back to Sally. "Did she just say that her sister killed you?"

"Uh, and me," Peri piped up.

Sally nodded and then held her hands up. "Okay just wait before you freak out and call us crazy. Can I just try and explain why we're here?"

"Is it going to keep me from calling you crazy?" Anna asked.

Peri let out a snort. "Oh, totally."

Sally ignored Peri's remark and kept her eyes on Anna. "You know that you are a Gypsy, right?"

Anna nodded.

"Okay, well that's not the only thing about you that is special. You have probably never heard of the Great Luna, but she is the creator of the Canis lupis. After she created them she realized they would need someone very special to be able to care for them in times of sickness or injury so she looked at the people of the world and saw that the Gypsy people had the most affinity for magic. Within the Gypsy females she looked for those with pure hearts, and gentle spirits and she chose them to be healers for her children. For centuries now Gypsy healers have been living with and taking care of the Canis lupis. To ensure that the healers would stay with their packs and to protect them, the Great Luna made them compatible true mates to the Canis lupis." Sally paused and glanced at Peri. "Have I missed anything?"

"Aside from all of the recent developments, no I think you've done a very good job of explaining it, although judging by the look on Anna's face she indeed thinks you're a few coffee beans short of a full cup. See what I did there," she pointed to the Starbucks logo, "because we're in a coffee shop?"

Crina and Sally both chuckled.

"Ask," Sally said to Anna whose narrowed gaze held her captive.

"Who is the Great Luna? What is a Canis lupis? Magic, pack healer, true mates?" Anna's voice grew with each word and then as if losing the wind from her sails she slumped down into her chair like a deflated balloon.

"The Great Luna is a deity, she's a Creator," Sally explained. "The Canis lupis, well they are a little harder to explain."

"They aren't hard to explain Sally, it's just hard for the human brain to wrap their little cells around the notion of something so supernatural," Peri interrupted. She looked at Anna and said deadpan. "Werewolves, as in huge, furry, for some reason absurdly handsome to a near ridiculous amount, body changing beasts."

Anna's mouth dropped open but when nothing came out Peri reached out and gently pushed her chin up to close it.

"Anna," Sally reached out and touched the girl's arm to get her attention. Anna's head turned and her gaze met Sally's. She didn't look terrified yet, just shocked, so Sally decided to continue. "They are real and we can prove it to you, although not in the middle of Starbucks. But let's finish answering your questions first okay?"

Anna nodded slowly unable to formulate any words.

"So as for the other, well, magic is just that, its magic. There is no science behind it and no way to explain it. As for the whole pack and true mate thing, now that you know what we are talking about 'werewolves,' well that explains the pack part, I guess. There are werewolves all over the world and they live in packs, with a hierarchy to keep them in line. Werewolves tend to be quite violent if not kept under tight control."

"Ya think," Anna let slip out and then slapped her hand over her mouth. "Sorry," she mumbled through her hand.

Sally waved her off. "No worries, you got nothing on my friend Jen so don't worry about anything that might pop out because of shock."

"Are you a Canis lupis?" Anna asked Sally finally able to find her voice.

Sally shook her head. "No, I'm like you."

"Like me?" Anna asked slowly.

Sally nodded with a smile. "A Gypsy healer."

Chapter 7

"The world has advanced more than I could have ever imagined. As I withered away in the darkness, life outside continued to move forward, to grow and change. It's so big, so full of wonder and danger and I want to experience it all, but I want my mate by my side. Until she commits to me I can't fully enjoy all that this life has to offer. How do I get her to see that she is the kaleidoscope through which I want to see the world?" ~Lucian

"Is she alright?" Lucian asked Peri as he waited for her outside. He had not put up much of a fight when she had asked him to stay outside because he really was enjoying himself. There was so much to see and look at and when he didn't understand something he just sifted through Peri's thoughts for the answer. She didn't particularly like that, which only made his smile grow bigger because for some reason aggravating her was a strange form of foreplay. Well, that's what she accused him of doing anyways and he wasn't going to disagree with her.

"Well, she hasn't run out screaming, she isn't crying like a wuss, and she hasn't passed out. So I'd say, so far she is doing pretty darn good."

Lucian chuckled under his breath as he leaned back against the building. He kept scanning his surroundings after having been told by Costin that Lorelle had been spotted, but so far he hadn't seen anything suspicious. He had, however, seen way too many half-dressed females and he was beginning to

102

wonder if any of them had mates because there was no way in all of creation he would let his mate walk out of their house dressed in such a state.

"Let?" Peri's voice broke through his thoughts. She was beginning to spend more and more time in his mind and it warmed his heart and caused his wolf to rumble in delight. They wanted her to feel comfortable with them, to want to be with them.

"Would you really want to walk around with that much skin showing?" He asked, truly curious of her answer. *"Does it not bother you that because these females do not cover themselves I see all that is uncovered?"* He felt her rage rush through him and for the first time realized she was every bit as possessive of him as he was of her. She was just much better at hiding it.

"It would behoove you to keep your eyes on the clothed portions of those bodies." Jealousy dripped from her words and he felt the insecurity beneath it. Lucian was moving before he even considered what he was doing. He pulled the door open to the building he had been guarding. Scents assaulted him but he quickly picked out one, just as his eyes landed on her. His strides were long as he made his way to his mate. She turned just as he reached her. She wasn't surprised to see him; she simply stared up at him. Lucian ignored the other eyes that were on him and focused only on her.

He leaned down close to her ear breathing his scent on her, enjoying her reaction to his closeness. "Don't you know?" He whispered.

"Know what?" Her voice was breathless.

"There are none who hold even a crumb to the beauty I see in you. Perizada, I would rather gaze on your form clothed in burlap sacks and animal droppings than on the half-dressed or naked form of any other."

Her lips quirked up in a sly smile. "You sure know how to sweet talk a woman, Lucian," she teased but he felt her relax. She had needed his reassurance, even if she wouldn't ask for it. She had needed to be reminded that even in the midst of others only she held his attention.

She looked up at him and to his surprise she leaned up and pressed her lips to his. It was quick, but he felt it to his soul. His wolf stirred, growling deep in his chest as he reached for her. She leaned into him giving him the touch he so desperately craved. He tried not to snarl when she turned her attention away from him and back to the human girl.

"Anna, this is Lucian, he is a Canis lupis male," Peri told the girl.

"Mate," Lucian growled unable to keep the wolf in check. "I am her mate."

Anna's eyes widened as she looked up at him. She met his eyes but dropped hers immediately and looked away. He could smell her fear and part of him was repulsed, the wolf was glad, if she feared him she was less likely to try anything stupid that would put his mate in danger.

"Perhaps it's time to go somewhere more private," Sally spoke up from across the table.

Peri stood up and Lucian released her though he didn't step away from her.

"Anna, are you willing to continue this in a not so public setting?" Peri asked the girl matter of fact like. "I give my oath as a high fae that no harm will come to you."

"A high what?" Anna's eyes were suddenly as round as saucers.

"Oh, my bad, we didn't go over that part did we?" Peri said flippantly. "Oh well, never mind we'll get back to that. Look, if we leave you here, which we won't, my sister is going to come back for you. I can promise you that she will hurt you. Those are your options."

"I'll take door number one please," Anna said dryly, though her eyes were still pretty big.

"Excellent," Peri smiled. Lucian took her hand and led her from the store trusting Sally and Crina to make sure the human followed. Once they were outside they waited for Adam, Sorin and Elle, who had been canvasing the blocks around them, to join them.

"She didn't try to throw hot coffee on you or anything?" Elle asked Peri.

"Why would she do that?" Peri asked with a raised brow.

"Peri, I've known you for centuries. You can be quite abrasive and more often than not deserve a little hot coffee poured on you," Elle retorted.

The group around them tried to cover up their laughter with coughs but Peri wasn't fooled.

"Well if I'm abrasive, you lot are annoying, like a wedgie that just keeps getting deeper and deeper, you are a pain in my a–,"

"Beloved," Lucian purred interrupting his mate's rant.

At the sound of his voice, Peri's head snapped around to look at him. She'd only heard him use that rumbling purr a couple of times and it called to her. The deep timber poured over her like warm silk, wrapping around her body and caressing her skin. She felt the rumble inside of her, vibrating against her nerves until she just wanted to climb into his lap and beg him to pet her. *What the hell*, she thought as she pulled her gaze from his. Her breathing was shallow and her palms were moist with sweat. She saw him out of the corner of her eye moving towards her but she held up a hand to stop him.

"I need a minute please," She said gently through their bond.

"It's normal, Peri, it's just the bond. Our souls are demanding that we complete the mate bond, that's what you're feeling love, it's alright." He tried to reassure her. It might have worked if they had been alone but there were witnesses to her loss of control and it was humiliating.

"Peri?" Adam's voice cut through Peri's thoughts. "Hey, you alright?" Peri had known Adam for a very, very long time and thought of him like a brother. He always had her back and he knew her very well. She looked at him and she knew the minute he understood what had caused her to act like a love sick lust monkey.

"It's normal, I went through the same thing," he told her.

She did not want to talk about this, not here, not now, and frankly not ever. "We don't have time for this," she snapped. "We need to get Anna to safety and then we have a crap load of new developments to discuss."

Elle could tell that Peri wanted to move onto something besides what was going on with her in that moment. "Where are we going, Peri? Did the Great Luna tell you yet?"

"For now we're going to take them to my house in Farie" Peri informed them.

She took Lucian's hand but didn't look at him and then grabbed Anna's hand. "You might want to close your eyes and whatever you do please do not puke on me. It tends to make me angry." She didn't give Anna time to respond but instead flashed them to the fae realm.

Peri stared out at the forest from behind the house where she had just deposited Anna and Lucian. She had immediately flashed herself from the room to the forest beyond the house. This was her realm. She knew this land and could navigate it even with her eyes closed, so as she began to walk she did just that. She closed her eyes and let her mind clear of all the things that were bombarding her. She let go of the worry about her sister. She pushed away the thoughts of the five healers who needed her help and lastly she pushed away her doubt about Lucian and she just allowed herself to feel. She didn't like feeling out of control, she didn't like feeling like she couldn't prevent herself from acting on some behavior. It made her feel weak and she liked that even less.

"There is an awful lot of not liking *going on out there,"* she heard Lucian's voice.

"Do you feel out of control like that?" Peri asked him.
"Worse," he admitted.
"Why?"

"Because I am male," he chuckled causing her to laugh as well which she knew had been his intention. *"Peri, I know it is harder for you to endure because you are not Canis lupis. You have been around us for a very long time but that is not the same thing as being one of us. You've been*

around mated pairs but now you are experiencing all that you saw. I understand that it's confusing but I would really like it if you would talk to me about it instead of running from me. Let me bear this with you."

She huffed. *"But you're the problem. How am I to let you bear this with me when you are the reason that I can't keep control?"*

"Then complete the mate bond with me and the problem is solved," he told her matter of fact like.

"I'm glad it so simple for you, but it isn't the same for me. There are things we've yet to discuss, important things that you need to know. I mean we are essentially talking about marriage here, Lucian."

He growled. *"No, this goes beyond the human marriage. This is permanent, there is no out clause, no divorce decrees."*

"Exactly, you just argued my point for me. This is something so very serious and shouldn't be rushed."

"It's as natural as breathing to me Peri, I do not fear being tied to you for all time."

"Well babe, you should." She sighed. She looked back at the house. She wasn't in the mood to deal with a scared human who knew nothing of their world. She had her own problems and yet she knew that she would have to set them aside and deal with Anna and four other healers that were still out there. She turned to walk back to the house, instead of flashing, using the time it would take her to get there to get herself focused and ready to work. There would be time to deal with her love life after the healers were safe and after her sister was pushing up daisies. She only hoped that her control would hold out. She had this horrible feeling she was going to attack

Lucian in a lust induced state right in front of some innocent girl scouts. Wouldn't that just be peachy?

∞

Costin wrapped his arms around Sally and pulled her back against his body. He needed her touch, needed to reassure himself that she was still real and not some elaborate figment of his imagination. He leaned his head down and kissed the spot on her neck where his mark was. His desire flared when she trembled from the touch of his lips. He breathed deeply, allowing her scent to wash over him marking him as hers. When he lifted his head his eyes collided with the human girl. He knew by the way her eyes widened that his own eyes must have been glowing as a result of his wolf being so close to the surface. She dropped them quickly and he looked away from her, not wanting to upset her before Sally had a chance to explain more about what was going on. Sally patted his hands that rested on her stomach and his wolf let out a contented sigh as his arms tightened around their mate.

"You okay?" She asked him.

"Restless," he admitted. Traveling outside of their territory always put him on edge, and knowing the woman who had been responsible for his mate's death had been so close to her once again had his wolf wanting flesh between his teeth.

Sally looked up at him and kissed his chin. She smiled when he growled at her, not happy with the small form of affection. He tilted her head back further and captured her mouth with his. Sally gave into his silent demand and let him take control of the kiss, turning her around and pulling her closer to him. His hands were in her hair and hers were wrapped tightly around his neck by the time he pulled back. He gave her a victorious wolfish smile and nipped her bottom lip.

"Feel better?"

Costin smiled. "A little, that was just the appetizer."

Sally rolled her eyes and turned back around to face the room to find Anna blushing and obviously trying to look anywhere but at them.

"Sorry Anna, I didn't mention that wolves are extremely affectionate and demanding in the return of their affection?" Sally smiled.

"He's one too?" Anna motioned towards Costin who was still holding Sally in his arms.

Sally nodded. "Gypsy healers always mate with a Canis lupis," she told her.

"I think I need to sit down," Anna stumbled to a love seat.

"That's probably a good idea because I wouldn't want you to pass out when Costin phases," Sally agreed.

"You want me to phase?" Costin questioned.

"Well I think of all of the people here I'm the least jealous so if she gets a glimpse of your fine body I won't rip her throat out," Sally explained.

Costin nodded. "Good point, love."

Sally stepped away from Costin and took a seat next to Anna. "Costin is going to prove to you what your mind is still telling you is an impossibility. Please don't run, okay? Werewolves are predators and they like to chase things, especially scared things. You ready?"

Anna looked at Sally like she had lost her mind. "Am I ready to watch your husband change into a wolf?"

Sally smiled sweetly. "Okay when you put it like that it sounds really absurd." She turned to Costin. "Might as well just go ahead, babe."

Costin kicked off his shoes and slipped off his socks then took off his shirt and winked at Sally when she blushed. When he went to unbutton his jeans Anna was on her feet.

"Wait, wait, whoa, hold up, why are you taking your clothes off?"

Costin folded his arms across his impressive chest and let out a tired sigh. "Because if I phase with my clothes on it will tear them and I didn't bring an extra pair with me. I'm not going to get naked, Sally says she's not jealous but I won't put your life at risk just on her word." He gave his mate a playful smirk and then quickly removed his jeans so he was left standing in his boxers.

Anna stared in disbelief as a beautiful specimen of a man suddenly was a wolf. His body shimmered and morphed magically, there was no other way to describe it, into a wolf. He was huge, with a thick grey coat of fur. Suddenly he threw his head back and let out a low deep howl.

Anna slammed her hands over her ears as did Sally. Adam, Sorin, Crina, Elle, and Lucian came into the living room to see what was going on. When the howl ended he sat down on his haunches and looked at Sally as if waiting for something.

"Was that really necessary?" Sally glared at him.

He let his tongue lull out to the side and gave her what could only be deciphered as a grin. Sally tried to look mad but her lips curved up into a smile.

Anna still had her hands over her ears and she was just staring at the wolf before her. She couldn't take her eyes off of him, and though she had just watched a man turn into a wolf before her very eyes, she still didn't want to admit that it was real. But how could she not? How could she argue that there was no such thing as werewolves when she had witnessed, *was* witnessing it? She watched as the huge wolf walked over to Sally and laid his massive head in her lap. Sally ran her hand over his fur and he closed his eyes and let out a low rumble.

"Anna, you still with me?" Sally asked, not taking her eyes off of her wolf.

"Well if you just fell into a rabbit hole and wound up in wonderland then yes I'm with you." Anna ran her hands across her face, rubbing her eyes and working the stress out of her forehead where a headache was beginning. She closed her eyes and wondered if when she opened them she would realize this was all just some strange dream and she was still asleep on her stool in the store. No such luck as she blinked and the wolf still sat with his head in his mate's lap.

"Well you still haven't had a meltdown or attacked anyone," Peri said leaning on the door jam. "Either you really are this calm, or you're a sociopath. Did you torture animals as a child or wet the bed?"

"Would it make you feel better if I told you I was having an inner meltdown?" Anna asked her.

Peri raised a brow at her and pursed her lips as she thought about it. She waved a hand at Anna and said, "I'm not worried, there's still a lot you don't know, plenty of time for you to have a two year old moment." She eyed Costin. "I think she gets the point, why don't you put your human skin back on along with some clothes and then rejoin us?" Costin gave her a snort making it clear he heard the order beneath the question and didn't appreciate it. He lifted his lip in a silent snarl but then turned, grabbed his clothes up in his muzzle, and trotted out of the room.

"Okay," Peri said as she walked further into the room and took an empty seat across from Anna and Sally. She looked up at Lucian whose steady gaze had been burning a hole in her since she had entered the room. "I suppose we should fill her in on my sister."

Lucian nodded. "She needs to understand the danger," he agreed.

"So you've learned that there are things that go bump in the night," Peri said as she looked at Anna who seemed to have come to some sort of decision and was sitting up a little taller, looking a little more alert. "Without boring you with too many details or just totally blowing your tiny little mind, I'm going to tell you about a few other things that you didn't know existed along with the Canis lupis. For now I'm going to try and only give you information that you need to know and then we'll see how you're doing."

Anna nodded and continued to watch Peri as she gathered her thoughts.

"As I told you in the coffee shop, I am a *high* fae. I am one of seven, well six now, of the high fae on the council. I am from this realm where we currently reside called Farie. The human realm is just one of many in this universe. My people are the most powerful of all the supernatural beings and because of that we have always acted as the supernatural police, for lack of a better term. But that is just one of our many roles. Another role that we play is a sort of ambassador between supernatural beings that don't always get along. The Great Luna, remember she's the one who created the Canis lupis, assigned us to different packs around the world so that we could watch over their Gypsy healers and help them with their magic. I was assigned to the Romanian pack a very long time ago. Now," she took a breath and let it out with a humming sound before continuing, "there is a lot of history that has happened and you will learn all of that in time but what you need to know is that in the past year things have been changing rapidly. A very young dominant male found his true mate and that seemed to be the catalyst for others who have since also found their true mates. There was also a witch that was defeated and a warlock that rose to power and fell almost in the same breath. That is where my sister, Lorelle, who you had the unfortunate pleasure of meeting, comes in.

"It didn't seem that unfortunate," interrupted Anna.

"Excuse me?" Peri narrowed her eyes.

"I just mean, she seemed pleasant enough. I mean, now that I remember it, she was a bit abrupt…"

"Regardless of whether she was playing the Molly Manners routine," continued Peri, "she is a high fae like me, but she has allowed darkness to infest her heart and soul and she has chosen to seek selfish ambitions. She teamed up with the aforementioned evil warlock and tried to kill off some of the

114

Romanian pack mates." She motioned to Sally. "Sally was one of the ones she actually succeeded in killing, and I myself was also defeated."

"How is that possible?" Anna interrupted. "I'm sorry, I don't mean to be rude and I'm not calling you a liar but even seeing a man turn into a wolf before my eyes doesn't have me believing in the dead coming back to life."

"Well let's just say it's good to know a deity," Peri smiled knowingly. "Again, there are things you will learn in time. For now, you need to understand that Lorelle is dangerous and if she is interested in you, it isn't because she wants to be your BFF. She got away after Reyaz, that was the warlock, was killed and I had planned to go after her, but the Great Luna informed me that first I needed to seek out five Gypsy healers that needed protection. That is why we showed up in your store. You," she pointed at Anna, "are the first of those healers. You are important. You are unique and you have powers that you don't even know about. You have a place in the supernatural world and we are going to help you figure out where that place is."

Anna stared at the woman who had just informed her that not only was she another species all together, but that Anna was a part of that world as well. Her mind was grasping for reality, for truth, because she desperately wanted everything Peri had just told her to be true. Up until this point her life had been page after page of disappointment. Call her pathetic, but she was in need of something extraordinary because ordinary just wasn't cutting it anymore. Before Peri had even begun telling her all the crazy crap she was spouting, Anna had decided to just dive into this mess headfirst without a lifejacket and sink or swim she would take it. She was eighteen, her mom had taken off, so she was alone and she was so very tired of being alone.

"Okay."

Sally's brow furrowed slightly. "Okay? Are you for real this time?"

Anna laughed. "Yes, this time my okay is for real. I'm not saying that at some point I won't just have a toe curling meltdown, but for the moment I'm where I'm supposed to be. I don't know why I know that, but I just do."

"Psht, please, you haven't met Jen yet," Peri scoffed. "Take your worst meltdown then add about fifty two-year olds, a few dozen female cats in heat and the crowd at the water amusement park as they watched that whale, Shampoo have a snack on his trainer—then you can picture what a Jen meltdown is like."

"Damn," Anna muttered.

"Exactly."

"And I think you mean Shamu" Anna said.

"I tell you that you're going to meet a girl whose tantrums are comparable to twenty-four female cats in heat and you're worried about the name of the whale, really?" Peri asked dryly.

Chapter 8

"I'm beginning to wonder how much longer
we can live in secret alongside the humans. The
darkness that we thought we had contained in
our realms is seeping into this one. I felt it as I
stood in the forest of my homeland. Like a tiny
crack in a large dam, it's just a trickle. But that
would change over time. We would be fools to
believe that it won't affect the humans. But then
we might be bigger fools to think they would
accept us as we are." ~Perizada

The gentle rumble of deep voices and occasional
laughter floated through the house as the group
relaxed after a stressful day. Peri sat next to Lucian on
the back porch staring out into the night sky. He
slipped an arm around her waist and pulled her closer
to him so that all of her left side was pressed to his
right side. She shivered and blushed when he
chuckled.

"In fifty years will that still happen?" She asked
him.

"In fifty years will I still pull your body close to
mine?" He asked, purposely misunderstanding her.

She cut her eyes at him with a coy smile. "You
know what I meant. Will your touch still affect me
like that?"

"How does it affect you?"

Peri could tell that he wasn't teasing this time. He
truly wanted to know, was eager to know exactly what
it was his touch did to her. "It's like electric current
flows through me and the point of entry is wherever

your skin is against mine. I can feel the heat from your body soaking into me and it's like my cells can't get enough of you so they try to absorb quicker as if they were dehydrated and you were the tiniest drop of water."

He leaned closer to her so that his lips were close to her ear. Peri tried to remember to breathe as she felt his breath on her as he talked. "In fifty years when I touch you, that feeling will be multiplied by a hundred."

"Then it will probably kill me," she said as a breathy laugh escaped.

Lucian rotated until he was kneeling in front of her, pushing her knees open to slip his large frame in between them. He put his hands on her hips and pulled her to the edge of the seat as he stared deep into her eyes. "No, because your need of my touch will have grown to match your reaction. You will absorb it just as you do now. You will shiver, your lips might tremble, and your face will feel flushed, but you will be very much alive."

Peri held his gaze as she reached up and ran her fingers through his blonde hair allowing the strands to slip through her fingers. She was so attuned to him that she could feel each silky strand as it brushed her skin, could hear the subtle whoosh and smell the masculine musk of him. Her hands slid down the back of his neck to his shoulders where they rested.

"I love your touch," he whispered hoarsely to her as his eyes slipped closed. "To any Canis lupis touch is paramount to being healthy, but to me who went so long with no touch from another living being," his eyes suddenly opened and the wolf stared back at her with glowing eyes, "I truly am ravenous for it. I crave

118

it, not just touch Peri, *your* touch. Like a starving beast whose body is devouring itself from lack of nutrients searches for the tiniest morsel, I look for your touch. No matter how small, I find myself constantly bracing for it. Every time you get anywhere near me I have to bite back the whine of my wolf, who is just as frantic for you. I truly fear for my control when we're close, and yet I can't make myself stay away from you."

Peri sat speechless, looking at the broken man before her. His body was tense, his muscles bunched up beneath her hands. His eyes were so full of pain that she felt the hurt of it in her own soul. He had been deprived of one of the most important things in a pack—touch—for centuries and now that he had a mate he felt as though he was mentally begging for her to touch him all the time. And Peri was so wrapped up in her own crap that she hadn't even thought of his needs. As she stared into his eyes, an idea formed in her mind and she quickly blocked it from him. She took his hand and stood, pulling him up with her.

"Come with me," she told him gently and pulled him off the porch and deeper into the forest. She walked, pulling him along with her until she found the spot that she had often come to when she needed to think. The trees had grown tall with their branches stretching out to each other creating a canopy, a secret cove.

Peri let go of his hand and then raised her hands and began to whisper. Little sparks of light shot from her palms, floating all around the hidden cove casting a soft light over the area. When she stretched her hand out over the ground and began chanting, she could admit she was showing off just a tad, thick grass shot up from the ground creating a mattress of plush vegetation upon which to recline.

She slipped her shoes off and stepped onto the thick grass. She took a seat and then looked up at Lucian. "Lie here," she motioned to a soft patch of grass.

Lucian didn't ask why, he just did it, without question, trusting his mate and needing to be near her regardless of the outcome. Once on his back Peri positioned his arms alongside his body. She slipped his shoes off and then his socks and wasn't surprised to see that he even had sexy feet.

"Do you trust me?" She asked him.

"Without question," he responded.

"Good, close your eyes," she instructed. Then she took the hand closest to her in her own and closed her own eyes. There were perks to being a high fae with more power than one being should be given, and her touch starved mate was just about to get a crash course lesson in those perks. She pushed her power into him, similar to the way the gypsy healers could get inside of their patients to see what areas of their body needed healing, Peri's spirit slipped into her mate. She spread her power throughout his body, over all of his nerves, his muscles, and tissue. She literally draped him in her. She heard his intake of breath and felt his wolf stirring. She pushed deeper until she was in his mind and there she poured her essence into him. As her power pulsed inside of him she used their bond to communicate not just with words, but also with thoughts. She pictured touching his face, his lips and knew he felt it when he returned the favor and used their bond to touch her.

"How?" He asked her.

120

"I'm not like other women, mate," she teased.

"I feel you, everywhere, all at once." His words were choppy with emotion. Peri felt the tears slipping down her own face as his emotions rushed over her.

"Is this okay?" She asked hoping she hadn't overstepped her bounds.

"There are no boundaries for you, beloved. You, and only you, have open access, all the time, any place for any reason," he reassured her having felt her doubt.

"As do you," she told him and realized just how much she wanted him to realize that she understood him. She understood the touch thing, that was something she had seen with the mated pairs, and pack mates and she knew it was vital. She would never refuse him her touch, would never take away something that he lived without for so long. She might not be quite ready for the Blood Rites or completing the mate bond, but she was getting there. Admitting that she needed his touch and being willing to give him the touch he needed was getting one step closer to being ready.

Her eyes popped open when she felt his arms around her and his lips on hers. He pulled her down on top of him, running his hands up and down her back as he explored her mouth with an expertise that was both alarming and exciting. He caught her by surprise but she was quickly catching up and giving as good as she got. He rolled until he covered her, his firm body pressing her smaller form into the soft grass. His hands trailed up her neck and into her hair, pulling a groan from him as the silky strands caressed his deprived skin. When he finally pulled back to look at her, Peri was breathless and drunk with desire.

121

A slow smile formed on his lips as he brushed a few wisps of hair from her face and then used that same finger to trace the swollen lips he had just tasted. "You look ravished."

"Do I?" She asked innocently.

"Mm-hmm," his chest rumbled as he continued to stare down at her with unabashed want.

"Well you look hungry," she teased.

"Oh I am, beloved. I am famished." He kissed her forehead and then her cheeks and then her chin. "Lucky for me I find that there is feast before me."

"Is that so?" She asked as he tilted her head back and kissed her neck and then her collarbone and then lower still at the swell of her breast.

He felt her tense. "Relax, Peri, I'm not going to bite you." He didn't hide the disappointment in his voice because he wouldn't lie to her. He wanted to bite her about as much as he wanted to do other things to her, but he would wait until she was begging him, every bit as desperate for him as he was for her.

When she started laughing he propped himself up on his forearms over her and stared down at her beautiful face. "What is it that you find so funny?"

"You think I will beg," she said through a ripple of laughter that was shaking her stomach and in turn shaking him.

He nipped her chin and then leaned down and gently bit down on the flesh on her neck below her ear, where his mark would be very soon. He tugged gently and her laughing abruptly stopped and was followed by a gasp. Her hands gripped his biceps, holding on to him as if she would fall into oblivion if she let him go. Lucian released her and said through his own increased breathing, "There is no shame in begging your mate for what you want, what you need."

"Would you ever beg me?" Her voice was a whisper.

He stared into her pale green eyes, captivated by an ancient beauty that revealed glimpses of an even more beautiful soul. "Perizada," her name rolled off of his lips in a tone he had never used before, because no one but his mate would ever hear him beg. His hands slipped up her sides until one cupped her face, his thumb stroking across her lips and the other ran gently through her hair. "I need you. I need to feel your skin against mine, I need to smell your scent dancing around me," his voice shook as spoke, his eyes drinking in her reaction to him. "I need to taste you, your flesh, your desire, your blood," he paused and let his warm breath fan over her face. "Peri,"

"Yes," she answered quickly.

"Beloved, please, I beg of you, let me taste you."

Peri decided in that moment that he would never be allowed to call her beloved in that tone of voice again, ever. She knew that he was just trying to make a point and she heard him loud and clear, the man was not too proud to beg and damn if he wasn't good at it, really, really good.

"You're good." She wasn't too proud to tell him. "And when I say good I mean I would nearly let you rip my clothes off and have your way with me." Okay so maybe now she was sounding a little desperate, sue her.

"Is that a request?" He asked with want and need pouring off of him.

As she stared back, her lips parted with indecision, she could see the glow in his eyes beginning to dim and felt a small pang of regret as his wolf slipped back unsatisfied and unfulfilled.

"Don't do that," he told her gently.

"What?" She asked innocently.

"I told you, we wolves are patient hunters. He will wait."

"We should probably get back to the house. I need to find out who our next mark is." She tried to sound matter of fact like, but even she heard the reluctance in her voice.

"Next mark? You do realize we aren't assassins right?" He teased as he helped her up from the ground.

"How do you know what I do in my spare time?" She asked coyly as she wrapped an arm around his waist letting him tuck her in close to him as they walked back.

"Do I need to be worried that I'll be your next mark?"

She laughed, *oh he walked right into that one.* "You're definitely my next mark handsome, but killing you is not what's on the agenda." And then she added because Jen was rubbing off on her. "Unless death by pleasure is the way you want to go."

∞

Lorelle knew she had stalled for long enough. She knew that she would have to answer the magic that Volcan had put inside her and she wasn't too keen on the idea of seeing what would happen if she just ignored it. The problem was, no matter how many times she told herself to get moving, she couldn't. All she could think about was what the human had said. She didn't have to see Perizada to know that she was alive. She girl had said that the woman she had met looked like she could be Lorelle's sister—that was confirmation enough. Then, to add fuel to the fire, the healer Sally was certainly alive and Lorelle knew for a fact that she had been very dead not too long ago. Since she had left the human in the coffee shop talking to the healer who was supposed to be dead, Lorelle had been pacing on the edge of the dark forest fighting the pull of the magic inside of her that demanded she go find the next healer.

She reasoned that she needed to consider what it meant that not only was Peri alive, but that she was also seeking out the very same gypsy healer. Did that mean that Peri knew about all the healers? And if she did, was she going to be taking them to the wolves?

"Dammit," Lorelle huffed into the silent forest. "Why couldn't she just stay dead? Is that too much to ask after you've killed your sibling? I don't think it's unreasonable of me to expect her to do me the courtesy of keeping her too perfect self in the damn ground!" Lorelle let out a slow breath as she composed herself after her brief, but much needed rant. She still had a job to do if she wanted to break free of Volcan.

She closed her eyes and felt his magic moving inside of her, pulling on her will to go in the direction that it demanded. She fought the urge to cringe away and instead let it lead her to her next target. She flashed, letting Volcan's spell direct her path. When she felt herself become still, she waited several heartbeats before she opened her eyes.

"Okay," she said slowly as she looked around. "This is not what I was expecting." She stood on a sidewalk at the edge of a lawn that looked as though it hadn't seen a lawn mower since before Lorelle was born. The house beyond the jungle of a yard was dilapidated and Lorelle wondered how a stiff wind didn't just blow the shack right over. She looked left and then right and saw that the houses on either side where in the same sad shape as the one before her. The entire neighborhood was like a forgotten ghost town. The only signs of life were the cars that littered the street and driveways and the slight noises she could hear coming from inside some of the pathetic dwellings.

Letting out a loud sigh, she made sure to cloak herself as she crept up the walkway. Dry weeds burst through the cracked cement like bony hands reaching from the grave. She couldn't imagine a healer living in these conditions, but then she couldn't really imagine anyone living in these conditions. Lorelle's own life had always been a one of privilege and ease. How quickly things change when you decide to off your sister and join forces with evil.

She didn't bother to knock, she wasn't going to do things politely this time, not if there was a chance that Peri could show up at any moment. The door flew open with a loud bang as she held her hand out pushing her magic forward. As she stepped across the threshold she was surprised to find, in stark contrast to the crumbling mess outside, a clean, though sparsely filled, living area. "Huh, learn something new every day," she muttered to herself.

"Can I help you?" A sharp voice had Lorelle nearly jumping in the air, not because she was afraid of a little human, but because said human shouldn't be able to see her.

Lorelle turned to look at the owner of the voice and her eyes widened. The girl was younger than the first one she had visited, but not by much. But that wasn't what surprised the fae. The shocking thing about the youth was her sheer beauty, as if she'd been hand chiseled by the Great Luna herself. In a place so very ugly, this girl stood out like a diamond in the rough. *It was a shame that Volcan was going to get his grubby hands on this one*, Lorelle thought. But then she also thought, *better her than me*.

"Actually, yes, yes you can," Lorelle smiled wickedly. She made a motion with her hand at the wall in front of her, smiling at the little gift she knew her sister would eventually find, then she leapt across the room and grabbed the girl's arm flashing as she did so, instantly transporting her far from her hovel, away from her life, and away from any future she ever thought she might have.

Lorelle thought for an instant as she dropped the girl off in the dark forest that she might have felt something akin to guilt, but she knew it was impossible for her to feel guilt, not after the things she had already done. She chalked it up as indigestion, ignoring the fact that she'd never so much as had a stomach ache in all her millennia alive. Indigestion was better than guilt any day of the week in her book.

∞

Volcan felt Lorelle's presence in his forest, felt her fear, her shock and anger. She had been there for several hours and he cursed his limited form that he couldn't go to her and force her to do his will. He didn't have time for her to deal with the fact that her sister, whom she so proudly declared dead by her own hand, was indeed alive. He had known that Perizada was alive, but who was he to burst the fae's bubble? All that mattered at this point was that she get him the healers. He needed their magic if he ever wanted to be more than a spirit again. He had been patient long enough. For so long he had existed trapped in this castle that once had been a place of power. Now it was a prison.

Lorelle had wandered into his home seeking refuge from her own sins, and now thanks to her need of sanctuary he had his tool. If he could just be patient a little longer he would be free, and then they would pay. All those who thought they could destroy him, they would see what true power was.

He finally felt Lorelle leave and when she arrived back he felt another presence. It was pure, light, goodness and though he wanted to touch that with a fifty foot pole, he smiled because it was a healer. The very thing that could destroy him for good, could also restore him. So it was with all light, it could give warmth, and cause growth or if exposed to it for too long or in too high a quantity it could reduce the world to ash. It was a risk worth taking. He was tired of simply existing. His time was coming and soon he would remind the fae council of what true power really was.

Chapter 9

"The words leftover, relic, remnant and the like at one time held a negative connotation. Now, knowing that I am a member of the remnant of gypsy healers in this world, I see those words in a whole new connotation. Because no matter how big or small the remainder is, I am a part of something good and pure. I am not alone, I have a purpose." ~Anna

"Do you know where we're going next?" Peri asked Sally as they all gathered in the living area of the home in Farie. Sally sat in Costin's lap looking as tired as Peri felt.

Sally nodded. "I called Rachel just to check my information. From what I could get from the girl's mind it would be best if we went in small. She's going to be skittish."

"What leads you to this conclusion?" Lucian asked.

"She doesn't come from the best circumstances," Sally explained. "Some of the things she's seen are downright disturbing. She's poor, and from what I can tell she doesn't trust anyone because of the things she's seen."

"Am I right in saying that you don't think any males should accompany us?" Peri asked.

"Yes. I think it would definitely be best if just females went," Sally agreed.

"Peri," Lucian started.

Peri held up her hand to stop him. "I know you don't like the idea of us going without male protection and while I appreciate your concern you have to remember who I am and what I'm capable of. Now that Lorelle has entered the picture, time is of the essence and we have to get these healers to safety. We've dallied long enough as it is."

"I am very aware of who you are and what you are capable of, if you remember your illustration of your power to me just a short time ago." Lucian's words had Peri's skin flushed a delightful shade of red. He continued even as he enjoyed her reaction. "Though I know these things I am still your mate, your protector, your shelter and there is nothing you can do or say that will keep me from following you into any amount of danger no matter how great or small." His eyes held her steady gaze making it perfectly clear that he would not be swayed. He was going with her and there wasn't a damn thing she could do to stop him.

"Fine," she finally said after several tense seconds. "You, and you" she snapped at Costin and Sorin, "are going to have to trust me to take care of your mates. One huge male we might be able to hide, but not three so you both will stay here." She didn't give Costin or Sorin time to argue before she moved on to give orders to the others. "Sally, Elle, myself and Lucian will go retrieve this next healer. The rest of you will get some rest."

"I can't let you go without me," Costin murmured against Sally's ear as she hugged him. "Every word Lucian spoke is true of me as well. You are mine. I will not risk you, not even for another healer."

Sally pulled back to look up into his eyes and it pained her to see the fear for her safety. She knew

130

exactly how he felt because she too could not imagine letting him leave her behind as he ran headlong into danger. But she also knew that sometimes you had to do things you didn't want to do because it was the right thing, not the easy thing, but the right thing. And frankly it just sucked. "You have to know that I understand how you feel and your feelings are valid to me. But you also know that I am a healer and with that comes sacrifices that we have to be willing to endure. We have to get this girl out of harm's way so that she can live the life she is supposed to. What of her mate Costin, shouldn't he get the chance to be with her? If it is difficult for her to be around men then let's not start out her experience with our world by terrifying her with three huge, intimating males. Trust me to be careful, trust Peri to protect us, please."

Costin stared into the eyes of his pleading mate and knew that she was right. He would concede. He wouldn't like it or pretend to be okay with it, but he would do what he knew he must.

"You will come back to me in the exact condition you are leaving in. If there is so much as a scratch on you I will never let you leave my side again." Costin took her face in his hands and almost violently smashed his lips against hers. He kissed her with a passion that would help her remember why she should be careful, why she should desire to return to him as quickly as possible. When he finally released her the look on her face was one he had seen many times, but only behind the closed doors of their bedroom. "I love you," he whispered to her.

"I've no doubt of that and just as you have no doubt that I return that love." Sally turned away from her mate's intense stare, thoroughly shaken from his kiss. The sooner she left, the sooner she would be back in his arms.

Elle too was in a heated argument with Sorin, but in the end he too accepted the inevitable and released his mate to go. He shook with the need to snatch her back and shackle her to his side. Instead of acting on his impulse he stood watching her every move, willing her to be safe and to return to him whole and untouched.

Sally took Elle's hand as she stepped away from a rigid Sorin, and looked up at Peri. "Her name is Stella, and we're going to start with a place that seems to preoccupy her mind. I looked it up on my phone; it's in New York City, in the Bronx. It's a club she works at called The Core."

Peri nodded. "Okay, Elle, be sure to be cloaking when we flash. Let's make this quick and painless."

They flashed leaving the others to wait anxiously for their return.

"Did my mate seriously just head to a club in the Bronx without me?" Costin asked, his anger still evident in his sharp tone.

"We didn't even think to ask them of their destination before we let them talk us into staying behind," Sorin growled, obviously not any happier about it than Costin.

"In your defense, Costin, Peri would have bound you to keep you here if she had to," Adam told him as he pulled Crina closer to him, silently thanking the Great Luna that his mate had not gone into such a situation without him.

Costin growled. "I've already experienced that once and don't care to repeat the event."

132

"She could have kept him here?" Anna asked from where she sat on the floor, legs folded in front of her. She looked skeptical at the idea of little Peri being able to keep powerful looking Costin from doing anything.

Costin's smile stretched wide across his face revealing white teeth, but there was no mirth in it. "I suppose I could enlighten you on some things. It might distract me from killing something because of my Sally traipsing around one of the most dangerous cities in the world without me. Sorin, Crina," he motioned for them to sit and then looked at Adam with a tilt of his head, "if you all will please have a seat and join me in regaling our new healer with our recent history. I wish Wadim was here. He's the Romanian pack historian and has a penchant for storytelling."

"Where should we begin?" Adam asked.

"She would probably like to hear Jacque and Fane's story," Crina offered.

Sorin smiled and cleared his throat as he nodded. "It was a clear, summer night when I pulled the limo up to the curb in Coldspring Texas," he began remembering back to that night over a year ago.

∞

"Can I just say that New York in the summer smells about as good as a well-used port-a-potty," Sally grumbled as she rubbed the stench from her nose. Peri and Elle had flashed them to an alley which was apparently home to several dumpsters, one overweight homeless man, two mangy tabby cats, and something that might have once been a dog…maybe.

"Well the quicker we find this club, then the quicker we find the girl and you get the idea," Peri said with a wave of her hand. She headed for the opening of the alley, obviously expecting the others to follow.

Night had fallen over the city but even without the sun shining down the summer heat permeated the air. The blacktop from the street and the concrete beneath their shoes seemed to release the heat it had soaked up throughout the day. As they emerged onto the sidewalk Peri didn't miss a beat as she grabbed the arm of the first person walking past.

"I'm looking for the club called The Core," she told the guy who was staring at her in awe. He tried to speak but nothing he said made any sense. She let go of him with a huff. "Remind me to only ask questions to females."

"Peri, I have the address on my phone," Sally pointed out, "You don't have to ask directions."

"You could have mentioned that back there in the alley and before I was nearly drooled on by the human male," Peri snapped.

"You are worried," Lucian's voice invaded her mind. He had stepped away from their group and blended into the shadows. Peri was impressed with his ability to take in new things with such composure; she was sure she would have been gawking like an idiot at the tall building and boxes with wheels on them.

"Is it that obvious?" She asked back.

"Try not to take it out on your allies."

"Can I take it out on you?"

134

"I have told you, I will be whatever it is you need me to be."

As his words echoed in her mind Peri fought the need to go to him and beg him to wrap her in his arms and make all the bad things in the world go away. She had accepted that Lucian was her mate, that he had the other half of her soul, but what she wasn't accepting as well was that the half of her soul that he possessed seemed to be a pansy ass girl.

"No, she is simply someone who knows it's okay to let her burdens be carried by the one who was born for that very purpose," Lucian rumbled.

"Okay we need to head that direction." Sally's voice interrupted before Peri could respond. She turned to see the healer pointing away from the bright lights and deeper into the belly of the city.

"Lead the way Sally. Elle you and I will cloak us, I don't feel like dealing with any stupid humans; it's bad enough I have to deal with stupid supernaturals."

"We love you too, Peri fairy," Sally laughed.

They walked quickly down the sidewalk, completely unnoticed by those around them. Lucian trailed them closely, and the only reason Peri knew he was there was because she could feel him. She imagined that living in the Dark Forest for all those centuries taught him a thing or two about blending in.

After several blocks, which grew darker with every step, Peri was beginning to think that Sally's phone was leading them into the depths of hell and not to a club. When they finally came upon the neon sign, sporting burnt out letters causing it to read "Th ore" instead of "The Core," she knew she was right. The phone was indeed leading them into a *version* of hell.

Half-clad bodies trickled through the dilapidated door and each time it opened they could hear the rumble of music and smell the stench of sweat, lust, and alcohol.

"You're going in there?" Lucian asked as he materialized from the darkness around them.

"Believe me, this is not my idea of a good time," Peri told him.

"We totally should have brought Jen," Sally spoke up with a smile.

Elle nodded. "She would have definitely enjoyed this."

"What are they wearing?" Lucian's appalled voice had all of the women turning to look at the door as two women dressed in halter dresses that left little to the imagination giggled their way into the club.

"I told you to prepare yourself," Peri warned. "It's not my fault your imagination could not fathom the depths to which the human depravity has plunged."

"Hey," Sally snapped, "We aren't all depraved."

"Sally, you're a gypsy healer and therefore uncharacteristically wholesome, you don't count."

"Isn't the one we are going after a healer?" Lucian questioned.

Peri nodded. "And I bet your furry little butt that her innocence will shine like the sun in this dark hole."

"We aren't dressed for this, do you think they will let us in?" Sally asked watching another group of scantily clad women go into the club.

Peri looked them over and then nodded. "Oh, I can handle that." She mumbled something under her breath and then snapped her fingers.

"Sweet!" Sally grinned as she looked down at the knee high boots, black skirt, and fish net top with a red halter style bra underneath. She looked at Elle who was wearing the same outfit but with a hot pink bra that matched her hair, and then to Peri who again wore the same outfit but with a silver, metallic bra. "Um Peri, are we supposed to look like triplets?"

"We go in, we get the girl, we come out. I'm not real concerned with how original our outfits are," she said sharply.

"That's an awful lot of flesh showing, mate," Lucian's deep growl rumbled through the night as his voice bounced off the walls of her mind.

"Play your cards right and one day you might just get to see the rest," Peri teased knowing that no amount of her telling him to be reasonable would make him reasonable. She was pretty sure that reasonable and Canis lupis could not ever be used in the same sentence. His response was several swear words in his native tongue.

"Let's do this," she said with a determined glint. Her hand paused on the door and she turned to where she knew Lucian stood once more wrapped in shadows. "Keep your wolf in control. We do not need a blood bath in here because you lose your cool. I need you to remember something for me," she paused waiting.

"What is that beloved," his voice carried through the dark night.

"I am yours." With that she opened the door and ushered Elle and Sally into the dark club. She knew he would slip in behind them and she tried to use a little magic to keep him from being noticed.

Elle was flirting with the bouncer as she convinced him that Sally was indeed old enough to be in such an establishment and then before they knew it they were being ushered into the sea of dancing bodies. Sally's hands rose in the air as she and Elle shimmied their way through the crowd. Peri used her magic, surrounding herself with it and the humans around her instinctively moved away to give her room. She saw a male dance up to Sally and out of nowhere Lucian was suddenly there calmly pushing the drunk guy in another direction. It didn't surprise her that he was looking out for, not only his own mate, but those of his pack mates as well. His eyes met hers briefly as he melded back into the crowd disappearing. Suddenly the room got quiet as the music was turned down. All heads turned towards the bar where several spotlight where now shining.

"I have a bad feeling about this," Elle whispered as she moved closer to Peri tugging Sally with her. All three stood and watched, frozen with the rest of the crowd as three females jumped up on the bar. They moved in synch with each other, every motion obviously practiced. When they finally turned to face the crowd Sally gasped.

"What were you saying about her innocence shining like the sun?" Sally asked Peri.

Peri groaned. "Let me guess, Stella is the dark beauty in the center that no one can take their eyes off of?"

"Ding, ding, ding, we have a winner," Sally muttered.

"Even the humans are drawn to the healer in her," Elle said as she watched the faces of the crowd.

"Uh, Elle," Sally chuckled, "I don't think it's the healer in her they're drawn to."

Peri snorted. "If only Jen were here."

"She would totally be jealous of Stella's moves," Sally agreed.

"Peri, what do we do?" Elle asked as the crowd began to cheer the dancers on.

"Watch and learn; variety is the spice of life after all and mated pairs are together for a long, long time." Peri laughed at the skeptical look in Elle's eyes. "Well we can't very well just snatch her off the bar," she clarified.

The music continued on and the three girls danced. Thankfully no clothes came off. As soon as the girls were done they were being ushered quickly from the makeshift stage and through a door behind the bar.

"Can you see if there is a back entrance, maybe they will use it for an exit," Peri sent the thought to Lucian.

She saw him slip through the crowd and knew the only reason she was able to see him was because he allowed it.

"Lucian's checking on a back entrance," she told Elle and Sally.

"Are we just going to take," Sally paused as her eyes caught a movement that was incongruent with the atmosphere. Suddenly, where there had been an empty space across the room from them, there was Lorelle. Her eyes met Sally's drawing a gasp from the healer.

Peri's head snapped around and her eyes met her sister's for the first time since Lorelle had left her dying the dark forest. Peri grabbed Sally's arm as she snapped, "Elle outside now!"

They flashed from the building ending up on the sidewalk outside of the club. Sally's eyes, wide with fear as she remembered her encounter with Lorelle and the outcome, which had been her own death.

"Talk to me, Lucian," Peri reached out for him as if she had been doing it all of her long life.

"There is a door back here," he showed her the image in his mind of the door he was staring at. *"I can hear voices through it."*

"We have company. We need to get the girl and leave now," she told him, then looked at Elle and Sally. "We're going to flash to the rear of the building and meet Lucian. I'm going to get Stella and then we're going to get the hell out of dodge." She didn't give them time to answer but grabbed both of their arms and flashed to the location Lucian had showed her through their bond. They appeared beside him in an alley that ran behind the club. A weak fluorescent light hung precariously above the club's rear door, buzzing and sputtering, providing the alley's only illumination. Peri felt his hands on her waist as he leaned in close to her ear. "I heard her name being spoken just beyond the door," his deep voice rumbled.

Peri nodded. "I'm going in to get her and then as soon as I'm back here we are going straight back to Farie. Lorelle was in the club." She felt him tense and sensed his anger. She patted his hand. "I got this, Lucian. You watch the girls for me." Then she was gone.

∞

140

Stella wiped the sweat from her neck and face and then tossed the towel in the dirty clothes basket next to the lockers. She heard one of the other dancers yell her name and tell her goodnight. She didn't even have the energy to respond. She was tired of dancing. She was tired of late nights at the club and then long days at the diner where she worked. She was sick of the leering men, grabby hands, and nasty comments. And the club customers were bad too, she chuckled to herself. It might not have bothered her so much had her background been different, but then her childhood had been filled with nightmares. It had left her so scarred that she didn't think she would ever be able to tolerate the touch of man, not matter how loving or gentle. She could barely stomach her brother's hugs, but she tried hard not to show him, she didn't want to hurt him. He no idea what she had endured at the hands of their father, literally his hands. And if her brother had known, he would have killed their father, and then she would be all alone with her brother behind bars. Bile rose in her throat at the thought of the one man who had taken her childhood from her. There had been no mother to love her or care for her. The woman who bore her and Derrick had been the product of generations of alcoholics and drug attics. After Stella had been born she left the hospital without so much as an *I don't want this kid*. Her parents hadn't been married, and to this day she still didn't know why their father had chosen to keep them when it was so obvious that he had no love for either of them. As soon as Stella turned eighteen, her brother had moved them out of their father's apartment. Though he hadn't known about the horror she went through, he did know that Willie

141

James was a no good scoundrel, not worth the precious oxygen that he took from the world.

She graduated high school and started working at the club where Derrick worked as a bouncer because he wanted to know where she was, that she was safe. She had argued that being eighteen meant that she was an adult and didn't need his supervision; he disagreed. Then she had argued that it was weird that he was okay with her dancing in a bar but he had argued that she wasn't taking any clothes off and he kept an eye on her and always tossed out the scum. The pay was good, and that was the only reason she was doing it. She was saving up. She was getting out of the city, putting the memories of her shattered youth behind her like dust kicking up from the back wheels of a car; as soon as she had enough money of course.

She grabbed the oversized t-shirt that she kept to wear after her show and pulled it over the skimpy outfit. She slipped out of the dance shoes she wore to help her slide over the bar and put on her only pair of tennis shoes and then closed her locker. She was just turning to leave when she heard her name. It wasn't her name being said that shocked her into stillness, it was the sound of the voice saying her name. It was nearly musical in cadence, beautiful beyond words, causing chill bumps to rise on her arms. She turned slowly to see a woman with white hair and pale skin. She looked young, but her eyes told a different story than the youth of her face. Stella was about to ask her who she was when a hand clamped around her arm.

"We have much to discuss, sister, but Stella and I have pressing business, so it will have to wait for another time. Toodles." Stella looked at the woman who held her arm and her eyes widened at the sheer beauty of her. She looked like the woman across the room, only brighter, as if the sun followed her wherever she went. "Please try not to puke," the woman said and then they were swallowed by darkness just as the other woman shrieked, "PERI!"

Stella tried to pull away from the grip but found that the woman was much stronger than she looked. She blinked, attempting to see through the darkness and just as quickly as the blackness had engulfed them, there was light again. She realized they were in the alley behind the club, where the dim glow of The Core's back light illuminated only a small area around her. There were three other people standing there, looking expectantly at the woman who still held her arm.

"You know where to take them, let's go," the woman said and then they were overcome by darkness again. This time it lasted longer and she understood why the woman had asked her not to puke because the feeling was disorienting, causing her stomach to get a little queasy.

Stella's thoughts were racing as she tried to cope with the obscurity around her and the sick feeling in her stomach. Who was the lady who had called her name, who was the lady who grabbed her arm, how did they know her name and what in the hell was she doing to cause them to move from one location to the next without so much as a here let me get the damn door for you? Okay so she had a lot to work through, but living in the Bronx she knew the first rule of any situation was don't panic. Her brother always told her that panic equaled stupid and stupid equaled dead. Yeah, he was just full of warm fuzzies like that.

After several minutes in the dizzying black hole she was abruptly surrounded by light and people. She looked from face to face as they stared at her and she was sure they were waiting for her to bolt or freak out. They obviously weren't from New York. New Yorkers don't freak, they get pissed and then they get even. She took stock of the males in the room and instinctively took a step back, attempting to put as much space as possible between them and herself. She didn't trust men, not any, save one. She noticed that when she took the step back each of the men wrapped their arms around the respective women standing next to them, almost as if they understood that she feared them and they wanted her to know that she was of no interest to any of them.

"I'm going to go out on a limb here and say this isn't your everyday, run of the mill mugging," Stella said in her best New Yorker accent.

She heard a small snort of laughter and turned her head to see the beautiful woman who had grabbed her looking at her with a smirk. The man, revision, huge, handsome man holding her didn't look at Stella, but just somewhere in the vicinity of her.

"I don't know what they're feeding you healers these days but it's made you much less sweet and innocent than what I'm used to." The woman called Peri smirked.

"Forgive me for just a second if I don't really care what you're used to since you just kidnapped me and worked some weird mojo on me," Stella said in as calm a voice as she could muster.

144

"Oh I like her," one of the girls that had been standing in the alley spoke up. Stella would like to say her pink hair was unique, but in her line of work she saw all sorts and pink hair was tame.

"So you haven't killed me yet, and at the moment you are all staring at me like I kidnapped *you*—which I didn't. So," she turned and saw an empty chair, she backed up slowly to it and sat down, crossing her legs attempting to appear as confident as possible and then looked back up at the group. "I am guessing by your bossy, take no crap attitude, you would be the leader of this outfit," she said narrowing her eyes at Peri. "How about we cut the crap and you tell me what you want so I can get back before my brother tears the Big Apple apart looking for me."

Peri sat on the arm of the chair that Lucian had taken. She stared at the gypsy healer across from her in what she knew was a look of respect. Then again, the girl was from New York, and worked in a club as a dancer, she had to be made of tough stuff. Her dark chocolate skin was smooth and even, with the obvious freshness of youth. She had large almond eyes that were a very light brown which was striking against her dark skin. Her hair was fairly long past her shoulders, straight and shiny, held back by a scarf she had tied as a head band. She had full lips, high cheek bones and a no nonsense attitude that Peri found herself smiling at.

"You are correct," Peri finally breathed out as she leaned into the hand Lucian had placed on her lower back. "I am in charge of this ragtag looking outfit."

Stella chuckled. "Um, no offense, but only people who have gone under the knife or have their

145

pictures photo shopped look as pretty as you freaks do, so ragtag you are not."

"She's going to give Jen a run for her money," Crina laughed to Peri.

"Yes, like Jen, she doesn't seem to have a filter," Peri agreed. "Tell me, Stella, do you believe in the supernatural?" Peri watched as the healer's eyes narrowed.

"I believe in God if that's what you mean," she answered confidently.

"Lucian," Peri said her mate's name but didn't take her eyes off of Stella. "I think you should just show her. Let's just rip the band aide off fast. Then after she has her fit we'll break it all down for her. Then we need to move onto the next one."

"Are you sure you want *me* to?" Lucian asked calmly in his deep voice.

Peri turned her head to look at him. *"You're beautiful in your wolf form."*

Lucian smiled at her, obviously pleased at the compliment. He leaned forward and kissed her chastely on the lips before standing. "We should probably go outside for this." Lucian was a large wolf and with this many people in the room, he knew there would not be enough room for him.

They all followed him out the front door into the front yard of the house. The night air of Farie was cool and refreshing, a stark contrast to their previous surroundings. The sky was full of stars too innumerable to count.

Stella noticed the only other girl who looked as lost as she felt and managed to ease herself closer to her. "You're not one of them, are you?" Stella asked the girl.

146

"I'm Anna," she answered. "And according to them I *am* one of them, and you must be too if you're here and they're about to show you this." She motioned to the incredibly handsome guy who was removing his shirt.

"Uh, why is he undressing?" Stella asked as her chest began to tighten and the familiar feeling of dread welled up at the idea of knowing a man in any intimate way. She had no desire to see a half dressed male, no matter how magnificent he was.

"I can't even begin to answer that, but rest assured he won't hurt you and he won't even look your way," Anna said, obviously picking up on Stella's distress. "He belongs to that one." She pointed to the one called Peri. "And they are quite committed to each other."

Stella wanted to believe Anna, but she had watched too many married men come in the club and slip their wedding bands into their pockets, as if that somehow made them free agents.

Lucian turned to face the group and looked at Peri. "I'm going to leave the breeches on."

"Good call," Peri nodded and smiled at his lapse into a manner of speaking long past.

There was a shimmering in the air around Lucian and then his human form slipped away the pants falling as rags to the ground, and in its place was a massive white wolf.

"I don't know what you slipped me, but you could make a killing in the Bronx," Stella muttered as she stared at the massive wolf before her, where only moments ago a man had been.

Sally smiled sympathetically at the new healer. "Believe me, chick, if we could bottle this crap and make some money off of the stuff we live, we'd be rich."

"Uh, hello. People like Anne Rice *are* freaking rich because of the stuff we live, and they don't even know it's real," Crina piped in.

"How do you know she doesn't know it's real?" Adam asked, joining in the banter.

"Are you implying that Anne Rice wrote her books based on facts?" Sally asked skeptically.

"I'm simply saying that…,"

"I'm so sorry to interrupt what is sure to be a conversation that I might actually care about later, but could someone please explain to me where the man went, and where the wolf came from?" Stella jumped in cutting Adam off. "I mean, this may be normal to you people but even in the Bronx we don't have werewolves."

"Oh, I wouldn't be too sure about that…" Peri said with a twinkle in her eye as she stroked the huge white wolf.

Chapter 10

"If you have ever lived in someone's shadow then you know what it is like to feel second best. To feel as though you are the credits that nobody wants to read at the end of a fantastic movie. Though you may have played a major part in the production, you are but a passing thought to the viewers. I have played second fiddle to my sister long enough. I have been the afterthought to her triumphs for as long as I can stand. I am done; I have reached the end of my rope." ~Lorelle

Lorelle stared at the empty spot where the healer had been standing. She was frozen with shock. Her sister had been right there within her grasp and she had just stood there like a daft fledgling as her prize was stolen. That was two. Two healers ripped right from her grasp. Two healers that would have gotten her closer to her goal of escaping yet another evil man hell bent on ruling the world. Why couldn't men just be happy with killing their obnoxious sibling and being the powerful one on a council? Why did they always have to strive for world domination and all that crap? With no reason to linger in the dim, smelly room that scantily clad women used to change their clothes, she flashed herself back to the dark forest, back to the place that had been her salvation until Volcan showed up.

As soon as the sounds of the city were gone and the familiar darkness of the forest surrounded her, Lorelle resumed her pacing. With three girls accounted for, there were only two left. She *had* to get those two, there was no getting around it. If she failed to produce more healers than Peri stole, she was sure Volcan would somehow magically zap her even in his bodiless form.

"I hate to bother you since you seem busy in thought, but my mom will be expecting me home soon, or well I think soon. I'm not really sure of the time," a sweet, innocent voice broke through Lorelle's concentration. She turned her head slowly to look at the girl and for all her contrast to the healer known as Sally, this one reminded her of the Serbian pack healer. Where Sally had tan skin, this one had milky pale skin, where Sally had brown eyes, this one had green eyes and where Sally had long dark chocolate hair, this one had strawberry blonde hair cut to just below her ears. Again she was struck by just how beautiful she was for a human. She had that glow about her that was common in healers, though to humans they would never understand why they were drawn to the girl. She wasn't short or tall, simply average and she was just beginning to show the curves of womanhood. She looked much too innocent for this world. Much too innocent for the unimaginable things she would be facing in the near future and here she was simply worried about getting home to a mother who expected her, but would never see her again.

"Are you not more worried about the fact that a stranger somehow transported you to a forest that looks dark enough to hide only the most horrifying creatures?" Lorelle asked.

The girl crossed her arms in front of her and shivered as she looked around the forest as if seeing it for the first time. Lorelle was sure that at any moment she would fall apart in tears begging to go home and then she'd have to knock a backbone into her. But the human surprised her.

"I've seen things that I can't explain before, and I've learned that asking questions doesn't mean you will always get answers. I've also learned that sometimes you will get an answer that you wished you'd never asked for. So I typically try to stay *out* of the know, if you know what I mean."

Lorelle's eyes narrowed on the girl. "What's your name, healer?"

"Jewel," she answered simply.

"Jewel what?" Lorelle snapped.

The girl looked down at the ground as if the grass suddenly was the most interesting thing in the world. She muttered something so soft that Lorelle didn't hear her.

"It can't be that bad," she growled.

Finally Jewel looked up at her with a flash of defiance in her eyes, daring Lorelle to laugh at her. "Stone. Jewel Stone is my name."

Lorelle stared at her for several seconds before she burst into laughter. "I was wrong, it is that bad," she said through the chuckles that racked her body.

"It is *not* that funny," Jewel stomped her foot. This only caused Lorelle to laugh harder. Finally after several minutes she composed herself and looked at the obviously ticked off healer.

"Well, Jewel Stone, if I were you I'd change my last name. That's just a little free advice from me to you."

"I would prefer some advice on how to get home. That's what I really need to know. Not how hilarious you think my name is," Jewel stated calmly, attempting regain her composure.

Lorelle's brow rose as she finally began to see a little backbone rising up in the unassuming looking healer. "The best advice I can give you, healer, is to accept your fate. Sometimes in life we don't get choices, this is one of those times. Enjoy your time in this forest because it is bound to be the most pleasant left in your short life." Lorelle didn't let her conscience be touched by the fear that flared up in the green eyes on Jewels pale, pretty face. Instead she let Volcan's magic once again pull her, dragging her away from the forest and the frightened healer, to her next victim—to the next life she would destroy. She decided this time she wouldn't ask for a name. She didn't want to know. She didn't need to know because knowing their name made them a person, made them somebody's daughter, niece, or sister.

Then again, maybe she was doing somebody's sister a favor by taking their sibling away. Maybe their healer sister outshined them for all of their lives with her gentle nature and unpretentious ways. Maybe, just maybe, she would keep feeding herself her own crap and it would begin to taste like chocolate.

∞

"Do you think it was wise of us to leave Stella so soon after telling her about all of this?" Sally asked Peri as they stood outside a dilapidated old home in the Chicago suburbs. The entire neighborhood looked as though it could use a good coat of paint and the world's largest lawn mower.

"Right now we don't have the luxury of wisdom," Peri said though not unkindly. "We have three more healers to rescue from the talon-like clutches of my bitch of a sister and I can't be holding a bottle out for these young healers while holding their hand and singing *Hush Little Baby*."

Elle laughed as she stepped up beside the two women. "You're descriptions always do get better the angrier you become."

"Bite me, Elle," Peri growled.

"That's not my job, Peri, but I know someone who could assist you," Elle winked at Lucian who was staring quizzically at the two. He was still confounded by their banter and had openly admitted that most of the time he simply ignored them.

"Are we going to do this or what?" Adam asked.

"Why, are you in a hurry to get back to your mate, Adam?" Costin asked with a chuckle.

"Like you wouldn't be chomping at the bit to get back to Sally if she had been left behind," Adam said with an unapologetic shrug.

Peri turned to look at the group behind her. She had made all of the males come with them on account of what Sally had explained to her about Stella and left Crina with the two new healers, knowing she could handle them if need be. She stared at the four huge, devastatingly handsome men and frowned. They weren't very inconspicuous in the rundown neighborhood as their beauty, and that's what it was, shone like polished copper against tarnished silver. "Can you all please quit your incessant griping for five minutes so we can get this thing done? I swear it's like dragging three year olds across the damn globe while they scream I want my lollipop."

"Well, she is lickable," Adam mumbled.

153

There was a snort of laughter from the other males, including Lucian, which earned them all a glare from the females.

"Ladies, the men obviously need time to mature, so why don't we go in and save the day while they deal with their thirteen year old libidos." Peri motioned for the girls to follow her, ignoring Costin's response of, "It's more like sixteen year olds, if you want to be accurate."

"Sally, that one is yours," Peri huffed.

"At the moment I don't claim him," Sally said as she tried not to laugh.

"That's not what you were singing this morning, Sally mine," Costin's rich voice whispered in her mind.

"You shouldn't dwell on the past, Costin Miklos, nothing good ever comes of it," She teased back.

"I beg to differ. Every time I remind you of my past kisses, you give me more, and by more I don't just mean kisses."

Sally choked as she felt her mate's hands in places not appropriate for a mate's hands to be while rescuing a girl from the clutches of evil.

"Costin, I swear if your mate falls over in the throes of ecstasy I will declaw you and let Jen neuter you," Peri called out as she reached the door.

"How does she always know?" Costin asked as the males joined them on the porch.

Lucian chuckled. "She's just that good," he answered with pride in his voice.

"Shh," Peri held her finger up, hushing the males though she sent Lucian a caress of affection through their bond, pleased by his praise. She pushed the unlocked and unclosed door open slowly. As she stepped into the room she didn't have time to react before Sally gasped and the males all snarled.

"Is that blood?" Elle asked as she stepped closer to the wall. Sorin was by her side as his instinct to protect her took over. He and the other males, besides Adam, had their noses in the air trying catch any scents that might tell them something of what had happened in the home. Adam roamed through the house checking to see if there was anyone present and when he returned back to the main room where the group still stood staring up at the defiled wall, he shook his head at Peri.

"Dammit!" Peri shouted as her power surged though her along with anger and a sense of failure that she was not accustomed to. Lucian took her chin in his hand and pulled her face up to look at him. His steel colored eyes stared intently down at her as he spoke. "This is not your fault. You expect too much of yourself."

"I'm supposed to save them Lucian. It is my *job* to save them," she told him almost desperately.

"I know, love, and we will. We will get her back. That is what I am for, remember?" He pressed a kiss to her forehead before looking back up at the wall. "Adam, get me something from the girl's room please," he told the fae.

When he returned Lucian took the shirt Adam handed him and he sniffed it, then he stepped up to the wall and sniffed the blood. "It's not hers."

Peri and the others let out the breaths they had been holding.

"What does it mean?" Sally asked.

Peri read it out loud as she thought about the words.

"You freed one, but in doing so, you condemned the world. He has returned, though he never truly left. I will take what you think is yours, and you will pay for all you have done to me."

"I feel like one of us should whisper *He Who Must Not be Named has returned,*" Sally mumbled.

"What is with you Americans and your movies?" Elle asked.

Sally shrugged. "How else can you enter a fairy tale, fight in an epic battle, or win the hot guy?"

Elle gave her a pointed look.

Sally looked sheepishly at her mate and then back to Elle. "I'm sort of living that aren't I?"

Elle held up her hand with her forefinger and thumb slightly a part as if to say, *just a tad.*

"You're sister sucks at rhyming," Adam told Peri.

"Rhyming would have been a tad more dramatic," Peri agreed. After reading it one more time Peri raised her hand and ran it through the air in front of the wall and, just like that, the blood, and dooming words were gone as if they had never been.

"We shouldn't linger here, Peri," Lucian told her softly in his deep rumbling voice.

She nodded. "You're right. Sally, where's the next one. Let's just keep going. If we go back to Farie we might linger too long and then my soon to be bloody sister will snatch another one out from under us."

Sally closed her eyes and sifted through the memories she and Rachel had been getting from the healers they were searching for. She smiled. "We're going home."

"To Romania?" Peri asked as her brow creased.

"Bigger than that," Sally smiled.

The rest groaned. "Seriously, we have to go to Texas?" Adam huffed along with the others as they had heard Sally talk about Texas enough to want to beat their heads against a longhorn, or whatever it was she was always talking about.

"What?" Sally asked innocently. "Everything's bigger in Texas."

"Bloody hell not this again," Peri snatched arms and motioned for Elle and Adam to do the same. "Show me where we are going in your beloved Texas Sally so we can get there and get out before my own ego grows out of control just from being in that blasted state."

Costin grinned wickedly. "Wait if your ego will grow just from being in that state does that mean my...,"

"Shut it wolf," Peri snapped and then looked at Sally expectantly.

"You can see in my mind?" Sally asked.

"Not usually but your mind is so open right now that if you think something directly to me I will get it," she explained quickly to her.

Costin growled at the idea of one more person have access to his mate's mind, but Peri ignored him. She didn't have time to placate jealous wolves at every turn.

Peri waited as Sally closed her eyes and sent her the image. Peri shared it with Adam and Elle and then they were gone, leaving the sorrowful looking house in worse condition than when they had arrived. For a mother would now come home to that house to find her greatest fear realized, a child gone without a trace and without any hope of returning.

∞

Heather Banks stood on the front porch of her small home as the Texas heat beat down on her. Even the wind only brought warm air that did nothing to sooth her overcooked skin. She was convinced she was keeping Burt's Bees Body Butter in business with the speed in which she used it only to turn around and buy more.

"Another day in paradise," she mumbled to the tumbleweeds that she was sure were rolling by. The land around her had once smelled of rich, green grass, fragrant blooming wild flowers and that little underlying hint of fertilizer, and not the bagged kind. Now all she smelled was dirt, dead things, and more dirt. The drought had been hard on all God's creatures in this part of Texas, whether human or otherwise. For months not a drop had fallen from the sky, and she knew the small town of Shady Grove wasn't the only place affected. She tilted her head up to the sky and prayed that God would have mercy on them, if only for a few minutes. She imagined the angels looking down at her and remembered how her mama use to tell her that when it rained it was the angels tears as they wept for the lost souls of men. Heather wondered as she stood with her face aimed at heaven if the lack of rain meant no souls were being lost, or if the angels were just tired of weeping over so many. Then, not for the first time, she thought, *is there something more?* Her eyes closed and her heart ached for what she did not know. "There's got to be something more," she whispered so only the angels heard.

She heard the familiar sound of tires crunching her rock driveway and smelled the gas fumes of the old Chevy as her longtime friend pulled up. By the sounds of the prancing paws in the back, Cheryl had only brought three dogs with her this time. She heard the door slam and the tailgate creak as it opened.

"One, two, three," she counted as the paws hit the ground and smiled at being right.

"Why in seven hells are you standing out in this heat cooking like a Ball Park on a weenie roast when you have a perfectly good air conditioner inside?" Cheryl hollered more loudly than necessary. Then again, Cheryl did everything more loudly than necessary.

"Oh come on, Cheryl, it's a beautiful day! The sun is shining and the birds are singing,"

"I know you're blind, Heather, but ya ain't stupid," Cheryl interrupted.

Heather laughed. "Okay so it is hotter than Hades in August in South Texas, how's that?"

"Gettin' there," Cheryl huffed.

"So who'd you bring me today?" Heather asked as she knelt down and held her hand out. She felt wet noses against her hand and arm and once they had her scent she reached out and ran her fingers through each dog's fur.

"I've got Hillary, Bill, and Chelsea; they're all Australian shepherd mixes."

Heather rolled her unseeing eyes. "They do realize that this is Texas right?"

"We just train 'em, we don't name 'em. You know that, Heather," Cheryl chided.

"That, *and* make fun of their name choices," Heather said with a shake of her head. She stood back up and stretched her arms over her head. "Suppose we better get started."

"Well, their names aren't getting any better with us just standing here like blooming idiots."

Heather followed after Cheryl and the three dogs, counting under her breath only by habit now. She didn't need to count to know how many steps the training building was from her house, she could walk to it in her sleep. She snorted to herself at that thought, because without her sight sometimes it felt like she was doing things in her sleep.

She felt the cool air of the building the minute Cheryl opened the door and the familiar smell of the many and varied dogs that had passed through her door. She smiled as she heard the excitement in her three current students as Cheryl let them loose to get some of the energy out of their systems. Dogs were a lot like children; they listened better if you just let them run it out.

"So where are they at in their training?" Heather asked.

Cheryl was just about to answer her when the training room door opened and the warm air blew in bringing with it a strange and oddly scented group of people.

Heather's head snapped around as she heard the shuffling of feet and smelled the distinct musk of men, feminine smell of women and a tiny hint of fur. She started to take a step in the intruders' direction but was stopped when Cheryl put a hand on her arm.

"What can we do for ya?" Cheryl asked the group. She watched as a brown eyed, brown haired beauty stepped forward and smiled with all the innocence of a bunny rabbit. Cheryl would have

160

believed it except for the fox at her back. The man that stepped up behind her was tall, built, as they say in Texas, like a bull bought for studding, and inhumanly handsome. His narrowed eyes spoke that of a predator, and any on the other side of that woman was his prey.

"We're sorry to interrupt," the girl spoke and they heard the Texas lilt in her voice. "My name is Sally, and this here," she pointed to the fox, "is Costin my ma—," she paused then seemed to correct herself, "husband. We wanted to talk to Heather if we could."

"You sound awful young to be married," Heather spoke up. Her heartbeat sped up and she used all of her senses to reach out and "see" who it was that had entered her training building. She knew beyond a shadow of a doubt that this was her "something more."

"Well, he hit me over the head and drug me into his cave, so what could I do?" Sally joked.

Heather relaxed just a bit, though Cheryl didn't remove her hand from her arm.

"What do you want to talk about? Do you have dogs that need training?"

There was a burst of feminine laughter and Heather turned her head slightly as if to look at Cheryl. "Am I that funny or do I have a booger or something on my face?"

"Pfft, please, Heather if you could see this bunch you would not be asking me that. They're not," she paused and then finally finished as their laughter died down, "normal."

Chapter 11

"I can see your face with the touch of my fingertips. I can feel your breath though you're a world away. I can hear your voice clearer than the purest tone. I can smell your skin sweeter than the richest morsel. I know you. My heart sees you better than my eyes ever could." ~ Heather

"We do not have time to deal with the human, love," Lucian purred through their bond.

"Does everything you say have to sound as though you're about to have your way with me?" Peri asked irritated at her reaction to him, especially when she needed to be paying attention to the matter at hand.

"I promise you that when that time comes you will have no doubt of my intentions, now please deal with the human so that we can abandon this place before you sister graces us with her presence."

"Good grief, give you males a little bit of power and suddenly you're giving the orders," Peri muttered under her breath before she flashed right in front of Cheryl. She looked the startled woman in the eyes and said, "I do apologize for this because you will have one hell of a headache when you wake up." She touched wide eyed Cheryl's forehead and as her body began to crumple Peri slowed its decent so that the human didn't hurt herself. Then she turned to Heather who was looking right at Peri, though Peri knew the woman couldn't see her.

"What did you do to Cheryl?" Heather asked in a surprisingly steady voice.

"I didn't hurt her if that's what you're afraid of," Peri assured her.

"Well what else would I be afraid of, that you had turned her into a pig that oinked the national anthem?" Heather asked as her hands landed on her hips and she looked up where she knew the tall woman's face to be. She could feel the woman's breath on her hair which told her she was definitely taller than her, which wasn't hard since Heather was five foot nothing.

"I thought everything was bigger in Texas." Heather heard a deep voice mutter and then a grunt which assured her that the male who had spoken received an elbow to the gut.

"Well I see being blind hasn't made you docile." Heather could hear the grin in the woman's voice and though she sensed that this woman was no one to trifle with, she didn't feel threatened.

"And being able to see hasn't given you manners."

There was a collective groan from the group still by the door. Heather turned her head in their direction. "Should I be shaking in my boots? Is that why you, let me see…," she paused to listen to their breathing, to the shuffle of their feet and the little noises they didn't even know they made. "You *six* stand over there looking like I've just insulted the Governor of Texas by telling him I voted against the death penalty?"

"I don't even know what that means," one of the girls muttered.

"Don't ask, it's a touchy subject in these parts," another girl responded.

The woman standing closest to her cleared her throat bringing Heather's attention back to her.

"All you need to know at the moment is that we will not hurt you. But there is another who will if you don't come with us."

Heather considered her options, not that she really had many. Shoot, she knew she was a blind girl from a small town in Texas with no family to speak of and living on next to nothing. She wasn't so blind to believe that something big wasn't happening, something *more* had finally come.

"Will Cheryl be alright?" She asked tentatively.

"She will be fine. She will wake up believing that you found a long lost cousin and have left for a nice long visit."

"I'm not coming back am I?" Heather's forehead wrinkled as she thought about never "seeing" her little house again, or never spending time training her beloved dogs for people who needed them so badly.

"You might one day convince your mate to bring you back for a visit," the woman said as she took her arm gently in her small but firm hand.

"My what?" Heather asked just as she felt a powerful pull against her body. She didn't know what was happening but she knew she wasn't in Kansas anymore.

Peri let go of Heather as soon as they appeared in her home across the veil in Farie. She stepped away from her as soon as she was sure that the young woman had her bearings. The others appeared seconds after her and stepped back to give her room.

"Another one?" Stella asked as she, Anna, and Crina came into the room. She stared at Heather with unapologetic curiosity. "And she's blind. Are you trying to make the beginnings of a bad joke? A stripper, a gypsy and a blind girl walk into a fairy house."

"Been gone two minutes and already this is more interesting than my life," Heather chirped.

"We don't have time for introductions or explanations," Peri ground out as her hands clenched at her sides. She could feel the last healer slipping away from her, could feel her sister getting closer and she couldn't let it happen, not to another one. "Heather, here's the group, group this is Heather. In case you are just that dense, she *is* blind. She is not deaf, she is not stupid, and she is not going to answer every ignorant question that pops into your heads."

"She also can speak for herself," Heather added dryly.

"Pipe down, Helen Keller," Peri retorted. "Just because you can't see doesn't mean I will treat you any different than any of the rest of these know it all's."

"She's all bark and no bite," Sally added unhelpfully.

"Literally," Lucian added.

Peri's head snapped around to glare at him. He shrugged. "Sarcasm, I learn quickly."

"I would like to point out that, since you said I'm not stupid, that Helen Keller was blind *and* deaf. I can hear your screeching voice just fine."

"What is with you people? You're supposed to be frightened and confused and yelling about wanting to go home? You should be frantic with worry about your families or blubbering on about Mr. Whiskers who will pee all over your house if you don't change his litter box at exactly six o'clock." Peri stared, huffing and out of breath, at the three girls who didn't seem the least bit afraid.

"Maybe what's behind us is much scarier than what is in front," Anna spoke up for the first time.

"It can't be that easy, but I don't have time to psychoanalyze three gypsies who are obviously not in their right minds. Those of you going, grab a hand," Peri nodded to Crina, "You got this?"

Crina nodded. "I'm good, go get the next one and bring my mate home safe."

"Sally, where we headed?" Peri looked at the healer, her shoulders tight as if awaiting some horrible verdict and, in a way, she knew she was.

∞

Lorelle felt as if she were on some elaborate race against time, only it wasn't time she was contesting with, it was her sister and her own life. She knew Volcan would follow through on his threat, if she didn't deliver more than one healer he would destroy her. How he would go about doing that, she had no clue, but who's going to argue with a spirit that has somehow survived for centuries in a place that was supposed to have been basically quarantined? Yeah, she wasn't going to either.

She had left Jewel standing in the dark forest, no doubt more than a little confused and scared and allowed the pull of Volcan's magic to take her to the location of the next healer. As she opened her eyes and took a deep breath of salty ocean air, she could only hope that her sister hadn't beaten her there. She didn't know how Volcan's magic worked or how she was able to pick out the healers from all the other Joe blows in the vicinity, she just knew. Then again wasn't that why it was called magic, something unexplainable, something that should be unattainable but somehow made possible?

Lorelle heard a sea gull call out only to be answered by another and then another. She turned in a slow circle to find the very big ocean behind her. Light brown sand made for what she was sure was a nice beach, if you liked nice beaches and liked being half dressed with a bunch of strangers bouncing around in what amounts to a giant bath tub like rubber duckies, then yeah she was sure those yahoos enjoyed it.

She closed her eyes and tried to focus, tuning everything else out. "Come out, come out wherever you are, little healer," she muttered under her breath. *Okay, creepy much, Lorelle,* she chastised herself. That was when she felt it, the goodness, the wholesome purity that only came with a healer. She followed the direction of the power to a diner just off the beach. The sign read *Crustaceans, they're what's for dinner.* Lorelle's eyes narrowed and her lips puckered as she read the ridiculous sign. "Seriously, that's what you came up with?" She retorted as she paused for just a moment to watch the people who unknowingly found themselves in the presence of a predator. A small smile escaped as she considered the irony of the ocean at her back with sharks swimming to and fro, hunting, and searching for that perfect meal; just like she was.

∞

"I swear if one more person snaps their fingers at me for a refill, or tells me their fries are too chewy or too crispy, I just might have to accidently spill my pitcher of water on them," Kara whispered to Lisa.

"I hear ya, waitressing in the summertime with the tourists blows serious crab chunks," Lisa huffed and blew a stand of hair from her face as she quickly wrapped silverware into napkins to put on the clean tables.

"I've got one year left Lisa, one year and then no more greasy burgers or pushy customers."

"Where ya gonna go, Kara?" Lisa asked, smacking on the gum that she seemed never to spit out. "Not to be a total buzzkill, but with no family and no money, your prospects are looking pretty grim."

Kara knew Lisa wasn't trying to be cruel; she was just honest in that way that made you want to stuff a Twinkie in her mouth and tell her not to chew. "I've been working since I was fourteen and saving my money," Kara explained. "I have a plan. It's not like I live in some fantasy land where I get saved by some white knight or some crap like that. I know exactly where I'm going and what I'm going to do." Lisa started to speak but Kara held a hand up stopping her as yet another customer snapped their fingers at her and pointed to their half empty drink glass.

"More lemonade?" Kara asked politely though she wanted to tell the rich tourist to get their own damn lemonade. Kara didn't know what was wrong with her lately. Usually she wasn't so testy. Usually she had more patience with people. But for the last couple of weeks she had been restless and short tempered.

"I really shouldn't have to point it out to you; it is your job to take notice of these things," the lady griped.

"I do apologize about that, ma'am," Kara told her as she picked up the glass and hurried to fill it and then return it to the woman before she could say anything more. She honestly didn't know how much more she could take. She worked constantly in the summer to save money because she couldn't work as many hours during the school year. Her foster mom, or really it was more like foster grandmother because Pearl was ancient, hardly had enough money to feed the hoard of cats she kept, let alone take care of Kara. But Kara didn't complain because at least Pearl let her be. She didn't hit her, yell at her, tell her she was a burden or touch her in ways that made her want to peel off her skin. She did, however, treat her like one of her precious kitties from time to time and that was pretty disturbing.

Grab your bootstraps, pull yourself up, and carry on, Kara thought to herself as she ground her teeth together. There was, after all, nobody to do it for her or even offer a helping hand. She was on her own, always had been. There were times that she feared she always would be.

It was late afternoon when Kara felt something shift in the air. She turned to Lisa who was wiping down the fountain machine and frowned. "Do you feel that?"

Lisa paused and looked around expectantly. "Feel what?"

"I'm not sure, it feels dark, or evil," Kara shivered, though it was still quite warm outside.

"Kara, I'm not sure what to think about you when you get your little *feelings*. I'm not saying I don't believe you because, hey, I'm totally open minded and all that, but sometimes you kind of wig me out."

Kara smiled. "Sometimes I wig myself out." She was trying to keep it light because she didn't want Lisa to know just how ominous the feeling in her gut was. Something was wrong, like seriously wrong.

She stepped out onto the outside of the pier and began wiping down the tables and folding down the umbrellas that shaded them. Her eyes roamed over the beach that was beginning to empty as the beach bums and tourist began to head home, or just for dryer endeavors. It was as her eyes scanned back to the left that she saw her. Just as her eyes met the cool blue eyes of the indescribable beauty, she felt another pull to the right only this one was bright and full of hope. Her head swung around and she was sure she was seeing double as she looked at a woman who looked nearly exactly like the woman on her left.

"What the," Kara mumbled. She stood frozen, and her eyes widened as suddenly more people appeared, literally just appeared around the woman on her right. "That didn't just happen," Kara mumbled. "That's not possible, it's not real. I'm just tired." She was trying to reason with herself and failing miserably, especially when the women began to talk.

"You cannot have her, Lorelle," the woman on the right said coolly.

The woman called Lorelle laughed and it made Kara's skin crawl. "You aren't going to stop me this time, Perizada."

Okay, so that's a strange name, Kara thought and then added *really you're worried about her name and not the fact that they appeared out of thin air?*

"You have a weakness that I do not," Lorelle told Perizada. "You care. You care for humans and the miserable existence they call life. So how are you going to save one healer when there are dozens more in danger?" Lorelle lifted her hands and Kara watched as the woman literally shot light from her palms directly at the diner.

She heard the other woman yell but didn't wait to see what she and her band of suddenly appearing people would do. She dove off of the pier into the sand below, all the while yelling Lisa's name. The explosion was not near as big as Kara thought it should have been and when she looked up she saw why. The woman named Perizada had her hands out in the direction of the diner as well and was doing something to minimize the damage that the first women's strike had done. Suddenly there were feet by her head. She looked up slowly and into the face of Lorelle, the woman she had first seen, the woman who felt like malice and emptiness all rolled up into one.

"You are coming with me," she told Kara as she snatched her wrist and jerked her onto her feet. She didn't appear that strong, but she lifted Kara as if the girl weighed nothing at all.

"Ah-ah-ah, Lucian," Lorelle chided pulling Kara against her chest and wrapping a hand around her throat. "Move any closer and I will snap her neck."

"You will not. You need her, though for what I do not know," the huge man she called Lucian said calmly. A little too calmly for the circumstances if you

171

asked Kara, which he did not. In fact he didn't take his eyes off of the woman holding her. His silver eyes seemed to glow as he bore down on them.

"If you were sure that I would not kill her, then you would charge me. But you are not sure; therefore, you will stand there like the helpless male that your species constantly produces and watch me take what you think belongs to you." Lorelle tightened her grip on her as more of the group appeared.

"This isn't over, Lorelle." Perizada's eyes could have burned holes into Lorelle with the anger that her gaze bore. "Oh and don't bother looking for the other healers, I think the score stands at 3 to 2. As usual you're losing."

Please don't taunt the woman who might snap my neck, Kara thought as she stared at the group across from her. They all looked ready to kill, and she had no doubt that even the smallest among them could.

"I grow tired of being in your bitchy presence, Peri. Rest assured you have not seen the last of me, and boy do I have a surprise for you. My master will not be pleased you have thwarted his plans."

"Then I imagine it's your own ass you should be worried about," Peri snapped.

Lorelle shot another bolt of light at the group just as darkness swallowed them. Kara tried to close her eyes and take slow deep breaths because she knew at any moment she was going to puke all over the not nice lady who wanted to kill her. Then again that might not be such a bad thing.

Kara felt her feet hit the ground and stumble forward, her face nearly colliding with the grass and dirt beneath her. Thankfully her palms slammed into the ground first stopping her from getting a mouthful of earth. She pushed herself up quickly, not wishing to be vulnerable to the threat she knew Lorelle posed and quickly looked around. Forest surrounded her and Lorelle was several feet away staring at her as if she had grown a second appendage in an unsavory location.

"If you're going to cry and moan please get it out of your system now because I get irritated with bumbling twits, and when I get irritated I do painful things." Lorelle's lips tightened as she spoke and her whole body seemed to tense up.

Kara didn't respond to the remark but instead turned to see a girl around her age emerge from the forest. She was fair skinned with strawberry blonde hair and radiated gentleness. She wore worn out jeans and a grey t-shirt that said ARMY across the front that looked like it might have actually been in a war.

"Are you like her, or me?" Kara asked wanting to know exactly what the score was.

"Last I checked I couldn't just vanish into thin air only to reappear somewhere else," the girl told her.

Okay, so two to one, Kara thought. *But judging that the one can shoot light blasts from her hands really makes it more like two to one thousand.* So not so great odds.

"I am going to make this as simple for you two as possible because frankly I don't like talking to you. You both are descendants from a long line of gypsies; please tell me you know what a gypsy is?"

"A nomadic people that primarily lived in Europe until they began to migrate to the United States in the 1800's," Jewel recited quickly.

Lorelle's eyebrows rose. "Let me guess Wiki is your one true friend?"

173

Jewel didn't seem offended as she answered. "I work in a library; you learn stuff when you work in a library."

Lorelle shrugged. "Whatever, okay so you know what a gypsy is. Well you two little lovelies have gypsy blood somewhere in your heritage. Don't ask me where because frankly I don't give a damn. Because of your gypsy blood you have an affinity for magic that regular, mundane, humans do not," Lorelle took a deep breath and then continued on. "And because of that you have been chosen by the Great Luna to be healers to the packs of Canis lupis around the world. Any questions?" She held up her hand to stop the two girls who had both opened their mouths. "Wait, I forgot, I don't care."

She closed her eyes briefly and rubbed the frown that was forever gracing her lips with her hand. Finally she looked up at the wide-eyed healers. "I would tell you to stay here, but really where are you going to go? I'll be back," she thought about it and then waved a hand carelessly, "before you can starve to death." Then she was gone, just poof gone.

"Ow!" Kara squawked suddenly and rubbed her arm where the very guilty looking Jewel had just pinched her—hard. "What was that for?"

"Just wanted to make sure I wasn't dreaming. I've read that in dreams that even when things happen that should be painful you don't actually feel any pain," Jewel explained.

"We may not be dreaming but I haven't ruled out that we might be trippin'," Kara admitted as she looked around the dark, densely populated forest.

"You mean drugs?" Jewel's voice rose just a little revealing the doubt she had about Kara's conclusion.

"No, of course not, I meant Lucky Charms." Kara closed her eyes and let out a deep sigh. "I'm sorry, that was rude. I sometimes get a little testy when I'm stressed out. This situation qualifies as extremely stressful."

Jewel smiled in a way that Kara knew she was forgiven, and more than likely Jewel was the type that forgave way too much, way too often. "I think we might need to consider that what Lorelle said is true," Jewel told her matter of fact like.

"You mean believe in magic, gypsies with powers and Canis lupis, which if I'm not mistaken are werewolves?" Kara crossed her arms across her chest as she met Jewel's steady gaze.

"Exactly," Jewel beamed obviously pleased at Kara's conclusion.

"What did you say your name was?" Kara asked.

"Jewel."

Kara made an *ah* motion with her mouth as if Jewel's name explained everything. "Well Jewel, I'm Kara and I'm here to tell you there is no such thing as magic and if there was I would have figured it out a long time ago and gotten myself the hell out of Dodge."

Jewel nodded as if she totally understood what Kara was saying. "Well, I don't know where Dodge is, and I'm sorry if it was a horrid place for you, but it's hard to refute the evidence that we have and I think we could better spend our time trying to figure a way out of this instead of trying to make sense of it."

Kara wanted to laugh at the girl's obvious innocence. She wished she was still that innocent but it's hard to stay innocent when you're a product of the system. No parents, no love, no security, and that equaled jaded. But instead of sharing all of her baggage with Rainbow Bright over there, she simply nodded and said, "I'm guessing you have a plan?"

Jewel smiled mischievously. "Like I said, you learn a few things when you work in a library."

Kara didn't know if that should comfort or frighten her.

Chapter 12

"Defeat has never been an option. I may lose a skirmish, I may have to retreat and regroup, but I will not lose the war. There is too much at stake, although I don't even know what is at stake. There are too many unknown variables. What I do know, what I am utterly sure of, is even if I have to go to the furthest depths of hell to save the healers my sister has stolen, I will do it, and I just might toss my sister into the pit while I'm at it." ~Perizada

"You need to rest," Lucian's voice came from behind her.

"There is no rest for me. I will find none until I have done what I was charged to do. You were a warrior, you know what it is like to have orders that you must carry out, to have those who have been entrusted into your care to keep safe, and then fail them." Peri held her voice steady even though she was torn up inside.

"You are doing all that you can, love. You cannot expect more of yourself than you have to give." Lucian's arms wrapped around her and his breath on her neck sent a thrill through her that she wanted to enjoy but couldn't.

She pushed his hands away as she rounded on him, her eyes narrowed and flashing with the power that she fought to contain. "Why can't I?" She nearly yelled. She knew her anger wasn't at him, not really, but he was a convenient target and he had wandered into the lion's den. "I am a high fae, thousands of years old, with power and wisdom beyond which the likes of even your mind can imagine so tell me why I shouldn't expect more of myself? Tell me how I could possibly have let my sister get her wicked hands on those girls and then lay down for a little nap, or curl up in your arms and enjoy the feel of your skin and the breath from you lungs!" She was gasping for air as her hands fisted at her sides.

"I could help you if you would only let me. I could bear this burden with you," he told her in his infuriatingly calm way.

"Ugh! Not this again! Are you serious? You want to bring up the whole mate thing at a time like this? You really want to go there, because I can't think of ANY reason for us to take time away from searching for these girls so you can bite me and *claim* me like I'm your property only to then have your...,"

"DO NOT SAY IT," he suddenly snarled at her. His shoulders pulled back and his chest rose and fell with deep breaths of anger. His eyes had begun to glow and now were blazing silver that swirled in time to the beat of Peri's heart.

She had pushed him too far.

"I am done waiting," he growled though not nearly as loud.

"Excuse me?" Peri tried to sound threatening but it came out more as a pathetic whisper. The weight of the task the Great Luna had set before them was weighing her down. She felt as though the lives of the entire world depended upon her, and she had no idea who, other than her sister, that she was fighting. She felt guilty for her divided attention. She should be focusing on finding the healers that Lorelle had captured and yet she found that she couldn't keep her mind or heart off of the determined wolf.

178

Then she felt angry for having to feel guilty when all she wanted was to be loved the way Lucian was promising to love her. Most of all she wanted to feel safe and for the first time in her very long life she found the place she could go and feel completely safe —Lucian's arms.

"I have been patient with you, Peri. I have helped you, protected you and loved you from the distance where you have kept me. I have given you time, but it is not helping you or me. It is simply preventing us from being whole. You cannot do what the Great Luna is asking you to do until you deal with us. You would not be divided in your attentions if your soul was whole." Lucian's voice, though firm, was full of understanding.

"So you want me to what? Just take a mini vaca and have a honeymoon while Lorelle and whoever her evil master is continues doing who knows what to those healers?" Her voice had once again grown in strength as her temper once again flared. "And what am I supposed to tell the little healers Lucian? What am I supposed to say to them when I finally find them, because I *will* find them, tortured and drained of their magic? I'm sorry I couldn't get here sooner but I had to get MY ROCKS OFF!"

"ENOUGH!" Lucian's voice reverberated off of the walls of the house behind them and shook the glass in the windows. His wolf had surfaced and though he appeared angry he was in complete control. Peri had yet to see him lose control and in that moment it seriously pissed her off that she felt so out of control.

"I have come to find your brass and completely immodest ways rather endearing, but I will not allow

179

you to cheapen the mate bond. I will not allow you to turn something that the Great Luna intended to be sacred and eternally binding into some form of quick fix for raging hormones. I have been trapped in a realm for over two hundred years, alone, without any form of companion and yet with the way that you speak about the physical love between a mate and his female you must find it surprising that I have not ripped your clothes off. Let me clue you in on something that either this day and age has warped for you or you actually never knew; what happens between a mated pair on their bonding night and on any night after that is not about *getting your rocks off*," he gritted out the words with disdain. "It is about love, sacrifice, commitment and a willingness to be vulnerable with your mate. It not only solidifies the bond between mates but it also creates a level of intimacy that you will never share with another, nor should you. It binds your souls together making you whole once again."

Lucian held Peri's gaze as he spoke and Peri knew that everything he was saying was true. She knew that he was right and she did need him as if he were the last breath in a world being sucked dry of oxygen.

"I love you, Perizada. I don't know when it happened but I know that I love you. You are my mate and when you are ready to admit that you need me, use the bond and I will return to you."

Peri took a step towards him as she felt her heart crash into her toes. "You're leaving?" The desperation in her voice normally would have made her cringe but in that moment she didn't care how she sounded.

"I do not wish to hurt you with cruel words said in anger and I am afraid that is what will happen if we continue on like this. I will not be far and I will keep you safe." He walked over to her and stared down into her eyes. His hand reached up and traced her cheek more gently than a hand so large should be able to. Peri's eyes fluttered closed just as his warm, firm lips pressed to hers. It was over much too quickly and he was gone when her eyes opened and the tears finally came.

∞

Lucian drew on his wolf's speed, needing to get as far away from his mate as possible before he let his wolf take over and simply claim what was theirs. Not as a man claims property as she had so eloquently said, but as a lover claims the heart of the one he longs for. If she would let him, he would give her everything she needed and when he could give her no more, he would petition the One who could. If she would only let him he would conquer her demons and give her rest for the first time in centuries, just as she would give him rest.

Lucian phased into his wolf form without thought as soon as he was out of sight. He didn't know where he was going since they were in the fae realm and he didn't know their land as well as his own, all he knew was that he needed to run and possibly kill something. He didn't want to leave her, especially since she did not bare his mark, and their bond was not complete. But just as he told her, if he stayed he was going to say something that he would not be able to take back or do something she would regret. Because what she did not understand was that he was on the verge of biting her with our without her consent and he did not want to do that. The man did not want to do that. His wolf just wanted their mate. He wanted her marked, bonded, mated, and by his side where she belonged. The wolf did not understand why their mate was being so difficult and had decided they should just take matters into their own hands. Lucian chuckled to himself and told his wolf he had a lot to learn about their mate if he thought forcing something on her was a good idea.

His paws moved swiftly across the ground. He barely made any sound at all, even with his large form. He had learned to be invisible while living in the dark forest. *Living,* he snorted to himself, *I was not living, I was simply surviving.* He tried not to let his mind revisit those memories of three centuries in a land where evil had saturated the very soil he walked on and the air he breathed felt like noxious fumes to his lungs. Now he held his own darkness at bay only with the knowledge that he had hope because he had found his mate. Even after all those years alone, all those days and nights wondering if he would ever see his family again let alone have the opportunity to find his true mate, she was here, she was real and alive and breathing. Just knowing that eased the ache in him if only a little.

He felt her pain and confusion and it took every amount of strength in him not to turn around and run back to her. She needed time, be it ten minutes or ten months; time to think and work through her frustrations. He would stay as a shadow in her mind and once he returned to the house he would talk to

Adam about taking him along once Peri was ready to make a move again. No matter what she thought, he would never really leave her. Even if he wanted to he could not. He not only loved her, he liked her. Liked her spunk and tenacity, liked her bravery, her devotion and selflessness. No, he would not give her up, he would wait, like the patient hunter he was and when she was finally ready he would answer her call. He finally slowed to a walk and found a spot next to a tall tree and lay down in the late evening sun. His wolf did not want to relax, he wanted to go back, to take their mate and show her that she was theirs and belonged with them. Instead of doing what his heart and soul longed for he closed his eyes and imagined a day when she would finally be his, the way he was already hers.

∞

A knock at the door startled Peri, ripping her from her tearful meditations. That alone told her how distracted she was, to be snuck up on, even by a quiet, little healer.

"Come in, Sally," she said wearily.

"Tell me," was all Sally had to say.

Peri kept her back to the healer as she told her everything that had been said between her and Lucian. She knew that something in every healer compelled people to share their burdens with them because it was in their nature to want to help, no matter how jaded they might have become. But usually that compulsion didn't work on Peri. But she was beginning to realize that the normal rules didn't apply when your heart was breaking.

"I drove him away," Peri admitted. "I knew I would. I knew he wouldn't be able to put up with me, hell I can't put up with me half the time. He left and you know what, Sally, I don't blame him one bit for going."

"You have to know that he's not really gone. Peri he can't leave you any more than you could leave him. He's giving you time, and though it might have come out in words of anger, it's a gift that some true mates don't get."

"It may be a gift to me, but to him it is the equal of torture. I know it. I can feel it inside of him, see his pain through the bond and it's driving me mad." She finally turned around and looked at the American who became a healer, a mate, and a friend. "I have always had two things to do; look out for the healers and make sure the wolves played nice. There was a brief time that I stayed away from the human realm but as soon as you appeared I returned to do what I have always done."

"And now the rug has been pulled out from under your feet," Sally offered with her trademark gentle smile.

"I don't think I could have landed any harder on my butt if I tried," Peri admitted.

"What do you want to do?"

Peri clenched her eyes closed as she took a deep breath through her nose. "What should I do?"

Sally chuckled, though she meant no disrespect towards the fae. "The powerful Perizada asking the American from Texas what she should do. Have to admit, Peri, never thought I'd see the day."

"Well if all you're going to do is gloat with your Texas size ego then you might want to use that nifty bond to call out for help from your mate. I grow weary of being emotional and find I need to turn somebody into something I can squish with my shoe."

"That's the Peri fairy we all know and love," Sally laughed but quickly smoothed her face. "But seriously, you need to do what is best for you and Lucian. Peri, nobody doubts your desire, or ability to rescue those healers. But even the strongest heroes have to rest and do the things necessary to make them capable of being the best. Every Alpha knows that without his true mate he is weaker than the others. Every male knows that there is a darkness that grows inside of them because the animal they share their bodies with harbors violence, the need to dominate and have the desire for the kill that the man does not. There is one thing that keeps that darkness at bay. What a gift we are to the males of the Canis lupis species. But he is just as much a gift to you." She reached out and laid her hand on Peri's arm allowing the magic that only healers were endowed with to flow into her. It was peaceful, as though water had been thrown on the fire inside of her quenching the burning inferno.

"Now imagine *that* times infinity," Sally whispered. "That is what the mate bond is. That is what you will know once you give yourself to him and he to you. Tell me Peri, how would anyone deny you that, or expect you to save the world without it?"

Sally turned and left the room as quietly as she had come, pulling the door closed behind her. Peri was speechless, which was a rarity for the fae. Sally had just turned her world upside down. She had given her a glimpse, just a glimpse of what the bond between true mates brought. It was like rain drenching the dry earth after years of drought. If felt as though, for that brief moment in time while Sally had touched her allowing peace to fill her, she was whole. Every cell healthy, every nerve relaxed, every beat of her heart suddenly had purpose. How could that be? How could one as imperfect as her find contentment with one as imperfect as him?

"Because you complement one another, Perizada," Peri heard the Great Luna's voice fill her room and that same peace returned only filled with a finality that Peri knew only came with the deity. *"True contentment comes when you accept your weaknesses and embrace your mate's strength. You will both find fault in the other, but you will choose to see past the fault to the soul that lies beneath them and you will choose love. When you make that choice there is no room for doubt, fear or hesitancy, there is only room for honesty, trust and hope."*

"I want to," Peri whispered to the once again empty room. "But I'm scared, I admit it. I fear a love that deep, that complete. Because if I ever lost it, how would I survive?"

"You can never lose me. I was yours before our time, and I will be yours long after it has past." She should have known he would be listening, should have known he would feel her pain and put his own aside so he could attend to her.

Lucian's breath stopped in his lungs as her voice filled his mind. *"Come back. P-p-please, come back."* Her broken cry was a stab to his heart and he was back on his feet running without even thinking.

He phased and grabbed a pair of pants that were lying on a shelf as he entered the house. One of the females, most likely Sally because he was learning she just did things like that, must have put them there for him knowing he would need them. He slipped them on and then followed Peri's scent and the sound of her heartbeat to her room. He pushed the door open without knocking and she was in his arms before the door closed behind him.

She wrapped herself around him and buried her face in his neck. He could feel her tears on his skin and it broke something inside of him.

"Shh, love, I am here, I am not leaving. Please, beloved, stop crying," he cooed to her trying to get her to calm down.

"I'm sorry, I just didn't know how to be what you need. I don't know how to be a mate but I don't care that I don't know how, I just need you with me. Please don't leave, you can have me, I'm yours, please just don't go," her cries bubbled out of her. Her fear of losing him now greater than the fear of looking like a desperate twit had finally allowed her to submit to the bond, to accept that he was meant for her as she was meant for him.

Lucian ran a hand down her hair and back and then pulled back so he could look at her. "Will you complete the mate bond, Perizada? Will you be my mate, my love for all of eternity?"

"Yes, I'm yours, I've always been yours," she said as her eyes met his. "I love you, Lucian, I love you."

Lucian picked her up and carried her to the bed. He laid her down and then lay down next to her propping himself up on an elbow. "Do you know the covenant words?"

She nodded.

"We'll say the words that will bind us as mates and then we will complete the Blood Rites. I have a request."

"What?" She asked curiously as her finger tips ran down his shoulder and arm.

"I want to do the Blood Rites at the same time," he paused, unable to continue, afraid of offending her. He came from a time when such things were not discussed until after the bond and Blood Rites were complete.

Peri's eyes widened. "You mean you want to bite me while...,"

"As I take you as my mate, blood and body, becoming one," he finished for her.

She should have known that only her mate could have made her, a three century old high fae, blush.

"I have the privilege of having a high fae at my bonding ceremony," he told her with a smile as he stood up and pulled her with him. He walked her over to a chair and gently took her shoulders pushing her down to sit.

Peri watched him walk into the bathroom and heard water running. When he reemerged he was carrying two dripping wash cloths with steam rising up off of them and a towel. He knelt before her and lifted the hem of her dress, placing it on her knees. As he took her left foot in his hands and squeezed the water from one of the cloths he looked up at her and Peri saw what it truly meant to be loved by a mate of his race.

Lucian held her gaze captive as he spoke the words that would make her his for all eternity in this life and the next. He used on older version of the vows, one that he had learned might not be as well accepted in this day in age, referring to himself as his mate's servant. "On this day I kneel before you, as a servant to my mate, to ask if you will make me whole. Will you give yourself to me? Finally calming the beast inside, bringing order to chaos, shining light where there has been only darkness? Will you bind your life to mine, your fate to mine, and your soul to mine and, in doing so, complete the mate bond?"

Peri pushed herself out of the chair and onto her knees even as she answered words that she had heard at every Alpha's bonding ceremony that she had taken part in. "On this day I kneel with you, my mate. I will make you whole as you will make me whole. I will give myself to you, calming the beast, bringing order to chaos, and shining light where there has been darkness. I will bind my life to yours, my fate to yours, and my soul to yours and complete our mate bond. I will take you for my own, my mate, and my Alpha." Peri didn't stop there but added words that her people spoke when two fae were united. "I bind my magic to you, my powers will be your powers, and the ancient knowledge I carry will now be yours as well. No other shall know me as you will, no other will hold me captive as you do. I, Perizada of the high fae, have so spoken these truths and covenants. So shall it be as I have said and as Lucian Lupei has said. Two hearts in one accord for eternity."

Lucian took her face in his hands and tried to be gentle as he felt her power flow through him. His body shook with the intensity that it carried and he felt as if the light pouring into him from her would burst forth from him. Like the rays from the morning sun that surged up as it rose chasing away the shadows of night, Peri's light chased the darkness that had been taking over inside of him. He stared into her eyes, afraid to look away and realize it was all a dream, a magnificent fantasy his mind had created because he so longed for her.

"It's not," she told him as she pushed the blonde locks that had fallen forward from his forehead. "This is real. I don't know why it happened or how I could possibly be so blessed but we are here and you are mine."

As out of control as Lucian felt he was sure that his kiss would be nearly violent. But his wolf reined him in, allowing him to capture her mouth with his own in a kiss that began slowly, almost hesitantly until they couldn't get close enough.

Finally she was his, his bonded true mate. When he pulled back her skin was flushed and he could see the slight tremble in her hands as she ran her fingers through his hair. He knew she couldn't be comfortable kneeling on the ground so he stood and scooped her up carrying her back to the bed where all of this had begun. He laid her down and followed her body with his own pressing her gently into the mattress. A low rumble rose from his chest as their bodies made contact and he fought the need to turn her head and sink his teeth into her beautiful flesh. He didn't bother trying to remove their clothes because his mate's magic would take care of that. Instead he focused on her, showing her with his touch, his kiss, the little nips with his teeth and the thoughts sent through their bond of just how much he loved her.

When his teeth finally found their mark he felt the bond solidify, as if two pieces of metal had been soldered together and now stronger because of it. He was in awe of her beauty, held mute by her reaction to him and changed forever by the adoration that shone in her face as he pulled away from her neck. He knew now why the males that were bonded never wanted to be without their mates. He understood how they could become addicted to their company, their taste, and their light. And as his mate fulfilled her part, taking his blood and binding her flesh to him, her life to him, he thanked the Great Luna that she had not forgotten him and she had not forsaken him. She had given him a true mate, his perfect match and showed him what unconditional love truly looked like.

Peri knew she should wonder over the fact that she was able to bite her mate and then she actually swallowed his blood, but there was no room for wondering. Her heart was overflowing with an amount of love she never knew was possible. Her soul was dancing in sheer delight at finally finding her other half. Nothing could have prepared her for how she would feel during the Blood Rites because there was nothing it could be compared to. There was a passion that ran so deep inside of Lucian that she was sure she would drown in it. Every touch, every whispered word against her skin, every breath in her ear testified to the esteem, respect and love he had for her. Never before had she ever been handled with such care and never again would she have to go without it.

"What about the personal vows that mates are supposed to write themselves?" Peri asked as Lucian held her in his arms, the warmth of their love still fresh on her flushed skin.

He propped himself up on one elbow so he could look down into her eyes and so she could not only hear the sincerity in his voice but see it on his face. "I would give you the world if you asked it of me. I would forsake all others if you said that's what you needed. For every bit of pain you've suffered I would take it as my lot if it meant you would never have had to endure nor suffer it again. For every night spent alone and every day spent in the service of those who were put under your care I would hold you in my arms and take your burden as my own. I have lived too long without you, Perizada. We both have endured longer than any should have to without their other half and I vow to you that never again will you stand alone. I will be by your side always. I vow my allegiance first to our creator, the Great Luna, because without her I would not exist and I would not have you, and second I vow my allegiance to you, my beloved, my mate."

Lucian hoped that his words conveyed what his heart and soul was feeling, though he didn't know if that was possible. There was so much inside of him, so many emotions battling for first place and though they were all important he knew the one that shined above all others was love. Because when he looked at her through the eyes of love her faults faded away, her weaknesses surrendered to his strength, her needs became his own and all he could see was the beautiful woman given to him so that he could serve her, provide for her and tie his fate to hers for all time.

Peri's eyes glistened with tears and Lucian's face blurred briefly before he wiped them away. She took a deep breath and wondered how she could follow that up. How could she compete with the incredible selflessness that he exhibited towards her?

"It's not a competition, Peri," he whispered to her, wiping away yet another tear.

After several more minutes of gazing into his eyes she finally began to speak. "I have roamed this earth, as well as other realms, for longer than my mind cares to remember. I have seen pain, death, life, joy, sorrow, sacrifice, hate, love, and so much more lived out in the hearts of man as well as other species. I had accepted my purpose in my life, resigned myself to a life without the enduring love of a mate, spouse, partner, or any other term given to such relationships. I have obeyed the Great Luna and lived out her design for the fae and our place in the universe and I have been thankful for what she has given me. But when I look at your face, when I feel your soul connect with mine, when I hear your heartbeat and see your love I know that had I been aware that this was possible, I could not have been satisfied without you. I too give thanks to the Great Luna for wisdom, her faithfulness and her unconditional love of her children. You are one of those children, and for so long you were lost to us, to me, but I know she protected you because the darkness did not consume you. I love you, Lucian, more than I ever thought I was capable of and if you will be patient with me, if you will let me make mistakes and love me anyways, give me grace as I find my way in this new life, I will endeavor to give you the same respect. You are mine as I am yours and nothing save the Great Luna herself shall ever separate us."

"I still need to give you my offerings," Lucian told her as he ran his fingers through her hair, reveling in his allowance to touch her when he wanted.

"It is enough for tonight, wolf, let it lie for now. We have much to do, so many trials ahead of us but let's just be this tonight."

Lucian kissed her forehead gently and wrapped her in his arms as he spoke quietly against her ear. "As my beloved desires, so shall it be."

The night wrapped around them as they lost themselves in each other. A man with the soul of a wolf lost for so long now held in the arms of his mate. A woman of a race boundless in power given great responsibility now held in the arms of the one who wants her only for the female she is and not the position she holds. For this night they abandoned all else and accepted the gift of unconditional love. For this night they were simply a man and a woman becoming one, body and soul.

Chapter 13

"The most convincing lie is one sprinkled with truth, when the listener has trouble separating what could be with what is not. How else would good, innocent people be so easily led astray? Learning how to feed such falsehoods to a common human is difficult, but learning to convince one as powerful as a fae, a high fae at that, well that is an art form. But then I've always appreciated a good challenge, especially if the demise of one so pure is the end result." ~Volcan

"Two is not enough!" Volcan bellowed at Lorelle.

She crossed her arms in front of her chest and tried to look unaffected by the incorporeal evil fae who held her fate in the palm of his, probably talon clad, hands. She had known he would throw a tantrum because really, the eviler they are the bigger the fit. She waited to see if there would be more, of course there was.

"How could the others have slipped from your grasp? I gave you the power to be pulled directly to them. Your sister on the other hand, would have had to use a tracking spell which would have taken time."

"You obviously have forgotten how resourceful Perizada can be when she sets her mind to it," Lorelle quipped.

"I DO NOT CARE!" He roared.

See, bigger fit, Lorelle thought.

"All I care about is what you do or do not do. You must draw her out, exploit a weakness that will have her crawling out of hiding."

"I won't have to, she will eventually come looking for the two healers I took," Lorelle explained. "She has hero syndrome and feels it's her place to protect everyone less powerful than herself. That makes her an easy target."

"She must not be that easy if you failed to kill her on your first attempt," Volcan taunted.

Lorelle gritted her teeth to keep from using American slang she had learned that would essentially tell him to go jump off a cliff. She didn't figure he would like that too much.

"What do you suggest, Volcan, since you are obviously so smart and I am so very, very beneath you?"

"Flattery will get you nowhere with me child. Only results! Now...," he nearly crooned the word. "where would your sister be hiding the little healers?"

Lorelle thought about it for a moment, though she knew the first location that had flitted across her mind would be the correct answer.

"There is a house in Farie that she uses often as a base of sorts. She used it to harbor the wolves at one time. That is where she will be holed up." The air around her shifted and she knew that he was moving. In her mind she pictured a large serpent slithering around her, head undulating and tongue flicking out to taste her scent. She shivered at the thought and swallowed down the lump of dread that had made its way into her throat.

"I'm going to give you the power to dreamscape. I will need one of the healers, but pick the weaker of the two, I do not need much power for such a task. I want you to enter your sister's mind while she is

196

unguarded and plant seeds of doubt along with realistic possibilities."

"What kind of doubts and possibilities?" Lorelle's brow rose as she considered his request, well more like command. She knew her sister well, and knew that Peri was not easy to sway. She was as hardheaded as stone gargoyle when she wanted to be.

"You need to convince her that there is still one more healer out in the world to be saved. As much as I do not want to reveal myself just yet, if you must you may tell her of my power. She will believe that I could know such a thing, she will remember just how powerful I once was and she will not take the risk that you are lying to her. She will take it upon herself to ferret out the non-existent girl."

"Okay," Lorelle said drawing out the *o* as she thought about his plan. "My sister ,though a proud, conceited fool, will not believe that there is one more healer if it was the Great Luna who informed her of the five, which I'm positive is how she found out about them. She would know it was a farce."

"Fine, figure out something she will believe," he all but growled.

"Then what?"

"The healers she has acquired will be unprotected and ready for the taking." The satisfaction in his voice was beyond creepy.

"They won't be unprotected. Peri would never be so foolish. She will leave wolves, and maybe even one of her fae lap dogs to watch after the humans."

Volcan's anger seemed to go up a notch as Lorelle felt the air around her drop in temperature.

"You doubt my power? Even now I am still more than capable of removing a few meddlesome wolves and fae children. All you need do is allow me to funnel my power along with one of the healers into you and you will be able to smite your enemy with barely a lift of your finger."

Lorelle's mouth watered at the thought of wielding such power. To be able to kill those who had wronged her, who had interfered with her first attempt. Her head tilted ever so slightly as she considered her quest. Kill, *no*, she thought, *I can't kill them, the consequences would be too dire.*

"I think the best thing to do would be to put the wolves playing sentry and the fae out of commission," she told him as she studied her nails.

"Killing them would be more permanent," Volcan so unhelpfully pointed out.

Lorelle squeezed her hands into fists so tight that her knuckles turned white as she struggled with her desire to smack the air where she thought he stood in hopes that she might actually make contact with his face.

Letting out a slow breath she answered. "I realized that death would be a more lasting result, it would, however, also enrage the most powerful Alpha the Canis lupis has ever seen. And he has managed to unite the packs once again, so it would not only be his wrath we would have to endure, but the wrath of many Alphas. They don't take kindly when one of their own is murdered, believe me I know." She could tell he hadn't liked her implying that he wasn't strong enough to take on the wolves so she quickly added, "I've no doubt that you could hold your own for a time, but it would be unwise to underestimate the wolves. They hold the favor of the Great Luna, she has joined their race with the fae, combining their magic making them even more powerful. I just feel it would be in your best interest to build more of your power before you strike; perhaps getting your physical form back, for instance."

Volcan was quiet and she could tell that he was considering her words, no matter how much he didn't like them. He was a strategist and she had no doubt that he would want to consider all angles before acting, or at least centuries ago he would have. Now he did seem more like a petulant child that just wanted his toys back. She kept waiting for him to blurt out *you can't come to my birthday party*. She nearly laughed at the image of the great Volcan reduced to a four year old tantrum.

"I admit that your concern holds merit," Volcan murmured as if it pained him to say such a thing. "Although the Great Luna has rarely involved herself in the matters of her wolves."

"It appears that the more they seek her out, the more she answers." Lorelle frowned as she considered her words and realized how true they were and frankly it was irritating to the last nerve that hadn't been danced on by the great and mighty butthead before her.

"Fine, do not kill them. But make sure they will not be able assist Perizada for quite some time."

She nodded, not really caring if he could see her or only feel her presence. "When do you want to do the dreamscape?"

"Tonight, we have no time to waste. Retrieve one of the healers," he paused and Lorelle could almost feel his humor. "I hope you are not queasy at the sight of a little blood."

Lorelle didn't respond as she flashed from the disturbing nature that seemed to enshroud his essence. She considered all the ways to deal with the healers and though she could just force the girls to cooperate, she decided a little brain washing would be more effective in using their magic. A willing subject was much easier to draw power from, and attempting to use healing magic for the opposite of healing was no easy task. She honestly wasn't even sure that it was possible but then she was not about to tell the world's most malicious toddler, all be it in a grown up form, that he couldn't do something. She was at times admittedly impulsive, but she wasn't a complete and total idiot— at least not yet.

∞

"Though I hate to question your infinite knowledge from all of the books you must have read on escaping magical forests, but do actually know what you're doing or are we just wandering aimlessly?" Kara asked Jewel who was in front of her, diligently traipsing through the thick foliage and unforgiving limbs that seemed to reach out and slap them periodically.

Jewel's breathing was slightly labored, evidence that she indeed sat most of her day with her nose in a book instead of doing physical activity. Say for example lugging a tray full of food and drinks around for fourteen to fifteen hours a day. "I'm looking for higher ground," Jewel explained attempting not to sound like a puffing freight train. "If we can get high enough to see over the trees, we might be able to see where the forest ends and normal, untainted land begins."

"What do you mean by untainted?" Kara asked.

Jewel stopped, abruptly causing Kara to run into her back, bouncing off of her surprisingly sturdy frame. "You can't tell me you don't feel it." Her eyes widened as she looked at Kara with alarming intensity.

"Feel what?"

Jewel shook her head and mumbled something under her breath that sounded like *ignorant muggles*. In the little time Kara had spent with the redhead, it did not surprise her that she used a Harry Potter reference in their circumstances, and maybe it was fitting.

"I don't tell many people this, or at least not people I'm not close with," Jewel stiffened her shoulders as if preparing for some sort of blow before she continued. "My mom is a fortune teller." She watched Kara's face carefully and Kara knew she was waiting to see if she was going to laugh at her.

"What does that have to do with the evil queen and her apple tree?" Kara asked, unsure of why Jewel's mother being some quack that liked to convince people she knew something about their lives that hadn't happened yet, mattered at a time like this. "No offense but I don't really care what your mother tells or doesn't tell. I just want to get back to my life, no matter how pathetic it may have been. I have a plan and I need to stick to the plan if I'm going to,"

"Get the hell out of Dodge?" Jewel asked with a small smile on her lips.

Kara laughed. "Exactly."

"Just hear me out, and try to listen with an open mind. For these few minutes while we talk consider the possibility that there is more to the world than what we know. Consider that you are more and that you weren't taken simply because you have great hair and a nifty nose piercing."

"You think *I* have great hair?" Kara's voice rose and octave.

"*And* a nifty nose piercing," Jewel pointed out. "Because of what my mom does, I have always been exposed to the otherness in the world. I have always been aware that things are not always what they seem. People are often more than what we perceive them to be. When I first arrived in this lovely wooded prison I played dumb to Lorelle. I didn't want her to know just how much I understood, because knowledge is power, especially to the fae."

"Wait, hold up," Kara blurted out. "You knew about this? You know what she is and you believe her?"

"My mom often kept tabs on what was going to happen in my life, though she rarely told me because she didn't want to influence what was to be. On this instance she decided to break her code of silence because she felt I needed to know, needed to be ready. She said she had always known that I carried magic inside of me, but it was untapped and out of my reach. She began to tell me about the things in this world that humans did not know about and being the curious spirit that I am, I began to research it. It's hard to find any credible information, but every now and then I'd come across a blog on the internet or a brief mention in an old book of someone encountering something or someone that they didn't know how to explain."

Kara stepped back and leaned up against a tree, needing to feel something solid and real as she listened to the tale Jewel weaved.

"My mom told me that soon I would encounter such a being. She said it was my fate, my path to follow and not to fight it. But she also said to keep my wits about me, to listen and to remember that sometimes the most beautiful things I would encounter were actually evil wrapped in alluring trappings. This Lorelle who has taken us is one such beautiful thing. This lush forest, is so much more than that. It is dripping like a festering wound with the infection of malice and if you will open yourself up, for just a split second to the possibility that you are indeed special as the fae has indicated, you will feel it and you will see it." Jewel took a step towards Kara, her hand reaching out, imploring her to take it. "If you let me, I can help."

Kara considered the innocent looking girl before her wondering if she was one such beautiful thing that was attempting to lure her into a magical world she had invented in her little head. But then she sensed goodness in Jewel that she had rarely come across in her life. Jewel was pure, untainted, even though she talked of magic, malice and otherness, she was light, warmth and peace. She looked around the forest with the firm tree at her back. She couldn't deny that this was real, it was truly happening and if that was the case then what Jewel said might be true. She didn't like the possibility of things she couldn't explain. But as her eyes returned to Jewels hopeful green ones she inwardly shrugged thinking what else did she have to do than attempt to *feel* the evil that Jewel spoke of.

She took Jewel's hand and wasn't surprised to find it soft and warm, unlike her own that were rough from being washed constantly because of clearing nasty tables and washing dirty dishes day after day. "What do I need to do?" She asked her.

"Close your eyes and picture yourself opening a door in your mind." Jewel waited until Kara complied. "Take a deep breath and let it out slowly and picture yourself walking through that door into the forest, but as you cross through speak these words in your mind; *reveal the truth, remove the lies, unbind the light inside of me to shine through the darkness.* Then open your eyes and tell me what you see."

Kara did exactly as Jewel told her, and because she truly wanted to know what was happening, what she had been literally snatched into, she believed for just a minute that anything was truly possible. *Reveal the truth, remove the lies, unbind the light inside of me to shine through the darkness,* Kara chanted to herself as she pictured a white door opening before her. She lifted her foot to step over the threshold but the second her foot was beyond the threshold, she nearly jerked it back. Before she even saw it, she felt it, her skin crawled and she gritted her teeth forcing herself the rest of the way.

She opened her eyes once fully through the door, just as Jewel had instructed and she could see it. Black ooze dripped from the trees burning holes into the leaves that it touched, and grey fog rippled through branches and under bushes. A pungent odor rushed into her nose causing her face to scrunch up as though she'd sucked on a lemon.

"This is what you have been seeing the whole time we've been trekking along?" Kara stumbled over her words a bit as she continued to inspect the seemingly changed forest around her.

"No, not the entire time. I only see it that way when I open myself up. You can keep the door closed, so to speak, so that you aren't bombarded with the nastiness of this place. So, do you believe me now?" Jewel's eyes narrowed on the former waitress.

"I have to admit that your argument coupled with the evidence is quite convincing," Kara admitted.

"What are you, pre-law?"

Kara let out a snort of laughter. "First of all, how old do you think I am? And second, the lady I live with is obsessed with crime shows and Judge Judy."

"Would you like to close this off," Jewel offered, "before we continue to chat?"

Kara nodded and closed her eyes once again. She took hold of Jewel's hand and pictured the door. As she pushed it open and stepped back through she let out a breath and with it all of the nastiness that she had breathed in.

When she opened her eyes she was once again in the forest that, though still dark and uninviting, no longer dripped with black nasty stuff or had rippling fog that was seriously just wrong in so many ways. Somehow this version felt much less threatening.

"Now," Jewel interrupted Kara's thought of, *thank goodness I'm back in the tad bit less evil forest*, moment. "Your disposition indicates that you are eighteen or nineteen. Your appearance, however, does look a little younger than that. The way your eyes narrow like a hawk's and dart around, constantly watching your environment reveals a much older soul

205

and one who has seen too much for her few years." Jewel clucked her tongue as she examined Kara and then said, "I'm going to go with sixteen or seventeen."

"You're good," Kara smiled but it did not meet her hawk like eyes. "I'm sixteen going on fifty."

"I'm seventeen," Jewel divulged as her eyes drifted up and her lips pressed together.

"There's nothing wrong with being seventeen." Kara grinned.

"Maybe not but it's just so, so…," Jewel stammered. "Mundane, that's what it is. I mean it isn't sixteen which is supposed to be sweet, and it isn't eighteen which is supposed to be the coming of age, leaving your childish ways behind you to become a mature woman."

"Maturity is overrated," Kara grumbled having experienced firsthand that sometimes maturity comes much too soon to the innocent.

"Maybe for those who have had it thrust upon them," Jewel said knowingly. "I've seen things in my short little life that most will never see, but I imagine from the haunted look in your eyes I've never seen what you have."

Kara pushed away from the tree deciding that the conversation was veering in a direction she did not want to go. Her past was her past and she wouldn't use it to gain sympathy or pity.

"So if we're going to find this higher ground to see if we can get out of this cesspool we should probably keep keeping on." She motioned for Jewel to once again take point and began to follow her. "So what do you think Lorelle wants with us anyways?" Kara asked.

"Probably to hook us to some machine and suck the power from our bodies until all that is left is flesh withered like a dried up prune." Jewel's tone was so straight forward that Kara didn't know whether to believe her or not.

"Uh, are you being for real right now or is that something you read in one of your books?"

"Nope, saw it on the Princess Bride, only Westley, that's the guy who got captured and attached to a machine, was having his lives sucked from his body, not power."

Kara cleared her throat. "Okay, but are you insinuating that based on a movie, our outcome could be the same?"

Jewel turned back to look at Kara with a mischievous smile and gleam in her eyes that showed a slightly different side to the studious girl. "Rule number one when dealing with smart people, do not believe everything they say. In fact believe only half of it and consider the rest dressed up with big words that are meant to keep you from understanding what part is truth and what part is not."

"So you're saying I shouldn't believe anything you say?" Kara asked attempting to clarify Jewel's statement all the while wondering if what had just happened indeed had been some mind trick.

"No, I said smart people, I said nothing about dealing with geniuses."

"Modest much," Kara mumbled.

"Confident," Jewel corrected. "I may have grown up with a crystal ball reading, tarot card shuffling, scry throwing eccentric lady, and maybe sometimes I'm ashamed of how weird people considered her and consequently me. But having knowledge and exhibiting the ability to use it, not just obtain it, now that is something I *can* be proud of."

Kara said nothing in response to Jewel's passionate explanation. What could she say? I'm proud to be an orphan, or waitress. Nope, that wasn't going to fly, which was exactly why it was hard to believe that she, Kara Jones, could possibly be special in any way particularly a magical one.

∞

Lorelle followed the two healers, unseen through the forest, listening and observing the girls. She had definitely been surprised at what the one called Jewel had revealed. She had not let on in any way to Lorelle that she knew what she was or what was happening. That was one she would have to watch. *It's always the quiet, smart ones,* she thought.

Just as they rounded a corner she stepped out from the trees directly in their path, so close that Jewel nearly ran right into her chest.

"Is it possible that maybe you could put up a *fae crossing* sign so we are better prepared for the sudden appearance?" Kara asked as she stepped up next to Jewel.

"So you've decided you believe in all of this then?" Lorelle asked raising a thin, perfect eyebrow at her.

"I'm getting there." Kara shrugged.

Lorelle studied them, looking past the human covering to the gypsy magic inside. Jewel was slightly more powerful than Kara, but she suspected it was because Jewel had been exposed to magic her whole life. Decision made, she grabbed Kara's arm moving as quick as a viper strikes.

"Well, lucky you, I have something that will completely convince your little mind that everything your intelligent gypsy sister told you is indeed true."

Before Lorelle flashed, she heard Kara tell Jewel, "I guess I'm about to find out if there is a magic sucking machine or not."

Lorelle rolled her eyes at the healer as she flashed them back to Volcan's mansion. She laid the girl on the table in the large dining hall as he had instructed her and put a binding spell on her. Lorelle could tell the moment Kara realized she couldn't move, her eyes took on that deer in headlights look and the vein in her neck began to pulse as her heart sped up. Lorelle had also put a *hold your tongue* spell on her because frankly she was tired of listening to the incessant chatter.

She felt Volcan's presence enter the room and her back immediately went rigid. A strange screeching sound began to rise and Lorelle realized it was coming from a very frightened Kara. Her eyes were looking around wildly, like a cornered animal searching for a way out. She must sense Volcan, Lorelle decided, or maybe he was speaking to her in her mind, it was quite the open book after all. She was the youngest of the healers, and her lack of knowledge made her vulnerable to intrusion from other magical beings.

"Is the other one as powerful?" Volcan's voice graded like sandpaper across her nerves.

"Even more so," Lorelle told him, when she wanted to say *I'm not a freaking idiot, you told me to bring the weaker of the two and looky-there that's what I did.* She once again held her tongue, just barely.

"She knows nothing of her heritage, of her abilities," Volcan said as if Lorelle didn't already know.

"Correct."

"She will not be able to heal herself and I'm not ready for her to die just yet. What of the other one," he snapped. "Is she aware of her power?"

She nodded. "To an extent she is."

"Bring her. She will keep this one alive." Volcan waved her off like a common servant.

Lorelle flashed herself to the power and energy she knew to be Jewel's. The girl led her there like a beacon and didn't even know it.

Jewels eyes widened at Lorelle's once again sudden appearance.

"Hope you learn as fast as you claim to, little healer," Lorelle muttered as she snatched the girl and returned to Volcan.

Chapter 14

"You know how you believe that you're too powerful for anyone or thing to be able to touch you? No? Okay let me briefly explain. I am one such as that. Powerful, cunning, vigilant, never defeated—until I was. And let me tell you, it freaking sucked." ~Peri

"The first wisecrack Costin makes I swear I'm turning him into a rock and tossing him into a lake," Peri grumbled as she and Lucian finished dressing. The morning had come much too fast and with it the painful reminder of what was before them.

First, she had to face the wolves, literally, and her two comrades, and three clueless healers after completing the bonding and Blood Rites with Lucian. She imagined this is what new brides felt like when it was customary for the newly married couple to live with her parents for a time. It just wasn't right. Nobody should have to look in the eyes of people they truly knew after a night like that, especially if said people had already experienced a night like that.

"The blush on your pale skin is lovely," Lucian purred.

"Just because you're my mate doesn't mean I won't turn you into something unsavory," she warned.

"Maybe," his voice dropped even lower. "But I've no doubt you would not leave me in such a state for long, not after…,"

Peri put her hand over his perfect lips stopping his words. "I get it; you are the only one truly exempt from my wrath blah, blah, blah. Try not to gloat, okay?"

"I would not dare," he smiled and it was one that he gave only to her. Peri took his offered hand and followed him from the room, all the while hearing the drums of her impending doom. It was worse than even she could have imagined.

They entered the kitchen that was clamoring with people moving to and fro. Suddenly they all stopped as though it had been choreographed and turned to look at the pair. Grins that Peri swore would split their googlie-eyed faces in half, spread across the lips of all, save the new healers who just looked as clueless as ever, as the group gawked at them.

"Really, is this necessary?" Peri attempted for calm but she was pretty sure her voice trembled as she said it.

"Welcome to the group," Costin grinned at Lucian.

Lucian's head did the wolf tilt thing as he looked back at the younger wolf. "What group?"

"M squared, W squared, A," Costin said a little too proudly.

Sally's head dropped forward as she groaned. "I have got to stop letting you hang out with that female Serbia Alpha."

Lucian stilled looked confused so Costin added. "Mated Male Werewolves Anonymous."

Adam reached over and knocked fists with Costin as he laughed. "Good one."

"You do realize that doesn't make sense because werewolves is one word right?" Crina pointed out.

"Technicality." Adam winked at his mate.

"What is it for?" Lucian asked.

"Support, brother, because let me tell you once the females gang up on you it is game over, bar closed, dog house sleeping, done."

"Costin, I'm going to turn you into a rock," Peri spoke up repeating what she had told Lucian. "And then I'm going to toss you in a lake."

"Why can't you turn me into something useful like Sally's bra or the locket she wears around her neck," he whined.

Sally gasped and turned several shades of red as she glared at her mate.

"I get the bra thing, but I'm not even going to touch the whole locket thing," Adam retorted.

"Nestled between the mountains, brother, nestled between the mountains," Costin beamed like a clever child.

Sally was too speechless to even move but Crina beat her to it. "Peri you force his phase and then Sally can shave his pelt like one of those labra doodles that the Americans find so cute, then I will put a pretty little bow on his big dumb head."

Costin pointed to Crina but spoke to Lucian. "See, didn't tell you? They gang up on you and you can either run for the sake of your pelt or beg forgiveness like a trained lap dog."

"What is your choice?" Lucian asked seriously.

Costin gazed at his mate adoringly as he slowly backed out of her reach. "I do so love her lap," he said in a voice that should not be used in the company of others.

The room erupted into laughter, with even Peri smiling at the fool bartender who was beyond smitten with his little healer.

Sally was still glaring at Costin when the laughter died down. "This isn't over, Costin Miklos."

"Oooh I hope not, Sally mine." He winked roguishly.

Lucian drew Peri further into the room and pulled a chair out for her to sit in. She took the offered chair without comment, which no doubt surprised the others, and turned to look at the three humans.

"Feeling a little lost?" She asked them. Peri watched as Heather, the tiny blind healer filled with so much spunk she practically floated, turned in her direction.

"From your angle it looks like we have been found."

Peri stared at the girl wondering what made her so brave. She was the oldest of the group but she was also the blindest. "I would think you would be the most frightened of the group considering you don't have your sight."

There was a collective indrawn breath in the room. Peri huffed and flicked her hand at them. "It's not like she doesn't know she's blind, good freaking grief."

"Decorum, Peri," Elle spoke up.

"Yeah, I have none," Peri admitted brazenly.

"I'm not offended," Heather assured them. "Though I don't think Peri believes what she is insinuating, that I am helpless because I can't see what is going on around me. I am probably as perceptive as these people you claim are werewolves."

"So do you not believe us because you can't see them?" Crina asked.

Heather's head turned unfailingly to Crina's exact location. "I see them, with my ears, my skin, my nose, and the air that I breathe in and taste in my mouth. I do not believe any less because my eyes fail me, I believe less for the same reason the seeing believe less, because such beings are not supposed to exist."

"What about you two?" Peri motioned to Stella and Anna. "What do you believe?"

"I can't deny what I've seen," Anna said. "And I can't deny that I'm intrigued," she admitted somewhat sheepishly.

Peri nodded, her lips turned up ever so slightly. Then her piercing gaze fell on Stella and her eyes narrowed. "Can you honestly tell me that you don't want this to be real, that you haven't hoped for an escape all of your life?"

Stella's eyebrows drew together as she crossed her arms in front of her. "You don't play fair."

Peri chuckled. "Not very often."

"What about my brother?" She asked her.

"Is that the only thing holding you back?"

"I want to know he is okay. He will be worried sick about me, and that's not something I can live with no matter how incredible this all seems."

Peri let out a resigned breath. She hated dealing with human family members, it was messy and she only did messy on the battlefield. "Your brother has been dealt with."

Stella jumped out of the chair she had occupied. "What do you mean dealt with, because in the Bronx, dealt with is in no way reassuring?"

"Good grief girl, sit down," Peri grumbled. "We didn't kill him. I have more interesting things to kill than a measly human."

215

"Peri, that isn't reassuring them," Sally pointed out.

"I'm not trying to reassure them."

"Okay, good to know," Sally quipped back.

"His memory has been altered." Peri held a slender finger up to stop Stella from speaking. "No, it will not hurt him. Yes, he will be fine. Yes, he still remembers you. No, you cannot tell him or contact him, and yes I'm sure it will not hurt him for the fifteen times that you are bound to ask me."

Stella's lips tightened against her white teeth. "What *does* he remember?"

"Oh, did I not mention that?" Peri asked dryly.

"Peri, could you please play nice for once in your life?" Sally whined.

"Uh, excuse me, but I have played nicely once in my life and what did it get me? Three insufferable humans, believe me once was quite enough," Peri countered. Looking back at Stella she decided that the truth was best, especially with someone who had endured so many lies in her lifetime. "He thinks you finally did what you've always said you would and gone off to college. My magic enables me to make suggestions in the human mind. If those suggestions happen to be ones that the person truly wants, it makes it much easier. Your brother truly wanted you to get out."

Stella nodded at her, seemingly satisfied for the moment of Peri's explanation. Peri knew that later, when the girl had more time to think she would once again come demanding more information. *Humans,* she thought, *too damn curious for their own good.*

"As for you two," she looked back at Anna and Heather. "Scenarios that were believable have been given to those closest to you. Take everything I said to Stella and apply it to your situation because I will not repeat myself; it annoys me to do so."

"It would be months before my mother even realized I was gone," Anna admitted.

Peri ran a finger across her chin as she looked at the only one of the girls who looked like a gypsy. "Yes, you had an unusual upbringing. You have always been aware of your heritage."

Anna nodded. "But that doesn't mean I believed in the magic my mom claimed we possessed."

Peri clasped her hands in her lap and took a deep breath. "Okay, to review, we took you because you are gypsy healers. You have an affinity for magic that other humans do not. You are highly important to the Canis lupis race. As we explained, they are werewolves. There are twelve packs all over the world. Some are larger than others. Some are more receptive to the joining of the packs while some are just buttheads. What is important that you know, though you won't understand it until it happens, is that you each will become members of a pack. You have a true mate, which will be a dominant male, capable of protecting you, one who holds the other half of your soul. These males sometimes live centuries before they find their mate. Some of them are slightly scary, and some are like Costin," she motioned to Sally's mate who had his arms wrapped around his still slightly irritated mate with his chin resting on her head.

"What she means is incredibly handsome and fun to be around," Costin clarified.

"And oh so humble," Crina added.

"We have explained a little about the fae, which Adam, myself, and Elle happen to be. I am a high fae, a member of the Council that governs over the fae as well as the supernatural world. Recently, the Great Luna has once again begun assigning fae as ambassadors of sort to each pack. They also serve as a guide to help the healer in the pack learn and grow in power. Typically a healer does not come into her power until she turns eighteen. What we are beginning to realize is as the magic in our world has begun to change so have the rules.

"You three are of age, and though you may not be aware of your power, it is there inside of you, I can see it, the wolves can feel it, and other supernaturals will be able to as well. Healers are sought after, not just by the Canis lupis who wish to protect them, but also by those who would use your powers for evil. That is why you have been brought here. You each have a destiny, but it is not in the human world. If you attempt to run from this destiny you will be endangering your life, and depriving a worthy male the opportunity to be whole, to love you, and to tame the beast inside of him." Peri stared at the three girls as she finished, her words hanging ominously in the air and the group behind her eagerly awaited their response.

"Okay, I'm pretty sure that we weren't told *all* of that," Heather commented. "And I have really good listening skills, so I would remember hearing such information."

The others chuckled at her reference to her senses, and Peri could tell that Heather was going to be a huge blessing to the pack that had the honor of gaining her.

"We might have given you the condensed version," Peri conceded.

"Why do you think we are all taking this so well?" Anna asked.

Sorin, Elle's mate, was the one to answer her which was significant because he only spoke when he truly had something to say. "If I may," he looked at Peri and she gave him a nod to continue. "I had the privilege of watching three American young women, such as yourselves be brought into our world just last year. None of them were aware of the supernatural world. Each of them, however, felt as though there was something missing in their lives. I believe this feeling, this sixth sense if you will, is what allowed them to transition as smoothly as they did. You three seem to be even more receptive to what you have learned, and I think that is because you are going to be powerful healers. The magic in you is strong and though you may not have been aware of it, your soul has been."

The three women seemed to consider this.

"I had no clue about gypsies or healers," Sally spoke up, "even after I learned of the werewolves' existence. It wasn't until I turned eighteen and started having some freaky stuff happen that the wolves were clued in that I was a healer."

"Are you happy?" Stella asked pointedly.

Sally smiled at her and the natural peace that surrounded a gypsy healer flowed off of her, touching the others in the room. "More than I ever thought possible. I'm not saying I don't miss my parents, and I actually do get to talk with them occasionally," she pursed her lips at Peri. "But if you're asking me whether I would choose a human life over this one, the answer is not in a million years."

Peri stood then, smoothing down her clothes and stepping around the chair to grasp the back of it. "I understand that it is a lot to take in, but," she bit out, "we don't have the luxury of sharing some Dr. Phil moments and blubbering over what is, what might have been or what should be. We failed to rescue two of the five healers we were sent after. They were captured by the evil I spoke of. Unfortunately I have to claim the one who took them, as she is my sister. Believe me she is wicked and yes, I would like very much to drop a house on her." Peri noticed Elle giving her an odd look. "What?" Peri shrugged. "So I like human movies, bite me." Her fingers snapped at the already grinning Costin. "Not a word rock boy."

"How can we help?" Heather asked, once again exhibiting the fearless nature she seemed to possess.

"For now the best thing for you three to do is stay here, don't freak out and ask Crina and Elle, who will stay to protect you, as many questions as you like even if Crina complains about it. Elle is much more even tempered than the she-wolf, as you will find in most fae. I am the exception," her eyes flared as her power rose. "The rest of us are going hunting."

"When are we leaving?" Adam asked, all playfulness gone. Regardless of his relaxed attitude, like Costin, when it was time to fight, he was all business. Until he started killing things, that seemed to make him giddy, which Peri admitted was a tad disturbing.

"When does evil like to come out to play, comrade?" Peri asked him.

"When darkness falls,

The devil will play,
Lurking evil calls,
To draw you away."

Anna's voice, though nearly a whisper, filled the ears of all present. Her eyes had been unfocused as she spoke, but once silent she looked up at them. "It was a gypsy rhyme my mother use to tell me," she explained. "It was meant to remind the listener to be ever alert during the devil's play time."

"Or you could just say at night, that would have been a tad less creepy," Crina offered, her hands clenched up by her chin staring wide eyed at Anna.

"It was also a ward of sorts," Sally said looking curiously at her. "Your mother was protecting you with magic she knew she held."

"She told me that as well," Anna admitted. "I never believed her."

"There's a first time for everything," Adam smiled at her.

"I have a feeling we are going to be experiencing a lot of firsts," Stella grumbled.

A wicked smile spread across Peri's lips. "Oh, healer, you have no idea."

∞

"I know we need to sleep because we will be out all night dodging the devil," Sally said as she lay next to her mate. "But it is so hard to even doze when I know it's daylight outside."

Costin turned on his side and propped himself up on his elbow. He smiled his *bedroom only* smile that

221

made Sally's palms sweat. "There are other things to do in a bed besides sleep."

Sally laughed. "Is that all you think about?"

"What else should I think about? I'm a young, viral, married, mated, male."

"I think you mean virile," Sally corrected.

"Not important," Costin replied.

"Kind of is babe. Viral means you have some sort of nasty contagious, probably weirdly named issue. It's really not something you *want* to go around claiming."

"I know what I *do* want to go around claiming," he nearly hummed to her.

Sally raised an eyebrow at him. "Sometimes I seriously think you need some sort of counseling. You and Jen could join a support group together or something."

"Sally?"

"Yes."

"I'm going to make you tired now so you can sleep."

Sally tried to keep the ridiculous giggle out of her voice when she answered. "I will endure such treatment, if I must."

"You must," he whispered in her ear as he gathered her close. He smirked when, despite her words, she surrendered to him quite willingly.

Chapter 15

"Let me in, let me in, sister mine. A wolf in sheep's clothing knocks at your door. I am harmless it whispers to your mind. Just open it a bit, and then a bit more. Now, shut the door, shut the door, sister mine. Lies for the truth are what are in store." ~ Lorelle's spell

Lorelle knew her sister well. After all, centuries together revealed much. She knew that her sister hunted at night, which meant she would slumber during the day. Of course, getting Volcan to understand that meant they needed to do the dreamscape sooner rather than later was like ripping her own finger nails off one by one.

"How can you be sure? If you attempt to enter her mind while she is awake she will know, and then she will be on guard even when she sleeps," Volcan argued.

Lorelle reached for all the patience she had left, which wasn't really much to begin with, before she responded. "I feel it unnecessary to point out that you have been out of commission for some time now. While you were floating around aimlessly, no doubt licking your wounds, I was with the living, in particular, my sister. I know how she thinks. I also know she has taken a mate, so she will be a tad distracted in her thinking no doubt."

"How did you learn about the mate?" Volcan asked his voice thick with suspicion.

"I saw them together when we happened upon one another when we were getting the healers. I could sense the bond between them and his protectiveness towards her was undeniable." She waited for him to respond. After several minutes still nothing. "I feel I shouldn't have to reiterate that time is of the essence. But I will if I must."

"You tempt my wrath," he snarled.

"Well, you try my sanity—we're even."

"I concede," he finally said sounding like the sullen child he wasn't. "But if you fail, I will remove a limb in a most painful way."

Lorelle pressed her lips so tightly together she was sure they would meld into one big lip. She wanted to point out the he needed her, but he would only point out that he apparently had minions that would keep her from escaping. Knowing her luck, he didn't have a single minion and she was only held captive by her fear.

"Healer," Volcan growled, his disembodied voice seemed even creepier without being able to see the face behind it. "Come here."

Lorelle motioned to Jewel who had been standing against the wall across from the table that Kara laid on. She had been bound so she couldn't run and with a flick of Lorelle's wrist the binding dropped away.

"If you attempt to escape I will cut out her eyes," Lorelle motioned towards Kara. She had found that threatening someone else instead of the one you are trying to make cooperate heeds better results.

Jewel nodded as her eyes darted from Kara back to Lorelle. She knew who the predator in the room was, and she knew that Lorelle wasn't bluffing.

"You will need a fae blade," Volcan's voice interrupted the staring match between the two.

Lorelle held up her hand and out of nowhere a very sharp, very real knife appeared.

"What is your name, healer?"

Lorelle watched Jewel's hair ruffle as Volcan's presence swept around her. "He's speaking to you," she told her.

"Didn't Lorelle already tell you my name?"

Lorelle nearly smiled. This little healer was wise. She knew the power of willingly giving your name to one such as Volcan.

"Perhaps," he sneered. "But I do not trust her and want to hear it from your lips."

Lorelle tapped Kara's unblinking eyes with the tip of the knife as she watched the resistant healer struggle with what to do. As soon as the knife made contact she gave in.

"Jewel," she blurted out. "My name is Jewel."

"Full name," Volcan prodded.

Letting out a resigned sigh she answered. "Jewel Stone."

Volcan chuckled and the sound was like sand paper rubbing against his lungs as it rumbled up through his unused throat.

"The woman who birthed you must have been aware of magic in the world to give you such a name."

Lorelle wondered what he meant. What was special about the girl's name? Thankfully, Jewel asked so Lorelle didn't have to look like an idiot.

"What is significant about my name?"

"It really is tiresome that you know so little of your heritage," Volcan droned. "As one such as yourself, having a name that is of an element is powerful, and you have a name with three elements.

Stone, which is of the earth, and Jewel which is created from the earth, air, and even some water. Your powers often use the elements to heal, which is of course what you were created to do."

"And you think my mother knew this?" Jewel asked him, momentarily forgetting the situation.

"Most definitely. Your mother was more knowledgeable than you are letting on."

"Now that we've had our lesson for the day, can we please continue," Lorelle questioned, irritated by the fact that she had not known about what Volcan spoke of.

"Lorelle, run your blade down the inside of each forearm of the girl. Then carve these symbols on her forehead," he filled Lorelle's head with the images of which he spoke. Carve these on the furthest part on both sides of her face close to her ears, and the last one on her throat. Please be careful on the throat and don't slice too deep. If she bleeds out before Jewel can heal her I will be most displeased."

"I don't know how to heal her," Jewel spoke up before Lorelle moved to begin cutting.

"Your instincts will kick in," Volcan assured her.

"I understand the blood sacrifice, but may I ask what the symbols are for?" Lorelle knew it was dark magic, which was why she had no idea why she was going to be carving the healer up like a turkey.

"If it will make you work any faster then I will explain it," Volcan snarled.

Lorelle waited until he began before she touched the blade to Kara's arm and ran it down the flesh, splitting it open effortlessly.

"The symbols were created by me, using magic that most would never dare. Wherever a symbol has

226

been cut into the flesh, it gives me the ability to harness their power. No spell needed. Each location of the symbol is significant."

By this point, Lorelle had just completed the symbol on Kara's head. Blood ran, streams of red down her arms, and now on her face. To Lorelle's surprise the healer was still awake. She hadn't passed out and she hadn't made any noise.

"The symbol over the head will give me access to the power of her mind, the symbol on her cheeks near her ears, give me access to the power of her hearing, and the symbol on her throat allows me access to the power in her words. You may not realize this but when a healer uses their magic to heal someone, she uses all of her senses, at the same time. She is not limited to focusing on one thing only."

"What about the sense of touch?" Lorelle asked as she carved the last symbol onto Kara's neck. The healer was now a mess of blood and anguish.

"Do not use touch," Volcan ordered. "You must not touch your sister in any way while in a dreamscape. She will feel my power in you. She will feel the healer's power and she will know that you couldn't possibly be telling her the truth, not if you were under my influence."

"The human body only has seven pints of blood," Jewel spoke up. "I just thought maybe you should know that since it looks like Kara has lost at least one so far."

Lorelle could tell she was trying to remain calm, using her facts and reasoning as her anchor.

"Touch her, slow the flow of her blood." Volcan's voice was just a whisper.

227

Jewel's mind was screaming at her to do something, to fight somehow, to save Kara. But she didn't dare act against the fae or the evil voice that surrounded her. She knew the only way to help Kara at this point was to do as she was told. She reached out and grabbed Kara's hand. It didn't feel as warm as it should. She closed her eyes and thought about how her mother used to say that in order to access her power for the first time she would need to truly want it. Jewel couldn't think of anything she wanted more in that moment than to have power to save this girl who was slowly becoming her friend.

As soon as that thought entered her mind she felt a rush of energy course through her body, straight down her arm and through her hand into Kara. She saw in her mind what she needed to do, how her magic could help. She constricted all of the veins that had been cut and also slowed Kara's heart to slow the pressure. When she opened her eyes she could still feel her power working in Kara, like the running of an engine unseen boxed up in a car, the sound always in the background of everything else. She saw that it was working, the blood flow was slowing. So she hadn't rescued them, but she had been able to save Kara. *This time*, she thought, *but what about the next time?"*

She continued to hold her friends hand as she watched Lorelle's face take on a faraway look. She appeared dazed and uncoordinated. She leaned forward stiffly and dipped her fingers into the blood that had pooled on the table. Jewel tried not to gag when Lorelle lifted those very fingers to her mouth and sucked on them like they were the last dove ice cream bar on earth. She looked back down at Kara, determined not to watch the fae do any more disgusting acts all the while hoping for a miracle. She was pretty sure this was one of those situations that warranted one.

Lorelle hated the way it felt when Volcan took possession of her body. Unlike the first time she resisted the intrusion, causing her to be uncoordinated for a few seconds until he forced his will on her. Then to her utter horror, because though she may seriously be bloodthirsty for her sister's death, she did not mean it literally, Volcan dipped her hand into the healer's blood, defiling her even more as he licked it from her fingers.

"Why let such powers go to waste?" He whispered into her mind.

"Maybe because there is something seriously wrong with someone who wants to suck on a blood popsicle?" She snapped.

"Oh, so wanting to maim and kill your sister makes you normal?"

Dammit, it's not a good thing when the psycho has a point.

"Enough of this," Volcan rumbled. *"Focus, find your sister. Picture the house you spoke of, the room she occupies and the bed she sleeps in. Imagine a window opened to her mind and slip in that window."*

Lorelle pictured her sister, could see the room and bed perfectly in her mind. She could see Peri laying on her side with a large arm wrapped around her waist. That would be the mate. She pushed closer until she was right beside her ear and pictured the window. It was open and she imagined it beckoning to her. Without any resistance she pushed her consciousness into her sister's usually well-guarded mind.

"I figured you would come," Peri's voice surprised Lorelle as she whipped around to find her sister lounging lazily on a settee. The room around them became stark white, nothing adorning the walls.

"How could you possibly know?" Lorelle asked.

"Do you think me a fool?" Peri's brow rose as her unnerving gaze held Lorelle still.

"I think you are so arrogant that you turn yourself into a fool." Lorelle tried to tear her gaze away from her sister's but she couldn't, not until she felt Volcan pour a little more power into her. It was wrong, dark mixed with light, grey and dull as it filled her.

"There is only one place you could have gone to lick your wounds sister," Peri drew the last word out, sounding a little snake like. "None have reported to me that you have been in their realms, not that any would let you in. So that leaves only one place—a place that recently has been reopened for dark business. Tell me, Lorelle, am I wrong? Are you not residing in the dark forest, perhaps even Volcan's castle?"

"You know nothing!" Lorelle shouted letting her rage get the best of her.

"Calm yourself, remain dignified in the face of your enemy. When you lose control, you reveal weakness." Volcan commanded.

"Why are you here, Lorelle," Peri asked, obviously choosing to let her little outburst slide.

"I thought you might like the chance to save your little healers. I came to propose to you a challenge. You know how I dearly love riddles and races against time."

Peri's eyes narrowed. "Why would you be willing to give up the healers? You must have been desperate to capture them to risk showing yourself to me."

"Come now, Peri, you know I have always enjoyed a good game. Not to mention I do love to see the devastation on my opponents faces when they fail," she taunted.

"Playing with the lives of healers is not a game; it is suicide. If they die, you will as well." Peri stood slowly and Lorelle only refrained from taking a step back because Volcan would not allow it.

"Maybe for you, dear sister, but for me it is proof of my superiority to you. Are you scared you will not be able to make it in time?"

Peri took another step forward and her frown deepened. Ignoring her sisters question she asked, "What have you gotten yourself wrapped up in this time? What magic is it that I sense in you? It is familiar to me, and yet I cannot place it." Peri's head shifted side to side as if a different angle might suddenly shout the answer at her.

"You needn't worry about me. What you need to worry about are the two healers in my possession. I propose a little wager, Sweet Sister. Solve the riddle, make it to the destination in time, and you can have them. But if you fail…I will not only keep these healers but you will give me the others as well."

Peri's face tightened as she glared at Lorelle. "Why would I bargain with the lives of the ones I know are safe?"

"Because if you do not then the ones in my grasp will surely perish in a most horrific way. Can you live with that, Perizada?"

231

"You're bluffing. You won't kill them. You need the healers for something, I'm just not sure what."

Lorelle threw her head back and let out a throaty laugh. "I've already taken everything I need from them. They are useless to me now." Lorelle lied, knowing that her sister wouldn't be able to determine the truth in her dream. Lorelle watched as her sister struggled with her need to protect the healers in her care and the need to save the ones that would otherwise die at the hands of her sister.

"What is the time frame?" Peri finally asked through clenched teeth.

"You have exactly twenty four hours from the minute I finish telling you the riddle. Are you ready, perfect Peri? Are you prepared to fail and have to look into the eyes of the healers who have trusted you to protect them and tell them you bargained their lives and lost?"

"Give me the damn riddle and then be gone!" Peri growled.

"Pushy, pushy. Fine, listen closely, I will only say it once.

Pitter, patter, pitter patter rain drops fall,
The bitter wind bites down to the marrow.
Little bird, little bird don't you fall,
You won't come back a little sparrow.
It aches, It aches, hunger and thirst,
Glisten, glitter to the bistro they go,
Tick tock, tick tock, who'll be first,
Dusk sets, dawn rises, can't be slow."

Volcan pulled Lorelle's consciousness from Peri's mind so quickly it nearly made her physical body sick. Her eye's opened as he rushed from her body nearly

232

dropping her on her knees. She had to grab the table that the healer still laid on to hold herself up.

"What sort of riddle was that?" Volcan barked.

Lorelle laughed as she told a frightened looking Jewel to heal her friend. Then she answered him. "One that my sister will understand, if she is able to figure it out," she paused, "with so little time to spare in searching for the healer. People, even high fae, don't think quite as reasonably when they are rushed, especially when lives they are charged with are on the line."

She felt Volcan's pleasure at her explanation and she nearly vomited.

"Maybe I judged you too quickly, Lorelle. Maybe, just maybe, there is hope for you yet."

Lorelle closed her eyes as she tried to push out the last of the lingering darkness Volcan left behind, all the while thinking, *I'm not sure I want that sort of hope.* That, however, wasn't her final thought. Her final thought as she flashed the nearly dead healer back into the dark forest was that it was too late. It was too late the minute she sliced Kara Jones open and tasted her blood.

Chapter 16

"You would think, as I did, that century old fae would be unaffected by the pop culture of this time. You would think, as I did, that century old fae had a high standard for which they set in regards to every area of their very long life. You would think that, and you would be wrong."
~Sally

"What is it?" Lucian asked sitting up in bed nearly as quickly as Peri had.

Peri held out her hand and a pen and paper materialized. She began writing furiously, the scratching of the pen the only sound in the room. Lucian waited, ever patient for her. He could feel her distress, sense that something had happened while she was sleeping but what he did not know. Finally, several seconds later she looked over at him. Her eye blazed with an anger that only came from one thing—betrayal.

"Tell me," he said softly but firm enough that it was clearly still a command.

"There is no time for me to say it twice. I need you to gather everyone except the new healers and bring them here."

He wanted to argue, wanted her to trust him enough to share with him and only him, but he recognized that for the insecurity that it was. He would not let something that had no merit come between them.

"I do trust you," Peri told him as she laid her hand over his larger one that was resting, possessively, on her thigh. "And I need you to trust me."

He was up and out of their door with no more than the sound of a gentle wind as he moved with the swift and quiet way of his wolf. Peri stared at the paper in her lap. The hastily scrawled words glared back at her, daring her to try, taunting her to play her sister's game and run the risk of looking like the fool she said she was. How had it come to this? Once again a riddle stood between her and the life of another, although she wasn't even sure this healer really even existed. But could she take that risk? "What if, what if, what if," she chanted to herself and then added, "What if's never added a single breath to the one baring the question."

Her attention was drawn away from the riddle in her lap and she looked up to see the room filling with what she had come to think of, to herself of course, as the Special Seven. She figured that covered a wide range of meanings that applied in some way to each one. Jen, the queen of giving ridiculous titles, would be proud.

Lucian took his seat next to her while the others either took to the floor or perched on anything capable of holding them up. Their groggy eyed faces, lined with sheet indentions and impressive bed heads were suddenly alert as her words penetrated the fog of sleep.

"I have spoken with Lorelle,"

"How?"

"What?"

"When?"

The barrage of questions flew at her, each in a different pitch and emotion. Peri started to quiet them down but she didn't have to. Lucian let out a low growl, deep and rich, one so similar to another Alpha that could command a room with the simple act. Everyone went still and quiet.

"Please allow her to finish completely before you ask your questions. It will slow things down if you do not," Lucian said in the same deceivingly polite tone that his brother did. Deceiving because usually, for his brother Vasile, the calmer the tone, the deadlier his anger had become.

Peri continued as though she hadn't been interrupted. "She came to me in a dreamscape, don't ask what it is, there is no time to explain it. While in the dreamscape she proposed a challenge. She gave me a riddle and a time frame. If I figure out the riddle and make it to the destination in time, then she will release the two healers in her possession. If I fail to make it in the time frame give, not only will she keep the healers, she is demanding I give up the ones in my care. I sensed very dark magic in her and around her, leading me to believe that whoever is the bearer of such magic is her puppet master. If it is who I think it is, then there is a real possibility that she will not follow through with her end of the bargain. That said, I have twenty four hours to decipher a riddle she recited to me which is supposed to disclose the location of the girls." She paused and looked at their utterly shocked faces and let out a deep breath. "Go." She said giving them permission to commence rapid fire question time. In hindsight Peri realized that might not have been the best way to handle it.

"Enough," Lucian commanded pushing an abundance of his power into the room so that all of the wolves were on their knees and the fae's eyes bore holes into the floor. "Sally, you begin," he told her coolly.

Sally cleared her throat before speaking. "Do you think we should take her seriously? What if it's just a ploy to distract us, or what if they, I'm sorry to say it, are already dead and it's just a trap?"

Peri shrugged. "I honestly don't know. My sister has become quite the deceiver and while I have my doubts about her motives I would rather be cautious than run the risk of leaving two girls in the hands of Lorelle and whoever else is yanking her chain if there is a possibility we can save them."

Surprisingly there was a moment of silence before Adam finally spoke up. "So what's the riddle? We only have twenty four hours to solve it and find the girls."

Peri nodded. "Okay then." She looked down at the paper in her lap where her hastily scrawled writing stared back up at her. "Remember it's a location that we are looking for." Then she read.

"Pitter, patter, pitter patter rain drops fall,
The bitter wind bites down to the marrow.
Little bird, little bird don't you fall,
You won't come back a little sparrow.
It aches, It aches, hunger and thirst,
Glisten, glitter to the bistro they go,
Tick tock, tick tock, who'll be first,
Dusk sets, dawn rises can't be slow."

"Don't every one speak up all at once," Peri added dryly when she finished reading and looked up at the blank faces staring back at her.

"I need a pen and paper," Sally said suddenly snapping her fingers as if they would suddenly appear in her hand. She glared at the high fae when Peri snapped her fingers and a stack of paper and pens *did* appear on the floor. "Must be nice," Sally muttered as she snatched up a piece of paper and a pen.

Peri shot the healer a smirk before looking back down at the riddle before her.

Silently, one by one, the group picked up paper and pen and began writing down the riddle, going over in their minds what it could possibly mean.

"So it's a place," Elle said as she tapped her lips with her pen and stared at the words she had just written. "Well would the pitter, patter, pitter patter, bit indicate that it's a place where it rains a lot?"

"Bloody hell, that narrows it down to a few hundred countries, not to mention cities," Costin growled.

"We have to start somewhere," Crina added.

"Did she specify if it was in the U.S., since that is where she obtained them in the first place?" Sorin asked.

"Nope, why on earth would she give us a hint like that?" Peri answered snidely.

"Okay if the pitter, patter is rain, then the bitter wind bites down to the marrow must mean it's also cold in this place and windy," Adam suggested.

"What the crap does a little bird have to do with a place?" Sally looked up at Peri. "This isn't straight forward, she's making a play on something Peri. Little bird and not returning as a sparrow, that means something, it's a reference to something but I don't think it's the place necessarily."

"What do you mean?" Peri asked her eyes narrowed as her ears perked up at the healer's words.

"I'm not totally sure yet," Sally admitted. "But with references like the little bird, the glitter and glistening and the bistro, I mean seriously what would those have to do with a place? It seems more like she is referencing something that would point you in the direction but not necessarily describe the place itself."

Once again the room dropped into silence, the only sound was the scratching of pens and the occasional growl of frustration.

A knock on the door several hours later had a few heads popping up as Peri absently said, "Enter." She didn't look up from the paper she and Lucian stared at to acknowledge whoever had knocked.

"Is this some secret meeting that we aren't supposed to know anything about?" The sound of Stella's voice breaking the ominous silence had everyone in the room finally looking away from the words that were frustrating them. Not only was Stella standing there looking curious but the other two healers were right behind her. Anna attempted to look around her shoulder while Heather's head was tilted slightly obviously listening to every detail.

"If it was secret, then we did an awful piss poor job of keeping it that way, don't you think? And being as old as I am there are very few things I do piss poor anymore." Peri rolled her eyes as she reached up and stretched her arms and back. She was stiff from being hunched over for so long and the much needed stretch seemed to help wake her up a tad. "If you insist on standing there in the doorway, please do come in and make yourself useful," Peri told the three healers who stood staring at them curiously.

The three girls pushed into the room and walked around the sitting bodies. Anna helped to guide Heather around everyone until they reached the bed where Peri and Lucian sat. As they sat down on the floor Anna looked up at Peri. "So how can we help?"

Elle chuckled. "Something seriously has to be wrong with them. They are taking this all way too well."

Peri ignored her comrade and explained what she had told the rest of the group hours earlier. She then read the riddle to them, pointed out the pen and paper and told them to get to it. They didn't have to be told twice.

Heather mulled the words of the riddle over and over in her mind. She repeated them under her breath committing them to memory as she tried to work through what the meaning was behind them. Sally had mentioned, after Peri had filled them in, that she thought the riddle was eluding to a location by referencing something else. So Heather focused her attention on the things in the riddle that weren't so obvious. She considered each line, breaking them down in her mind, and attempting to give meaning to them in any way that might make sense. It was going to be a long day she decided, as the murmurs around her continued.

∞

Jewel watched Kara unblinkingly as she sat propped up against a tree in the dark forest where once again Lorelle had basically tossed them. She stared at her unconscious friend, willing her to

240

continue each labored breath that rattled through her weak lungs. She had lost a lot of blood in the little ploy executed by Lorelle and her evil master. Jewel gave thanks to whatever god or goddess she needed to for allowing the magic in her to do what it was obviously intended to do, and that was to heal. She would not have been able to forgive herself if she had had to watch Kara die on that table at the hands of a vile shadow person and an evil fae with an inferiority complex.

For so many years she had read book after book of fairy tales, fantasy, sci-fi and the like about evil and the good that conquers it but never in a million years did it prepare her to face it. Even after her mother's many adamant attempts to convince her that there was so much more to the world they lived in, she could never have imagined someone like Lorelle or something as horrible as watching Kara's blood flow from the huge cuts in her arms and the horrific designs now carved on her skin. As she stared at her new friend and the symbols on her face and neck she considered this new ability to heal and slowly made her way to Kara's side.

"I'm sorry I couldn't do more, Kara," she whispered. "I'm sorry I'm not brave or bold like you and didn't fight back. But, I'm going to try something now, something that might make up for a tiny sliver of my failure." She took Kara's hand in hers and tried not to shiver at the cool temperature of her skin or the clammy feel against her own flesh. She closed her eyes and pictured the power that she could feel inside of her own body swirling around like ribbons of gold behind her closed lids. Her body felt warm as she attempted to once again control it and push it towards its intended goal. Jewel thought about each symbol and the location and one by one she pushed her healing power to them. She watched in her mind's eye as the cells regenerated and the tissue healed and slowly began to close. Sweat formed on her brow as she attempted to minimize the scarring as much as possible. Jewel attempted to remove as much of the symbol as she could in hopes that the distorted pieces would keep the evil from being able to use Kara.

When she opened her eyes and started to pull her hand away she sucked in a breath as Kara's hand clenched around her own preventing her from severing the bond. Jewel looked at Kara's skin and wanted to weep as she saw that it had worked. There was a small amount of scarring in some places but for the most part the symbols were gone, though she knew the damage did not only lay in Kara's flesh. It was also branded forever in her heart. The pain she endured at Lorelle's cruelty would not be easily forgotten. Jewel wished desperately that she could take that pain away, but she knew the only healing that would work for that was time.

Kara's hand continued to stay tightly closed around her own as she continued to sit by the unconscious girl. She knew they had to figure out a way out of this nightmare because if they didn't it was only going to get worse. Her mother had spoken of such evil and she had honestly believed that nothing that vile could possibly exist, not in their world. She was wrong, so very, very wrong. Now the only thing left to do was to wait. Wait for Kara to wake up, wait to see if she would be able to move, wait to see if Lorelle or her horrid master would come seeking them again. Waiting had always sucked but in that moment Jewel decided that never in her life had she hated waiting so bad. *Hurry up and wait*, she thought to herself as she leaned back against the tree behind her and continued to hold on tightly to the first true friend she'd ever had. She closed her eyes and tried to put away the things she had seen. She reached for the good she knew to be true. She reached for her mom's love, strange though she may be. She reached for the books that had kept her company for so many long nights. She reached for every ray of sunshine she had ever felt upon her skin. These things she had to think on because the alternative was too dark, too scary.

"Remember Jewel," her mother's voice echoed in the quiet places of her mind. "Darkness, pitch as night, will come to you. It will surround you and threaten to take from you everything you hold dear. You must not succumb. No matter how it suffocates you, you must look for the light and latch onto even the tiniest flake because even the smallest amount can pierce through the blackness, showing you a way out."

At the time Jewel had thought that her mother's speech was better suited to some fairy tale book, not as advice to her teenage daughter. But now, as she sat surrounded by that very darkness her mother spoke of, she understood. She needed to find the light. She knew with light there was hope, and hope was something she could work with.

∞

Heather's head was beginning to throb with the effort to stay awake. They had been at it for hours and hours and night had fallen once again. They were no closer to figuring out the riddle than they had been when they started. Frustrations levels were running high and she was sure that at any moment Peri was going to make good on her threats to turn them all into some disgusting insect. She squeezed her eyes shut tight and let out a deep breath, attempting to relax the tense muscles in her back. She needed to think about other things for just a few minutes. Maybe stepping back and then returning to it would help her see the riddle with new eyes. *Ha, new eyes that's a good one*, she laughed at herself, as she frequently did.

Her mind drifted off to the things she would be doing had she not been abducted by a crazy fae and her apparently too hot for words mate along with their merry lot of supernaturals. In the evening she typically listened to audiobooks. She had always loved books. She loved the rich details they provided, the intense relationships and the intriguing plots. They were so much more exciting than her life, well until now that is.

Her latest book was not one she thought she'd ever be listening to, but one of her friends had balked when she had said she hadn't read them, stating, *everyone and their dog has read them, how have you not?* Heather had refrained, barely, from the smartass remark of I can't see in case you haven't noticed. She knew her humor about her situation made some people uncomfortable. So that was how she found herself listening to the Twilight Series. Yes, yes, it was way overdue and she was way past when it was cool to be a twihard, but it was pretty good for the most part. She had only read the Anne Rice version of vampires so it was interesting to see them viewed differently, complete with sparkling bloodsuckers…and that's when it hit her, like a bolt of lightning shooting straight into her mind.

"It aches, It aches, hunger and thirst,
Glisten, glitter to the bistro they go,
Tick tock, tick tock, who'll be first,
Dusk sets, dawn rises can't be slow."

The words ran through her mind and their meaning slipped into place. It aches hunger and thirst, just as a vampire thirsts for blood. Glisten, glitter, the vampires in Twilight sparkled. *Okay,* she thought, *what about to the bistro they go?* The only thing she could think of in regards to that was the restaurant that Bella and Edward dined at together, although it could also be literally referring as humans as their restaurant. *Eww, that's just wrong,* she scowled. The tick tock, who will be first is obvious, Lorelle or Peri. She thought back to the beginning of the riddle, about the little bird not falling, maybe she means not to fall in love. Because if she falls in love with Edward and he changes her, she will come back a vampire, not the innocent sparrow she once was. It was a stretch but she'd run with it for now. Then there was the part about the rain and cold, this was an obvious reference to the weather of the location.

Heather took a deep breath and let it settle into place. If her breakdown of the riddle was correct, then Lorelle was talking about Forks, Washington. Part of her wanted to blurt it out, to shout it at the top of her lungs because they had been at it for so long. But then there was a part of her that wasn't fully convinced that what she had deduced was correct because, really, it was ridiculous. How could an evil fae like Lorelle possibly make a riddle up based on a freaking teen book series from the twenty first century? It didn't make sense, not that anything in the past twenty four hours had made sense. After deliberating and arguing with herself she finally dropped her head and raised her hand.

"If you ask me if you can go to the bathroom I'm going to…,"

"Turn her into a cockroach, we got it Peri," Elle interrupted.

"Just so long as we're clear," Peri said as she turned her attention to Heather. "You don't have to raise your hand. Just speak up, someone will start listening eventually."

"Once I tell you what I think the riddle is referring too you're going to think I'm ridiculous so raising my hand like a juvenile seemed appropriate."

Peri didn't comment but simply waited for her to continue.

"Do you happen to like paranormal teen fiction?" Heather asked the fae, feeling totally foolish.

Peri's eyebrows drew together as she leaned forward with her elbows braced on her knees. "Maybe, what's it to ya?"

"Does your sister know you like paranormal teen fiction?"

Peri rolled her eyes. "Yes and she thinks I'm an idiot for it, but seriously some of the hunks in those books are beyond swoon worthy." There was a low growl to Peri's left. She reached over and patted her mate's leg. "Don't worry wolf, they don't hold a candle to you."

"I think the location is Forks, Washington," Heather finally blurted out. The room was silent, and

246

Heather could feel the stares boring into her. She knew how it sounded but she was hoping that now that she had said it, maybe one of the other young girls would see it too, provided they had read the Twilight series, but then who hadn't right?

Several minutes of silence crept by when finally someone spoke up.

"Bloody hell," Sally laughed. "She could be right, Peri. Now that she's said that I'm looking at the riddle from that angle and it just makes sense."

Heather quickly went over the ideas she had thought out and Sally agreed with her, seeing the correlations as well. Slowly, others that were familiar with the series began to speak up and share their thoughts.

"I agree," Peri finally said. "Why I didn't see it sooner I don't know, but knowing my sister as I do, this is exactly something she would do. Something so simple and obvious in many ways and yet so ridiculous that you wouldn't give it a second thought."

"What do we do now?" Anna asked.

Peri looked at the clock on the wall. "We have twelve hours left until the time limit Lorelle set has expired. So we're going to shower, eat and then a group of us will head to the infamous Forks to hopefully rescue the healers my sister claims are there."

There were murmurs of agreement as they began to file out of Peri and Lucian's room. When they were finally alone, Peri let out a sigh as she looked at her mate.

"I can't believe she used a teenage romance book to give the location; that just shows that she isn't in her right mind. She is obviously certifiably nuts."

"That Heather is a bright one," Lucian added as he took Peri's hand and pulled her up from the bed.

"I imagine she uses her mind a lot more than the average person." Peri closed her eyes as she stood in front of her mate. She tried to imagine what it would be like to not be able to see, to only be able to rely on her other senses. "I wonder if she ever feels as though she is trapped inside of herself. It seems a lonely thing, to not see the world, the colors, the beauty and even the ugly in it."

"She sees it, love," Lucian told her as he pulled her into his arms and pressed a kiss to her forehead. "She just sees it in a different way."

"So it looks like we're going to Forks." The words rolled dryly from her lips as she pulled away and headed for the closet to search for clothes. "I suppose it could be worse."

Lucian chuckled. "How so?"

"We could be heading into a dark forest with a crazy warlock on the loose and a power hungry fae at his beckon call. Been there, done that, would prefer not to ride that roller coaster again. However," she poked her head out to look at him. "something tells me we will be returning to the dark forest for a totally different kind of ride, and if it's because of what I think it is, it's going to be rough."

"Saving the world was not meant to be easy," Lucian teased.

"Maybe not, but they could have made it a hell of a lot less deadly if you asked me, which nobody did, which once again proves to be mistake of epic proportions."

"Epic?" Lucian asked with a raised brow.

"Totally epic," she confirmed as she walked out of the closet fully dressed.

"Well remind me not to make that mistake then."

"No worries, mate of mine, any mistakes you do make I assure you, you will only make once." She winked at him as she waited for him to finish dressing.

"How generous of you," he responded dryly.

Peri grinned wickedly. "Truly my kindness knows no bounds."

∞

Volcan's mind wandered back to a time long past. It was a time when he was powerful, feared and respected. Those had been the days when his endless hours of work began to produce fruit. He had managed to take ordinary humans and endow them with magic. It wasn't natural, it wasn't what Fate had ever intended to happen, and for those reasons the magic twisted and morphed into something even darker than he had thought it would be. As the magic settled into the humans it blackened their souls and ripped any form of humanity from them. The evil wrapped around them as a snake wraps around its prey, squeezing the life from them. The light faded from their eyes and all that was left was the withered soul in a body never meant to house such power. He had thought his plan ingenious. He was going to corrupt the human world, and bring them under his rule. He was supposed to have been a king. But his creation turned on him, choosing not to obey him but to go their own way. They formed covens amongst themselves and scattered to the winds, leaving him to face the wolves and his kind, alone.

It was a long and bloody battle and ultimately it was his near demise. None knew that a piece of his tattered soul had survived, they underestimated the amount of power he held and so he waited. Like a lion biding its time as its prey wonders oblivious to the danger just beyond the brush, ready to pounce when the time was right. His time was coming. Once again he would rise from the ashes and take back what was his and this time he would be victorious. No other outcome would do. He would watch as the wolves howled in pain and frustration as they watched their healers, possible mates, be used for his own purpose. He would have no mercy, and once every ounce of magic had been reaped from them, he would toss their bodies, limp and lifeless, before those who could not save them. Yes, his time was coming, all he needed was to be patient for just a little longer.

Chapter 17

"I feel a change coming, like the wind has suddenly reversed its direction and all of nature must catch up to follow. I'm restless, my soul inside of me cries out for the one who would complete me and yet I fear that very thing. What do I have to offer one such as precious as a true mate? But change is coming, that much I know. Whether I'm ready or not, it's coming." ~ Dalton Black, Colorado Pack

"Tell me again why we are making a stop to see Dillon Jacobs?" Adam asked as they walked up to the Colorado Pack mansion.

"Because I feel it's better to go in over prepared than under. Dillon would be quite irritated to know that we had been taking healers from the US, which he considers his territory, without his knowledge. So what better way to inform him than to ask for his assistance?" Peri answered as she stepped up to knock on the large wooden door. Before her hand could connect with the wood, Lucian had his arm around her waist pulling her back and swinging her around so that she stood behind him.

"In what universe do you think it is okay to waltz up and knock on the door of another Alpha, especially one that I haven't even met?" Lucian asked her through their bond.

Peri crossed her arms in front of her chest and let out a loud sigh. "By all means wolf, knock until your heart's content."

Lucian ignored her impertinence and rapped three times on the door. He took a step back causing everyone behind him to have to do the same.

"Protective much?" Peri teased.

"For the time being, this is my pack, my responsibility, and no harm will come to what is mine." Lucian's voice rang with a finality that none dared argue with.

Finally the door swung open and every one's head save Lucians turned up to look at the mountain of a man standing before them. The man's eyes met Lucian's briefly before dropping and then moving on to those behind him. When they fell on Sorin it was obvious he was a familiar face.

"What brings you to our territory, Sorin of the Romania pack?" His deep voice rumbled out of his massive chest.

"Dalton," Sorin said with obvious affection. "It's good to see you. We have come seeking Dillon's aid."

Dalton's eyes narrowed as he once again allowed them to sweep over the group. He gave a nod to Costin and another to Adam and Peri. When they landed back on Lucian it was obvious he made sure not to meet the other wolf's eyes.

"You look familiar and yet not," Dalton admitted.

"I am Vasile's brother, I have been away for quite some time," Lucian explained.

Dalton noticed the markings on Lucian's neck and his eyebrows drew together. "You are mated?"

Lucian stepped aside and wrapped and arm around Peri's waist pulling her against him. "Perizada is my true mate."

"We had heard that fae and wolves were mating," Dalton admitted and his voice lacked emotion but the glint in his eyes exposed the truth, he was intrigued. "But it is still strange to see it."

"Not to be entirely rude," Peri said as she cleared her throat. "But time is of the essence, we really need to speak with Dillon."

Dalton gave a single nod. "Of course, come in." He led them to the large living area and motioned for them to take a seat. "I'll let my Alpha know you are here." As his huge form left the room, it suddenly felt a lot more spacious.

"Okay he looked large the first time I met him, but for some reason he looks as though he's grown. Can werewolves grow once they are mature?" Sally asked with wide eyes.

Costin growled low and Sally swatted him. "Just because I noticed the size of a guy does not mean I want him, Costin."

"I'm going to ignore how that remark sounded only because I know how innocent your mind tends to be Sally mine," Costin told her as he sat in one of the chairs and pulled her down onto his lap.

"That was actually a pretty good one," Peri admitted with a chuckle.

The room went quite as they all felt power sweep across them filling the space. Dillon walked into the room glancing quickly around and Peri knew he was looking for his daughter Jacque.

"She isn't here, Dillon," Peri told him.

"Is that a good thing?" He asked the fae.

"It is a necessary thing. Her presence wasn't required for this mission, and there was no reason to put her into harm's way needlessly."

Dillon walked further into the room and drew his power back so that it wasn't an overwhelming force. Dalton walked in behind him and took up a silent sentry position against the wall next to a massive rock fire place. For some reason, the muscles in his face tightened and he seemed incapable of standing still, shifting his weight from one foot to the other every few minutes.

"To what do I owe the pleasure of your visit? Oh and congratulations on your mating," said Dillon, appearing to ignore the fidgeting of his bodyguard. When Peri looked at him in confusion he added. "Jacque filled me in. Lucian, I am not old enough to have known you before but I have known Vasile for some time and I am glad to see that he has regained a brother that he had lost."

Lucian gave the Alpha a respectful nod but did not respond more than that.

"We have a situation," Peri began. "Well really we have five situations…"

"These situations are all in the U.S.?" Dillon frowned.

"Well, they were, but they have been moved out of necessity. Three of them are in my possession and two are in the possession of my sister, of all people. I am asking for your help because there are just too many unknowns and I prefer to have adequate ammunition behind me in such circumstances."

Dillon took a seat across from her folding his hands in his lap taking on a relaxed pose, but Peri was not fooled. He was Alpha, and always prepared to attack at a moment's notice.

"Start at the beginning, condense where you can since Dalton explained that you were on a time constraint of some sort."

Peri shook her head with a sigh. "Well hold on to your tail Alpha because I'm about to blow your mind." Peri began explaining to him all that had transpired from the conversation she had with the Great Luna all the way to the dreamscape and riddle with Lorelle. When she revealed the news of the healers both Dillon and Dalton had sucked in shocked breaths and Dalton pushed away from the wall taking a step closer to the group causing low growls to erupt from the males. Dillon had raised an arm to halt his wolf but kept his eyes on Peri.

He sat in stilled silence after Peri was finished. His green eyes began to glow with the presence of the wolf as his protective instincts rose at the mention of gypsy healers. Every Alpha worth his salt knew what having a gypsy healer in the pack meant. More successful births, healthier wolves, peace, and another true mate to one of the dominates, the ones most prone to give into the darkness that grew inside of them year after year as their wolves overtook more and more of the man. Dillon immediately realized that one of the healer's might be a mate to someone in his pack. Sure it wasn't a guarantee, but the odds were decent. There were twelve packs, two of which already had healers. That left five healers for ten packs—a 50/50 chance, he liked those odds. His jaw clenched and unclenched as he turned over the possibilities in his mind. Hope warred with the disappointment he knew the males in his pack would feel if one of the precious gypsy healers did not belong to one of them.

"So you want my pack to accompany you to this town where the other two healers are supposed to be awaiting your rescue?" He asked, unable to stop the growl that accompanied his words.

"Call me crazy, but I had a feeling if a battle broke out in your territory without your knowledge you wouldn't be too happy," Peri answered dryly.

"You would not be as old as you are if you were not wise. But then, perhaps because you are as old as you are, crazy has crept up on you as well." Dillon smiled as he stood quickly and turned to Dalton. "Get Lee, Phillip and Aidan."

Dalton nodded and left the room still looking rather flustered.

"Myself and my first three will join you. My mate and my fourth can stay and handle pack business for me. What is your risk assessment?" He asked turning to direct the question at Lucian.

"Lorelle is unpredictable, and powerful in her own right. She is working for some master of unknown identity and power, which leads me to the conclusion that the risk of injury and or casualty is moderate to high."

"It sounds so ominous when you put it like that, Lucian," Sally whined. Costin rubbed her back soothingly and pressed a kiss to the spot just below her ear.

"You know that I will protect you," he whispered in her ear.

"But who will protect you?"

He growled. "Not that I need protecting but if it will appease you I will jump behind that Goliath called Dalton at the appropriate time." His eyes sparkled mischievously and Sally laughed which had been his intention. No need to tell her that there was no way in hell he would ever hide behind another nor would he ever fail to protect his mate.

The wolves Dillon had requested filed into the room joined by Dalton and Tanya, Dillon's mate. She walked over to Dillon and looked up into his eyes, her own filled with hope. "Healers," she whispered.

"There is no guarantee that one will be for our pack love, don't get your hopes too high."

"When are you pessimistic wolves going to learn that hope is one of our greatest gifts in this life? I will hope, mate, because we have many males," her eyes darted to Dalton and back to her mate, "who are in desperate need of their true mates. Not to mention that a healer would raise the spirits of others who haven't found their mates yet, giving them more time."

Dillon stroked her cheek gently and pressed a soft kiss to her lips. "You hope then, and should that hope be shattered I will be here to gather you up." He turned then and looked at his wolves. He motioned to Aidan, his fourth. "You and Tanya will oversee the pack. Do not speak of this with any one."

"Yes, Alpha," Aidan said dropping his eyes in submission.

"Peri, I assume we will be traveling fae style?" Dillon's lips tightened at the idea. Alpha wolves did not like to be out of control and flashing with a fae most definitely took the control from their hands.

"Earn enough frequent flyer miles and you just might win a trip to nowhere," Peri smirked as she reached out her hand for Lucian and Sorin who stood on her other side. "Please keep your seat belt fastened until the seat belt light has gone off and return your trays to the upright position." Then she was gone along with the two males.

"She's a little odd isn't she?" Tanya asked.

Sally laughed. "Oh, you are being too kind, she is more than a little odd. She's like a lion with the head of a giraffe and the tail of a pig kind of odd."

"Wow, that was some impressive comparing and surprisingly accurate," Adam praised as he took Costin and Sally's hand. "We'll be back for you, Alpha," he told Dillon before he too flashed.

Peri returned and motioned for Dalton and Lee to take her hand and once again she was gone. Adam was right behind her waiting for Dillon to say his goodbyes to his mate. Phillip took Adam's hand and Dillon quickly did the same. The darkness swallowed them as Adam flashed.

Tanya watched as her mate disappeared before her eyes. She blinked back tears as she once again turned her thoughts towards the healers Dillon had told her about. Dalton, one of their most dominate males, slipped into her mind as well. He, of all their wolves, needed a true mate most of all. He was damaged nearly to the point of no return. He was faithful to Dillon and he took his duties seriously, but he spent too much time alone when he wasn't with the pack. He refused any form of touch even though wolves craved it and thrived on the reassurance of their pack mates. Even when in his wolf form he kept his distance, protecting and watching from afar, but never truly joining in the hunt. She decided then and there that she would do whatever she could to ensure that the healers be allowed to visit their pack. If she had to beg the high fae herself then she, an Alpha female, would lower herself to such tactics because that's what you did when you loved those who were yours. You laid your own pride aside to ensure that those in your care had what they needed. If she had to go before the Great Luna herself and petition on Dalton's behalf then that was what she would do. She refused to lose him, and her wolf was fed up with seeing him be taken more and more by the darkness.

"Hang on a little longer Dalton," she whispered fiercely. "There is still hope."

∞

Lorelle looked out over the town of Forks. The small town seemed too quiet and it was disturbing. She had planted a false trail that would lead Peri and her merry band of do gooders to a deserted cave near the coast. She had left her a message, one that would make it quite clear what a fool she had been to believe the lies Lorelle had fed her. She wished she could stick around to see the enraged face of her sister when she realized she had been duped, but she had better things to do—like kidnap three other healers. She flashed from her location and found herself standing before the veil to Farie. She could no longer flash directly into her realm because she had betrayed her race. To enter through the veil was going to be extremely painful, but it was either endure the pain of the veil or die a horrible death at the hands of a deranged spirit.

With that thought taking center stage, she walked towards the veil and began stepping through it. At one time she simply would have felt a warm sensation flowing over her as she crossed over, but this time, this time it was like sharp points being slowly stabbed into her flesh. Starting from the top of her head and moving over every inch of her, down to the bottom of her feet, she felt the invisible piercing needles penetrating deeper and deeper. The air was thinner and she found it hard to breathe, causing her lungs to scream out in pain begging for more oxygen, and with every gasp she only found that there was no more air to be had. She wanted to howl at the agony but with no air there was no sound to slither up her throat and out of her mouth. She continued to push, feeling as though she were walking through some sort of viscous liquid causing her movements to be sluggish and uncoordinated. Just when she was seriously considering turning back she felt one of her legs break through to the other side and the pain in that foot and leg was relieved immediately. It gave her the push she needed to continue forward. After several agonizing minutes, she found herself standing in the bright forest of Farie. The fresh air burned her lungs and the positive energy that flowed through the realm felt like bugs crawling across her skin. Shaking off the uncomfortable feeling, she flashed to just outside the house that belonged to Peri, one she had used as a safe house of sorts for more than one species over the centuries.

She disregarded the idea to send her power out slowly and sparingly because the council would know as soon as she crossed into the veil of Farie. But thanks to a little dose of Volcan's magic mixed with gypsy healer blood, her location would not be so easy to pinpoint. As her power seeped further into the house, she began to feel the magic of the three healers, Elle, and a she-wolf. Her mouth dropped open in shock that her sister would be so stupid as to leave only two guards for her precious healers. She truly was as foolish as Lorelle had claimed. *This is going to be like taking candy from a baby,* she thought as she began to gather her power, pulling on the energy that Volcan was feeding her. She refused to think about how he was doing that, about his presence that seemed to always be lurking in the back of her mind. She was beginning to suspect that the two times he had possessed her he had not fully removed himself, that he had left some sort of residue in her mind of himself and it made her want to dig in her brain with a spoon until she found it and scooped it out. Gross? Maybe. Necessary? Without a doubt.

A knife materialized in her hand and she sliced the palm of her hand. Blood magic was strictly forbidden for the fae, but she had crossed so many lines at this point that it really didn't matter. She needed the power. She needed the darkness if she was going to take these healers from Elle and the she-wolf. Failure was not an option and she would cut every damn inch of her body if she needed to in order to succeed in her task.

∞

"Can you explain this whole true mate thing a little better than the brief explanation Peri provided," Anna asked Elle and Crina as they sat around the kitchen table sipping the hot chocolate Crina insisted they have in order to talk.

"Crina would be better to explain than me," Elle said truthfully. "I'm mated to Sorin but it's still very new to me. She's been around the wolves her whole life and knows much more about the mate bond than I do."

All three healers directed their attention on the she-wolf waiting expectantly. Crina took another sip from her mug and then set it down in front of her. She pulled her knees up to her chest as she settled her feet on the edge of her chair. Her delicate features concealed a deceptive strength. As she tilted her head to the side looking up at the ceiling as if the answers were written on it, she looked even younger and more innocent.

"True mates are one of the Great Luna's greatest gifts to her children," she began. "It goes beyond the marriage bonding that humans practice. It is far more permanent as two halves are bound together making one. It is more than the joining of bodies; it is the joining of spirit as well." She looked down to the healers across from her and blew out a breath causing her cheeks to puff out. "With me so far?" All three girls shook their heads no. "Good," Crina smiled and continued. "Now, the most important thing you need to know about true mates is the part you play in it. The males of our species have a beast that resides inside of them. Over time the darkness that the beast harbors begins to spread in the man. They fight it for as long as they can because they are noble, but they can only combat the darkness for so long before it overtakes them completely."

"What happens if it overtakes them?" Stella asked, leaning forward with her elbows resting on the table.

"Their wolf takes control and they become feral." Crina's eyes softened as she pressed her lips together considering her next words carefully. "You are the light to that darkness. The females of our race are considered precious to the males. When a male finds his true mate he finds peace for the first time in his long life. You help him control the beast, and as healers, your light shines all the more bright. In turn, he will be your protector, your confidant, your lover, your best friend and the other half of your soul. Your mate will treasure you as no other ever could. He will be possessive to a fault, more than likely bossy, jealous and prone to temper tantrums. But," she raised a finger at their worried expressions. "he will also make you laugh, hold you when you need to be held, do anything in his power to bring you joy, serve you, live for you and die with you. He is yours forever and you are his."

"Whoa," Heather said breathlessly.

"Understatement," Stella added.

"Um, that last part," Anna spoke up with a scrunched up brow, "what do you mean by die with you. Did you mean die for you?"

Crina shook her head. "Nope. Once you complete the Blood Rites with your mate your fate is bound to his and his to yours. If one dies, the other joins."

"Suck a banana," Stella breathed out.

"Gross, but oddly appropriate," Heather agreed as she took in the information Crina had just shared.

"That's pretty heavy," Anna told the she-wolf and then looked at Elle. "Did you know that when you took Sorin as your true mate?"

Elle nodded. "It's not something you can turn away from. You can try but you will only be torturing yourself and your mate."

263

"And you're telling us that each one of us will, without a doubt, be mated to a wolf?" Stella asked.

"Healers are always true mates. You must be protected and a human could never protect you as a Canis lupis can," Ella answered truthfully.

"Are all wolves so," Stella searched for the right words but Crina beat her to it.

"Sexy, intimidating, overwhelming and again, sexy?"

The girls laughed, even Elle joined in.

"Exactly," Stella agreed.

"It's a wolf thing." Crina smiled. "I've yet to see an ugly wolf. Don't ask me why but they are all built solid as if they worked out all of the time. They're handsome, and rarely humble about it."

"Good to know," the sightless Heather smirked. "I'd hate to be mated to an ugly beast and not even know it."

Anna nearly spewed the hot chocolate she had just sipped as she laughed at Heather's words.

"Have you always been able to find humor in your circumstances?" Elle asked unable to imagine having such an ailment.

"I can't change it," Heather shrugged. "I can either be miserable wanting something that will never be, or I can find joy despite my disability. It also seems to make other people more comfortable around me if they see that I'm not a walking nerve of sensitivity over it."

"I have the highest respect for you, Heather Banks. You are a female of great worth and your mate will be blessed to have you." Elle's voice rung with sincerity and Heather smiled, treasuring the words for what they were—acceptance.

Chapter 18

"I ache everywhere. Breathing takes effort and moving is out of the question. There was a time that I thought working as a waitress at a restaurant with rude tourists was quite possibly the worst fate ever. Nope, not even close. Being sliced up be a psychotic fae, now that was something to rate up there with things never to do. Waitressing is looking pretty good in this moment, like dove chocolate good." ~ Kara

"Do you feel that, Peri?" Adam asked as they walked through the wet town of Forks.

"If you mean that nasty, greasy slime that's gliding across our skin, then yes I feel it," she answered as she searched for the trail of magic she knew her sister would have left for her.

Lucian lifted his nose into the air and took a deep breath. "I smell her," he told his mate. He pointed left down a side street. "She went that way."

The group turned and headed in the direction Lucian had indicated.

"Adam keep that cloak up back there," Peri called back to the fae who took up the rear of the group while Peri took up the lead casting her own cloak over the group.

"So just for fun, what are the chances that we'll run into some vampires?" Sally asked lightly.

The group chuckled while Peri rolled her eyes. "Let's just deal with one psycho at a time, okay, healer."

"So they do exist?" Sally gasped.

"You should know by now, Sally Miklos, that there are some things that prowl the night that are better left alone never to be discovered. Let's just leave it at that alright?" Peri closed the topic as simple as that.

Lucian continued to smell the air, following the scent of Lorelle and the foul residue of magic she had left behind. As the town began to end and trees became their surroundings the group grew more and more edgy. The wolves were all letting out low rumbles despite being in their human forms. Suddenly they emerged onto a beach. The ocean stretched out before them as far as the eye could see.

"It's harder to smell her here," Lucian told Peri. "The salt in the air is masking it."

"I can still feel her magic," Peri assured him. "We can follow it."

Peri led them on as her gut began to twist with uneasiness. As they came upon a cave where the trail of her sister's magic was the most concentrated, Peri felt her heart stutter as she saw the message written in blood across the cave wall. Once again she was the only one who could see it, because none of the others appeared to be on the verge of losing their cool. Her eyes roamed across the message over and over and with each pass she grew more and more angry.

"What is it, Peri?" Lucian asked, picking up on her rage.

Peri began reciting the words, slowly at first, then increasingly faster as her voice became louder and louder:

"No chance of rescue ever existed,
So easily you have been misled,

Running blindly you persisted,
Like a fool believing what I said.
Lives will be lost the price for your choice
Your chance for victory has now passed,
This I decree, this promise I voice.
For once dear sister you came in last
Your precious magic is now bound,
You cannot pursue, you cannot save,
What you have lost is never to be found,
While you forever rot in this cave."

"BLOODY HELL!" Peri's voice rebounded off of the walls of the cave as her power swelled inside of her. "She thinks to trap me? She thinks to hold me hostage with magic that she has stolen from another? Who the hell does she think she is! She led me on a wild goose chase and like the fool she declared me to be I ran after her with my head up my ass."

"So this was a distraction," Dillon spoke up. "Why would she need to distract you, Perizada?"

She turned to look at the Alpha and everyone near her took a step back, except for Lucian who took a step towards her. "She's going after the three healers we saved." And as the words left her mouth she knew without a doubt that was what her sister was doing. Elle and Crina were tough, but if Lorelle was sharing dark magic with someone powerful they would be no match for her.

"Crina," Adam roared as he realized it just as Peri did. "Peri we have to go now!"

"We're going with you," Dalton spoke up for the first time since he had met the group.

Peri narrowed her eyes at the wolf but then dismissed the suspicion and looked back to Adam.

"She has bound our powers," she told him and her words were cold as ice.

Adam turned with a snarl worthy of a dominate wolf slamming his hand into the cave wall causing it to rumble and shake around them.

"She may have bound your powers, but I would bet that she did not think to bind ours," Lucian told her calmly.

Peri turned to look at her mate and as their eyes met, she felt it. He was pushing the strength and power of his wolf into her. She closed her eyes and let herself sink into the rightness of it. He was hers. What was his belonged to her as well, and he was giving it freely. A minute later she felt even more power flooding her and she recognized it as Adam's. She could feel Lucian's uneasiness at this but he allowed it because he knew that, in that moment, if they were to escape, there was no room for jealousy. Peri's eyes snapped open when yet again more power rushed in. This power was pure and good. Sally was standing in front of her touching her hand, smiling sweetly as she shared the healing magic that lived inside of her.

Peri felt the light inside of her begin to shine outward, as her glory was revealed. She was radiant, filling the dark cave with light and warmth. But underneath all of that radiance she was pissed. "If you are coming with us then you had better find a placc to touch myself or Adam because we can't come back for anyone," she told them as she closed her eyes and focused on the magic Lorelle had used. "Adam, be ready to flash in a moment's notice, I will only be able to force the door open briefly."

268

Peri pushed all of the magic rippling through her into the web of darkness that Lorelle had cast on the cave, ripping and tearing though the strands. Her teeth clenched together painfully as she willed the opening in the spell to become large enough for them to flash through. Just a little bigger, almost there, her heart raced and finally the straining hole was big enough. She held it, even as the web tried to begin to repair itself. *Not on my watch*, she thought as she yelled. "NOW!" She and Adam flashed and she knew they had just barely made it before the web had once again mended the threads that Peri had destroyed.

They arrived outside the veil opening instead of in Farie where they should have ended up.

"What has she done now?" Sorin growled as his patience at not being able to get to his mate began to wane.

Peri focused on the entrance to her realm as she shut out the grumbling voices around her. Her teeth bit into her lip and her hands clenched at her sides. She had to get to those girls. She couldn't let Lorelle take them, not after already failing two of the other healers. If she lost these healers Peri wouldn't be able to live with herself. If they suffered an ill fate, which was sure to happen in Lorelle's care, then there would be no peace for her ever again, mate or no mate, Peri would meet her end.

"That isn't going to happen," Lucian growled in her ear as he wrapped an arm around her drawing her back firmly into his chest. "We will save them, Peri. We will save them and I will destroy your sister for putting you in this position. I hope you will not hate me, but I have no mercy for someone who would torture my mate in such a way." He pulled her closer and kissed her neck. "Do not count me out just yet, beloved. I do not make promises that I cannot keep."

Peri's head fell forward as she felt the weight of the task before them fall squarely on her shoulders. "Even if we save them, Lucian, what will be left of them if we get there before they are killed? You know why healers are sought after. You know the pain they will suffer. I've seen the devastation wrought on the tortured mind. It is not pretty, and should they not find their true mate, then the probability of them ever healing from such an experience is slim to none."

"Then it is better we get there sooner rather than later," he kissed her neck one more time before letting her go. "Get us through that veil, Perizada." Through their bond he added, *"I have complete faith in you, beloved mate. Draw on the love for those girls rather than the rage for your sister. Allow it to fuel your power. There is no power greater than sacrificial love. It can destroy the strongest of enemies, pierce the darkest of nights, and heal the most damaged of hearts."*

"Wolf, I love you, truly I do and because of that I have to be honest. The Hallmark card moments kind of make me throw up in my mouth."

Lucian chuckled as he watched his mate begin to weave her power into a spell. *"Then I suppose you should learn to enjoy the taste because, as you know, we old ones tend to be set in our ways."*

Peri didn't turn around but let out a dramatic sigh. *"Well there goes my idea of changing every annoying thing about you and shaping you into a docile little lap dog I can swat with a newspaper when I'm irritated with you."*

"Sorry to disappoint you," he teased.

"That's okay, wolf. I haven't given up on turning you into a nice handbag or rug."

∞

Elle felt it first and was on her feet moving towards the front door as she yelled. "Spread out, do not clump together."

Crina was right behind her, all the while motioning with her arms for the healers to spread a part as Elle had instructed.

Stella hurried over to the farthest wall in the kitchen while Heather headed for the living room and Anna for the stairs.

"Why do they want us to spread out?" Anna hollered out.

"Some sort of tactical maneuver," Heather offered.

Crina hurried in from the dining room and nodded her approval when she saw that the healers had done what they were told. "Lorelle is here. If you are clumped together it would be easier for her to flash all of you away if she gets past us, which she won't," she added with a low growl.

"I'm going out, Crina," Elle told her from her position at the front door. "I think Peri has the house warded so only certain fae can flash inside, but I don't know if she revoked the invitation from Lorelle."

"Be careful Elle. Sorin will tan your pretty hide if you get yourself hurt."

Elle grinned. "Now where is the fun in being careful?"

The she-wolf laughed and waved her off. Elle slipped out of the door closing it behind her.

Contrary to her words, she stepped cautiously away from the house, her eyes roaming quickly around her, searching for any sign of Lorelle. She could feel her, knew she was there, but couldn't see her. She nearly growled in frustration as she made a circle around the house with no results. Finally fed up she yelled, "Come out, come out wherever you are." She waited, still nothing. "Surely you aren't scared of little'ol me, Lorelle, you're twice my age. You have to know your power dwarfs my own." Again she waited. She knew that if she could strike just the right nerve Lorelle would reveal herself out of sheer pride. "Peri was right; you are too scared to fight your own battles so you hide behind those more powerful than yourself. Come back when you're ready to face me like a warrior." She turned to go back into the house, but when she felt the heat of magic flying towards her she turned and threw up her hands to block the cheap shot Lorelle had just taken.

Lorelle stepped from the cover of the woods, her long flowing dress so similar to those Peri wore, only hers was tattered and worn. It might have been black at one time but now it was a dingy gray that made her skin look pale and sickly.

"It is not wise to taunt a high fae, Elle, mate of Sorin, warrior of the fae. You provoke that which you cannot defeat." Lorelle's voice carried on the wind and seemed to caress Elle's face.

Elle brushed it away, cringing at the evil that saturated it and met Lorelle's gaze. "You are not welcome here, Lorelle. You have betrayed your race. You have worked with the enemy. You have murdered, and for those things you have been sentenced to death by the high council. For the sake of your sister, surrender yourself and end this madness."

Lorelle threw her head back and laughed. "Do you take me for a fool?" She asked as the laughter died down leaving an evil smirk on her thin lips. "I came for the healers. We can do this the easy way, in which you simply hand them over, or I can relieve you and your wolf of your duty. And by *relieve you of your duty* I mean rip your still beating hearts from your bodies." Lorelle, of course, had no plan to kill them, but there was no need for them to know that.

"I would never hand over innocents to one such as you. You will have to kill me first."

"So be it," Lorelle said coolly as she threw out her hands releasing a black fog that swirled around Elle and the house. She began walking towards Elle, using the vapor as cover. Had she not been focusing very closely, she would have missed the sound of metal whooshing through the air. She side stepped to the right just in time to see a silver knife fly past her. She wondered why a knife thrown by Elle would not hit its mark. The knives fashioned by the fae were spelled to always hit their intended target, but Elle's had flown right by her. She continued forward, dodging over and over the knives that Elle hurled at her. Getting closer to the house she began to wonder why she wasn't closing in on the fae. Elle had been right there in front of it. Lorelle turned as she slowed the fog from thickening and began to be able to see around her. She was less than twenty feet from the front door of the house where her prey stood, with an, *I know something you don't know* smirk on her face.

It didn't take her long to find out what that something was. Lorelle heard a low growl behind her and turned just in time to see a huge grey wolf lunge for her. She didn't have time to get her hands up before the wolf knocked her to the ground. She hit the earth with a cruel thud knocking the air from her lungs. Gasping for air she turned her head back to see the wolf running and she shot out her hand, her dark magic heading full speed for it. She knew she had hit her mark when she heard a loud yelp from the wolf. It wasn't a killing blow, it was more of a mess with me and I'll fry your tail off blow.

Lorelle climbed to her feet, still gasping for air and caught sight of Elle. She had her hands raised and her lips moved as she weaved some sort of spell. Light shot from her hands coming straight at Lorelle, but she easily reflected the spell, sending it hurtling back towards its creator. With Elle caught off guard by the move, Lorelle took advantage and shot her own blast of light. She watched as the bolt hit home and the younger fae crumbled to the ground. She wasn't out, not yet. She looked up at Lorelle with rage in her eyes and once again flung her hand out. Fire erupted from her palm and Lorelle felt the heat of it on her face just as she doused it with water from her own hands. She could see the frustration in Elle's face and was completely surprised when the female took off at a dead run heading straight for her.

Lorelle started throwing spell after spell at the fae but one after another Elle deflected them. She dodged and ducked until suddenly she was upon her and plowed straight into Lorelle's stomach. Once again the air was forced from her lungs but she somehow managed to stay on her feet. Elle stepped back and swung out her arm and Lorelle felt the palm across her face just as she heard the loud smack.

Before she could raise her arms Elle was punching her in the stomach, kicking her shins, and slapping the side of her head just over her ears causing a ringing sound that disoriented her even more. She couldn't believe it; she was getting her ass kicked without magic. She continued to take the abuse Elle dealt out, but while the other fae was distracted she let her power build inside of her. She would let the young fae think she was winning and then she would hit her with a jolt that she would never forget and if she was lucky, she might live through.

∞

Heather could hear the shouts and growls outside. She could feel the heat from the power the two fae were wielding and wondered, not for the first time, what the things that emitted the noises looked like. Energy built around her, so much that it was nearly strangling her. She heard Crina's loud yelp and since then had not heard another sound from the wolf. That had her worried. If Elle was out there dealing with Lorelle alone, what chance did she have at beating her? Perhaps if Lorelle caught sight of one of the healers she so desperately wanted it would distract her. And who better than a poor little blind girl who couldn't defend herself to walk out into the fray?

Heather took a step towards the door, and another and another. Her mind was made up. She could not just stand here and do nothing, not when she could help. She knew Peri and the others would be back very, very soon. Elle and Crina would have

275

done that mind to mind stuff they have with their mates. They would have called in the cavalry, so she only needed to keep Lorelle distracted long enough for them to arrive. When she knew she was near the door she reached for the knob, turned it, and jerked the door open before her fears could keep her from acting. Stepping out quickly and closing it behind her she turned towards the noise. She could hear Elle's rapid pants along with flesh connecting to flesh. It sounded like a good old fashioned brawl.

Heather made her way to the railing in front of the house, purposely bumping into it, cursing in frustration as if she hadn't known it was there. She reached her arms out in front of her as if searching for something to guide her, feeling like a fool, but she figured it would contribute to the whole helpless look.

"Heather, go back inside!" She heard Elle's command and ignored it. She continued her stumbling trek forward, all the while listening to the sounds around her, tasting the power as she breathed in and smelling the rotten magic that no doubt rolled off of Lorelle.

"Is she blind?" Lorelle's voice asked incredulously. "Seriously, a blind healer?"

Heather heard another smacking sound and guessed Elle must have made contact once again with Lorelle's face. It was in that moment that Heather realized what she was feeling. Something was tugging on her own emotions and all at once she felt her anger rising, along with a sense of hopelessness that nearly dropped her to her knees. Lorelle was feeding her magic with their negative emotions; she had to be. What else could she possibly draw dark magic from in a place like Farie? She was taking the butt kicking

276

from Elle while she was storing up magic inside of her and Heather imagined it wasn't just because she wanted to save it for a rainy day.

"Elle you have to get away from her," Heather shouted. "She's going to blow any second; you have to get away!"

Elle did not heed Heather's warnings. She continued her ruthless assault and only paused when all of the sudden the air filled with a different kind of power. The ground began to shake and growl, snarls and barks filled with the promise of death resounded through the air. Heather couldn't see them, but she felt them. *The cavalry*, she thought with relief, *we're going to be alright*. She repeated this thought over and over but even with help on the way, her gut screamed that they weren't out of the woods yet.

"LORELLE!" A voice like thunder boomed and Heather had to cover her sensitive ears. She knew that voice—Peri—and she sounded pissed.

She started to take a step back but was stopped when a strong grip wrapped around her arm. Fingernails dug into her flesh and she stumbled when she was jerked up against the person holding her. She knew it was Lorelle, simply by the evil that surrounded her. She tried to jerk her arm free but Lorelle's grip was too tight.

"One healer will have to do for now," Lorelle said loudly. "But don't worry, sister. We will return whatever is left of her when we're done." Heather sensed a change in the air and knew Lorelle was doing that thing they called flashing. Mere seconds later she tripped as their feet hit solid ground and Lorelle shoved her forward.

"Through the veil with you healer, and don't think you can escape. Even if you could see you are no match for me." She pushed her again and Heather stumbled forward. Her body felt weightless as she moved forward until suddenly she was standing on solid ground again. At the same time, Lorelle followed closely behind her. She heard the fae's vehement cursing and then felt her vice-like grip once again grab her arm. Whatever they had just passed through had been painful for Lorelle. Her strong hand was shaking and her breathing was labored. Heather briefly entertained the idea of trying to escape. Perhaps whatever pained Lorelle had weakened her enough that the healer could get away. But then she nearly laughed at the idea of her running head long into a tree because she wasn't familiar with her surroundings. For now she would have to cooperate. But the great thing about being blind was that people always underestimated her. They thought her helpless, unable to act independently or care for herself. *Morons*, she snorted to herself. Lorelle would soon let her guard down and when she did Heather would be ready and then she would show the wicked witch just how helpless she wasn't.

∞

Kara was still unconscious when Jewel's head jerked up from the brief nap she had allowed herself. She felt Lorelle's familiar dark power and just like usual she was suddenly standing before them. Only this time she wasn't alone.

"I brought you two a new playmate," Lorelle sneered as she pushed the girl towards them. She stumbled a bit before righting herself and then turned, keeping the fae in front of her.

"That was not necessary," Jewel said without inflection in her voice. "We are quite fine on our own."

Lorelle shook her head with a huff of laughter. "Just think of it this way, little Jewel, the more there are of you, the longer it will be in between your turns."

"Turns for what?" Heather asked.

"That's need to know information healer, and you most definitely aren't on the need to know list. Bye," she grinned and then added in a lower, much less friendly voice, "for now." Then she was gone.

"No matter how many times I see her do that, it still freaks me out," Jewel muttered, then looked up at Heather and smiled. "I'm Jewel," she said attempting to sound as welcoming as possible. Though in a place like the dark forest, with evil living in the very air they breathed, it was hard to sound very inviting.

Heather turned to in the direction of Jewel's voice. "I'm Heather. At the risk of sounding like an utter lunatic, I take it that you are a gypsy healer as well?"

Jewel nodded but then realized when there was no reaction from Heather, that what she had initially suspected was true—she was blind. "That's the rumor," she added to her nod.

"I'm sure you've deduced by now that I can't see jack, so could you please fill me in on where the wicked witch has deposited us?"

"No worries, I hear Jack isn't very handsome so you aren't missing anything."

"That was pretty good," Heather chuckled. "Just shy of being lame, but good nonetheless."

"Sorry, I take my laughs where I can get them these days. Anyways, to answer your question, it's a forest, but not your typical nice, full of life forest. It's dead, with darkness and malice cloaking everything."

Heather grinned. "Good description."

Jewels eyes filled with the tiniest bit of joy at the compliment. "Thanks, I read a lot. Like, really a lot."

"Me too," Heather said seriously. When Jewel didn't respond she snickered cheekily. "I'm just yanking your chain, Jewel. Although I do read some, just not in the same manner you do, obviously."

Jewel let out a cautious snicker, still unsure of whether it would be rude to join in on the joke.

"Is there another healer here?" Heather asked. "Lorelle said she brought you *two* a new playmate."

"Oh yes," Jewel said quickly. "Kara is here but she's unconscious."

"Is she going to be alright?"

"I think so or at least I hope so. She's lost a lot of blood," Jewel explained. "Lorelle used her in some sort of spell that her master conjured."

"So Lorelle isn't acting by herself." Heather made it a statement instead of a question.

"Nope, she's just the puppet. There is definitely someone more powerful pulling her strings," Jewel agreed.

"How long have you two been here?" Heather asked as she slowly took a seat on the ground where she stood.

Jewel made a clucking sound with her tongue as she thought about her answer. "Honestly, I have no idea. Night and day sort of run together here. Lorelle brings us some sort of bread stuff every now and then. For something so small it is rather filling." She paused to see if the other girl would ask anything else and when she didn't she asked her own question. "Have you always known you were a gypsy healer?"

Heather laughed though it wasn't an entirely happy sound. "Never had a clue and never would have thought such a thing existed. I'm a blind seeing eye dog trainer from a little town in Texas. The most exciting thing that happens there is someone's prize bull escaping and happily giving out free stud services to any cow in heat."

A burst of unexpected laughter shot out of Jewel as she pictured the very descriptive scenario from Heather. Had she never read any western books, she would be clueless about the whole stud remark, but as it were, she was quite clear on those types of services. She regained control of herself and wiped her eyes from the moisture that had gathered there. "So if Lorelle isn't the one who told you what you are, then who did?"

"Well, apparently like any good story has its villains, so too it has its heroes. Lorelle has a sister named Perizada and she is a high fae, only she hasn't crossed over to the dark side. Peri has been trying to get to us supposed gypsy healers before Lorelle could. Unfortunately she didn't make it to you and Kara."

Jewel felt a pang of jealousy in her chest at not having been found by the good team first, but then quickly pushed it away. If she hadn't been here she wouldn't have been able to help Kara.

"So what's your story?" Heathers question pulled Jewel from her pity party.

"Well," Jewel began, her voice taking on a story telling tone. "I'm from a suburb in Chicago. I live with my mother and I'm seventeen years old. I work at the library and in the fall I will be…," she paused then corrected herself. "I would have been starting my senior year in high school."

"So no dad in the picture, what does your mom do?" Before Jewel could answer Heather quickly added, "And do you think she's freaking out by now?"

"If you didn't know about all this gypsy healer stuff, I would be totally embarrassed to tell you this, but as it is I'm not sure how much stranger things could get. My mom is a fortune teller. She's the community joke to most people, making me the teen joke, hence the working at the library and escaping into adventures buried in the pages of books. And," she took a deep breath and let it out, "no I don't think she *is* freaking out right now. She's not freaking out because she had a premonition that this, or something supernatural like this, was going to happen to me."

Heather considered the girl's words for several minutes. She wondered if, even though her mother knew that Jewel would be facing something dark, something not of this world, she was still scared for her daughter. She wondered what it would be like to have someone worrying for her. She tossed that thought out the window. She was not one to wallow in self-pity, or dwell on the *what might have beens*, or the *what she wished could be*. She chose to live in the present and accept it for the gift it was.

Something that Jewel had said was nagging at her. *I'm not sure how much stranger things could get*—those were her words. It was then that she realized just how little Jewel truly knew.

"Not to burst your bubble Jewels, but things are going to get quite a bit stranger for you and Kara."

"What kind of strange?" Jewel slowly asked.

"The furry kind." Heather's vague answer did not appease the hungry-for-knowledge librarian.

"Specifics," she coaxed.

Heather blew out a puff of air before she answered. "The werewolf kind of strange."

Jewel was shocked silent, her eyes growing impossibly wide, before she finally whispered. "Shut the front door."

"There would be no point," Heather said dryly. "These wolves would growl and snarl and rip your door to shreds."

Chapter 19

"Pain must come before relief can happen. Sorrow must be endured for joy to be felt. Darkness must descend for light to reveal. Battles must be fought for peace to follow. Trials must be faced so you can learn to overcome." ~ Great Luna

Peri's head whipped around as Alston, Nissa and Dain, all members of the high fae council, appeared behind them. "Could you possibly move any slower?" She growled at the group of her peers. "She was RIGHT HERE! In our grasp! And where were you three?"

"We knew she had arrived Peri, but we could not pinpoint her location. She had dark magic assisting her," Alston told her sounding every bit as frustrated.

"Dark magic? Really? Imagine that, the sister that was in cahoots with the warlock that tried to kill off half the wolves is meddling in dark magic. What did you expect she would be using, Chris Angel's Magic for Beginners?" Her words were met with silence as they each realized the implications of what just happened. She should have flashed, Peri thought to herself, but instead she ran with the wolves, ran with her mate, where she had felt she belonged. If she had flashed, might have been able to keep Lorelle from taking Heather. But her choice had cost them and it was a high price.

"I am sorry that we were not able to stop her, Perizada," Dain spoke up, his deep, cool voice breaking through the stillness that had descended after the magic had dissipated.

Peri didn't look at him but simply waved him off, too irritated to placate anyone at the moment.

"I'm sorry as well, Peri," Elle spoke up gripping her side where one of Lorelle's spells had made contact. "I told Heather to go inside. I told them to *stay* inside. I'm sorry I couldn't protect her."

"It's not your fault, Elle," Sorin said softly as he pulled her into the shelter of his arms.

Crina came limping over, still in her wolf form and whined at Peri's feet. Peri stared at the she-wolf and her gut clenched at the injury her sister had caused. Here was another one hurt while under Peri's protection. If anyone had failed, it was her. The fae stared at the ground at her feet, unblinking.

"Sally, fix Elle and Crina up please," Adam said after a few moments had passed in silence. "I'll get these four wolves some clothes so they can phase back."

Adam jumped up the steps and was through the front door and back in a flash, bringing some T-shirts and wind pants, which the wolves took between their teeth. They trotted in a line around to the side of the house. Barely a moment later, four men came jogging back fully clothed.

"Where are the other healers?" Dillon asked breathlessly, scanning the house and the surrounding area, a slight look of panic in his eyes.

"Dillon, I understand that you are concerned for the healers," Adam began in a calm voice. "Obviously, the implications are staggering." A low rumbled rolled out of the three wolves that belonged to Dillon.

285

"Easy, boys," Adam said slowly. "You can't go barging in there salivating over them like they are a couple of pieces of prime rib. It's been explained to them that they will have a mate, but who that male is could take time to find. They haven't had any time to adjust to this world. We need to bring them along slowly. Let us go in first and prepare them, give them the respect they deserve." Dillon gave Adam a slight bow of his head but his eyes held the fae's.

Lucian's head nudged his mate's leg pushing her in the direction of the house. Before she turned to go Alston spoke up. "When were you going to inform the council of your findings?"

Peri's eyes narrowed on her long time comrade. "When it was time for me to tell you. This mission was given to me, not the council. And when the Great Luna decides that it is a matter for the fae council, then I will gladly inform you of anything and everything. Until then please keep the information you have learned today to yourselves and for the love of sane beings everywhere if Lorelle is within your grasp don't let her get away." She turned her back on them without waiting to see if they would respond, effectively dismissing them.

Lucian nudged her again, she started moving and her hand found his warm fur and she took a handful of it and held on. She needed his strength, needed his unending composure, because she was on the verge...of something. What that something was, she wasn't sure. Maybe on the verge of snapping, or having a meltdown of epic proportion, or quite possibly she was on the verge of nothing, of just shutting down. For the first time in a very, very, *very* long time Peri felt completely inadequate for the task she'd been given.

Sally shuttered at the eerie silence that filled the room as everyone but the Colorado wolves gathered. Costin, Crina and Lucian had phased and dressed. Sally had worked her magic, literally, on Crina and Elle. Apart from a few lingering bumps and bruises, both ladies were now almost fully healed, and Stella and Anna looked thoroughly shell shocked. All in all, it was an exhausted, defeated looking bunch. It tore at her heart to see her pack mates, her comrades in such devastation. They were all natural born protectors. Failing was not an option, losing was not in the cards and cracking under pressure had no place in them. They were warriors of the most lethal and dedicated kind. Sally knew what they were feeling. Her mate's emotions were pouring into her and even she, a healer could not bring him comfort.

In that moment she had never wished so much that Jen, her out spoken, fiercely loyal and loving, albeit sometimes embarrassing friend, was with her. Jen would know what to say to rally the troops. Jen would be able to step up and tell them that they better check their emotions at the door, flip totally into battle mode and lock and load. She'd probably add the word bitches to the end of her speech because that was her style, but regardless of that she would inspire them. As the silence continued and the blank stares remained on their faces, Sally dug deep. She reached for her inner Jen, the place where she found strength, courage and the ability to be a badass. Stepping away from Costin into the middle of the room, she cleared her throat. Her eyes met each and every person's. She let them see that though she was a healer, though she brought comfort and light when they needed it, she could also bring strength and the willingness to fight even though there seemed no chance at victory.

"We have become pack." Her voice was strong as she turned in a slow circle. "Through the tribulations we have faced, the pain we have suffered, and support we have given one another. That is what pack is. It doesn't matter if you are fae, wolf, or healer. Joined together in a common goal, with different strengths and weaknesses yet learning to thrive because of them and not in spite of them, is what it means to be pack. And when we endure adversity, when darkness gains a foothold, when one of our own is battered, bruised or incapacitated, pack doesn't hang our heads in defeat. We yell the battle cry so our enemies will know that we are coming. They are our prey and the hunt is our specialty. Three of our own are incapacitated. We will not waste another minute with our eyes down, our tails tucked between our legs wallowing in what we failed to do. We will try again, and again and again, and the only way we will stop is if every single one of us is lying dead on the battle field." She turned and looked at Peri, her eyes narrowing in on the fae. "Perizada, high fae, mate to Lucian, lead your pack or get out of our way."

Peri's jaw tightened as she stared at the one person least likely to say such a thing to her. The bold command had obviously caught everyone else off guard as well because there was a collective sharp inhale around the room. She took a step towards her and another, keeping any emotion from showing on her face. When she stood less than a foot away she leaned in next to Sally's ear. "Remind me not to let you watch Braveheart anymore." A sigh mixed with chuckles reminded Peri just how good wolf hearing was.

"The healer is right," Peri looked at her mate, met his cool stare and nodded. "You know the dark forest, you should lead us." His only response was slight tilt of his head in conceding her request. "Now…," Peri, beginning to sound and look more like herself, rubbed her hands together as she looked at Anna and Stella.

"Why does that look on her face make me want to run?" Anna muttered as she leaned closer to Stella.

"Probably because something humorous is about to happen at our expense," Stella answered not taking her eyes off the fae.

"Sally," Peri glanced at the healer. "Let Dillon know that we are ready for the first one. Only one," she warned.

The snarl from Costin just about caused the girls to yelp. "I don't think so!" he barked at the fae.

"Oh yes, what was I thinking?" Peri's said as she rolled her eyes. "Adam, you do the honors."

Adam nodded and headed for the door. Peri looked at the two girls with mirth in her eyes.

"What was that all about?" Anna whispered.

"Because Costin has severe *obsessive-over-his-mate issues*, he seems a bit reluctant to send his pretty little healer out amongst the other wolves, especially wolves of a different pack than his own," Peri replied. "Adam is not a wolf, though if he was he would be pretty high up on the dominance scale. As such, Dillon will not feel challenged by him. If I sent Costin, or heaven forbid, Lucian, Dillon's wolf might feel the need to assert his dominance as an Alpha. Frankly we don't have time for a pissing contest."

"Mmm," Anna hummed. "That totally makes sense."

Stella's brow rose as she looked at her. "Really?"

Anna puckered her lips and shook her head. "No. Not really."

"Good because I was about to feel like a clueless twit," Stella quipped.

The room plunged into silence when the door opened and Adam walked back in, followed by an imposing figure.

"What the crap do they feed those guys?" Anna whispered to Stella, who simply shrugged as her eyes stayed fastened on the new comer.

Stella searched for any sign that this male could be what Crina and Elle had described as a true mate. He was over six feet, though only by a few inches. He was handsome, which just seemed to be a common denominator with the male wolves, with sandy brown hair worn short and brown eyes. She could appreciate that his clothes hugged his form nicely showing off a well-toned body. She turned her head slightly in Anna's direction and spoke quietly through clenched teeth. "You feel anything? Any tingles or vibes that make you want to crawl up in his lap and smile adoringly at him?"

Anna snorted. "I got nothing," she admitted.

"Me either," Stella admitted.

This time Anna leaned towards Stella. "He's hot though."

Stella's eyes sparkled in appreciation of him. "That he is, my gypsy friend, that he is."

"He can also hear you," said the object of their perusal.

Both girls had the sense to look embarrassed, though only mildly.

"I'm Lee," the large man stepped forward and held out his hand to Stella, who shook it and then Anna who followed suit. "It is an honor to meet you, and I will admit it is disappointing that one of you beautiful ladies is not mine."

He didn't give them time to respond but quickly stepped away melding into the group that lined the walls.

"Bring in the next one, and tell him to be quicker. The gypsies aren't going to bite." Peri chirped, then added, "Bloody hell this is going to take all day."

"Patience is not a strong suit of yours, is it beloved?" Lucian's smooth voice floated through her mind.

"Not when I have a sibling to kill."

"Fair enough."

Once again the door opened and this time two males followed on Adam's heals. Adam looked at Peri and shrugged. "Dillon's not a patient man."

"Wolf after my own heart," Peri muttered.

"Okay this is just getting ridiculous," Anna huffed as she took in the two males. While they were both large men, one was a veritable giant; his mere presence seemed to take up any space left in the already full room. He was handsome, but not in the traditional sense. His was rugged, raw, and completely unknown to the man himself. It was obvious in the way he carried himself. He was confident, completely sure of himself with his broad shoulders pulled back, yet somehow he still managed to look relaxed. It was not the look of a man who knows how he affects the opposite sex. His face had a strong, square jaw with a sharp, straight nose and his upper lip was slightly plumper than his lower. His cheeks were just high enough that it kept him from having that pretty boy look. His dark brown hair caused his pale blue eyes to look even stranger than they already were in their nearly translucent state. Anna could admit he was quite the specimen, but that was all he was to her.

"Anything?" She asked Stella.

"I get more sensations from my Ben and Jerry's ice cream."

"My name is Dalton Black. It is an honor to meet you." He bowed slightly but did not offer his hand. He also didn't mention that neither female was his true mate. He simply stepped aside to let the other male come forward.

"I'm Phillip Wright," he smiled a boyish grin and kissed each of their hands. "Very nice to meet you ladies." Phillip was leaner than the other two males though taller than Lee. He wore his black hair in a short military cut. His face was rounder, though not less handsome, and his eyes were the color of Spanish moss.

Both girls returned his smile and then looked at Peri who frowned. "Well, that was uneventful."

The door opened one more time and another male walked through who was quite a bit shorter than the first three, though not any less sturdy or handsome.

He nodded to them both as he smiled, though his eyes looked sad. "Healers, I'm Dillon Jacobs, Alpha of the Colorado Pack. It is an honor to meet you, to welcome you into our world, though it is hard not to be disappointed that one of my males was not yours."

Stella didn't know if she should apologize or give condolences to the obviously upset males. She looked at Anna whose pressed together lips and flighty eyes told her she was just as unsure as she was.

"It is what it is," Peri announced. "Now that the butt sniffing is out of the way, it's time to make a plan. Dillon, you and Lucian should come up with a battle strategy. Lucian knows the dark forest. He can tell you what vantage points would be best and where weaknesses lie. For the sake of what little sanity I have left, keep the dominance crap to a minimum."

"Adam, you and Elle will take the wolves outside and fill them in on your abilities and how you can best assist them during the fight."

"Do you really think it will come to that?" asked Elle.

"I have no idea. We know that my sister is working with someone or something powerful. We don't know what we are going to be up against. It's best to prepare for the worst. I won't be caught unawares again." The powerful fae practically ground out the final words through gritted teeth.

She turned to Sally next and smiled a smile that Sally had seen several times, one of which had been just before they had taken on Desdemona, the witch they had killed. It was a smile that told her that Peri couldn't possibly have near as much sanity as she claimed. "Sally dearest," she cooed. "You, Strip Tease over there, and the actual genuine looking gypsy, are coming with me."

"Where exactly is that, Peri?" Sally asked with a friendly smile, but her narrowed eyes belied it.

293

"I've gotta pocket, gotta pocket full of fae stones," Peri sang as she headed towards the kitchen leaving the girls to follow.

"Mother of pearl, she's making up her own words to the tunes of pop songs," Sally groaned.

"Is that a bad thing?" Anna asked.

"Let's just say when Peri starts trying to be creative with today's popular culture it's a *she's gotta plan that's probably going to get us killed* thing."

Stella scrunched up her face. "Good to know."

"I'm pretty sure there is nothing good about that piece of information," Anna pointed out.

"True. However, it might make things a little less tense if we go to our deaths with a catchy jingle stuck in our heads courtesy of our completely not psycho fairy."

Sally laughed as she motioned them to follow her. "You gals are going to fit right in."

Anna's brow rose. "To what? Our coffins?"

∞

"I suppose three is better than none." Volcan's voice grated over every nerve in Lorelle's body. She had dreaded facing him after she had failed to retrieve all of the other healers, but she knew there was no getting around it. Better to deal with his tantrum and then be done with it then stew about it. To her surprise he didn't throw the three year old fit she had been expecting. He acted somewhat rationally, well as rationally as a deranged, power hungry spirit could.

"They are all quite powerful, they just don't know it, don't know what they are capable of," she explained.

"I almost hate to bleed them dry without them being mated. If they were mated they would hold even the power of their mates. But I suppose I shouldn't be stingy."

Lorelle bit her lip to keep from laughing. *Yes, worry about being stingy as if you aren't about to kill three innocent girls by draining their blood to gain their magic,* Lorelle thought. The humor of it was quickly doused as she considered that she wasn't any better than Volcan. Who was she to judge him? She was the one, after all, who had delivered the healers to him. She had sentenced them to a horrible death. She pushed the thoughts from her mind because she was perilously close to feeling as though she still had a conscience.

"When do you want to begin?" She asked him.

"As eager as I am," he purred in a way that made Lorelle throw up in her mouth. "the first healer needs to regain her strength. Let her body replenish her blood so that she isn't weakened. One more day should be adequate. Besides, there is a full moon tomorrow, and a storm is moving in. It would greatly increase the power of the spell to have all of the elements in their natural form to assist us."

Lorelle was about to leave when he added, "There is a clearing near the center of the forest, set up three altars. Use stone, not wood."

Lorelle flashed before she could say something that would get her killed. *Three stone altars? Seriously, who the crap did he think she was? Did he just expect her to pull not only one, but three stone alters from her butt?*

295

Lorelle's thoughts reminded her of how her magic had begun to change. The more time she spent in the dark forest, and the more she practiced dark magic, the harder it was for her to use any of her natural powers. Conjuring an element such as earth and the like, was child's play for most fae. Then again, most fae used their magic only for good, and not for selfish gain.

She flashed to the location he indicated and stood in the center of the clearing. Lorelle slipped her shoes off and pressed her bare feet firmly into the ground, letting the dirt gather in between her toes. The soil there was different from where she had grown up and lived. The soil beyond the dark forest was untouched by Volcan's magic and as such it was full of life. The soil she now stood on was dead. The only way to get anything from the earth around her would be by her own blood.

Once again she called up the fae blade that was endowed with magic. Unlike ordinary blades, fae blades could sense the intentions of the ones who wielded them. If the one holding the blade wanted to inflict a cut that would never heal, the magic in the blade would cause such an outcome. Lorelle ran the edge of it across her palm pressing deep. Quickly the blood swelled up through the parted flesh and ran like tributaries off of a river, into the grooves of her hand and over the edge. She watched in odd fascination as the red drops fell to the ground slowly at first, but then she squeezed her hand into a fist and the pressure pushed the blood out quicker. The drops fell in rapid succession, as though each drop was chasing after the one before it.

Closing her eyes, she focused all of her energy to flow through her body and into the ground beneath her. She pictured the stone altars in her mind and fashioned a spell to conjure the images there around her, solid and real.

"Blood that is spilt by my own desire,
To pay the debt for earth's sacrifice.
Stones, rock and grit begin to conspire,
Build me an altar not one but thrice.
Raise them up until they reach the surface,
Make them strong to hold their prey,
Let them last until they serve their purpose,
This I command and earth will obey."

Lorelle's eyes snapped open at the first tremor. She watched in silent satisfaction as her magic called and the earth answered. The ground rumbled and rolled as trees were uprooted and foliage destroyed. With every quake more and more rocks were pushed up through the soil. She realized when she saw steam rising from the rocks that her spell had gone deep into the earth. In order to fulfill her demands, her magic dug deeper and deeper until enough rocks had risen to form the three altars. One by one the rocks began to meld together until there were three separate large boulders. Then, as though a potter was shaping his clay, the three forms, seemingly maneuvered by invisible hands were smoothed and shaped until there before her sat three stone altars.

For a brief second Lorelle wondered where her applause was. Because frankly, she had just soaked the ground with her own blood, literally moved the earth by her own power, and fashioned three perfect altars where once only useless rocks had been piled. So

297

where in that dark forest of hell was her freaking applause?

"No doubt it's being given to my sister for making butterflies fly out of her butt," she muttered to herself as she walked over to one of the altars. She ran her no longer bleeding hand across the smooth stone. The different colors of the rocks had given the surface a mottled appearance and it would have been beautiful but for the dark liquid that streamed through the tiny crevices. She couldn't touch it, as though a clear sheet of glass separated the liquid from the surface. It moved like a snake, slithering around the stone, in between the different colors and when Lorelle looked closer she realized it was blood, her blood. Her very essence was flowing through her creations, but it wasn't beautiful, or awe inspiring, it was dark. It was deadly and she could hear the altars groaning for more blood, but not hers.

They were crying out for the blood that the healers would spill and as she pressed her hand more firmly to the altar she understood why. Dark magic was not natural. It went against the order of the universe. These stones had not been formed into altars by a master craftsman who understood the process of the undertaking. They had been called, commanded, to form into something that would serve as a platform for death. By her own spell, she had created them only to last until their purpose was served. The stones cried out for their task to be fulfilled so they could return to the ground from which they were so violently ripped. They wanted to return to their true purpose where life could take shelter beneath them and history could be indented and preserved on them and the surface far above the molten center could be protected by them from the earth's heat.

As Lorelle pulled her hand away and took a step back from the altar she knew she should feel something like remorse for what she'd just done. But she didn't see the horror of it. All she could see was the power it took to perform such a spell, power that had come from her and her alone.

Chapter 20

"I think I can, I think I can, I think I can. Isn't that what little ones are taught to say and believe? What happens when no amount of *thinking you can* changes what is? I can think 'til the cows come home that I can fix my eyes, but that doesn't make it so. At what point do we stop saying *I think I can* and just accept that we never will?" ~Heather

"Are you sure you're feeling good enough to walk?" Jewel asked Kara for the fifth or maybe it was sixth time, she couldn't remember.

"If you're not up to it we can just do what the cowboys used to do. When their horses were injured they'd shoot'em and then use their bodies for cover," Heather offered helpfully. "See Jewels, I know things too."

"I'm not sure whether I should be offended that you are comparing my worth to a horse, pissed that you want to shoot me, or creeped out that you would consider hiding behind my dead carcass in order to hide from the psycho fae," Kara admitted gruffly.

"You should in no way be offended at your worth being compared to a horse, Kara," Jewel said matter of fact like. "Horses have been held in high esteem throughout their existence. In the sixteenth century they were considered a symbol of power by the Europeans over the natives of North America. Some Native American's believe that the man and horse's spirit become one over time. And further back than that in the Iron and Bronze ages, horses were even worshiped in some cultures," Jewel finished and smiled helpfully at Kara.

Kara let out a half growl half sigh. "Not helpful, Jewel." Then she turned to look at Heather who was covering her mouth as her shoulders shook with the laughter that she was trying to contain. Kara had liked Heather right from the moment she said *welcome back to the crazy train, unfortunately there are no stops, no returns, and no refunds,* the minute she had regained consciences. From then on she and Jewel had been filling her in on what all had happened while she'd been out of it. For the most part she sensed they were being straight with her, but the little voice in the back of her head that was more often right than not, told her they were holding back something. There was something they weren't sharing and based on how fragile they were treating her it was because they thought she couldn't handle it. She pushed that worry aside when they started walking, only because she was then worried about poor, blind Heather hitting a tree or stumbling on a rock. Heather had quickly nipped that in the bud when she told her she could follow in Jewel's footsteps with no problem because she was about as quiet as a newly weaned heifer—whatever that meant. And then the five foot nothing woman did just that. She walked a few feet behind Jewel and was nearly as good as a shadow following its bearer. After that Kara quit seeing her as helpless and realized that she was a force to be reckoned with. She was older than her by a few years, she had known that before Heather had told her and not because she looked that much older. There was just something in her voice, and a maturity that only came with age.

Yes, she liked Heather, but that didn't mean she wouldn't give as good as she got to her new friend.

"Okay so maybe what Jewel said is helpful because I've decided the correct response to your suggestion is to be creeped out by you wanting to use my carcass. I can totally understand wanting to shoot someone," Kara said pointedly.

"I take that to mean that you are perfectly capable of walking your own blood drained body through this evil infested forest without Jewel asking you if you are alright every ten to fifteen seconds?" Heather asked.

"The only reason you two aren't more concerned is because you don't realize the possible consequences of all the blood Kara lost," Jewel defended.

"Why do I have the feeling she's about to tell us all those possible consequences?" Heather muttered under her breath to Kara.

"A healthy person can only safely lose ten to fifteen percent of their total blood volume without having serious side effects. Without sufficient blood volume dehydration can occur, and in the worst case scenario hypovolemic shock can occur, which means organs are dying because of lack of oxygen." Jewel responded quickly.

"Because she is," Kara answered the question Heather had asked before Jewel spewed knowledge that Kara was convinced was so congested in her head that she couldn't help but blurt it out because of the pressure build up.

Heather took a step towards the sound of Jewel's voice and reached out her hand. Jewel's eyebrows drew together but she took the offered hand.

"I appreciate your knowledge, and undoubtedly it is going to prove very useful, but sometimes we have to use the eyes in our head to understand a situation instead of all the, more often than not, useless facts we know. Look at her, does Kara appear to be in any sort of duress, other than being tired?"

Jewel looked at Kara and then back at Heather. "No."

"Good, problem solved, disaster averted," Heather grinned and released Jewel's hand.

"But," Jewel started only to then snap her lips closed when Heather held her finger up in warning. Jewel started to turn to start walking again but then turned quickly. "What if,"

"Nope," Heather cut her off, and then sighed. "Look, do you want me to sniff her and see if I can smell death on her?"

Jewel's eyes widened. "Can you do that?" She asked as her voice rose in awe of the blind healer.

"No," Heather snapped. "Now turn around and lead us the hell out of here, or *I'm* going to start leading. And let me tell you girls, you know things are bad when everyone has to follow the blind chick."

Kara smiled at Jewel and shrugged when she continued to frown. "Just think how boring things would be without her."

Jewel thought about it a minute as she turned to once again lead them through forest, then hollered over her shoulder, "True and if she gets too annoying I know like a thousand different pressure points on the human body to knock someone out."

"Good to know, Jewels," Heather chuckled good-naturedly.

They walked on in relative silence from that point for several hours, only stopping long enough to give their feet a break and catch their breaths. At one point during one of their breaks they felt the ground beneath them begin to shake. Kara, being familiar with earthquakes from her home in sunny Californ-i-a, immediately sunk close to the ground to keep from falling over in case the shaking worsened. After several minutes of tremors that made their teeth vibrate but never got any worse than that, it suddenly stopped.

"Was that an earthquake?" Jewel asked.

Kara shrugged. "It felt similar to the few I've experienced but, it was much milder."

"Seems like an odd place for there to be an earthquake," Heather pointed out.

That was the most that was said about it. It wasn't something they could do anything about and it didn't really affect them at that moment so they just continued on.

A short time later, Heather had to put her foot down again with Jewel when the gypsy genius started talking about drinking their urine to stay hydrated. That was where Kara and Heather drew the line.

"I'm just saying," Jewel started up again an hour after their last stop. "It's sterile; it's almost like drinking water."

"You know what they say about *almost?*" Heather asked.

"That it only counts with hand grenades?"

"No! That it never drinks its own flippin' pee!" Heather said fiercely as Kara, pulling up the rear, snorted and snickered at their ridiculous argument, one she was sure they never expected to have in their lives. She didn't notice that Jewel had stopped walking and in turn so had Heather. She ran right into Heathers back pushing the smaller girl forward with a loud, "Umph."

"What's the holdup, shorty?" Kara asked.

"Did you seriously just ask the seeing impaired member of our posse what the holdup was? And I will not take time to point out that based on where your breath hits the back of my head you must only be a few inches taller than me," Heather whispered, hurriedly tilting her head back just a tad so Kara would hear her.

"To answer your question Kara," Jewel spoke up, "The holdup is a deranged looking fairy in the middle of the trail."

Kara tensed upon hearing mention of the fae. Lorelle was back and it made her blood run cold. Not with fear, fear was for someone who hadn't been living in the system their whole life. No, her blood ran cold with rage. She had been a victim at one time, and she vowed never to be one again. Lorelle, forcing her still on that table, cutting her arms and face up reminded her of what it was like to be the helpless little rabbit. Kara smiled wickedly as she thought, *Lorelle's going to learn very soon that this little rabbit has fangs.*

"It's refreshing to see females like you three walking through the forest, pushing on and keeping hope alive, pointless, but none the less refreshing," Lorelle said with a grin that would make Cruella Deville look downright friendly.

"What do you expect us to do?" Heather scoffed. "Curl up in a ball, crying while we wait to see what sadistic plan you have up your dirty sleeve?"

Lorelle looked at her fingernails as if suddenly bored by the conversation. "You healers aren't like the ones I remember. I always thought healers should have more spunk especially being mated to such dominant males. But then, I'm just a high fae, what do I know?"

Kara's brow drew together. "Just so you know you are seriously dating yourself when you use words like mated, and males. Marriage and men suffice for it this day and age. I mean, when you use a word like mate, the first place my mind goes is to like animals doing their thing to continue on their species, right?" She looked to the other girls for agreement.

"Totally," Heather nodded.

"Well actually the word mate can imply many things, it just depends how it is being used in a sentence. It can be used as a verb or a noun and if you add the word *less* to it making it a compound word, it becomes an adjective." Jewel's words began to speed up as she started explaining. "And not only that but it's used differently in different cultures."

Lorelle pinched the bridge of her nose and muttered, "The world can't possibly be a better place with these three nut jobs in it." She grabbed the still talking Jewel by the wrist, and then snatched Heather's wrist and pressed it against Kara's so she could hold them both and then flashed.

Lorelle dropped them unceremoniously on the ground as they reappeared in a small clearing. The girls righted themselves, dusted what little dirt wasn't permanently attached to their clothes and looked at their surroundings.

"What's the lay of land ladies," Heather asked as she stood listening for anything new or different from

306

where they had just come. She took in a deep breath and caught the deep smell of fresh dirt, not top soil, but the dirt beneath the uppermost layer that stays moist from the lack of sunlight. It was as if a large pile was sitting directly beside her.

"Circular clearing," Jewel began in a technical, no-nonsense tone. "We are roughly in the center, the surrounding forest is about thirty feet away in all directions. From the direction you face now, at 3:00 clock stands three stone, what I would say look like altars."

"Why does it smell like fresh soil?"

Kara looked down at the ground. "It looks as though the ground has been plowed or something. It's all rough and the grass and plants are mixed in with dirt that was obviously not on the top to begin with."

"My, my," Lorelle cooed. "Aren't you three quite the trio? Now that you've so aptly described to the poor blind girl where she is, can you deduce who the lovely altars are for and what their purpose will serve?"

"We wouldn't deprive you of your moment to share with us the way in which you plan to kill us," Kara said as she took several steps closer to Heather while she spoke so the healer would know where she was. If they were going to survive this, and Kara was determined they would, then they'd have to work together and that meant keeping Heather aware of her surroundings in a place she was unfamiliar with.

Lorelle's face tightened and her lips grew thin across her severe face as she glared at Kara. She reached out her hand muttering a spell under her breath to force the three healers under her will.

307

Suddenly all three girls were moving forward without choosing to do so. Each of them tried in vain to stop, but their limbs were not their own, not anymore. "If you want to be rude, then I will reciprocate in kind. But you should know that unless you're willing to fight dirty, I will win," she sneered at Kara.

Jewel was the only one of the three able to give Lorelle a shred of difficulty. She was aware of the magic that was a part of her very being, unlike Kara and Heather. She wasn't entirely sure how to use it, but as her legs propelled her forward she closed her eyes and reached for the light that was a constant, warm glow in her mind. Just as she had pushed her power into Kara when she healed her, she now attempted to push it to the part of her brain that controlled her willpower. She had no idea how she knew where that was, but it was not the time to question this sudden knowledge. Her feet stalled a foot from the altar. She turned her head and saw that Kara and Heather were climbing up onto the altars. It was apparent that they were not in control of their movements because they were jerky and stiff. Jewel felt power roll over her and then against her will she took a step and then another. It felt as though dirty grease, thick and foul had been poured over her head and rushed down her body coating every inch of her. She ground her teeth together as her hands pressed down on the cold stone forcing her to climb up on to it. And just as her two comrades had done, she laid down on her back with her arms by her sides.

If ever Jewel had wanted to seriously injure someone it was in that moment, stripped of her will, unable to help her friends, watching the possibilities of a new future in a new world slip away. She stared up at the sky that they had been unable to see within the cover of the thick, dark trees of the forest and saw that night was coming. Slowly the blue faded to purple and finally to black. There were no stars, only a full moon staring back at her. *This can't be how it ends,* she thought to herself. *Everything is just beginning, the books I've read unfolding before me as people I didn't think could exist come to life.* She tried to bite back the tears that seeped from her eyes, tried to focus on all the knowledge she had, searching for anything that would help get them out of there. But there was nothing. For all of her supposed gypsy magic, as she lay there waiting for Lorelle and her evil master to do their worst, Jewel realized she was still just a human. Gypsy healer heritage or not, she was no more than a mere mortal.

∞

Kara tried over and over to move something, anything, on her body but it was useless. She felt like one of those quarters people super glue to sidewalks just to watch others try to pick them up. As though someone had poured super glue onto the surface, pressed her body onto it with firm pressure for twenty minutes and boom, presto, stuck for life. There was no pain, not yet anyway, just the unbelievable force that Lorelle used to hold them in place. She wanted to snort at Lorelle's use of magic to subdue them. Kara felt like it was cheating and wondered just how well Lorelle would fare in a good old fashioned street fight. *How would the harpy do then,* she thought and inwardly grinned. She'd learned to hold her own in many of the foster homes she'd been in, and it had been quite a while since she had gone hand to hand with anyone. After everything Lorelle had put them through, and was about to put them through, didn't she have the right to get at least one good fist to the gut or knee to the nose in on the fairy? As she lay looking up at the sky, she realized that it just wasn't in the cards of this game called life for her to have a happily ever after. She had thought, only days or maybe a little longer ago, that she was headed for college. She had thought that she had an actual future with endless possibilities, or at least a future without Pearl the cat lady treating her like one of her pets. Then Lorelle had happened, fae, gypsies and magic were suddenly no longer just a Disney movie away, they were knocking on her front door. The worst part of it all, is that she didn't open the door. It had been shoved open by evil. Kara spent her life avoiding evil— evil people, evil places, evil temptations and yet here she lay like a virgin sacrifice in a pagan ritual. As she closed her eyes to block out the bright moon she remembered something Pearl had said in one of her rare coherent moments. It was when Kara had first arrived at Pearl's house as her foster child. She was fourteen, angry at the world, and desperate for something more. She'd been fighting a lot in school and the second time she was suspended Pearl finally decided to say something.

"What are you fighting for, Kara?" She asked her.

"I don't want to fight, but what else do I do when mean people do mean things to me?"

Pearl walked over to the bed where Kara sat and took her hand. It was rare that Pearl ever touched her so Kara paid attention. *"There are all sorts of evil in this world and there are several ways to deal with them. You are so young and have faced way too much of it and for that I'm sorry. There is a time to fight evil, there is a time to resist evil, but when neither of those things are keeping evil at bay, then there is a time to turn in the opposite direction and run as far and as fast as you can. That is not cowardice; it's wisdom. You pick your own battles. You know the ones you can defeat and the ones you need to do everything in your power to get away from."*

At the time Kara understood what Pearl had been trying get across. But now, after having been snatched up without any warning or time to run away by an evil that is beyond anything she has ever faced, she wondered where it fit in Pearl's lesson. How was she to have dealt with an evil she never saw coming, never knew existed, and had no way to run from?

∞

Heather knew that she should be terrified, and maybe in some unknown place in her mind she was shaking in her boots, but consciously she was holding it together. Maybe it was because she couldn't see their enemy. Maybe she had some irrational enthusiasm because, though the probable outcome was death, it was the most exciting thing that had happened to her since she was fourteen and Corey Sheffield had led her behind the bushes and kissed her, tongue and all. She figured it was a crap shoot to try and figure it out while in immediate danger. So instead she focused her senses on the things around her. Unfortunately there wasn't much to go on. There were no usual night sounds, singing crickets, hooting owls, or the scurrying of critters that emerged only when the sun dropped from the sky. It was silent, except for the breathing of Jewel and Kara, which she knew differed from Lorelle's because theirs was short and rapid. Lorelle breathed as though it was a burden and she could use that time to do something else like kidnap girl scouts or cast evil spells on nice old ladies that would make them crawl across the ceiling like big nasty spiders. She sighed a lot, and huffed irritably, and periodically she even groaned out a long breath. In short, it was annoying as hell. She didn't smell anything different than the soil she had first caught a whiff of when they arrived, and up to that point the temperature had felt fairly comfortable. On the tail end of that thought the temperature dropped and cold crept up the length of her as though she was being slowly sheathed in ice. She sucked in a quick breath and heard the others do the same. Her chest was beginning to feel compressed with the weight of the invisible tomb, the intensity of the pressure on her whole body felt like it would push her straight through the stone she lay on.

"So glad you could join us, Volcan." Lorelle sneered.

Heather guessed that this must be the puppet master Jewel had been speaking of. When he answered the fae, she realized that Lorelle had been just a drop of lava, but Volcan, he was the whole damn volcano.

"As much as it disgusts me to say it, you did well Lorelle. They are powerful. With just these three, unable to control the power and therefore unable to protect it, I'm able to draw on it. It has been a long time since I left the walls of that castle." Volcan's voice was as cold as the atmosphere he created.

312

"Kudos to you for rejoining society, does that mean you don't need to drain the little healers in order to have access to their magic?"

"No." He snarled. "The power I'm siphoning now is nothing compared to what I will gain with their blood. Why, have you suddenly had a change of morals? Is your heart bleeding for the prey that you caught?"

"Wow, you really know how to take a question and run with it. I was just thinking of how less messy things would be if I didn't have to slice them up," she said, with what sounded to Heather like false indignity. "If you're done with your usual three year old moment, can we please get on with it?"

"Start with little Jewel Stone over there. Their blood has to be fresh, warm and full of life in order for me to absorb the power in it," Volcan explained as if he was talking about the weather.

Heather squeezed her eyes closed as the fear she thought she didn't have, reared its ugly head at Jewel's first scream.

Chapter 21

"I've seen fights in the club, drunk fights, gang fights, cop versus gang fights, and I thought I'd seen more blood in my nineteen years than I ever would again. As I stand next to the powerful fae who has tried to prepare us all for the fight that is to come, I know now that it had all been merely a drop in the river of blood that would spill this night." ~Stella

Sally looked out the window to the field where the wolves and fae were practicing battle tactics. She shivered at the memory of a similar field, filled with similar and in this case some of the same people, practicing in much the same way. Only it had been for a different fight. In that field they had prepared to face a witch of incredible power, and wickedness to match. It was the first time in a very long time that the packs worked together for a common goal, something that was bigger than themselves. It was also the first time the fae had rejoined the wolves in battle since the Werewolf Wars, and that was when the last known healer vanished.

Now, in a time where gypsy healers are being rejoined with the wolves they were intended to care for, on *this* field they prepared to fight evil once again. It is a different battle, on a different battleground, with a different foe, but the outcome must be the same. For the sake of the future of the supernatural world, Lorelle and her master must not be allowed to succeed. The power that a gypsy healer holds is pure, its purpose to serve and to heal. Like many things intended for good, it can be twisted and shaped into something different when in the hands of the wrong person. The longer Sally was a part of that world, the more she understood how the thirst for power distorts the truth, corrupts the virtuous, and destroys anything that would thwart it.

"You ready for this?" Peri's voice drew Sally's attention from the window and her thoughts.

She turned to look at the beautiful fae who, when she so chose, could look as harmless as kitten, but lying beneath that façade was a fierce lioness. "Are we ever truly ready?" Sally asked.

"Do we have a choice?" The fae parried.

She thought back over the past year, of all the trials they had faced, all the evil they had destroyed, all the lives they had saved. If not them, then who would have? If Vasile and the wolves hadn't taken a stand, if Peri and the others on the Fae council hadn't left the comfort of their safe realm, if the warlock king Cypher hadn't turned from the dangerous path on which he had started—on and on Sally could list those in the supernatural community who looked at the malevolent forces standing before them and said *if not us, then who*. They didn't put their hands up, take a step back and say this is not my fight. It may sound like they made a choice, a choice to bow out or join in. But when it comes to those who have refused to let darkness have a foothold they don't ever consider there being a choice, because every battle is *their* battle.

"If not us, then who?" Sally answered firmly.

Peri's lips turned up in a knowing smile. "Exactly."

"I know it's a little crowed in here," Dillon spoke above the chatter of the group gathered in what, at one time, seemed like a large living room. But add eight rather large werewolves and a few fae, two with the egos the size of small continents and a room tends to shrink. "We're going to have to deal with it for a few minutes because Lucian and I have a plan and it includes all of you, even the new healers, so everyone needs to be in the know."

From their perch on the stairs, Stella leaned over closer to Anna but kept her eyes on the room in front of her. She turned her head slightly so that her voice wouldn't be projected out into the room for the hearing of the werewolves. "Did you know we were going into battle?"

Anna shook her head. "I thought Peri said all we had to do, and I quote, was hold a pretty stone that showed up whenever the hell it felt like it, throw in some chanting, maybe a little sparks, and if things got really bad there might be a virginal sacrifice and voilà, battle done, sister killed, healers saved…,"

"Get the hot chocolate," they both finished together as Stella nodded. "So she conveniently forgot to add that we would be joining in the war cry."

Anna's lips turned up in a sly smile. "It could be worse," she whispered.

Stella's eyes widened. "What's worse than running into battle with huge freaking werewolves and fae that like sharp pointy things towards a psycho fae hell bent on draining gypsy's of their blood?"

"The werewolves could be on the opposite side of us," Anna pointed out.

Stella thought about the huge wolf that had started out as a man and decided Anna was right, it would be worse to be running head long into a fight with the wolves on the wrong team.

"Sally," Lucian's deep voice rumbled across the room. "You and the healers will be here," he pointed to a crude layout he had drawn on the wall of the dark forest. "There isn't much raised land in the forest—that's the highest point. Once you have done what Peri has tasked you with, you three will then make your way to the battlefield to gather up the other three healers. Two of them have not been around our species yet and we decided they would be most comfortable and trusting of other humans."

Sally nodded, "We're ready."

"More than likely Lorelle is not expecting us this night," he continued. "Her confidence in thinking that she has rattled Perizada and that we will need to regroup for a day or so will be her downfall. Because of this, we are going to attempt to sneak into the dark forest. Neither Peri, nor the other fae will be able to use a cloaking spell because it would draw too much power and Lorelle would recognize it. If ever there was a time that you wanted to see how silent your hunt could be, tonight is that time. Once we've determined their location, we will spread out," he waved his hand in an ark over across the drawing, "and move forward as one, low to the ground for the wolves, and utilizing the trees for the fae. There are eight wolves and three fae. The attack formation will be three wolves, then a fae," Lucian took a pen from his back pocket and made little markers on the wall illustrating his description, "Three wolves, then a fae, two wolves, then a fae.

317

"Do not break the ranks for any reason until Peri gives the command. Wolves, after your time working with the fae today, you know what they are capable of. This battle is not going to be a fang and claw clash. This is a battle between, for lack of a better term—sorceresses. They fight with magic. Because of that we will start out in our human forms. As we draw closer to the enemy we will draw attention away from Peri, Elle, and Adam by phasing to our wolf in their line of sight and in different intervals. This should hopefully help us get close enough to get the three healers."

"Not that I'm questioning you, Lucian," Lee, Dillon's second spoke up. "But how do you know they will at this spot in the forest. Why won't they be at the castle Peri thinks Lorelle has been hiding out in?"

Lucian looked to his mate and nodded for her to answer.

"That's a fair question since I haven't fully explained what I believe my sister is up to," Peri admitted. "Long story short, gypsy healers have always been coveted by dark magic users because their magic is so powerful. But extracting the magic from the healers is difficult. Gypsy magic comes from the life force of the healers—their very essence. To access that power, the healers have to be drained of all their blood. The one stealing their power has to drink the blood directly from the source while she is still alive."

"Like a vampire?" Anna asked.

Peri shook her head. "Well, vampires, if such a thing existed, typically only take blood for nourishment, not power. This is different. There has to be intent and dark magic at play when the blood is being taken if the thief wants to steal the power. I don't even think Lorelle, depraved though she is, would stoop to this level. I think I know who would and I hope I'm wrong. There was once a member of the high fae whose lust for power was stronger than any I've ever seen. By delving into dark magic so deeply, he was eventually able to amass enough power to create his own race of evil witches. We thought him killed centuries ago by a combined force of wolves and the fae."

"How is that possible?" Sally frowned.

"We thought the dark forest was forever wiped from memory. In our vanity, we didn't possibly think his power could best our magic. But we underestimated our opponent. I think Volcan's spirit lived on because of the malevolence that saturated everything in its borders." Peri took a deep breath and let it out slowly before she continued. "So, if I'm correct then Volcan wants to drain these healers for their powers, but he needs Lorelle's help because he doesn't have a physical form, yet. The combined power of the three girls just might be enough to enable him to take back his old form and his old magic.

"The draining of the blood is a ritual. It will be done outside, in the elements. The girls will most likely be incapacitated in some way by Lorelle's magic. If I can draw her attention, it will distract her enough that her spell will fail. Then the girls should be able to get free. All of that to say, this location Lucian has picked is a clearing, one of only a few in the dark forest and just happens to be where Volcan was killed. His blood saturated the earth there, which means that since he is still alive, he can use the magic that would have seeped into the soil. Blood magic is powerful; it's dark, and when it's the blood of the spell caster it's even worse."

"When you asked me to join this little party you said it wasn't going to be life threatening," Adam accused, though his lips held a sly smile.

"I lied."

Adam chuckled. "You can admit that you wanted it to be a surprise for me since you didn't get me a birthday present this century."

"Adam?"

"Yes, Peri."

"Remind me to get you checked out by a veterinarian when this is done. Your excitement for killing things is beginning to become disturbing, and I worry that I will one day soon find you furry, flea infested, licking your butt, and enjoying it way too much."

Then tension in the room dropped considerably as it filled with chuckles and snickers at the bantering. It was what Adam had intended, and was one of the reasons Peri put up with his crap.

"Alright," Dillon took over again. "The fae will be flashing us to our rendezvous point. Costin will assist Sally, Anna and Stella to their location and then rejoin with the pack. Remember," he narrowed his eyes at the group, "this is a hunt until it's not; that means we move as one, in silence until it's time to engage the enemy. Number one priority is to get the girls out, number two, destroy those dumb enough to take what it ours." A collective growl of approval rose up from the wolves in the room.

Anna glanced at Stella who was looking back at her with what she was sure was the same expression on her own face. "What the hell have we gotten ourselves into?"

Stella bit her upper lip. "I'm not sure but I keep waiting for them to paint themselves blue and suddenly acquire a Scottish brogue, or for one of the women to yell, *Spartan, come back with your shield, or on it.*"

∞

"Just for kicks, how are you going to get their blood into your form so you can use their magic?" Lorelle asked as she held the fae blade over Jewel's arm.

She felt his presence surround her as he answered. "Through you of course."

Wonderful, Lorelle thought to herself as she felt Volcan enter her mind and begin to take over. She wanted to fight him, but she wanted even more to not know what he was about to make her do.

Under his influence Lorelle picked up the healer's arm and slit her wrist deep. Blood immediately poured out and, before she could think, Volcan forced her mouth to the wound. She didn't notice the girl's scream. Volcan fixated her attention to the task at hand and she could feel his need, his greediness for the red liquid and she was sure that at any moment she was going to vomit, but she didn't because he wouldn't let her.

The iron rich taste coated her lips and mouth and Volcan used her voice to croon over his feast. As she felt the flow of blood slowing, she licked the wound clean to see that it was knitting itself back together. Volcan jerked her head up to look at the healer's face but only saw fear and pain there. She took the blade again ran it across the same wrist, nothing happened. Her eyes narrowed as she felt Volcan's rage begin to grow. He made her move the blade up a couple inches on her arm and cut. As with the first wound, blood poured out warm, fresh and smelling rich with power. Once again Lorelle found her mouth pressed to the wound nursing it for all it's worth. She could feel Volcan's power getting stronger, could sense him better inside of her as his being seemed to begin to solidify in that realm.

"What is the healer doing!" He snarled in her mind. She pulled back and saw that the second wound was also knitting itself back together staunching the flow of blood.

Volcan moved Lorelle's face over Jewel's, hovering mere inches away. He narrowed her eyes and drew her lips taunt across her face. As he spoke, the voice that emerged from her throat was not her own, it was his. He was getting stronger very quickly. "You think you can stop me, little healer?" He sneered at her. "You think to keep me from having what I want, what I need, in order to accomplish my goal? I will cut every inch of your young, ripe body if I have to. I will begin severing fingers and drinking the blood from the stumps, and if you're lucky I will cut your tongue from your mouth and drink from you like a man to his lover. One way or another, Jewel Stone, I will bleed you dry."

∞

Jewel's mind was a chaotic mess. Pain was pulsing through her arm where the blade had cut her. Even though she had managed to heal herself, the pain didn't go away. Lorelle's rancid breath blew across her face as the words left her mouth, only it wasn't Lorelle speaking, it was the one she had called Volcan. The dry, hoarse sound that shaped into words somehow grated against her skin like coarse sandpaper. Up until that point she had been holding back most of the tears, though she couldn't bite back the screams when she was cut. The pain from the slice radiated to every nerve in her arm, not just at the location of the wound.

Volcan's words were her undoing. The tears flowed freely even as she squeezed her eyes closed unable to watch what was happening to her. She felt another cut and then the nauseating feel of Lorelle's mouth against her flesh. The sucking noises and lapping of her wet tongue made her gut clench and she had to swallow back bile. It was harder to focus this time because her fear had increased, but she slowed her breathing and once again closed the wound. Volcan snarled at her and cut her again, deeper this time so it took a little longer for her to heal it.

She didn't know how long it went on like that. Cut after cut, only for her to heal them again and again, in an attempt to slow him down. *Why*, she thought to herself and cringed when she felt the cool blade begin on her other arm. *Why am I trying to slow him down there by increasing my own suffering? Why not just let myself bleed until the agony stops along with my heart?* Slowly Jewel began to relax and quit fighting the pain.

She quit healing the wounds, and for the first time that she could remember, she stopped thinking all together.

She was drifting, her mind unable to bear the pain any longer, slipped her into darkness. It didn't last long. A faint glow began to form and Jewel felt herself blinking, though she was pretty sure she wasn't awake. Her once cold sweat coated body was now warm and dry. She sat up and was met face to face with a woman who radiated peace. It flowed off of her in waves and her elegant white gown rippled around her. She was beautiful, but that wasn't what Jewel found herself focusing on. Jewel was engrossed by the compassion she saw in her eyes. This woman cared deeply for her, she could see it plain as day, but she didn't understand why.

"I am the Great Luna, mother of the wolves. Even the sound of her voice brought a measure of harmony to Jewel. *"I created them and love them, and I do care for you, Jewel Stone, daughter of Gem, knowledge seeker and gypsy healer to the Canis lupis. You are precious to me, and you are also beloved to one of my wolves. I know you are tired, I know you are in pain and feel that there is no hope, but I have not abandoned you. I will not leave you to this fate, for I have a purpose for you, daughter of mine. Don't give up Jewel. They are coming for you, he is with them and together you will prevail. Use the power inside of you to do what you were created to do—heal. Use the knowledge that comes so easily to you and outsmart your adversary. Remember that the smallest bead of light can illuminate the darkest shadow. Use your light."*

Jewel gasped as she felt the pain return full force. She blinked several times attempting to clear her eyes from the tears. She could feel Lorelle/Volcan still sucking at the wound and she immediately healed it.

She tried to focus on what the Great Luna had told her, tried to grasp at every word but only a few remained in her weak state. Don't give up. They are coming. Heal. Use your light. She wanted to cry out in relief, to somehow let the others know that they were going to be rescued, that this wasn't the end.

The next cut that Volcan made, now that both arms were covered in healed wounds that wouldn't reopen, was just below her left collar bone. Lorelle's hands had ripped part of her shirt open, allowing access to the flesh there. He cut deep, so deep that she wondered if he was attempting to carve out her heart. When she felt the lips on her skin right above her breast she gagged, jerking herself just a little up from the table. Volcan didn't notice, he was too intent on her blood. Jewel attempted to wiggle her toes and felt her lips draw up when she realized that she could. For some reason whatever spell Lorelle had used to keep them immobile was beginning to fail. This only increased her courage even more. She pulled the light and power from inside her soul up and began to heal the deep wound over her heart. She would keep healing the wounds Volcan made, keep attempting to slow him in his progress to drain her. He had already taken enough that she was feeling somewhat dizzy, but she couldn't do anything about that now. She pushed that worry aside and focused on what she could do.

Just hold on, Kara and Heather," she thought to herself. And as another laceration was made the words of one of her favorite quotes came to mind. *"A hero is no braver than an ordinary man, but he is brave five minutes longer."*

Over and over she whispered *just five minutes longer, just five minutes longer.* And though it sometimes came out in pants of anguish, she refused to stop saying it. Help was coming; she just had to hold out five minutes longer.

∞

In all the time that Kara had spent in the homes of those who didn't truly want her, she had seen true pain. She had heard the cries of children enduring terrible things. But in all that time, she had never heard such sounds as the ones coming from Jewel. She didn't consider the girl weak because of it. Kara knew from experience that strength was not measured by the ability to keep silent under torment. Rather, it was measured by those willing to persevere when the consequences of their actions reached beyond the little world they had built around themselves.

She could sense Jewel's power, remembered the way it felt when she had used it to heal her. Kara used that strength to giver herself courage, to persevere. If only for the sake of wanting to be as brave as her friend beside her, she would be, but her bravery was rooted in a deeper desire. She would be courageous, she would fight back, and she would face this evil, for all the times in the past when she wanted to fight for those who needed her but couldn't. For all the bruised faces, broken spirits, every loss of innocence she would endure. She would not go easily or quietly. If Lorelle and the one she called Volcan were going to take the power she barely understood, and the life she had longed for, then she would make them work for it and maybe, just maybe she would make them bleed for it.

∞

Heather didn't understand colors. She couldn't picture images in her mind, but she could feel. The depth of her feelings, the intensity with which she experienced situations in life was in no way hindered by her lack of sight. If anything, because she relied so heavily on her other senses, she could feel things more profoundly. Smells created recognition, whether positive or negative. Touch evoked sensations that captivated all of her attention all at once. Taste opened her mind to the beauty and pleasure of things her eyes would never let her see. Sound, sound was one that she sometimes wished she could turn off. When she heard things, she heard beyond the noise to the intent behind it. Laughter revealed not only joy, but what kind of joy. Weeping was not only sadness, it was also sorrow, relief, need, and so much more. Screams were not just the reaction to pain, but also determination to endure, anger from torment beyond control, or desperation for it to end.

The times when her disability frustrated her most were not when she couldn't find something, or make it to a location because she didn't have help. They were the times when it truly mattered that she *not* be disabled, that regardless of everything she could sense, the only thing she could do was wait, withstand the helpless feelings, and hope. She lay on that stone, her face turned up to a sky that, though she had never seen, had read descriptions of—descriptions that inspired a sense of awe of its vastness. She imagined it was a sky too beautiful for something so horrific to be happening beneath it. Unable to "see" that beauty that might somehow nullify the ugliness, she had to reach deep for an immeasurable abundance of hope. And even though it was probably a vain act, she did it anyway, for in between Jewel's cries and gasps for relief, she heard the young woman's plea, *just five minutes longer*. For those four words uttered by one brilliant, but young soul, she too would hold on, for five minutes longer, and then the next, and the next.

Chapter 22

"I have had those I cared for murdered right before my eyes. I have endured torture at the hands of indescribable evil. I have lived with the consequences of those experiences, and learned to deal in any way necessary. But even with those horrific things in my past, nothing could have prepared me for what we found this night. It will forever be burned into my memory and the only one who could heal it might never be mine."
~Dalton

Lucian pulled Peri to the side after the entire group had been flashed to the dark forest. His skin crawled with the memories of his time in the malicious woods. His throat burned as though a match had lit it on fire as he tasted the foul air. He would not allow the past to keep him from doing what he had to. Peri was his to protect and he would not fail her.

"I need to know that you will not detest me if I slay Lorelle," he told her gently as he ran his thumb across her cheek. "I know that you desire to be the one to destroy her and I understand your reasons for that. But if I get even a remote chance to take her out, I will not hesitate."

She looked up into his eyes and he saw the vulnerability that only she shared with him. Her eyes began to moisten but she quickly bit her lip and stopped the tears. "She needs to be stopped, whether by your teeth or my magic shouldn't be important. You are correct that because of all she has done, how she has betrayed her race, it is my right to snuff her pathetic excuse for a life out. But, if you get there first, I will not hold it against you."

Lucian could see the internal struggle that his mate battled. Whatever her words might say, Lorelle was still her sister, her flesh and blood. Regardless of the circumstances killing family is never, ever easy. He took her face in both his large hands and pulled her closer. He could feel the heat of her breath on his face and just by looking at her luscious mouth he could taste her. "Whatever happens this night, we will be together, in this life, or in the next. I love you, Perizada." He closed his eyes briefly as he thought about all the centuries without her, all the unbearable nights roaming, wondering if he would ever see his family again or find his mate. When he opened his eyes he realized he was not any less surprised to see her before him, real, tangible, his. "It could not have been anyone else, beloved. Do you understand?" His words were desperate and his eyes implored her to understand. "Your light, your passion, your temper, your desire, your loyalty, your love, they are all for me, as mine are for you. Before I go against every instinct I have and allow you to go into battle without me near you I need you to know how incredibly honored I am to be the wolf chosen for you." He closed the space between them and pressed his lips to hers. The familiar heat that flared every time they touched roared to life. Regardless of everything around them, of the looming danger ahead of them, he found himself lost in her taste, her scent, her touch. Only she could so fully command his attention, only she could soothe the beast in him that demanded their mate not fight. He felt her fingers run through his hair, felt her nails against his scalp and then down the back of his neck and he shuttered from the desire they invoked in him. As the kiss grew in intensity, so did his need of her, but now was not the time. *After* he told himself as he pulled back from the kiss with a final nip of her swollen bottom lip.

Peri stared up at the man that held her in his powerful arms. He held her so tightly against his body that she could feel his chest rise and fall as he tried to slow his breathing. He was convinced that *she* had saved him, that he needed her more that he loved her more, but he was wrong. Without Lucian she had simply been existing, nothing more. Life had lost its luster, surprises were very few and very far between, and loneliness was eating a hole inside of her that refused to be filled with useless things. If anybody had needed saving it had been her. He came out of nowhere, blindsiding her and causing her to question everything she had thought she wanted. He was relentless in his pursuit of her, and even when she refused him, he stayed, like the patient hunter he was. He held out until his prey was tired of running. When she finally fell, he had been there to catch her.

"Stay alive, wolf," she told him in her no nonsense voice as she tried to pull her emotions in check so she could do what she had to. "And try not to get injured too badly. Adam's thirst for blood is becoming legendary; I wouldn't put it past him to pounce on one of his allies just for the chance to kill something. I would hate for him to kill you because then I'd have to kill him and Crina would die, and then Vasile would flip his lid. It would just be a mess and you know how I feel about messes."

His eyes glowed as his wolf rose to her teasing. She had learned that Lucian's wolf loved to play, especially with her.

He smiled and it was all wolf. "I will consider your request, but only if you promise to return to me without a scratch on your delectable body."

Peri chuckled and patted his cheek. "You are such a funny male. Ridiculous, but funny."

He took her hand and led her back to where the group gathered around Dillon listening intently to his instruction.

"Lucian and I will take the outside of the arc. Lucian will be on the far right and I will be on the far left. In between us starting on Lucian's side will be Crina, Costin, and Elle. The next three wolves will be Sorin, Phillip, Lee and then Adam. Dalton and I will be to the left of Adam and Peri will be to my far left." He turned to Costin and motioned to the right. "According to Lucian the slightly higher ground is about half a mile in that direction. Take the healers and then get to your position as quickly as possible. We will begin moving forward before you return so take that into consideration when you come back."

Costin took Sally's hand and Anna and Stella fell into step with them as they headed toward the higher ground.

Sally looked at the tiny clearing where Costin had led them and frowned. "I thought he said it was higher ground. All I see is trees, and more trees. How am I supposed to know what to do if I can't see what is happening?"

"Sally mine, you got this. Just do what you were born to do and let the elements do the rest. This land needs healing; there have not been enough healers to accomplish that in a very, very long time. I know you and your partners in crime can do this, I have faith in you." He leaned forward and pressed a kiss to her forehead and she closed her eyes allowing his love for her to wash over her and chase away any doubts.

When he pulled away and turned to go the frown returned. "Is that all I get? A kiss on the forehead?"

Costin turned walking backwards as he gave her one of his heart stopping, dimple grins. "I want to make sure that we both have something to look forward to when this is over. Knowing you are waiting for me tends to make me move a lot quicker. Don't dilly dally, love, I've got plans for you." He winked and then turned, loping off into the trees and out of view.

"Wow," Anna's voice broke the silence.

Stella sighed. "I don't even want a man but even I can't deny that he is…,"

"Finger licking good, drool worthy, breath taking," Sally finished for Stella.

"I think that covers it," Anna agreed as Stella nodded.

Sally let out a snort. "Just wait, one of these days you both will have your own fur balls to pant over, though it's strictly forbidden to do it in front of them. They are nearly unbearable as it is so really stroking their ego is ill advised."

"Do you always talk like that?" Stella eyes crinkled as her mouth quirked up on one side.

Sally shook her head and let out a sigh as she turned and started looking at their ground zero. "No, unfortunately it's a side effect of being bff's with a slightly crazy, possibly delusional, definitely nymphomaniac who likes military lingo during stressful situations."

"Interesting," said Anna as she stood with wide eyes looking a little shell shocked.

"That's putting it mildly," Sally quipped. She pulled the backpack from her shoulders and knelt down to the ground to open it. Stella and Anna moved closer as she removed four stones. They pulsed with power, each emanating a soft glow of a different color.

"Were those in there when we left?" Anna asked. "I thought Peri said they show up whenever they want."

Sally shrugged. "Really they show up for the good guys when they are needed. To answer your question, no they were not in my bag when we left."

"So what would we have done had they not chose to make an appearance?"

"That's where the dancing naked part Peri was talking about would come into play."

"So glad they graced us with their presence," Stella added as she let out a relieved sigh.

"Me too," Sally admitted, but then added. "Because really, dancing naked would do nothing more than make things jiggle that just shouldn't jiggle and expose you to poison ivy in places that were never meant to have rashes." Not acknowledging their bewildered faces, she began to lay the stones out on the ground in a circle the way Peri had showed her. As she put each stone in its place she so named it. She laid down the white stone first. "Air, for the oxygen we breathe, the wind that cools our skin, and the destruction it can cause when necessary. Earth," she continued as she pressed the green stone to the

334

dirt. "For the life that shoots forth from it, for the fruit that it bears, for the home that it provides." Next was the red stone. "Fire, for the heat it provides, for the ways it can be used to bring about change, and for keeping those safe who have wielded it for such a purpose. Last, water," she laid down the final stone, which was blue. "For the life it sustains, for the thirst it quenches, and for the cleansing it provides. Air, earth, fire, water each on their own can cause destruction of unfathomable proportion, but together they not only destroy, they also purge, heal, restore, and renew."

Sally motioned for the two girls to take their places in the tripod around the stones. "I know y'all aren't familiar with your power, but it's there," she explained. "When you call it, the answer will rise up and fill you with energy, peace, and light. Let it flow through you, become a part of you so that way you can learn to direct it. Tonight we need to concentrate pouring our power into the stones. The power within them, combined with our own, will hopefully cleanse this forest of the evil that has saturated it for too long." She looked at both Anna and Stella and smiled using her own light to settle their fears. "Any questions?"

Stella's head tilted to the side as her hand found her hip. "Seriously?"

Sally laughed and it felt good. "Okay, bad choice of words. How about, let's do this."

The two healers smiled at her as they reached for each other's hands. Sally closed her eyes, focusing on her own magic, and hoped silently that Anna and Stella would step up and be what they needed them to be.

She felt the heat of her power flowing through her, surging forth as if it knew just how badly she needed it. Her mind moved quickly to give it direction and purpose. When her magic began pushing toward the stones lying before them, she opened her eyes and watched in fascination. They began to swirl and glow, each of them appearing as if their element was inside. Red burned with fire, blue tossed and rolled as if an ocean was teaming inside. White whipped and spun like the breeze on a windy day, and green looked plush and soft filled with grass and rich foliage. She looked up to see the other two healers, their eyes closed and faces tight with concentration. A small smile appeared on Sally's face as she stared at the two girls who would soon share her fate. These were her people. The wolves were her pack, of course, but these healers were actually like her. She couldn't help but find joy in knowing that she wouldn't be doing this alone. Yes, she had Rachel, but that was so different because Rachel was from a whole different era. But these girls were like Sally. She could relate to them and she hadn't known how badly she had needed that.

Her eyes closed once again and she continued to focus on pouring all of her energy into the stones. She had been in battles before where they had been victorious, and they would be again tonight. They had to be, because there was so much they all had to learn and so much good they could do. And as Costin shared his power with her when he felt her growing tired, she realized that more importantly than those things, these healers had mates who needed them.

Stella didn't really know what power Sally was talking about so instead she just focused on the part of her that always brought her comfort and peace. She pulled it around her like her favorite fleece blanket, sheltering herself from the cold world. As she began to feel herself growing warm she saw a faint glow in her mind's eye. *This must be it*, she thought. Now she had to get it into the stones. She didn't know how the image came to her, but she imagined a tunnel from her body, linked to the stones with branches at the end that divided the tunnel into four spouts. She pictured the light sliding into the channel she'd created and then pushed with all her will. She felt the energy leaving her body, rushing out of her in a steady stream and into the stones. She didn't know what was happening once the light reached the stones and she was scared that if she opened her eyes to peek then she would lose her concentration. So she would stand there as Sally had instructed, funneling this power until someone told her to shut it down. She felt the wind pick up around her, whipping her hair around her face, and heard thunder rolling in the distance, but still she did not open her eyes.

Anna couldn't believe how easy it had been for her to recognize the magic that Sally had described inside of her. She simply closed her eyes and did an inventory of her mind and there it was, a soft, humming, glow, waiting for a task, and so she gave it one. Replaying Sally's words in her mind she pictured the light flowing into the stones. Peri had compared it to pouring liquid into a glass, but to Anna it seemed more like a roaring river, surging forward, crashing against the sides of its constraints and then flooding through the mouth into the open water. Her light seemed to cover the stones like overflowing water and then seep into them. It was magical, and she watched it in childlike wonder.

All those years her mother had told her that magic lived inside of her and Anna had blown her off. She had thought her mom was crazy or smoking weed when she wasn't home. Now, standing there, named a gypsy healer, welcomed into the fold, and finally feeling like her *something more* was being fulfilled before her very eyes, she ached for her mother and for the relationship they never had because of her stubbornness. She hoped that her mom had kept the evil out as she always implored to Anna. She hoped she was safe and happy. Maybe one day, if they lived to see tomorrow, she could find her mom and tell her that she found her light and the darkness would never take her.

∞

Peri was silent, her breathing slow and measured. Her eyes were focused, but never still as they moved over the land, mentally marking obstacles to avoid. She looked at the wolves lined in what Lucian had called an arc, but she saw it as a half-moon and found it oddly appropriate. Volcan needed the full moon above them to make the power he was using stronger, but silently, unbeknownst to him a moon of another sort with deadly power was moving towards him.

"Everyone is in position, beloved," Lucian's warm rich voice rumbled in her mind.

"I'd say let's light this bitch up, but since we are going in as silent as possible that really wouldn't be appropriate."

He chuckled. *"Perhaps you should say, when you can't hear the wolves, that's when the wolves are coming."*

"Profound, and somewhat badass, I'll go with it," she teased.

"How generous of you," he growled back.

"What can I say, wolf? It's like a non-profit biz up in here. I just give and give and expect nothing,"

"Peri," he interrupted.

"What?"

"Give the order."

Peri rolled her eyes at his bossiness. She made a motion with her hand and when she lowered it the entire arc moved forward as one. The wolves, even in their human forms were impressively quiet and fluid, their movements not even rustling a plant. Peri, Elle, and Adam were fae—they were on a whole different level when it came to stealth mode. It was almost as if they became one with nature around them. They moved lithely, their feet not even leaving indentions in the earth beneath them. Peri could anticipate a dip in the ground, or a low tree branch that wasn't visible until right up on it. As for their senses, well they had a trick or two up their sleeves. Few species knew that when the fae went into battle mode, their senses jumped into overdrive. Everything was heightened. It was a credit to the wolves that she could not even hear them breathing.

They continued forward and when they hit the second tree line Peri saw Costin slide into position as if it was choreographed. Peri felt her heart speed up as they continued forward, step, pause, step, pause, it was a mantra in her mind. It felt as if they had been walking for miles when the first scream lit up the night. Peri threw her hand in the air stopping the males that would have reacted to the female's cry. They may not know her, but she was theirs because somewhere in the world, there was a wolf waiting for her.

All heads swung in her direction and she was hit full force by their collective power. Their glowing eyes revealed just how close their wolves were to taking this mission over.

"Control your wolves, Lucian," Peri growled. *"If we go charging in there they might slit her throat the second they see us. We stick to the plan."*

She could feel that he knew she was right, but the protector in him didn't like it. She felt Lucian's power roll across her skin and saw all of the wolves, save Dillon, take one step back in unison. The frozen snarls on their faces said they didn't like it, but he was more dominant than all of them and so they had no choice but to obey. She wondered why Dillon was able to resist the order; she knew Lucian was dominate to Dillon regardless of his Alpha status. She decided maybe Lucian had been able to leave Dillon out of the command out of respect. Wise wolf her mate.

Once everyone seemed to be in control, Peri motioned again and as one they continued forward. The screams continued, on and off as they progressed, and they grew louder as they drew closer to the clearing. She knew that Lucian was exerting a lot of energy keeping the wolves in check, but she knew he had to. Something in her told her that if they acted too soon they would lose at least one of the healers that were captured.

Peri covered her mouth as she gasped when the clearing finally came into view. Lucian immediately

340

reacted and surrounded her with his comfort through their bond. But no amount of comfort was going to calm her down. She was glad in that moment that she had chosen to be on the far left side because she was the only one who could see the altars. The trees were sparser in front of her, and heavier through the center where the others were headed. If any of the wolves saw what she was seeing, not even Lucian would be able to stop them.

Peri didn't know there were tears on her face until the wind picked up and she felt the moisture cool on her skin. The tall trees began to sway as it built in force. She looked up and suddenly the night grew a bit darker. Ominous clouds were building all around them. They billowed throughout the sky until the full moon was completely blotted out. They were plunged into complete darkness. She nearly smiled as she thought, *my girls got game*. She knew this change of atmosphere was no fluke. Sally and her two protégé were totally getting their magic on.

"Peri, we need to move, now." Lucian growled.

"Do you enjoy running head long into trees?"

He snarled. *"Of course not."*

"Then I suggest we walk quickly, not suddenly turn into a crazed pack of hyenas."

"I can't hold them all much longer," he said wearily, and she heard something else in his tone. *"Dalton is more dominant than he lets on. He isn't superior to me, but something has him near feral. I can't stop him much longer."*

"Fine, turn them loose. Let's see what Lorelle and her master can do."

Thunder conveniently roared just as the wolves, still human, surged forward. It covered the sounds of their low growls, and pounding feet. Peri ran, reaching for all of her senses to help guide her. The darkness abated when she finally reached the edge of the clearing. Lorelle had conjured fae light to hover above her prisoners, making them look like some sick horror show.

Peri started to step from the shadows but froze when she saw Lorelle suddenly stiffen over the body of one of the healers. She jerked and her limbs curled in unnatural positions until finally a thick, black liquid seemed to leak from the bottom of her feet. It flowed faster and faster, rising on top of itself. Lorelle's body slumped across the bloody mess of the healer, but Peri's eyes were jerked back to the liquid that was now solidifying. Slowly a skeleton formed, nerves and ligaments came next, then muscle and tendons wrapped around the bones covering them completely. For a split second, it looked as though a pile of meat in the form of a person stood there. But then skin rippled over the form, starting at the head and flowing downward until every raw bit was covered. Hair sprouted from the head, a startling white that fell against the pale skin. The face began to take on an appearance as the nose slipped into a long narrow shape; the eyes were a little farther apart than seemed normal and almond in shape. The mouth was lined with thin lips that held a grayish hue. The final adornment was a simple cloak. It wrapped around the form and Peri's mind finally registered what she was looking at—Volcan. All of this happened in less than a minute, but her mind was not processing it that fast.

Peri blinked when she heard a deep, scratchy chuckle and barely had time to block the red ball that he whipped around and threw straight at her.

"Perizada," Volcan bellowed. "How long has it been?" He stared where she stood in the shadows. She could tell he was trying to assess the situation. Was she alone? If not, how many were with her? Was his power enough? When the wicked sneer stretched across his face, she knew he had decided he was more than capable of dealing with whatever she brought. *Fool*, she thought and lunged to the right when another red ball flew at her.

"Come out, come out, wherever you are," he sung, sounding every bit as crazy as she remembered him to be.

"It's go time, wolf," She told her mate just before she flew out of the cover of the trees straight at Volcan. She hit his body with such a force that she surprised even herself. Her goal had been to take him completely unaware, and the pitiful thing about magic users is that they never expect to be attacked any other way.

"Hey Volcan," Peri chirped just before her fist connected with his face. "I'd say it's good to see you, but you're even uglier than I remember." She hit him again and again in quick succession while he was still trying to figure out what the crap he should do. It didn't last much longer. He put his hands to her chest and she felt a jolt slam into her and she soared away from him. She flew backwards through the air until she was abruptly stopped by a large pine tree. Before she could stand she felt bolt after bolt of his power crashing into her, pinning her in place. She wondered what the hell the wolves were doing, why they weren't ripping into him, and when she was able to get her eyes open she realized they were all standing around the edge of the clearing, some human, some wolf, but all pissed. The males in their wolf forms were ramming their heads into an invisible barrier that, by the way they bounced off of it, was as impenetrable as steel.

There was a short reprieve in Volcan's attack that gave Peri the opportunity to glance at her sister, who was no longer slumped like a rag doll over the healer. She held her hands up muttering under her breath as she built the shield's resistance. When she appeared to grow weak, her sister did something that made Peri scream at the top of her lungs. Lorelle, with a look of fierce determination on her face, turned and bit into the healer's leg like a rabid dog. The snarls of the wolves drowned out the girls' screams. Peri put her hand on the tree and pushed herself up. She was on her feet when she looked to see why Volcan wasn't blasting her ass and lost her cool, if she ever had it, when she saw him hovering over the next healer. He hadn't cut her yet, and Peri would be damned if she would let him.

"Not on my watch," she growled as she gathered her power ran towards the barrier and slammed her fist into it. A crack, able to be seen, formed and began crawling across it like a piece of glass that had been hit by a rock. She pressed her hands to the place in front of her and was able to melt away a space large enough for her to get through. She ran hard and fast towards Volcan and purposefully yelled about ten feet away. She anticipated his attack and was able to dodge it, giving her an opening. As she flew past him she landed another punch into the barrier and it weakened even more. When she turned to face Volcan again she was introduced to his fist as he slammed it into her jaw. She felt Lucian's rage and saw, out of the corner of her eye, the barrier crumple.

Peri grinned as blood dripped from her mouth. She looked at Volcan who was using his magic to fling wolves away from him. "Uh-oh, you're in trouble now."

Chapter 23
"The Canis lupis have a saying for those who would dare lay a hand on their mates or their children: *Better had the offender never been born than face the wrath of the male he had crossed."*
~Sorin

When Lucian saw Volcan's fist connect with Peri's jaw, a floodgate that he hadn't even known existed burst open. Power—raw and savage—erupted out of him and then the barrier was gone and he was running. The only thing he could see was a dead man, because that is what Volcan was, only now that he had hurt Lucian's mate, he would be a mutilated dead man. His wolf was hungry, and he wasn't picky about what kind of meat he ate. The flesh of his enemy would satisfy him even more than the hunt of a worthy opponent.

He lunged for the sorcerer and barely missed his throat when he was flung back. Lucian jumped back to his feet and began circling his prey. Volcan was focused now on a new threat as more of the wolves attacked him, but it was apparent that the blood of the little healer he had devoured had made him very powerful. That power was only made more evident when he threw up his hands and yelled something in a language Lucian didn't understand, and the mother of all bird attacks came raining down on them.

"Not this again," Peri said as she came up beside him, holding her hands above them using her power to deflect the nasty birds. "They're more annoying than dangerous," she yelled as the noise around them rose with flapping and cawing.

Lucian watched as one of the birds dove at Lee, its talons raking a huge gash in the wolf's arm. Immediately the wound turned black and the skin around it bubbled as if acid were burning it. "I think they are more than annoying this time, beloved," Lucian told her as they watched Lee hit the ground hard, his knee's buckling beneath him. Lucian started towards him and felt Peri at his side still protecting him.

Adam's scent whirled past him and he heard Peri yell. "SHEILDS, ADAM! THE BIRDS ARE POISONOUS!"

Lucian didn't turn to see if the fae obeyed, he was too busy trying to figure out how he was going to tell Dillon that one of his wolves was gone.

∞

Dalton's eyes bounced back and forth from the ruined mess that was once a healer, to the woman who had been the cause of her suffering. He didn't understand the overwhelming urge to protect the healer; he didn't even know if she was alive. He only knew that the minute his eyes landed on her, his wolf went feral. Had Lucian not already pulled him back, Dalton would have lost all control of him. As it was, he was hanging on by a miniscule amount of control. The other two healers where slowly sitting up, as whatever spell had been cast to hold them dissipated.

Dalton stalked his prey, deciding that he needed to neutralize the threat before he checked on the female. The one called Lorelle didn't even know she was being hunted, she was distracted by Crina and Elle who were holding their own pretty well against the hag. She was also battling the birds that her master had conjured—he must not want her if he hadn't protected her from his spell. He and the others were no longer bothered by the birds because of Adam's magic. So he was free to focus on his target.

He waited, watched as Elle threw knives and bolts of magic at her enemy. Crina, in her wolf form dodged forward just as Elle would strike against the fae, taking advantage of the distraction. She sunk her teeth into Lorelle's leg and then jumped away quickly, narrowly missing the spell fired at her. Finally his patience paid off.

Elle was hit. Her body took the blow in the left shoulder flinging the small fae around to fall on her stomach. Lorelle turned then to face Crina. The she-wolf lowered her body, getting ready to pounce, while Lorelle being the vain witch that she was, taunted the wolf instead of attacking. Dalton made brief eye contact with Crina, but it was enough for her to understand his intent. Faster than most wolves, Dalton lunged, phased and landed on the back of his adversary. His huge muzzle wrapped around her neck and his teeth sunk deep into her flesh. He heard the satisfying pop of the spinal cord. She hadn't even had time to scream. Blood coated his tongue, the taste and smell only serving to provoke his wolf further. He shook her still body violently, slinging blood all over his fur. She, who had hurt his little healer, was dead. He had destroyed her. With the wolf fully in control now, Dalton was unable to think of why it might not be a good idea to drag his kill's body across the ground next to the altar where she still lay in her own blood. It was a gift; it was nourishment that would make her strong again. Still holding onto the neck of the woman, he looked at the face of the girl he had killed for. Her eyes fluttered but did not open. He whined, imploring her to see him, to see what he had done for her. But she didn't move. The wolf's rage roared on and he sunk his teeth even deeper and shook his head hard, over and over, until Lorelle's head ripped from her shoulders. The rest of her body hit the ground with a thud as her head rolled a few feet away. Now he didn't know what to do. His wolf still wanted blood and death for the horrific things done to *her*. Dalton didn't understand it. He was every bit as angry as his wolf, but the man was able to reason and therefore stop himself from killing anyone who came too close to the altar where she lay.

He turned his massive head back to look at her, but her face was distorted with blood. He didn't know her, though he would protect her regardless of his feeling towards her because she was a healer. But as he gazed at her, he couldn't deny what his wolf was feeling. *Ours*, rumbled the wolf and Dalton agreed.

∞

Sally, Anna, and Stella were running full speed ahead through the thick forest. Sally held the red fae stone out in front of her and it blazed brightly lighting their path. They could hear the snarls, the shouts, and the birds and it only made them run faster.

Sally held back the scream of her mate's name as they burst onto the scene. It was not what she had been expecting. The first thing she saw was Costin and Crina in their wolf forms battling a man who she assumed was the infamous Volcan. Adam was throwing spell after spell at him and Dillon was attacking with hand to hand combat any time the fae was distracted. Behind the battle she saw two girls, one of which was Heather. Sally let out a small sigh of relief; they both looked to be in one piece. She watched as Anna and Sally moved past the two altars they had occupied, trying to get to the third but were brought up short by a massive grey wolf standing over the body on the altar. Every time the two healers took a step towards him, he growled and snapped his teeth. His muzzle was pulled back revealing wicked sharp canines and his eyes glowed a blue that made Sally think of artic glaciers.

She hoped that the two girls would take the hint and not move any closer to the wolf before she could get to them.

"We're going to go to the left here," she motioned to Anna and Stella. "I need to get a look at the injured."

They hurried to a tree where Elle was propped up. Sorin lay beside her in his wolf form, with his head on her lap as slow steady growls rose from his throat.

"Elle, are you okay?" Sally asked as she knelt down next to the fae and put her hand on her chest. Sally closed her eyes and pushed her essence inside of Elle, searching for any damage. There was nothing physically wrong, but she had been zapped of her power. Sally pulled back into her body and opened her eyes. "Sorin will be able to help you once he's no longer furry." Elle nodded and then motioned past

Sally. "Check on Lee," she wheezed. "He's been down along time."

Sally nodded and then walked quickly in a crouch, attempting to stay as small a target as possible while Volcan continued to fight. Lucian was kneeling beside the still wolf. Sally looked closer and saw that his chest didn't rise and fall. She put her hand on him but Lucian shook his head and patted her hand softly. "He is gone; there is nothing you can do for him." Sally felt the tears welling up in her eyes but quickly brushed them away when Lucian said, "Please check on Peri." She turned to see where he stared and Sally saw Peri's back as she leaned over yet another body lying much too still on the ground.

"There is nothing you can do," Peri said the minute she knelt down.

"Why do people keep saying that!" Sally bit out in frustration. This time she let the tears fall. She didn't know Lee or Phillip, but she was a healer, and when she couldn't save wolves, whether hers or not, it hurt.

Peri stood up abruptly and suddenly her body was glowing as Sally had seen it do on several other occasions. Most of those times were when she had moved past angry to downright homicidal, which was definitely the case now.

"ENOUGH!" She bellowed and her voice filled the air, overwhelming the snarls and shouts of the battle.

Peri stared past the wolves attacking Volcan and into his soulless eyes. He was too powerful for her, she knew it and so did he. *Bastard*, she spat inwardly. If she let this continue more would die before the night would fade and the light of day would reveal what was left of their battle scarred group. She had to make a decision. It wasn't what she wanted. It wasn't acceptable, but then neither were any more pointless deaths.

"Why couldn't you just stay dead?" Peri asked. She saw Lucian slowly stand and then heard him in her mind.

"As soon as he finishes his sentence we converge on him. If we get him, we will dismember him and then burn his body. If we don't, we will bury our dead, morn our loss and regroup to fight another day."

Peri trusted Lucian to somehow convey the hastily made plan to the others around Volcan while she focused her power.

"I think your sister asked the same thing about you. You and I must have something in common if death cannot hold us. Perhaps you should consider that maybe you're working for the wrong side. We could be great together, powerful beyond anyone's imagination. And if you need me to console you after you leave your mutt, I can fill the role as your lover. It—,"

He didn't get to finish his sentence before Lucian phased in the air as he dove towards his prey. Peri reacted a second later, throwing out her hands, concentrating all of her power on Volcan. Then a victorious howl rang out from the direction she had last seen Dalton., It was so loud that Peri was forced to slam her hands over her ears. Suddenly, the pulsing, violent energy was gone and so was Volcan. *Lorelle.* Her sister's name sprang to mind and she turned quickly.

Her eyes landed on the beheaded body of her sister and what little love there had been left for her caused a sharp pain in her chest. It didn't last long because Lorelle did not deserve her sorrow. She had seen Dalton attack her and had been about to help, but then she had caught the look in the huge wolf's eyes and knew that he was feral.

"Dalton!" Dillon's deep bark pulled Peri's attention to the final threat among them. The impressive wolf stood on the altar straddling Jewel's body. His head was lowered, ears flat and nothing short of ripping the face off of anyone who got close was in his eyes.

Lucian, still in his wolf form stood in front of her and pushed her, forcing her back away from the situation. She saw Sally heading slowly towards the enraged wolf talking in that sweet voice of hers. Peri could see the need in the healer to check on Jewel, to see if she could help her, save her. Costin moved forward in a dash and put his head in Sally's stomach and pushed her back so fast that she stumbled, but the other healers were there to keep her from falling. Costin turned then and faced Dalton with his own teeth bared promising a fight if he snapped at his mate one more time.

"This could get ugly really, really fast," Peri muttered as she watched Dillon take slow steps towards his wolf.

Peri knew there were several things in play at the moment, things that were making the normally controlled wolf a berserker. Her first guess would be that Jewel was his mate. She wasn't of age so he probably didn't understand why he's so protective of her, but his wolf completely understood, hence the standing over her bloody body and not letting anyone touch her. The second thing that was making the wolf lose control was probably the death of two of his pack mates, both of which had been above him in rank. This meant that he was now Dillon's Beta. The need to prove his dominance would be strong, as would the pain of losing part of his pack.

"Dalton, if you don't let them near her, she will die." The deep inflection in Dillon's voice told Peri he was talking wolf to wolf, Alpha to Beta. "Get control now or I will get it for you."

Dalton's glowing stare held Dillon's until a rush of power from the Alpha had the feral wolf dropping it along with his head.

"Get down!" Dillon ordered and under the Alpha's power Dalton could not disobey. He jumped from the altar, circled it once and then sat down next to Jewel's face. He was so large that even sitting his head was still above the top of the altar.

Dillon motioned for Sally to go to the girl but Costin would not move.

Peri huffed. "Bloody hell, do you damn fur balls want to hang out in this death trap all night?"

"Costin," Lucian's voice was soft, but powerful. Costin stepped aside and let Sally past but stayed right next to her.

Peri started to walk towards the altar when she realized that her mate, who had been in his wolf form had just spoken. She turned and looked at a very naked Lucian who had surreptitiously placed himself behind her. She raised a brow at him, but didn't leave him to suffer any longer. With a wave of her hand a pair of jeans covered him and a plain black shirt hugged his muscular chest.

That task complete, Peri walked over to where Sally was assessing the damage done to Jewel. Peri shook her head in disgust at what her sister had done. She had scarred this healer for life, and she didn't just mean the hundreds of knife wounds that covered her body.

"She's alive," Sally finally said. "But she needs a transfusion now."

"The blood of her mate will keep her until we can get her back to the house. I don't want to linger here any longer and a transfusion will take a while," Peri quickly explained.

Nobody responded and she started to get irritated until she realized that nobody else understood that Dalton was Jewel's mate.

She looked at the glowing eyes of Dalton's wolf and said. "Phase. Now. If you want her to live."

He phased instantly and Peri assisted with clothes nearly as fast.

"Have you figured out what she is to you?" She asked him.

"Aside from wanting to protect her," he paused and looked down at her face and then back at Peri. "There are no other signs."

Peri let out a deep groan as she crossed her arms in front of her and narrowed her eyes on him. "How is it, one as old as you is so ignorant of the gypsy healers' history?"

Dalton's stone façade was back in place as he looked at her. Peri had seen the flash of emotion in his eyes when he stared at Jewel, but he was in denial. *Dumb wolves*, she thought to herself.

"I'll say it again, and it will be the last time because, in case you haven't notice two of yours have fallen, Volcan got away, and I'm about two seconds away of zapping your ass, slitting your wrist myself and pouring your blood down her throat."

"Please," Sally's plea seemed to touch something in Dalton that Peri's threat did not. He gave her a stiff nod and then stared at the group of healers that had gathered around the table.

"Healers," Peri called. "Adam and Elle are going to take you to my home. Get cleaned up, get some food in you, and then fall apart if you need to." Peri looked at each girl and saw the same thing in their eyes—retribution. She knew that emotion well and it seemed that the little band of gypsies were going to be every bit as protective over each other as the wolves are to their own. She would rather see that in their eyes than brokenness or the lack of hope.

She watched them gather around Elle and Adam, every single one of them held their heads up. They didn't slump their shoulders, or curl in on themselves. They stood tall. Yes, there were still tears streaming down some of their faces, but they were not tears of defeat. They were tears from the loss of innocence, from feeling helpless when they wanted to fight, from seeing the guilty one get away. They cried for the right reasons, and for that Peri knew they would be okay, maybe not tomorrow, or the next day, but one day soon and for now that had to be enough.

"Dillon," Peri called to the Alpha who was carrying his fallen and laying them side by side to make it easier for them to be flashed. "I am forever in your debt. You assisted us when you did not have to, and because of it you have lost two good men. For that, I am truly sorry."

Dillon wiped the moisture from his eyes and shook his head at her. "There is no debt, Perizada.

356

We came to help protect and rescue the healers. They are pack to all of us until they are mated. They have the right to our assistance, and Lee and Phillip would rather have died while protecting the precious females, rather than have lived and stayed in Colorado to leave them to their demise."

"I will take them back to Colorado for you. Are you going to stay or are you going home?" She asked as she looked past him to Dalton who was standing with his back to them as he took care of Jewel.

"I need to stay at least until he comes to terms with this. I know that Lucian is dominant enough to handle Dalton, but he's not equipped to handle the ghosts that come with him."

Lucian nodded and Peri knew he probably understood a lot more than Dillon realized. But regardless, she had known Dillon would stay. Alphas are protective of their pack, especially ones that are injured, even if the injury isn't one that can be seen.

She was good on her word and quickly flashed the two fallen back to Colorado. Dillon had called ahead to let Aidan and his mate know so they were ready and waiting. When she arrived back in the clearing she appeared next to Lucian who stood back from where Dillon was speaking with Dalton.

"He hasn't taken his hand off of her since he phased and I don't think he even realized it," Lucian told her softly.

"They have a long road ahead of them." She felt an ache in her chest at the truth in her words. Lucian felt it too because he added, "But they won't be alone."

∞

"She's breathing easier," Dillon pointed out to Dalton whose jaw clenched and unclenched as he stared at the girl.

"What's—," Dalton began but had to clear his throat and no doubt shove his emotions back into the little box he had stored them in for so long before he continued. "What's her name?"

"Jewel." Dillon answered having heard the other healers discussing their injured friend. Dillon waited to see if he would say anything more, but Dalton was never one for small talk. He only chose to form words if there was no way to get around it. "Peri needs to take her to the house so they can give her the transfusion and Sally can begin to get to work on these wounds."

Dalton's growl at his words did not surprise him. If it had been his own mate lying before him cut to shreds he would be doing a lot more than growling.

"Only Peri and Sally will touch her," Dalton said slowly but purposefully.

Arguing with him would just keep the girl from getting what she needed longer so he simply nodded and then motioned for Peri to join them. Unsurprising, Lucian stayed where he was. He was a cunning, wise wolf who knew how dangerous a male wolf could be with an injured, helpless mate.

"If you will hold her in your arms, I can flash you both," Peri explained.

Dillon nearly smiled at the sly, old fae and her meddling. She knew as well as he did that the closer Dalton and Jewel were, the calmer he would be, even if he didn't realize it himself.

She turned and looked at him and winked. "I'll be back for you two—maybe," she added at the last minute before she and her cargo were gone.

Chapter 24

"This isn't over. He didn't win and we didn't lose. So maybe we didn't completely eradicate evil from the world, big surprise there, but we did save our girls, and Dalton beheaded my sister (it's always the quiet ones you have to watch out for). Now we're going to heal up a bit, rethink our strategy, gather some allies, and decide how many casualties is acceptable in the event that we have to zap all of Texas. Why Texas you ask? Because he is probably hiding out there. Uh, did you not see the size of that psycho's ego? He's like the poster boy for "everything's bigger in Texas." It's a totally viable option for where he ran like the yeller chicken (isn't that how they talk there?) he is." ~Perizada

"I have something for you," Lucian whispered in his mate's ear. Her back was pressed to his chest and he had pulled her as close as he could without actually absorbing her into his skin. They stood in the secret place where she had first taken him to show him just how powerful she was.

"If it's not Volcan's head on a plate with an apple shoved in his mouth, I don't want it," she grumbled.

He kissed her neck and let his touch sooth over her ruffled feathers. They'd only been back for two days and she was still extremely emotional, which she continually blamed on him because *you made me love you with all your Hallmark crap and beloveds this and beloveds that. If I'm emotional it's your own damn fault.* His response had simply been to kiss her to silence her.

Costin had advised him of that strategy, and he said Decebel, his Alpha, had been the one to fill him in on it. Apparently being mated to dominant wolves made the females talk faster, yell louder, and use foul language. When kissing did not work, he resorted to desperate measures, and he found that she did not seem to mind his measures, desperate or not, at all.

He continued to simply press his lips to her neck, waiting for his prey to come to him.

She huffed and turned in his arms. "Fine, what is it."

He smiled down at her. "I thought you did not want it."

A coy smile spread across her lips as she looked up at him and batted those ridiculously long lashes at him. So apparently she had figured him out as well. There was only one thing stronger than his desire for her and that was his love. She knew it, and exploited it when she could. "Wolf," she whispered as she rose up on her toes so her lips were just barely brushing his.

"Yes, beloved," he murmured as she held him captive by her eyes and the love that shined through them.

"I would like to see the gift you have for me."

"Then so you shall," he told her as he reached down to her hand and slipped the ring he had been holding on to her finger.

Peri stepped back from him but he refused to release her so she leaned her back against his arms forcing him to hold her up while she examined the ring.

"It's beautiful," she said softly. "Is it an infinity symbol?"

"It's called a lovers knot," he said. "It's an added bonus that it resembles an infinity symbol. So it's pretty fitting as a bonding gift I think."

"A lovers knot," she muttered as she tilted her hand this way and that so that the moonlight caught on the diamonds.

The ring had been in his family for a very long time and Vasile had kept it safe. When he realized Peri was his mate, his brother had given him the ring and with a wink said *good luck*. At the time he did not understand, it was crystal clear now what he had meant.

The ring was platinum, one solid piece that had been molded by heat into the knot. Then small diamonds had been set into half of it. He especially liked that one side was unadorned and the other shined brightly. It was a picture of them. He was simple, no fancy trappings, but his beloved shone like the sun at its highest peak in the day.

"There is no way to undo a lovers knot. Once it is tied it is permanent, just as we are permanent; bound to one another by our souls, our love, and our lives. The infinity symbol is a representation of how far I will go to show you how precious, how worthy, how beautiful and how loved you are to me." He reached for her hand and kissed the ring then pulled her back into the shelter of his arms.

Peri pressed her face into her mate's chest and thanked the Great Luna over and over for knowing what she needed more than she did. Lucian was all the things she wasn't and he made her better. She had no single idea what she could possibly do for him or how he could need her, but she knew that without him she would become callus and cold. The cool metal of the ring on her finger was surprisingly comforting. Even though she knew that he loved her, knew that he was hers forever, the outward symbol of the ring showing everyone that this is how he loved her, that this is what she meant to him, was something that soothed her doubts and quieted her fears.

"I love you, wolf," she whispered and knew that he would hear her.

"You are my beloved, Perizada, and if you need a ring on every finger and toe to feel confident in that, then that is what you shall have."

"I swear you're a walking Hallmark card," she told him as he picked her up and waited for her to flash them to their room. He laid her on their bed and followed after her, wrapping her tightly against him.

"You keep saying that, and yet I am beginning to believe that you have a thing for this Hallmark business."

"Why is that?" She asked with a smile.

"Because every time I say something that you claim is a Hallmark card, you take me to your bed."

Peri blushed at his old fashioned words and found them strangely more intimate than any of the language used in this day and age.

"Perhaps I like you there," she smiled.

"It is a good thing then, that I like being there."

They stared into each other's eyes and Peri drew on his strength, his never ending calm, so she could let go of her worries and fears. She didn't know where Volcan had run to. She couldn't track him down right that moment and she couldn't fix the horrible things the healers had been through, at least not in just a few days. But she could have this time with her mate. He was here with her, holding her, loving her, giving her everything he had to give. And she would give him nothing less than that of herself. She wasn't alone anymore. She didn't have to face the coming storm by herself and knowing that freed her to reach through their bond and whisper words she'd never whispered to anyone. *"I need you."*

His answer was always the same. *"And so shall you have me."*

∞

"How is she holding up?" Stella asked Sally as she entered the room given to all the new healers.

Sally took a seat on the empty bed that would be Jewel's if she lived, and looked at the faces of the four women. She couldn't call them girls, not after what they had been through. Anything girlish in them had been taken from them by Volcan and his puppet. She knew what it was like to have the rose colored glasses torn off.

"She's hanging there. Her mind is protecting her. Though that might have been a good thing while she was suffering at Lorelle's hands, now I'm worried she won't find her way back," Sally told them gently.

"You mean she might just stay unconscious?" Anna asked.

"Sometimes the mind is too damaged to handle the reality of something horrific. She has more cuts on her skin than I could count and several bites. I was able to minimize some of the scarring but it was a fae blade that cut her." She saw Kara reach up and touch the faint scar on her own forehead that had been marred by the same blade. She nodded to her. "She did a great job with yours, but on her there was just too many. I did the best I could." A tear slipped free and she quickly wiped it away. She was tired, two days back and not more than a few hours of sleep.

She hadn't asked any of the ladies before her to help with Jewel's healing because Dalton wouldn't allow anyone but she and Peri near the injured girl. He reminded her of another brooding male she knew, and like Decebel, Dalton was deeply troubled. He wasn't just quiet or antisocial, he had demons in his past. She could see it in his eyes when he stared at Jewel. And knowing the males of their race as she did, he was struggling with the idea of anyone, especially his mate, seeing those demons.

Heather listened to the weariness in Sally's voice. She was wearing herself out. But even with her mate Costin snarling at her to share the burden and get some rest, she respected Dalton's wishes and kept caring for Jewel on her own. Heather's stomach twisted into knots as she thought about the young girl and all she had suffered. Why couldn't it have been her? She had asked herself over and over. At least if it had been her she would never see the scars so it wouldn't really matter to her if they were there. But Jewel, she would see them every time she looked in the mirror.

"We'll be here for her," Heather spoke up suddenly. She could hear the rustling of sheets as they all turned their attention on her. "She's not going to have to do this alone. None of us are."

Anna smiled inwardly at Heather's words. For the past day they had spent their time talking quietly, sharing their stories of how they came to be sitting in a house, owned by a fae, in another realm. What amazed her was just how similar their circumstances had all been. No, they hadn't all suffered the same trials, or experienced the same loss. But they had all been alone in one way or another. And now, save the one who lay fighting for her life, they sat in a circle surrounded by the comfort of knowing they no longer were.

Stella caught Anna's eye and gave her a knowing nod. She understood what was happening in the gypsy's mind, knew that look in her eyes because she was feeling it too. Stella was perhaps the most guarded of the group. Her past was filled with memories that she constantly tried to avoid. It had been difficult when she lived in New York City and worked at that dingy club. As she sat here with Kara, Heather, Anna, and Sally, she knew that she might actually be able to heal the wounds that just wouldn't seem to close. She smiled to herself as she considered each of their pasts. They all needed healing, and where better for that to take place than surrounded by gypsy healers? If she had been asked that a week ago, she would have told you to lay off the dope, but it wasn't a week ago. It was today and she had seen and experienced things that she never dreamed possible. So for the first time in a very, very long time she had hope.

Kara listened as they continued to talk. They asked Sally questions about how she had become a healer, and about the wolves, and mates, and on and on the questions flowed. Kara saw it for what it was, a distraction from the pain they could all feel radiating off of Jewel. The only times she ever felt her distress abate was when that huge, incredibly handsome, and yet very scary looking man called Dalton would go in to her room. She didn't know what he did in there, if he talked to her, or held her hand, but whatever it was, Kara was convinced it was all that was keeping their little Jewel intact. When Sally tried to explain to them what it meant that Dalton could possibly be Jewel's mate, and how that would keep her alive and help her heal they had all been skeptical. Even after everything they still couldn't grasp the whole true mate thing. They had a few laughs about how bossy the wolves were and Sally shared with them a few stories of her friends Jacque and Jen who were mated to very dominate males and Kara had to admit that it would be nice to be loved like that. Okay, no it would be better than nice, but she wasn't going to hold her breath. Sally said it could take centuries for a male to find his mate, and with the pattern of her life, she would be the very last female on the planet that would finally find this man who would supposedly love her unconditionally. As Heather cracked another joke, which she was good at, and the girls grinned and laughed with much needed mirth, Kara decided for now this was all she needed. She'd never had friends or family before and she would bask in it for as long as she could.

Heather heard the door close as Sally left for the night. She had wanted to stay with them, claiming she needed girl time, but Heather figured what Sally needed was healer time. This girl who was even younger than Heather has so much responsibility and, even with her mate and the friends she so obviously loved, she had been lonely for those who could truly understand what she was. Sally had finally relented to leave when Costin had poked his head in the door and threatened to tell the group about Sally's first experience as a bartender. Based on Sally's reaction that was one story Heather would have to hear.

So now it was just them. Heather was so used to climbing into bed at night, surrounded by silence, encased in darkness, alone. It had never really bothered her before, or so she thought. But now, listening to the laughter, as Kara told Anna and Stella about their trek through the dark forest and about Heather threatening to shoot her like an injured horse, she realized how very wrong she'd been.

Epilogue

"Everything hurts. It hurts to breathe, to move, to talk, even to wiggle my toes—except when I feel his touch. I don't know who he is. I don't know what he looks like or what his voice sounds like or if he is even real, but I know his touch. Right now, it is my lifeline. Without it, I don't know if I will ever be able to claw my way back out of the darkness my mind has retreated to." ~Jewel

"Why are you standing out here?" Dillon asked him.

Dalton looked up from the place on the floor that he had been staring at for at least half an hour. He met his Alpha's gaze for a count of three and then looked away. He didn't like to talk. Talking led to sharing and sharing led to digging up old pain.

"Sally's in with her," he finally answered.

"Has she woken up at all?"

Dalton shook his head, but he didn't mention that she had spoken to him. It had only been a whisper and he had no idea what it meant. *Five minutes longer*, she had said softly. She had seemed restless and so he'd brushed her cheek gently with the back of his hand. She relaxed and whispered *thank you*. The simple appreciation she showed him in those words made him feel after having been numb for so long . But that hadn't been the worst of it.

Before Sally had entered the room to do whatever it is she did while she was with Jewel, Dalton had heard the healer walking towards the room. So he had stood up and started to let go of her hand. She had squeezed like a vice grip, her brow wrinkled and her lips trembled as she spoke. *Don't go. Please. I need you.* Her words had been a knife to his gut. *I need you.* They reverberated around in his mind digging into things better left alone. He couldn't remember the last time someone had wanted him, let alone needed him. The only way he was able to get her to release him was when he leaned down next to her ear and whispered *I'm always with you.* And if she was who Peri claimed she was, then he had been telling the truth.

"She seems better when you're with her," Dillon pulled him from his thoughts.

Dalton nodded.

"Why don't you want her to be your mate?" His Alpha finally asked bluntly, getting tired of his evasion.

"I never said that."

"Well you sure as hell aren't smiling like a dumb fool like most males who find their mates. Would it bother you if she was somebody else's?"

He gave no response.

"Would it bother you if another male tended to her instead of you? Held her hand, ran his fingers through her hair, whispered in her ear?"

Dalton's glowing eyes met his Alpha's and for the first time in his life his wolf challenged him.

"I'm going to forgive that because I goaded you. But because I'm granting you grace you are going to take the gift that is lying in that bed and treasure her, protect her, and heal her. Give yourself to her and take her as your own as is your right and privilege as her mate."

That was it. The tightly controlled pain that he kept safely locked away was on its way out. He made a beeline for the door and had to ignore the small moan he heard from Jewels room. Yet more evidence that she was his—it hurt to be away from her.

Dillon followed the huge wolf out. Dalton turned on his Alpha the minute Dillon was out of the house. "I know what a gift a mate is and I know what an honor being blessed as the mate of a healer is."

"Then what's the problem?"

"You said I could heal her," Dalton bit out. "That I could take her as my own and give myself to her." Dillon nodded and then waited.

"I can't be her mate, Alpha. I can't heal her when I'm already broken. I can't give myself to her when I cringe at the idea of being touched, and I can't take her as my own because then she will see what I am." Dalton closed his eyes and steeled himself to say words that shouldn't be hard to say, but felt as though something had clawed its way into him and was ripping them from him. "She deserves better than what I can give her. She is going to need a gentle mate after being handled so horribly. There is no gentleness left in me."

Dillon narrowed his eyes at his Beta as he watched the huge man feed himself lies written on his heart from a tragic past. He was definitely damaged, but who better to be the mate of a broken male than a healer? And who better to be the mate of a female who will have to relearn how to trust being touched and not cringe, than a male who has been there already? Dalton wasn't ready to see it yet. For whatever reason he believed he didn't deserve her and was trying really hard to convince himself he didn't want her. Lucky for him he has an Alpha who doesn't put up with self-pity. He has left Dalton alone for many years, allowing him to deal with his trauma in his own way, but that was about to end.

"Okay," Dillon said coolly. "If that's what you think, then I won't force you to take care of her any longer. You will stay here with me because they are going to need us to hunt down Volcan, but you can stay away from Jewel." Dillon noted Dalton's jaw tightening. It was time to go for the clincher. "Vasile called to let Peri know that some of the Alphas of the other packs are going to send their Betas to help with the search,"

Dalton snorted. "How kind of them to send their unmated dominates to a house that just happens to be full of unmated healers."

Dillon wanted to laugh. That was the most words he had ever heard out of Dalton's mouth at one time. He continued as if the Beta hadn't interrupted. "If Jewel hasn't woken up by then, it might be a good idea to see if the blood of any of the new males perhaps can do what yours did not."

Dalton went still, his hulking form like a chiseled statue, but for his eyes. They shot up to his, and though hooded by lids Dillon could see the barely contained rage. "What is it you are looking for their blood to do?"

"Bring her back," Dillon crossed his arms over his chest and tilted his head just a tad. "You didn't ask Sally why Jewel was still unconscious, did you?"

Dalton didn't respond.

"Well, maybe if you didn't even care enough about her to want to know what was wrong, then she isn't really yours."

Dalton watched his Alpha walk away, purposefully leaving those ringing words in the air. *She isn't really yours.* As he got his breathing under control and slipped back into his *talk to me and die* demeanor, he hoped for the little healer's sake that his Alpha was right.

From author:

Thank you so much for taking your time to read Into the Fae. It is my sincerest hope that you enjoyed it and will continue on this journey with the new healers. You can stay up to date one when books are due out, cover reveals, excerpts and book trailers by going to my site at www.quinnloftisbooks.com. Thank you again!

Please enjoy the following excerpts from:

Prince of Wolves, Book 1 The Grey Wolves Series By Quinn Loftis

Chapter 1

Jacque Pierce sat in the window seat in her bedroom looking across the street at her neighbors house; she wasn't really being nosy she thought to herself, just curious. "Yeah," she snorted, "only if you call curious sitting in your window seat eyes glued to your neighbor's house like a hound on the hunt at ten o'clock at night. I can call a spade, a spade tomorrow morning," she told her conscience.

The Henry's were having a foreign exchange student stay with them this year. They didn't have any children of their own, though Jacque didn't know if that was by choice or because they weren't able to have children. She had promised Sally and Jen she would get the nitty-gritty on the situation and call them.

So here she sat in her window, scoping out the neighbors house with her lights turned off and blinds cracked just enough to see and to top off her "James

Bond" experience, she even had binoculars! Now if she only had the nifty back ground music to go with her shenanigans. She had been sitting there for an hour already and was just about to give up when a black stretch limo pulled to the curb. Now isn't this strange, she thought, a foreign exchange student arriving in a limo? She put the binoculars to her face and adjusted them to get a better look, settling them over the passenger door to see just who would emerge. She knew this was a little much but honestly in a town of 700 there just isn't a whole lot of excitement and Jacque would take it where she could get it.

The driver got out of the limo to go around and open the back passenger door, but before he could get there the door was already opening, and the boy who stepped out of that limo had to be the most beautiful guy Jacque had ever seen, and that was only his profile. Wow, I mean wow, is all Jacque could think. Jacque couldn't even imagine what his entire face must look like. He was tall, probably six foot one or so, his hair was jet black, it was longer on top and she could tell that he had bangs that fell across his face sweeping to the left partially covering that eye. He had broad shoulders and from what she could see of his profile, high cheek bones, a straight nose and full lips. She quickly realized her mouth had dropped open and she was all but drooling over the handsome human being who had emerged from the vehicle. She watched as he and his driver conversed, it all seemed very formal until the driver suddenly hugged the boy with obvious deep affection. He must be more than just his driver Jacque thought.

Suddenly, he turned as if he had heard what she was thinking and looked straight at her window, straight at her. Jacque froze, unable to look away from the mesmerizing blue eyes that held her in place. All her thoughts seemed to fade into the distance and she heard, or thought, she wasn't quite sure which, the words, *"At last, my Jacquelyn."* Jacque shook her head, trying to clear the haze that had filled it. After she came to her senses from the intense stare she recapped in her mind what his face had looked like.

She was right about the cheek bones; nose and lips, what she wasn't prepared for was that his crystal blue eyes seemed to almost glow in the moon light. The hair that fell across his forehead and over his left eye only added to his mysteriousness. Over all he had a very masculine, very beautiful face. The shirt he was wearing was black and thanks to her handy dandy binoculars she was able to see that it fit closely to his form and showed off a muscular chest and flat stomach. He had a black leather biker jacket on, but past that she couldn't see because the car was in the way, but she imagined his legs were every bit as nice as the rest of him.

When she looked back at the street the mysterious guy was walking into the Henry's house. As she saw the door close she heard the voice again say *"Soon."*

Jacque sat there for a few minutes more trying to get her brain to work again, everything seemed so hazy. After blinking what felt like a thousand times she pulled herself together, picked up the phone and dialed Jen's number.

Three rings later Jen answered, "What's the word?" she asked.

Jacque took a slow breath and said "I think you better come over."

"I'm there chick, see ya in 5," Jen responded and then hung up.

Jacque grinned to herself as she thought about how great it was to have a friend like Jen who you could always depend on to be there when you needed her.

Jacque picked up the phone again and called Sally. She answered after one ring. She had obviously been diligently manning the phone, waiting for Jacque to call with details to the latest small town drama. "Jen is on her way over," Jacque said. "I need you to come too, we need to talk."

"Okay," Sally said simply and hung up.

Fifteen minutes later the three friends were gathered on Jacque's bedroom floor, hot chocolate in hand, because naturally, how can you have a girl powwow without hot chocolate?

"So, fill it and spill it," Jen said.

"Okay," Jacque said taking a deep breath, "so I'm sitting in my window seat, shades cracked lights off, binoculars in hand,"

"Binoculars, really, you honestly were using binoculars?" Sally interrupted.

"Well you said you wanted details, so I was getting you details," Jacque defended.

"Oooh, did you have the "Mission Impossible" sound track playing in the back ground cuz that would have been spy-tastic," Jen said enthusiastically.

"Actually," Jacque said distracted, "I was thinking more James Bond-ish, you know with the whole stake out thing,"

"No, huh-uh, that would be more like Dog the Bounty Hunter type stuff. But you couldn't be Beth 'cause you're not stacked enough on top, so you would have to be baby Lisa the daughter…." Jen rattled on.

"You are so, so not comparing me to Dog the Bounty Hunter's daughter right now and why are we talking about this anyway because it is sooooo NOT the point!" Jacque growled in frustration.

"Spy analogies aside, I was sitting there about an hour when finally a black stretch limo pulls up to the curb in front of the Henry's house."

"A limo? What foreign exchange student shows up in a limo?" Jen asked.

"I know right, that's what I was thinking," Jacque stated. "I assure you the limo is of no consequence once the person inside stepped out. Ladies, I saw the most gorgeous guy to ever grace my line of site."

"When you say gorgeous," Jen started, "are we talking Brad Pitt boyish good looks, or Johnny Depp make ya want to slap somebody?"

"No, we're talking Brad and Johnny need to bow down and recognize," Jacque answered.

"Aside from him being dropped off in a limo, and besides the fact that he is a walking Calvin Cline ad, it begins to get strange at this point in our story boys and girls," Jacque says in a spooky narrative voice.

"Like it wasn't strange already?" Sally asked.

"Well, okay strang-er. Just as he is about to walk up the path, he suddenly turns and looks straight at me, like he could sense I was watching him! Like, right in my eyes. I literally couldn't move; it was like I was mesmerized by him or something. Man when did

I start using the word "like" so freaking much?" Jacque said in exasperation. "Up until now it was strange, but now we are entering the world of "what the hell." As he is staring at me I hear a voice in my head and it said "At last, my Jacquelyn," then as he turned to go in the house and I hear the voice again say, "Soon."

Jacque stares expectantly at her two best friends waiting for them to tell her she's finally jumped off the deep end, but they just sit there staring at her. "Well?" Jacque asked. Finally Jen stirs taking a deep breath in, she looks down at her empty hot chocolate mug, "We're gonna need more hot chocolate."

"Agreed," Sally and Jacque say at the same time.

Jen returned with three fresh mugs of hot chocolate and Oreo cookies. Folding herself Indian style on the floor, she cocked her head to the side eyebrows scrunched together, "So let me see if I'm catching what you're throwing. Hottie exchange student drives up in a limo, steps out, rocks your world, looks into your eyes and speaks to you in your head? Am I getting the gist of it here?"

Jacque nodded her head sheepishly looking at the floor, "I mean, I guess it was his voice in my head. It could be a long lost dead relative who's been searching for me since they died and happen to find me the moment that hottie looked into my eyes."

Jen and Sally both gave Jacque the, get a larger spoon if you're going to shovel it in that big, look.

"What?" Jacque asked. "I'm just saying," she said throwing her hands up in the air in frustration.

Flopping back onto the floor Jacque groaned loudly and covered her eyes with the back of her hand, "Am I going crazy ya'll?" she asked.

"No sweetie, you been gone a long time now, we just didn't want *you* to know that *we* knew." Sally teased.

"Seriously, I know it sounds crazy, but I promise you guys I heard a voice, a beautiful, deep, masculine voice, in my head, and it knew my name! That is crazy, jacked up, put-her-in-a straight jacket, totally insane!" Jacque looked at them both with fear in her eyes; she truly did wonder if she had finally cracked.

There was after all, people in her family of questionable sanity, her mother being one of them. Jacque loved her mom and they had a good relationship, but she wasn't always in touch with reality. Jacque's father wasn't in the picture and never had been, he had bailed as soon as he found out her mom was pregnant. Thankfully she had two best friends who kept her feet firmly on the ground, which is why she was so fervently seeking their thoughts on this matter.

Sally finally spoke up, "I don't think you are crazy, Jac, really you're not. There has to be some sort of explanation. We'll figure it out, we always do."

"Yea," Jen added, "its two weeks until school starts. From now until then we are on scout detail." Sally nodded her agreement.

The three were quiet for a few minutes, each pondering ways to run into the new exchange student without seeming too obvious. Jen was lying on the floor looking up at the ceiling fan, her eyes following the blades as her mind turned its own circles, "We need to find a way to introduce ourselves to him so that we can each get a good look and see if Sally or I hear a voice in our head."

"My mom was planning on taking over a good'ole Southern meal for him since he isn't from here. We could ask if we could go over with her, or would that be too lame?" Jacque asked.

"No, I think that's perfect," Jen stated.

Finally, by midnight they had thought up a somewhat weak game plan, the whole of it revolving around going with Jacque's mom to the Henrys to give their new exchange student some fried chicken, 'taters, and corn on the cob. Seriously, how lame could you get, Jacque thought as she lay in her bedroom floor. Jen and Sally had quickly fallen asleep on the other side of her room each with their own blanket wrapped around them.

Jacque sat up and looked around her room, and thought, this was a place I feel safe and comfortable. The twin size bed with the new deep green bed spread her mom had bought her for her birthday, the stained-glass lamp with absolutely no theme whatsoever that sat on her small wood desk. She, Sally and Jen had carved various things on its surface. She looked at her dresser mirror which had pictures lining both sides, mostly of Jen, Sally and her in various places and poses; just a few hours ago I was just another 17 year-old getting ready to start my senior year, so normal she thought.

She had three homecoming mums hanging on the wall next to her bed, and on the other side of her bed was the window with a seat where she sat tonight, where her life had changed in a way she wasn't sure of yet. Jacque lay back down on her back watching her ceiling fan go around in a circle, the motor lulling her to sleep. Her last thought as she drifted off was of a full moon, whatever that meant.